The Guns of Valverde

"Lauded for her research as well as her terrific storytelling skills, Nagle gives life and depth to characters on both sides of the battle lines while telling a host of secondary tales. Pointing out human foibles as well as detailing the hardships and the horrors of war, this is a worthwhile read."

—*Booklist*

"Nagle, as before, does a deft job of weaving together the personal struggles of her characters with the broader texture of the war. Her portrait of the brutal campaign itself, of the unforgiving terrain where it was fought, and of the desperate adversaries who mounted it, is clear and gripping. Lively, compelling historical fiction.

—*Kirkus Reviews*

"P.G. Nagle once again presents the Civil War on the far western frontier in a manner that accurately tells the story of that region and time as well as the hard-as-nails soldiers who fought for control of the American Southwest. Well researched, her novel will give the reader the opportunity to absorb the excitement of those times, the rugged conditions under which the Union and Confederate partisans struggled, and the complex characters who followed the opposing flags in far off New Mexico."

—Don E. Alberts, Ph.D., author of *Rebels on the Rio Grande* and *The Battle of Glorieta: Union Victory in the West*

"Nagle vividly depicts its hardships and dangers. The Civil War history is accurate and colorful. . . ."

—*Publishers Weekly*

Forge Books by P. G. NAGLE

Glorieta Pass
The Guns of Valverde
*Galveston

*forthcoming

THE GUNS OF VALVERDE

P. G. Nagle

FORGE®

A TOM DOHERTY ASSOCIATES BOOK
NEW YORK

This is a work of fiction. All the characters and events portrayed in this book are either products of the author's imagination or are used fictitiously.

GUNS OF VALVERDE

Copyright © 2000 by P.G. Nagle

Map by Chris Khron

Edited by James Frenkel

A Forge Book
Published by Tom Doherty Associates, LLC
175 Fifth Avenue
New York, NY 10010

www.tor.com

Forge® is a registered trademark of Tom Doherty Associates, LLC.

ISBN: 0-812-58029-X

First edition: July 2000
First mass market edition: June 2001

Printed in the United States of America

0 9 8 7 6 5 5 4 3 2 1

In loving memory of
HARLEY W. KROHN

A great many people lent their advice, support, and expertise to the creation of this book. Among them are Daniel Abraham, Don E. Alberts, Peter de la Fuente, Ken and Marilyn Dusenberry, Robin Fetters-Naylor, Steven C. Gould, Sally Gwylan, Ralph Harris, Steven J. Jennings, Bruce and Marsha Krohn, Chris Krohn, Lynne Lawlor, Jane Lindskold, Maria del Carmen L. Martin, Laura J. Mixon, Jim Ed Morgans, James L. Moore, Avery Nagle, Scott Schermer, Melinda Snodgrass, Chuck Swanberg, Beau Tappan, Sage Walker, Vic Watson, Cory Weintraub, Dean and Natasha Williamson, and Ward Yarbrough.

Thanks also to the Artillery Company of New Mexico, the New Mexico Territorial Brass Band, the New Mexico Civil War Commemorative Congress, El Rancho de las Golondrinas Living History Museum, the Museum of New Mexico, the Palace of the Governors, the New Mexico State Archives, the University of New Mexico Library Center for Southwest Research, the Colorado Historical Society, Fort Bliss Historical Museum, Fort Bowie National Historic Site (Apache Pass), Fort Union National Monument, Yuma Crossing State Historic Park, Yuma Territorial Prison State Historical Park, Pecos National Monument, the Bureau of Land Management (Fort Craig), Picacho Peak State Park, The Rio Grande Press, and many others, especially the editors and authors of histories and diaries covering the New Mexico Campaign, without whose work the present volume would not have been possible.

UTAH TERRITORY

NEW MEXICO
TERRITORY
with Confederate Arizona,
1862.

0   50   100   150
SCALE IN MILES.

CALIFORNIA

Colorado River

CONFEDERATE

Gila River

Fort
Yuma

Stanwix Flats + Gila Bend • Maricopa Wells • Pima Villages •
Oneida •

PICACHO PASS +

• Tucson

MÉXICO

Golfo de
California

Copyright © 1995, 2000, Chris Krohn

GENERAL:

I have the honor and pleasure to report another victory.
. . . The Battle of Glorieta was fought March 28 by detached
troops, under the command of Lieutenant-Colonel Scurry,
and Federal forces, principally Pike's Peakers, under the
command of Colonel Slough. . . .

Pending the battle the enemy detached a portion of his
forces to attack and destroy our supply train, which he suc-
ceeded in doing, thus crippling Colonel Scurry to such a
degree that he was two days without provisions or blankets.
The patient, uncomplaining endurance of our men is most
remarkable and praiseworthy.

In consequence of the loss of his train Colonel Scurry has
fallen back upon Santa Fé.

I must have reenforcements. The future operations of this
army will be duly reported. Send me re-enforcements.

—*H.H. Sibley,*
Brigadier-General, Commanding

General S. Cooper,
Adjutant and Inspector General, Richmond, Va.

1

"Any cause that men sustain to death becomes sacred, at least, to them. Surely we can afford to pay tribute to the courage and nobleness that prefers death to even fancied enthrallment."

—Sergeant Ovando J. Hollister, 1st Colorado Volunteers

Kip Whistler strolled across a flat, sandy riverbank toward the copper-penny gelding called Firecracker, wondering if the horse was going to try to kill him. A flashy beast with flaxen mane and tail, Firecracker was aptly named and Kip knew his reputation. Some days he was the pleasantest fellow in the string, but he could explode without reason. He was consequently the least popular mount in the 1st California Cavalry, and kept getting traded around. Kip was counting on this fact.

"You're not really going to do this, are you?" asked Private Stavers at Kip's elbow.

"Course I am. Hell, Adam, it's just a race."

Stavers flinched at the profanity. Kip had known he would, which was why he'd said it. Stavers needed to loosen up some. Both of them had been in the California Volunteers for nearly half a year and Stavers still prayed over every meal, read from his bible every night, and dutifully wrote four pages to his mother in Chicago each Sunday afternoon after chapel, even though they were lucky at present to see a mail coach twice a month. Kip suspected his annoyance with this habit had something to do with his own lack of parents to write to, and he tried not to be too hard on Stavers, but his evil genius occasionally got the better of him. All the family he had was a stick-in-the-mud older brother who'd refused to loan him the money to buy a horse and join the cavalry. Elijah had offered him a banking job instead. A banking job! Might as well bury himself now and not wait for the funeral. Kip had walked out of his brother's office and straight to the recruiting tent for the 1st California Volunteer Infantry, trusting to fate to assist him in bettering his position.

Kip glanced up at Fort Yuma, looming over the Colorado River on its impressive, treeless bluff. He would have to get back there straightaway after the race, or he'd miss another band practice. From one cause or another he had missed altogether too many practices lately. His spirit just wasn't in the music, he guessed, and that was a sorry state of affairs. He had always loved music, and been good at it, from the day his legs were long enough to reach the pedals on Mama's parlor piano. It was hard, though, to get excited about polkas and waltzes when more stirring events were in the air. Not only was Colonel Carleton raising an army to assist the Commander of New Mexico in defeating the Texan invaders, but just two weeks ago Rebels in Tucson had captured Captain McCleave, a personal friend of Carleton's, and a military expedition was fixing to go to his rescue. The thought of watching the advance march away while he sat in the fort playing "The Girl I Left Behind Me" just about drove Kip to distraction.

The ferry was landing, Sergeant Aikins aboard it with Merlin, his big bay gelding. He'd refused to bring his horse across on the same boat with Firecracker. Old Jaeger, the ferrymaster, had merely shrugged and encouraged more spectators to cross with the animals. The second trip carried a lot more race-goers than had the first, Firecracker's reputation having commanded respectful distance.

Aikins, dressed like a city gent in his black wool coat and pomaded hair, led Merlin onto the landing, followed by Semmilrogge, the private who would be riding the bay against Kip. Aikins was a big fellow and he wanted a lighter rider for his pampered bay, especially since he'd bet a hundred dollars on the race. Semmilrogge was closer to Kip's size, a little heavier maybe and not quite as tall. He was a good rider, Kip knew. He and the rest of the cavalry rode every day, scouting or drilling. Kip hadn't been on a horse since he'd left San Francisco.

"Come on, Kip, call it off," Stavers urged him. "Bob's just trying to see how far you'll go."

"I know it," Kip said, looking over to where his backer, Bobby Zinn, stood holding Firecracker's reins. Zinn was a cavalryman also, several years older than Kip. He had first proposed the race over several pints of beer in a tavern in Colorado City, just across the river from the fort. Kip had agreed to it at once, partly for the money, partly because he thought it might be a chance to get transferred to the cavalry and active duty. And it was something to do. That in itself was enough.

Stavers stopped in his tracks a good ten paces away from Firecracker. Kip ambled on, past a flock of coots that scurried for the river's edge, their white bills betraying their hiding places in the tall marsh grass. He ignored them, keeping his eyes on the horse as it watched him approach. In all the stories of Firecracker's disastrous behavior, he had not heard, so far, that the animal was vicious. He dug a hand in his pocket and produced a lump of sugar which he offered on a flat palm. Firecracker's nostrils widened, then he lipped at it. Kip felt the massive teeth click shut just above his flesh. He lowered his hand while the horse chewed.

"You're not such a bad fellow, are you, boy?" Kip said softly. Slowly he reached up to Firecracker's neck and stroked his sleek coat. The sun made the short, smooth hairs gleam, little rainbow glints off their copper-brightness as powerful muscles rippled beneath. Firecracker was strong, there was no dispute about that. Kip ran his hands up along the withers, then down to the belly to check the girth. Firecracker grunted and swung his head toward Kip, ears flat.

"Don't like that? All right," Kip said, keeping his voice calm. Behind him he heard Stavers emit a feeble sound of dismay. Zinn had jumped, too, when the horse had swung his head. Kip glanced up at his backer.

"Keep his head down," Zinn said quietly. "Don't let him get it up in the air."

Kip nodded. The crowd of onlookers had started moving along the shore, some clustering around a starting line that had been scratched in the dirt a few yards from the river, some straggling toward the finish line a mile downstream to the west, where five men on horseback, the judges, waited. Kip and Zinn moved toward the start, with Firecracker following gentle as a lamb and Stavers nervously bringing up the rear. A crowd of men—soldiers from the fort and a few Colorado City men—stood around furiously making wagers in the warm sun. Already warmer than San Francisco ever got, and it wasn't even April yet. Kip knew the place would become a living hell in summer. Another reason for wanting to get out.

"You can bring him up right here, Sergeant," said George Johnson to Aikins, who led Merlin up to the line. Johnson was carrying a flag and looking important. He'd been given the job of starting the race, and now he looked over Kip's way. "You stand over there," he said, pointing with the flag to the far side of the line by the river. Firecracker, taking exception to the sudden flapping of cloth, whinnied a protest and reared, pawing at the air with his forelegs.

"No you don't, you bastard," Zinn muttered fiercely, hauling down hard on the reins while the spectators voiced disapproval and made more bets. Kip shot Johnson a dark look and followed Zinn up to the starting line.

"Don't you mind him, Firecracker," he said. "He probably did that on purpose." Giving the horse's neck a reassuring pat, he took the reins and mounted. Firecracker sidled under his weight but didn't buck, and Kip nudged him up to the line. Zinn went over to shake hands with Aikins while Semmilrogge mounted Merlin and grinned slyly at Kip.

"Where's your horn, boy?" he called. "Ain't you going to blow the charge?"

"Didn't know you needed it," Kip retorted.

"On your mark," Johnson yelled, holding the flag above his head. It hung limp in the still, dry air.

"Good luck," Zinn said, passing on his way to join Stavers, who had his hands clenched together in prayer. Kip nodded to Zinn, winked at Stavers, then turned his attention to his mount.

"Get set," Johnson cried.

Kip leaned forward over Firecracker's neck, shortened the

reins, and tested his balance in the stirrups. His heart was going rather fast, he noticed.

"Go!"

The flag swooped down. Firecracker tried to toss his head but Kip had him in hand, and only the slightest nudge with his heel made the horse surge forward. The spectator's roar of approval was quickly left behind in the thudding of hooves on hard earth. Merlin had gotten off a half length ahead, but Firecracker moved up easily until they were neck and neck. Kip spared a glance at Semmilrogge and saw him almost lying on Merlin's neck. He followed suit. Firecracker sped along the ground like a demon, and Kip felt a wild joy welling up in him. This was what he wanted—the freedom of a strong horse under him and no fences ahead! He let out a yip without thinking, but Firecracker didn't seem to mind. He just ran faster, pulling ahead of Merlin, eating up the ground between them and the finish. Horse and rider together flowed forward, steady rhythm almost more like wingbeats than hoofbeats, breathing in time to the gallop. Ahead Kip could see the judges clearly, and the flagman's head beyond a tall stand of river grass.

Suddenly the grass exploded as a cloud of coots fled the oncoming horses, slate-colored wings flapping heavily. Firecracker stopped short, sat back on his haunches, and reared, spinning away from the birds.

"Whoa," Kip cried, clinging on with his knees and trying to turn the horse around the right way again. Firecracker dropped his forelegs to the ground and immediately leapt sideways. Kip found himself sitting on nothing, then falling to the dirt in the middle of a cloud of dust. Coughing, he sat up and rubbed his right elbow where it'd hit.

"Shit," he said, watching Firecracker speed away after Merlin, toward the finish line. Damned horse might still win the race, but Kip wouldn't.

As he got to his feet and dusted himself off, he saw a solitary figure walking toward him from the starting line: Sergeant Casey Sutter, a member of Captain Calloway's infantry company, in which Kip had been a private for about fifteen minutes before being detached to the band. Sutter strolled up, arms folded across his chest. He was a bit shorter than Kip, a good ten years older, and weather-beaten into the bargain. He had been in the Regulars for years and had been stationed at Fort Yuma before, a fact which in itself had commanded the respect of all the recruits in the California Volunteers.

"That was impressive," Sutter drawled. "Anything broken?"

"No." Kip wished Sutter hadn't come, and resigned himself to getting dressed down. Instead Sutter surprised him by looking concerned.

"You're smarter than this, Whistler. What the hell are you trying to prove?"

Kip sighed. "That I can ride a horse nobody wants. Can't afford to buy one."

"Why do you want to ride at all?" Sutter asked. "You're sitting pretty. No drill, and you make more money than a line soldier—"

"I don't want to be left behind when the column marches for New Mexico," Kip said, starting back toward the ferry. Sutter fell in beside him.

Hoofbeats made Kip look back to see Semmilrogge and the judges riding triumphantly for home, with a few jubilant spectators for company. They tossed jeers and catcalls in Kip's direction as they passed, Firecracker placidly trotting along behind the party. No one had taken his reins; he was just following the other horses. Kip didn't bother trying to catch him.

"You won't be left behind, son," Sutter said. "Colonel Jimmy likes pomp better'n anybody, I reckon. He'll take the band along."

"I want to go with the advance," Kip said. "I want to help bring back McCleave."

"Why, for God's sake?"

"I can't stand just sitting here," Kip said. He was starting to sound petulant, he knew. Trying for a calmer tone, he added, "This war's important. I want to be part of it, not watching from the sidelines. I want to make a difference."

Sutter snorted. "You just want your ass in the saddle, instead of marching with that big old brass horn under your arm."

Kip laughed, which turned to a fit of coughing. Sutter beat on his back till it subsided. "Well," the sergeant said indulgently, "I'll talk to the captain and see what we can arrange."

"You will?" Kip looked up at him sharply, suddenly aching with hope.

"You won't get the cavalry. They don't have any horses to spare, not even bad-tempered nags—"

"He's not bad-tempered."

"—but maybe you can come back to the company as a field musician. Can you play the fife?"

"Yes," Kip said firmly.

"All right then. I'll see what I can do."

"Thank you, Sarge," Kip said, catching Sutter's hand and pumping it. "I'll make you proud."

"Don't thank me," said Sutter, trying not very successfully to frown him down. "You might not be so thrilled about it next week."

"Oh, I will," Kip said. Feeling suddenly lighthearted, he skipped a couple of steps along the shore. A coot peered out at him from the reeds. Kip grinned at it. He'd have to get his hands on a fife, and learn how to play it.

Icy water stung Laura Howland's hands as she reached for the shirt she'd left to soak. It was Pecos River water, frigid March snowmelt from the Sangre de Cristo Mountains, drawn at a riverbank overhung with icicles. She had left the borrowed washbasin in the sun for an hour, hoping it would warm a bit as the shirt soaked, but the day was too cold; a brisk March wind pouring relentlessly in from the plains to the east had kept the water near freezing. A shirt would ordinarily be boiled, but hot water would set the bloodstains on the cuffs.

Laura caught the cloth in numb fingers and began working it to ease out the blood. Her fingers trembled a little, possibly from the cold, more likely from the distressing emotions that arose as she remembered how the shirt had come to be stained. It was Captain O'Brien's shirt, but the blood was Lieutenant Franklin's.

She closed her eyes briefly, resisting tears. The woman who had called herself Charles Franklin had been wounded in battle and carried to Pigeon's Ranch by Captain O'Brien, had revealed herself to Laura and pledged her to secrecy, and had died in Laura's care while the battle raged around them. That a young woman of breeding and intelligence could forsake all and join the Colorado Volunteers in the guise of a man Laura had found incomprehensible at first, but on learning of it she had experienced a kind of revelation. Franklin had whispered of freedom, a freedom of unimaginable delight, and the idea had lodged itself in Laura's heart.

She glanced westward toward Glorieta Pass, where the battle had taken place, now hidden among the blue mountains toward which the sun had begun to descend. It had been only yesterday, her long, sorrowful watch while Franklin lay dying. Yesterday's events seemed strangely distant, almost as if she had dreamed them. She swallowed and forced her hands to move, kneading the cloth underwater to set free the blood which was all too real. It was the captain's only shirt, and she must hang it out to dry while there was still sunlight.

She glanced across the fire at Captain O'Brien, sitting before his tent, his greatcoat draped over his shoulders against the chill. He wore a frown of concentration as he bent over the pocket notebook on his knee. Laura had given him his first lesson today, and while he had quickly grasped the letters she had taught him, his hand was not yet accustomed to shaping them.

Laura left the shirt to soak a bit longer and picked up the captain's jacket. The blood that had soaked into the wool was mostly dry now, and she worked at it with a brush. What, she wondered, would be the consequence of her placing herself under Captain O'Brien's protection? That step, taken in anger at her uncle's sordid attempt to sell her into marriage (or perhaps something worse), would surely ruin her in the view of the polite Boston society she had once known, should they come to hear of it. She was, ostensibly, serving as a laundress while the captain escorted her to her friends in Santa Fé. It was an excuse that was only just respectable. Scrubbing the dust from the clothing of Company I was well enough for Mrs. Sergeant Somebody, but it was not what one would expect of Miss Howland, formerly of Church Street.

Boston, however, was a world away from New Mexico Territory. All the usual rules did not necessarily apply on the frontier, and certainly not in war times. She had no home, no family that she cared to acknowledge, no protectors save her army friends, yet she felt safe here, even happy. A hundred small freedoms she would never have enjoyed in Boston had become most dear to her in this country. Freedoms of which she'd scarcely been aware, until Franklin had spoken to her of similar feelings.

A gust of wind puffed fragrant smoke up from the fire. "Ach," the captain said, squeezing green eyes shut against the sting. Laura smiled, then busied herself with wringing out his shirt. It would not do to let her gaze linger on the captain's face, pleasant as it was to look at. She liked him, but she had not yet decided whether it was in her best interest to encourage his very evident affection for her. Laura felt a tinge of color coming into her cheeks as she stepped around the fire to hang the shirt on the little line strung between two tents: Captain O'Brien's, where she'd been sleeping, and that which had been Franklin's, currently occupied by the captain. She sensed his eyes upon her, and made a show of straightening the sleeves.

We are so very different, she thought. Not that she had any prejudice against the Irish. She had known any number of Irish gentlemen in Boston, and found them true-hearted, if rather exuberant, but the captain was—well—wilder. A soldier, a miner in Colorado. Heaven knew what before that. He was kind, and could be gentle, but was also quick of temper. He *wanted* to be a gentleman, she thought, but he was not one now, and she was not sure she had the power to make him one.

A thudding of bootheels; Laura turned to see Lieutenant Denning approaching in some haste. Denning was a good man, well bred, who would most likely become the company's first lieutenant now that Franklin was gone. He reached a hand to his hat as his eyes met Laura's, but his attention was on the captain. "Have you heard?" he called out before reaching the fire, "We're ordered back to Fort Union!"

The captain looked up sharply. "What?"

"A courier's here from Colonel Canby," said Denning, slightly out of breath. "The commander orders us to turn back at once."

"On a cold day in hell we will!" said the captain. He glanced up at Laura, coloring deeply, and muttered, "Sorry."

"Never mind," said Laura, and turned her attention to the lieutenant. "You must be mistaken, Mr. Denning," she said. "The Rebels have no ammunition—"

"Orders are orders," said Denning, disgust creeping into his voice.

Laura frowned. "Did Colonel Canby know about your victory when he wrote the order?" she asked.

Mr. Denning shook his head. "Couldn't have. His courier just arrived, and he was three days riding from Fort Craig. Half killed himself getting here."

"Well, then, surely—"

"It's *orders*," said Captain O'Brien, standing up.

"Colonel Slough read them in front of a dozen officers," said Mr. Denning. "There's no way to pretend they weren't received. He's miffed, though. He says it's an insult."

"Colonel Canby would never insult one of his officers," Laura said firmly.

"Colonel Canby don't know we've burned the Rebels' train," said the captain, folding his arms across his chest. "Here we are ready to kick the bas—the Rebels back to Texas, and there they are with no food and no bullets, but we're ordered back to Fort Union, and so we've no choice. We've got to turn back."

"Couldn't a message be taken to the colonel?" asked Laura.

"Not in time," said Mr. Denning. "Captain Nicodemus offered to ride straight back—"

"Nicodemus?" said Laura, surprised. "Would that be William Nicodemus?"

"I think so."

Laura felt green eyes burning into her. She pretended not to notice. "I should like to speak to him," she said carefully. "Is he at headquarters?"

"He was, last I knew." Mr. Denning shot a wary glance toward the captain. "I'd better tell the boys we're marching in the morning." He bowed toward Laura and strode off.

Her hands were cold, Laura realized. She put them into her cloak pockets, and turned to face Captain O'Brien. "Will you escort me to headquarters, Captain?" she asked.

She had observed that the captain's gaze occasionally took on an intensity quite intimidating to those who did not know him. Her late father would no doubt have disapproved of the way she now met and held this gaze, but she knew that the captain would interpret modesty as weakness, and if there were to be any hope of an understanding between them, she must not allow him to bully her.

"Captain Nicodemus?" he said, his voice tight.

Laura nodded. "A member of Colonel Canby's staff. I knew him a little last summer, when they were all in Santa Fé. He was a lieutenant, then."

"Got the colonel's whole staff wrapped about your wee finger, eh?" he said, his tone dangerously soft.

Laura raised her chin. "I wish to send a message to Colonel Canby. Would you be so kind as to escort me to see Captain Nicodemus?"

"And if I don't, you'll have Chaves, or Chapin, to take you?" His eyes blazed jealousy, but behind it Laura saw the hurt it had taken her some time to discern; the hurt of a man who believes his heart's wish is beyond his reach. Though her own heart was beating rather fast, she held his gaze calmly, willing him to understand what she could not say aloud. *You have no rivals. You need fear no competition. You have only to show you can behave like a gentleman. Win me!*

For a long moment, neither moved, then finally the captain glanced away. "I'll take you," he said roughly.

Laura breathed relief. "Thank you," she said, and handed him his jacket. He stared at her for a moment—the hard, hungry stare that had frightened her so at first—then he went into his tent.

Laura brought her gloves out of her cloak pocket and put them on; black and worn, like her gown. She really must do something about that. In these weary clothes, her appearance was barely civilized.

Captain O'Brien returned and stood blinking at her as if

deciding whether to continue being angry. She rewarded him with a smile. He ducked his head, turned, and strode off toward Kozlowski's ranch house, which was presently serving as headquarters for the Colorado Volunteers. Laura watched him for a moment, then allowed herself a small nod of satisfaction, and hurried to catch up with him.

"Who's the sick one?" the guard demanded from the doorway.

Jamie clenched his teeth to stop their chattering and squinted up at the man's silhouette. He and the other Confederate prisoners had been locked in Kozlowski's shed for a day and a half, and the sunlight blazing in the open door nearly blinded him.

"He is," Lacey McIntyre said beside him. Jamie shot him a glare.

"I'm not a s-sick," he said.

"You've been shivering all night." McIntyre's dark eyes showed concern. "Go on, Russell. You belong in the hospital."

"Come on, then," the man in the doorway said. "Get up."

Jamie reluctantly got to his feet, shaking off the assistance McIntyre offered. That was cruel, he knew, because Lacey didn't have many friends. He'd switched sides, so neither army trusted him much. Jamie tried to soften the snub with a smile, but the truth was, he was angry at Lacey for making him go. He wanted to stay with the prisoners—with Lacey, his friend—not be stuck in a damned hospital. He hated hospitals.

Something made him turn in the doorway and look back. Lacey nodded at him, and said something, only Jamie couldn't quite hear it because of the ringing in his ears. "Luck," it might have been. He nodded back, then quickly turned away. He hated good-byes as well.

Outside the sun was so bright he had to stare at the ground. He sneezed. Tears stung his eyes and he brushed them away. Scraps of muddy snow crunched under his feet. He hugged himself, partly because his arm was aching again and partly from the cold. He wished he'd picked up one of those fine Union overcoats from the battlefield at Valverde.

The thought of that day, more than a month ago now, made him shudder, and the guard glanced at him. "In there," the soldier said, indicating Kozlowski's tavern. Jamie walked through the open door and saw a dozen pairs of eyes looking up at him. The floor was lined with men stretched out under blankets or sitting up against the walls, every one a Union soldier. Jamie felt their eyes taking in his gray jacket—the nice one Momma'd made for him, with the lieutenant's bars from Captain Martin—and wished even more for the overcoat.

"Come on in, son." The surgeon got up from his knees beside a sleeping patient. "You been sneezin'?"

Jamie shook his head. "I'm not sick," he said.

The surgeon sat him down in the light from the doorway. "What's that?" he asked, pointing to the grubby handkerchief tied around Jamie's right arm.

"A minié ball grazed me," Jamie told him.

"Let's have a look."

Jamie sat still while the surgeon untied the handkerchief; hissed as the scab came away with the cloth.

"Better let me clean that up. Take your jacket off, son. Shirt, too."

Jamie did so, folding the uniform jacket carefully in his lap, fingering the rip where the ball had ruined Momma's handiwork. His other jacket was gone, now; burned with the rest of the supply train. Jamie closed his eyes. He didn't want to think about that.

The air was cold on his bare skin. He tried not to shiver and not to feel bad about how much thinner his chest was than those of the hardy Pike's Peakers still watching him, making him self-conscious. Damn them all, he thought bitterly.

"He looks cold," a voice said, not the surgeon's. Jamie looked up. One of the wounded men was looking at him, a sandy-haired giant with a big mustache, propped up on an elbow with his bandaged leg stretched before him. "Wants a blanket, I figure." he added.

"Yep," another said, a bushy-bearded fellow sitting with his back against the wall and his arm in a sling. "All his blankets got burned up, poor little feller."

Jamie clenched his jaw to control his fury. Damn these Pike's Peak demons, them and their barrel-chested major and the Irish captain who'd murdered the horses and mules. It was they who'd destroyed General Sibley's supply train. *His* supply train.

"Yeah, he wants a blanket all right," the first man mocked. "He's shaking."

The surgeon finished tying a fresh bandage on Jamie's arm. "Go sit by the fire, son," he said. "Don't want you getting sicker."

"I'm not sick," Jamie muttered as he shrugged into his clothes and moved to where he could stare into the flames. The Yankee men's eyes followed him and their voices whispered just out of hearing. He picked up a stick and poked at the coals, glad for an excuse to ignore his captors.

I'm not sick. I'm just sick at heart.

Fool. Bloody fool.

The words drummed in O'Brien's head, a march, unescapable, pounding along with his boots in the mud of the camp. He had walked straight away from his lady, turned his back on her, and yet she followed. He should say something to her, some kind thing to show he was not angry with her, but only at himself for being so clumsy. No words came. *Bloody fool.*

They got to the ranch house, a long, low construction, made of logs and busy with soldiers; a sea of staff officers and orderlies. He looked at Miss Laura to see if she meant to find this Nicodemus on her own, but she showed no sign of it. She stayed by him, saints knew why.

Colonel Slough's coach stood by the porch, the horses sidling in their traces with all the bustle about them. O'Brien reached a hand out to one of the leaders—matched grays, they were—and let it nuzzle his palm. A lad he recognized, one of Slough's aides, came out of the house with a burden of baggage.

"Bailey," O'Brien called, "where's that courier came from Canby?"

"In with the colonel, I think," said the soldier, jerking his head toward the house.

O'Brien looked at the house, not wanting to go in. Likely Chivington was in there, and the major was the last person he wanted to see. O'Brien had not forgiven him—would never forgive him—for making him slaughter horses. But here was his lady waiting, he hadn't a choice. He dared a long look at her, pretty wisps of gold blowing about her fair face, and felt the madness rising up in him again. Sure, he'd walk straight into hell for her, he would. Bloody fool.

Up the wooden steps, across the porch and into the house, with Miss Laura following. An orderly came at them with more baggage; O'Brien made the man step aside for her. Pleased with himself, he caught her eye, and the smile she gave him started a glow in his chest that spread right through him.

The door of the headquarters room stood open: Slough and Tappan inside shuffling papers and talking idly to Wyncoop, Logan, and another captain O'Brien didn't recognize. A lanky lad, dark, with a mustache as wispy as himself. The stranger looked up at O'Brien in the doorway, then beyond, and his eyes grew wide.

"Miss Howland?" he said, standing up.

She came forward with smiles, and all the men rose while O'Brien bit down on his temper. "Captain Nicodemus," she said. "I wasn't sure you'd remember me. Congratulations on your promotion."

Nicodemus grinned like a silly fool. "Not remember you? Course I remember! And thank you."

"May I have a few words with you, when it's convenient?" said Miss Laura, and no sooner said than he stooped for his hat and came toward her, offering his arm. She laid her hand lightly upon it, and as they passed him going out O'Brien smelled a whiff of her: clean, fresh soap and a hint of wood smoke.

He'd never thought to offer his arm. Damn bloody fool.

Wyncoop chuckled. "Your laundress has an old flame, eh, Red?"

"He's only a friend," said O'Brien, staring a challenge.

Wyncoop cocked an eyebrow, then shrugged. Slough went back to his papers, as did Tappan after a long look. Logan and Wyncoop picked up their conversation, and O'Brien turned away.

Miss Laura and her friend had got all the way to the porch before he caught up with them. He stopped by the door to let Slough's orderly pass with another bag, and hung back, listening shamefully to his lady talking to the courier. They were gazing out toward the old Indian ruin west of the ranch.

"Do you remember our picnic?" she was saying. "It seems so long ago."

The tall lad nodded. "That was the day I gave you up for lost," he said. "Thought Lacey'd won you. We all did."

O'Brien's gut began to burn. Still he stayed in the doorway, wanting and not wanting to hear more. Miss Laura only sighed, though, and pulled a folded paper from out of her cloak.

"Mr. McIntyre asked me to appeal to Colonel Canby on his behalf. Would you please see that the colonel gets this?" she said.

"I will. He won't like it," said Nicodemus.

"I know, but I promised to try," said Miss Laura, "for friendship's sake. I don't blame you for being angry—" She glanced up, and saw O'Brien. "Captain, I don't believe you have met my kind protector, Captain O'Brien. He has rescued me from a number of troubles."

O'Brien came forward. Nicodemus faced him and looked him up and down, then reached out his hand. "How d'ye do? Friend of Miss Howland's is a friend of mine."

O'Brien shook hands, watching the fellow's face, trying to read it. The young scrap had courted her, then. Well, if he thought to do so again, he'd soon change his friendly tune.

"Hear you Pike's Peak fellows scared the Texans right good," said Nicodemus. "They're calling you a lot of demons."

"More like angels, Captain," said a voice behind O'Brien, a voice there could be no mistaking. Nicodemus looked up, and O'Brien turned to see Major Chivington coming up the porch steps.

He had on his Sunday face, eyes fair brimming with hellfire and his beard freshly trimmed. A big man, the major—impressive when preaching, and a great hero with the lads.

"If we hadn't been here," he said grandly, "the Texans might have had Fort Union for the taking." He turned his attention to Miss Laura, and his fierce eyebrows drew together. "I thought you had escorted that woman to Glorieta, Captain."

"Aye, but it's full of wounded Rebels now," said O'Brien. "No place for her."

"Neither is this a place for her," said Chivington. "I believe our orders were explicit. There are to be no women traveling with this column."

O'Brien narrowed his eyes. "Aye, sir," he said slowly, "we'll leave her with the other laundresses at Fort Union, then."

"No," said Chivington, turning his glare on O'Brien. "I have tolerated her presence long enough. If she cannot go to Glorieta then she must remain here."

Miss Laura spoke up. "Major Chivington—"

"I don't believe I addressed you, *madam*," said the major.

"Now look here," said Nicodemus. "Miss Howland is a personal friend of Colonel Canby's—"

Chivington's eyebrows went up. "So I have been told. Perhaps Colonel Canby allows all manner of women to travel with his army, but the Colorado Volunteers do not."

"With all due respect, Major," said Nicodemus, straightening his lanky frame 'til he was nearly as tall as Chivington, "I think you've misunderstood this lady's position. She's a respectable lady—"

"Is she? Then I'm sure she will be very much more comfortable away from the army and the unwanted attentions of its less civilized members." Chivington spun on his heel and went into the ranch house.

Nicodemus turned angry eyes toward O'Brien. "That major of yours is a sight too headstrong! Don't mind telling you, that's why the colonel sent me racing up here with those orders. He was worried you Colorado fellows would go off half-cocked, and so you did!"

"I've no love for the man," said O'Brien. He looked at Miss Laura. "I'm sorry," he told her.

She gave him a sad smile. "So am I," she said. She glanced at her courier friend. "Thank you for defending me, Captain

Nicodemus. I think, under the circumstances, that I had better try to get to Santa Fé."

"The Confederates have Santa Fé!" Nicodemus said.

"If I can get to Mrs. Canby, I shall be quite safe."

"I'll take you there," O'Brien said. His voice came out husky, from the tightness in his throat. He swallowed.

"Thank you, Captain," she said, bestowing a smile upon him. "Perhaps if you take me to Glorieta, Monsieur Vallé can escort me to Mrs. Canby's house."

"You cannot seriously mean to go to Santa Fé!" Nicodemus said.

"I have no choice," Miss Laura answered. "I cannot remain here when all my friends are leaving. Poor Mr. Kozlowski has enough trouble on his hands."

"I won't allow it!"

Miss Laura turned a look on Nicodemus that O'Brien well knew could make ice water run in a man's veins. He himself looked down at the mud-caked boards of the porch, concealing his sudden glee.

"Th-the colonel wouldn't wish me to," he heard Nicodemus say.

"I cannot believe Colonel Canby would not want me to seek out his wife," Miss Laura said. "Please do not worry about me, Captain Nicodemus. I have good friends to help me."

O'Brien glanced up and saw her looking at him, smiling, and his heart gave a mighty squeeze. Ah, he hated to lose her, but he'd take her to safety. It was the best he could do for her.

She looked out toward the mountains, squinting into the westering sun. "It is too late today, I think," she said. "Perhaps in the morning? Early, before you're to march?"

O'Brien nodded. One more night. One more evening of talk by the fire; one more dawn listening to her softly breathing in the tent next to his. Precious hours to treasure.

She turned to her friend. "It was a pleasure to see you, Captain Nicodemus. Please give my regards to all my friends at Fort Craig." She put out her hand, and the courier shook it.

"Do be careful," he said.

"Thank you, I shall," she said, moving away. O'Brien made to follow.

"Miss Howland—"

She paused, and glanced back. O'Brien saw a hungry look in the lad's eyes, a look that roused a jealous fire in himself.

"Was I wrong?" Nicodemus asked. "About Lacey?"

Miss Laura was silent for a long moment. *Who is Lacey?* O'Brien wondered. He couldn't read her face.

Then, "Good-bye, Captain," she said, and turned to O'Brien.

He led the way down the porch steps, past Slough's coach, back toward the camp. All the way he could feel Nicodemus's eyes following them, and could guess only too well what the fellow was feeling.

Miss Laura was silent until they reached their camp near the end of Officers' Row. She stepped to O'Brien's shirt, hanging by the tents, and felt it.

"I had better hang it by the fire. It is quite damp still."

O'Brien stood staring, unable to think of a reply, while she moved the shirt closer to the fire. His lady—though he had no right to think of her as his—must leave him tomorrow, and the thought fairly paralyzed him. Wild ideas flew through his mind. If he flung himself at her feet and offered marriage, what would she say? He had no worldly goods to offer her, only himself. She might say no. Might laugh at him, even. A fairy princess like her, married to an old troll of a soldier? No.

He went into his tent and rummaged through what was left of his rations, producing a bit of cooked beef and some hard crackers. Miss Laura sizzled them together in a pan over the fire—saints knew where that pan came from; it seemed she could find anything she wanted—and the two of them ate in silence while night closed in over the camp.

"Well, Captain," she said when the last bit was gone, "where is your pocket notebook? We should have one more lesson."

O'Brien stared into the flames and shook his head. "No point in it," he said.

"That is not true."

Miss Laura picked up a twig, and scratched some letters

in the dirt. "What word is that?" she demanded.

"I don't know."

"Spell it out. You know all the letters."

"F," he said. "A, I, T, H."

"What word is it?"

"Fate," said O'Brien.

"Faith," she said, and her voice had gone soft. "You must have faith in yourself. You can learn this."

O'Brien shook his head. "You won't be here to teach me."

"Well, I'm sure Mr. Denning would—"

"No."

Miss Laura sat up and laid the twig across her knees. "It does not matter. You know enough now to start teaching yourself. And—we shall meet again, I'm sure. You must not give up!"

The earnestness in her voice made him look up.

"You can master this," she said, eyes bright, "and when you do, no one will be able look down on you, ever again."

That was true, he supposed. And oh, how he'd wanted that, but it seemed not to matter now. All that mattered was her company which he must lose tomorrow, likely forever. He looked down at the letters she'd writ in the dirt. She had more faith than he, he decided. She'd go to Mrs. Canby, to her friends in the regular army, and would marry one of the colonel's staff, and be very happy, and never think of him again.

He heard her stand, glanced up to see her checking his shirt. She hadn't had to wash it. He wouldn't have asked. Ah, she was a good lady; he didn't deserve her. He must try to forget it all. It had been only a dream anyway—a pleasant dream that had seemed very real—but already it was fading away, and the kindest thing he could do for himself was to let it go.

"Laura," he whispered, savoring the taste of the name she had not given him leave to use one last time.

"Pardon?" she said.

"Ah—siubhal a'rùin," he said aloud, his heart racing. "It's words from a song."

"Do you sing, Captain?" she said, smiling. She carried his shirt back to her seat.

"Aye," said O'Brien, watching her spread the shirt across her skirt before the fire. "Not as fair as you, though."

"Have I sung for you? I don't remember."

"Not for me," he said.

"Oh." She glanced down at the cloth in her lap. "Well, will you sing for me? Please," she said as he started to shake his head, and the fire glistening in her eyes took away all his will to deny her. He looked away into the flames, swallowed, and began to sing softly, barely above a whisper.

> "Siubhal, siubhal, siubhal a'rùin,
> Siubhal go socair, arragh siubhal go ciùin,
> Siubhal go do dorus, arragh èalaidh leam,
> Is go dhuit, mo mùirnin slàn."

He stopped, for the rest of the song had little to do with his feelings.

"That is lovely," said his lady. "What does it mean?"

"I cannot tell you," he said, feeling the heat rise into his face.

"Please?"

"No," he whispered. The fire popped, twice.

"Will you sing it again, then?"

He was trembling, he noticed. He moved a bit closer to the fire, and didn't look at his lady for fear that his heart would crack. Then he sang—*Come, come, come my love*—and she hummed the tune with him, making a tingle run up his neck.

"How beautiful," she said into the silence that followed. "And how sad."

He nodded, not wanting to speak for fear of breaking the spell. This moment would be a treasure to him, when she was gone. He dared a glance at her, all golden in the firelight. Steam had begun to rise from the damp fabric she held on her lap. She smoothed the sleeve with a fair hand, and he shivered as if she'd touched his own flesh. He closed his eyes.

The fire gave a faint, banshee whine. "Do you miss Ireland?" he heard her ask softly.

Surprised, he looked up at her. "Sometimes," he said. "But I wouldn't go back."

She nodded. "That is how I feel about Boston," she said. She lifted his shirt and felt it. "This is better. If you hang it inside your tent it should be fit to wear in the morning." She rose, and offered the warm garment to him.

"Thank you," he said, taking it.

"You are very welcome. Thank you for the song." She stood there a moment, looking softly down at him, then moved to her tent. "I'd better collect my things if I am to leave tomorrow," she said. She cast a glance at him over her shoulder, and smiled, and slipped into the tent. With a soft "Good night," she was gone.

O'Brien looked at the shirt that she'd held, that she'd washed for him. Another memory to treasure up. He added a log to the fire and sat fingering the shirt as he stared into the flickering flames.

2

"My mind her image still retains,
Whether asleep or waking,
I hope to see my dear again,
For her my heart is breaking."

—*The Girl I Left Behind Me*, Traditional Irish Song

It was cold in Glorieta Pass, even in midmorning. Laura pulled her cloak closer against the chill, and Captain O'Brien took his attention from the mules to glance at her. She smiled to reassure him, and he looked back at the road. He'd been quiet this morning, even more so than usual.

"I did not know you could drive," she said, trying to start a conversation.

"I was a teamster in New York," said the captain. He did not elaborate, and Laura kept silent while he negotiated the wagon around a narrow turn under the rising cliffs. She remembered the first glimpse she'd had of these rocks from the stagecoach upon her arrival in New Mexico—scarcely a year past—and more recently, the first time Captain O'Brien had escorted her to Pigeon's Ranch. That had been but four days ago. Four days and two battles, and considerable upheaval of life and of mind. She counted further back, to the day she had met Captain O'Brien and Lieutenant Franklin in Las Vegas, all of a week since. It seemed an impossibly short span of time in which to have made such friends, and lost one, and now to be parting from another.

Laura stifled a sigh and straightened on the hard seat of the wagon. Captain O'Brien was moody this morning, and she felt vaguely disappointed. She had thought—hoped?—he would express a desire to see her again, but he had said nothing. Perhaps he did not admire her so much as she'd believed. It would not be the first time, she thought, remembering with a small gasp of laughter the way she had flung herself—quite cold-bloodedly—at poor Lieutenant Franklin. Laura felt a blush rising to her cheeks. She had not known at the time that the lieutenant was a woman. Indeed, she had just broken up a fight between Franklin and the captain. The recollection sent a chill down her spine. The risks Franklin had taken! How had she found the courage? Laura suspected that had she herself not intervened, the captain would have half-murdered Franklin in the rage of his jealousy.

Where was that passion now? she wondered. She glanced at the captain's profile, seemingly chiseled from granite, and just as cold. Not a noble face, perhaps, but the eyes—set high between a strong brow and sharp cheekbones—were compelling. One could never forget such eyes.

Careful, Laura. Do not make a fool of yourself.

"It was clever of you to volunteer for this duty," she said as cheerfully as she could. "Monsieur Vallé will be grateful to have the wounded Texans out of his house."

"It was the only way I could think of to get you safe to Santa Fé," said the captain.

Colonel Slough had approved the detail at the captain's suggestion. While Lieutenant Denning marched the rest of I Company north with the command, Captain O'Brien and a dozen of his men now escorted two wagons—empty save for the one sick Rebel brought from Kozlowski's—to Pigeon's Ranch at La Glorieta Pass, where they would fill them with wounded Confederates to take into Santa Fé. Laura's presence with the detail had not been commented upon. She was sure Major Chivington was wishing her good riddance.

Behind them, driving the second wagon, Private Shaunessy began to sing.

> "I'm lonesome since I crossed the hills,
> And o'er the moor that's sedgy,
> With heavy thoughts my mind is filled,
> Since I parted with my Peggy."

"Shut it, Egan," the captain said, sounding annoyed. Laura glanced back at Mr. Shaunessy, who looked more amused than chastened. His eyes gleamed briefly at her from beneath the brim of his hat before he returned his attention to his mules.

A sound made Laura glance down at the sick man lying behind her. Surprising that an officer was being released, but then he was rather small, and wracked with fever. No doubt the surgeons didn't wish him to communicate his ailment to the Union wounded at Kozlowski's.

"Did you call?" she said to him.

No answer from the thin, strained face. The brown hair clung damply to his forehead despite the cool morning. He had thrown his blanket half off, and Laura reached back to pull it up again. He could be no older than herself.

"Emmaline?" he whispered.

"No," she said, "my name is Laura."

Captain O'Brien shifted in the seat beside her. She glanced up, but he was staring at the road. They were close to Pigeon's Ranch now, she believed.

"I'm sorry, Emma," muttered the Confederate. "I'm sorry."

"It's all right," said Laura gently. She smoothed his hair back from his face, thinking of Lieutenant Franklin's slow, tormented death. This man would live, she thought, unless the fever became very bad. It did not look like the smallpox she had seen so much of in Las Vegas, when she had taken shelter with Padre Martinez and helped in the hospital.

The wagon rounded another cliff, and suddenly they were at Glorieta. The snow had mostly gone, diminishing the evidence of the recent battle, apart from the fresh graves. Laura could not help glancing toward the canyon wall and the tall pine beneath which Lieutenant Franklin's remains now lay. A chill breeze stirred the naked fingers of a stand of young cottonwoods nearby, trailing a hint of wood smoke. Laura turned her gaze to the road ahead and to Pigeon's ranch house, strangely quiet now that there were no armies in the pass. Smoke was drifting from only one of the four chimneys. Probably enough wood for only one fire; between them the two armies had devoured everything in sight.

Including, she suddenly remembered, the burro that Captain O'Brien had purchased for her to ride. It had been in Monsieur Vallé's corral before the battle, but they had found no sign of it afterward. "Your burro," she said, turning to the captain. "Let me pay you for it."

"No."

"I know very well you spent your last dollar on that burro," said Laura, fishing among the few coins she had put in her cloak pocket.

"I'll not be taking your money," he said roughly.

"Then take some of Lieutenant Franklin's."

A scowl crossed his face, and he reined in the mules, rolling to a stop just short of the ranch house. Laura saw the muscles in his jaw working.

"You know the lieutenant gave me all h—all his money," she said. "Won't you allow me to share the gift?" When he didn't reply, she added, "You will need money on the march. Please, Captain. How much did the burro cost?"

He cast a furtive glance at her. "Ten dollars," he said.

It was a lie. A burro would have cost at least forty dollars in Santa Fé under normal conditions, and during a campaign of war—well, no matter. She would not hurt his pride any further. She counted ten dollars in silver and pressed the coins into the captain's hand.

"Thank you," she said. "I will feel better knowing you have it." She had not seen his eyes burn so sharply since the night before the first battle. He opened his mouth as if to say something, then closed it again.

"¡Hola, señores!"

Laura looked up to see Monsieur Vallé coming out of the house. She waved to him, and he hurried forward to help her out of the wagon.

"But what is this?" he said, raising his gray-flecked brows. "Is the army going to Santa Fé?"

"No," said Laura, glancing toward the captain as she stepped to the ground, "but I am. I've been banished."

Monsieur Vallé looked to Captain O'Brien, who merely said "We're here for the wounded." The captain flicked the reins, moving the wagon up to the door. Mr. Shaunessy brought up the second wagon, and the escort began to dismount, leading their horses into the stone corral behind the ranch house. Laura and Monsieur Vallé strolled toward the house.

"What does your brave captain want with the wounded Texans?"

"We're taking them to Santa Fé," said Laura. "Mrs. Canby has offered to take them in, but she would have to make several trips in her carriage to fetch them all."

"She is a saint, Madame Canby."

"Yes. I'm hoping she'll find a corner to spare for me."

Monsieur Vallé paused, looking down at her. "Is all well with you, ma chère?" he said softly.

Laura put on a smile. "Yes, thank you. I am fortunate to have so many kind friends." Her gaze strayed to Captain O'Brien, who was helping to carry out the wounded. How like him, she thought. He was not the sort to stand by and give orders, leaving the worst work to others.

"Come and say hello to Carmen," said Monsieur Vallé. "She will not forgive me if I let you go away without visiting her."

Laura nodded, her eyes still on the captain as she followed Monsieur Vallé into the house.

You're the greatest fool in creation, Alastar O'Brien. Granddad was right.

O'Brien cursed under his breath as he and Morris lifted another foul-smelling Texan into the wagon. What had possessed him to volunteer for this drudgery?

No trouble to answer that. It was all for the sake of his lady—Miss Laura—Miss Howland, he should say. But to drive into an occupied town with two cartloads of stinking Rebels at their backs? What a lovely romantic scene it would be. Why, she'd be fainting into his arms. From the stench if nothing else.

They went back into the house, and he glanced about, but she was nowhere in sight. That old Frenchman, Pigeon, had taken her off somewhere. Damn and blast.

If he, Alastar O'Brien, son of a career private in His Majesty's army and a farrier's daughter, were going to be such a fool as to speak to Miss Howland who surely had dozens of grand relations, he should have done so before they arrived here. Now there would be no more chance for privacy. Why had he not spoken before? Two days since, in this very valley, she had seemed to like him, and his heart had near sprouted wings. But she'd told him—warned him—that she expected his patience, and he'd thought there'd be plenty of time. And how should he speak to her, even if heaven should give him a chance? Sure, a fine provider he'd seem, with her own money—Franklin's damned money—jingling in his pocket.

Truth was, she deserved to be courted like the fine lady she was, and he hadn't the first idea how to set about it. He could almost wish Franklin alive. He was desperate enough to have asked the lad for advice.

Except that she had loved Franklin. He was sure of it. She never spoke of him but with tenderness, and if he'd lived, he'd have wed her himself. The thought was a knife in O'Brien's heart, and he sucked in a long, hard breath.

Best let her go, as he'd decided in the campfire's dying glow. He could do it, he thought, though it was harder than any of the battle work he'd lately been in.

"Daydreaming, Alastar?" Morris said softly.

O'Brien looked at the bearded ruffian lying at his feet, and at Sergeant Morris, squatting by the man's boots, waiting to lift him.

"That's Captain, to you," he said, taking hold of the fellow's shoulders. Did they not have any water in Texas, that they should be so unused to bathing?

"Aye, Captain," said Morris, grunting as they lifted the Rebel and hauled him out to the wagons. They were fast filling up. The wounded who could move themselves were climbing into Shaunessy's wagon, some painfully, all silently.

"How many more to be carried?" O'Brien asked Morris.

"Three, I think."

O'Brien swore as they lifted the Texan into his wagon, then climbed in and started moving the wounded men closer together to make room. The one lad they'd brought from Kozlowski's was taking more space than he ought. O'Brien shoved him ungently against the box. Miss Howland had seen fit to gift this stranger, this enemy, with her Christian name. If he hadn't looked half-dead already, O'Brien would have been tempted to murder him.

He frowned down at the fellow. Had he seen him before? In the canyon, or at the Rebel train? That was it. It was the lad who'd tried to defend the train. O'Brien had taken him prisoner, saving him from a bullet that some fool out of Wyncoop's company'd wanted to put in him. Looked like the reaper might take him after all.

O'Brien jumped down from the wagon. There she was, standing with Pigeon's wife over by Franklin's grave. As he watched she leaned forward and scattered a handful of pale flowers on the turned earth.

O'Brien looked away and busied himself with the last of the wounded, and with getting his men back in the saddle. By the time Miss Howland had said her good-byes and rejoined him on the box, he had his feelings firmly in hand. He kept his eyes on the road and his thoughts to himself as they drove over the pass, down through the canyon where Franklin had fallen in the first fight, and past the creek bed where O'Brien and his men had burned the Rebel train. The charred remnants had been scattered by the Texans on their way into Santa Fé, searching for food or anything left that might be of use, no doubt.

Miss Howland made a small sound beside him, and he glanced her way. She looked stricken, and he had to crush an impulse to gather her in his arms. She was staring at the scorched earth, the broken crates, the bits of blackened wood and metal that were all that was left of the wagons.

"It must have been dreadful," she whispered.

O'Brien didn't trust himself to answer. The worst horror was up the box canyon that had been the Rebels' corral. He urged the horses to a trot, the sooner to bring her away from this place of death. She didn't belong in a war, much as he hated to agree with Major Chivington. He was glad, truly, to be taking her out of danger.

Though it felt like riding into danger's mouth, just now. O'Brien was sharply aware of the Rebels at his back, and heartily glad they were wounded and weaponless.

"Kimmick, put out your flag," he called to one of his men, who undid a stick bundled in white cloth from his saddle and shook out the banner, propping it on his saddle-bow.

"It's still fifteen miles to Santa Fé," Miss Howland said in a small voice.

"They'll have pickets," O'Brien answered, glancing 'round. They were leaving the narrow entrance to the pass behind them, and beginning to drive between rolling hills spotted with scrubby evergreens. Sure to be a picket somewhere near.

As they drove west a band of blue mountains rose on the far side of the broken plain. The trail wound through hills better grown with scrub than those east of the mountains, but still it was an empty, lonely land. The rutted tracks curved gently northward, and glimpses of houses were now to be seen from the hilltops, and a thin trace of smoke from someone's fire. Before long they were rolling between small farm plots, and houses, and then into the town. The houses were all of mud, like the other Mexican towns he'd seen, but there were no Mexicans in sight. Tired, hungry-looking white men lay in the shadows of buildings and walls. Eyes looked out darkly from deep windows. O'Brien's skin began to crawl as if he were entering a room filled with vermin. He and his men were the only fellows in blue this side of the mountains, and he felt terribly exposed.

They splashed through a small stream, up a hill and into the town square. Here, at last, they encountered a picket of sorts; eight or ten fellows standing guard about the front of a long, low house on the far side of the square.

"It's across the plaza, and to the right," said Miss Howland.

O'Brien moved the wagon forward at a walk, keeping behind Kimmick's white flag. His escort kept close to the wagons, the lads looking as nervous as he felt. Two Rebels came forward to meet them, and he halted the mules.

"What's your business?" one said.

"Brought your wounded from Pigeon's," O'Brien told him.

The guard looked in the wagon, then consulted with his companion. "Can't leave 'em here," he said.

Miss Howland leaned forward. "Mrs. Canby is taking them in."

O'Brien drew a short breath. He hadn't thought it wise to

mention the wife of the Union commander, but the name had a surprising effect on the Texans. The guard's face softened.

"Go on, then," he said, jerking his head toward the street that ran away east of the long house.

O'Brien twitched the reins and drove 'round the corner, and in another moment Miss Howland was pointing at a wooden gate set into one of the endless mud walls whose few windows' looked out on a big Spanish church across the way. O'Brien pulled up at the gate. Miss Howland made as if to get down, and he had to force himself to move and assist her, when what he really wanted was to catch her up and never let go. He must leave her here, in the middle of this ants' nest of Rebels. He might never see her again. Numb, he stood by while she knocked at the gate. A voice from the other side said something in Spanish.

"It's me, Miss Howland," she said. "I've come with the wounded men from Glorieta."

A small door opened in the gate, and a Mexican peered out, then exclaimed, and smiled welcome at Miss Howland. They exchanged a few words, and he shut the door again, only to open the whole gate a moment later. It swung inward, revealing a short, dark passage big enough to admit a wagon, and a sunny garden beyond.

Miss Howland turned to O'Brien. "Juan Carlos has gone to fetch Mrs. Canby."

O'Brien nodded. He should bring the wagon in, now. Instead he stared down at Miss Howland. "Do you have any sort of weapon?"

She looked surprised, then smiled slightly, and pulled back her cloak to reveal a pistol strapped at her waist. "Another gift from Lieutenant Franklin," she said.

He had never seen a woman wearing a gun before, even the wilder women in Denver City. Somehow it didn't look wrong on her, though he couldn't like the necessity of her having it.

"Can you use it?" he said.

She nodded. "The lieutenant showed me how."

He searched her face, and she returned his gaze as calm as if she were at Sunday church and not in the middle of an occupied town. "Be very careful," he said at last.

"Thank you, Captain. I shall."

A noise from the house drew her attention away, and one of the mules sidled, and everything came into motion again. O'Brien led the team into the passage, disappointed in himself. With everything in his heart threatening to burst him open, all he could tell her was to be careful. She must think him a great idiot.

Go to, Alastar. Give it up, and be gone.

He turned to the wagons, seeking to bury himself in activity so as not to be thinking at all.

"Laura! Oh, my dear, I am so glad you have come!" Mrs. Canby hugged Laura without ceremony.

Laughing, Laura hugged her just as firmly, then stepped back and looked at Mrs. Canby's sad eyes, always so at odds with her smile. "You look tired," she said.

"Well, we have been fairly busy. How many men did you bring?"

"Seventeen, I believe. All that were in Glorieta, and one from Kozlowski's."

"Gracious. I shall have to put some of them in the parlor. No, the dining room, I think. It will be easier to move the furniture. Juan, pide a María que llevara las otras sábanas, por favor."

Laura swallowed, for her next words were not easy. "Do you think you could spare a corner somewhere for me?" she asked. "I'm not above the parlor, myself," she added with a small laugh.

Mrs. Canby turned surprised eyes to her. "I thought—" She glanced beyond Laura to the wagon where Captain O'Brien was helping unload the wounded.

"Major Chivington has forbidden me to travel any longer with the army," said Laura.

"Oh." A faint look of worry came into Mrs. Canby's face, then was banished by a kindly smile. "Of course, my dear. You know you are always welcome. You may share my room."

"Oh, I wouldn't—"

"Don't be nice, Laura," said Mrs. Canby, laughing. "It's the only place I have to put you. We shall be walking over a carpet of men as it is." She moved to the wagon in two quick steps. The captain looked up from his work. "Captain—O'Brien, is it not? I am deeply grateful to you for your help. Won't you come inside for a moment?"

He looked surprised, but gave a short nod. "Thank you, ma'am," he said. "Morris, you take over here."

Mrs. Canby gave instructions to Juan Carlos for the disposition of the wounded, then ushered Laura and the captain into her parlor. "I hope you won't mind the disorder," she said, indicating a heap of cloth strips on the table, waiting to be rolled into bandages. "We have been preparing for you, as you see."

Carpet. A sofa. A fire spreading warmth from the grate. They seemed unimaginable luxuries. Laura gazed around the room that had become so familiar to her in the past year, feeling as if she'd come home.

"Won't you sit down?" said Mrs. Canby, sinking gracefully into her chair. Laura sat on the sofa. Captain O'Brien, after a moment's hesitation, pulled his hat off and perched on the far end.

"It was so very kind of you to bring the wounded in, Captain. I was in a worry how to get them here."

"Kind of you to take them, ma'am," said the captain. "Caring for enemy wounded."

"Well, someone must care for them," she said gently, her sad smile curving her lips. "Would you like something to eat?"

"No," said the captain, turning his hat in his hands. "We can't stay long. We ought to make Pigeon's by dark, and myself I'd rather get back to Kozlowski's. Bad dreams come if you sleep on a battleground." He cast a glance at Laura, then hastily looked at the floor.

"Let me get you something to take along, then," said Mrs. Canby. "You must be tired of marching fare. No, it won't take a minute. I insist." She glanced at Laura as she rose, still smiling. "I'll be back shortly."

Dear, kind Mrs. Canby, thought Laura, giving them privacy in which to say good-bye. She glanced expectantly at the captain, but he seemed to have discovered some interesting quality about his hat. Well, she would make it easy for him, and perhaps he'd remember her kindly. She turned to him and held out her hand.

"Thank you, Captain, for all your care of me."

He shook her hand, and kept hold of it longer than was strictly proper, staring at her with a bewildered expression. Laura gently removed her hand from his grasp, smiling so he would not be hurt.

"Remember to practice your letters," she added, "for I shall quiz you when next we meet."

The captain's brows drew together. Had she angered him? Her heart gave a little flutter, a shadow of her alarm when they'd first met. She had feared him in earnest then; now she only feared offending him.

"Is there something . . . ?" she faltered, for his eyes burned green fire.

"Marry me!" he said hoarsely.

3

> *"Dear thoughts are in my mind, and my soul soars*
> *enchanted,*
> *As I hear the sweet lark sing in the clear air of the day.*
> *For a tender, beaming smile to my hope has been granted,*
> *And tomorrow she shall hear all my fond heart would*
> *say."*
>
> —*The Lark in the Clear Air*, Samuel Ferguson

Laura blinked, surprised, and glanced down to compose herself. By the time she looked up again, smiling, Captain O'Brien was at the parlor door.

"Captain?"

If he'd heard, he did not heed her, for he passed from the room and in two long strides crossed the foyer. Laura rose and hurried after him, but reached the breezeway only in time to see him driving one of the wagons away up the street. His men, standing about the placita, stared after him. Mr. Shaunessy, who had been in the act of backing the second wagon out of the gate, leapt onto the box and took up the reins. "Come on, lads," he shouted, hauling on the leaders, who snorted and backed into the street, then surged forward. The placita burst into motion, and in a whirlwind moment the Colorado men were mounted and gone.

Stunned, Laura walked to the gate and watched them disappear into the plaza. Mrs. Canby came toward her across the placita, one of last fall's apples in her hand.

"What happened?"

Laura turned dazed eyes toward her. "I'm not quite sure."

Fool. Oaf. Thón.

O'Brien heard hoofbeats overtaking the rattle of Shaunessy's wagon behind him, and glanced over his shoulder.

He half expected it to be Rebel guards following, but it was his own men.

No turning back. Inisg.

He went too fast through the stream; the mules' hooves skittered. He reined them in a bit.

No good to turn back anyway. He must have ruined whatever credit he'd had with her, shouting it at her like an order. An Diabhul, but he was the greatest fool in creation!

He kept up the pace until they were out of the town, then slowed the mules to a trot. He couldn't drive them so, even with the wagons empty. No use taking it out on them, poor brutes.

He stared straight ahead, for he wanted no conversation. The men had the wisdom to ask him no questions. He could feel his face burning.

He was made for a soldier, sure, and not for a ladies' man. Well, no matter. This would make it all the easier for her to forget about him.

He never stopped until they were back at Pigeon's Ranch. He'd have liked to drive past it, but the beasts were weary and needed water. He pulled up by the well, and for once left the work to his men, jumping down from the box and striding across the road, past the ranch house and corrals, to where a scrabble of rock went straight up to the clifftop. He wanted to speak to no one, and no one to speak to him.

The smell of melting snow and wet pine greeted him atop the hill. The ground was rocky and scattered with minié balls and buckshot, and the tree trunks were scarred and riddled. The fighting must have been bad up here. There'd been a number of bodies to haul down, he remembered, though others had done most of the work before he'd arrived with the burial detail. He stalked deeper into the twilit woods, wanting silence and solitude. Tall trees, mostly pines, made him think of Avery town and the mine he'd given up back in Colorado. He came across one great fallen trunk, roots frozen into claws grasping at the air. He sat down upon it, and buried his face in his hands.

It was a sickness, love. It stole a man's strength and his sanity. He'd heard a thousand tales to prove it, but he'd never been stricken himself, until now. Or not since he was a callow lad, chasing after the village girls in Racecourse, but that was nothing like this. Nothing at all like it. He had wanted Miss Howland with all his soul from the moment he saw her, and the only thing that had changed since then was that now he wanted her as his wife.

Well, you can't have her, man.

He'd behaved like a great, bloody idiot, and she'd looked away only because she was too kind to laugh in his face. The memory burned; her hatred would be easier to bear than her pity.

Forget her. No, impossible. The best he could do was to stay far away, and that the army would help him to do.

He should go back down to Pigeon's. If they didn't start soon, they'd be driving in the dark to Kozlowski's. The thought made him tired. He sighed, then froze.

A sound. He raised his head. There, again. Something moving in the woods.

O'Brien's hand went to his pistol. Coming toward him, shuffling through the trees. He drew and quietly cocked his gun, waiting, listening.

It was off to his left. He moved quickly and silently to shelter behind the fallen tree's gnarled, uptorn roots, bracing his arm on one and aiming out at the large shadow rustling toward him. It was a great giant of a Rebel. No, a bear. No . . .

He uncocked his pistol, and the sound evoked a snort. "Easy, there," he said softly, and slowly straightened to his full height, head and shoulders above the tree roots.

A horse, liver chestnut; a mare. For a moment he'd thought it was Franklin's bay, but that fine animal was dead, shot on the field at Apache Canyon. This lass was smaller, with mane and tail all the same, deep brown, only a small white star on her forehead to break it. She stood still, nostrils flaring, ears a-twitch.

"Easy, lass," said O'Brien, slipping the gun into its holster. "I'll not hurt you."

He took a slow step sideways, out from behind the roots. The mare snorted. He raised his right hand, palm up, inviting her to smell. She strained her neck toward him, sniffing the air, then sidled back.

"No, you're right. I haven't any sugar," said O'Brien softly. "Are you hungry, then? You've been out here since the battle, haven't you lass?"

She was saddled and bridled, though the reins were gone. Likely she'd trod on them and broken them. O'Brien took a step toward her, and she threw up her head, rolling her eyes at him.

"There, now. It's all right. No one to jump at you." O'Brien kept up a flow of gentle words, as he'd learned from his granddad in Racecourse. Horses were sociable creatures. They liked to be talked to, and sung to. He moved slowly closer, holding up his hand for her to smell. When he was just out of arm's length she gave a start and flattened her ears, eyes showing white.

"Ah, no, lass, you won't be playing off your tricks on me," he said, standing his ground. "Come, you'd like to be out of that saddle, now wouldn't you? Come along, then."

She allowed him to move closer, and condescended to snuff at his outstretched palm, then put her nose up to his face. He breathed into her nostrils, letting her take his scent, and slowly moved his hand to her neck, touching her oh, so gently.

"That's it, cailin. Good lass."

He stroked her, crooning softly, and moved to her side, where the saddle hung cocked toward him. He reached under the skirt for the girth, found it, and with a little fumbling, managed to loose it, catching the saddle and blanket before they slid to the ground. If she were going to bolt, she'd do it then, but instead she craned her head around to look at him, and *whuffed.*

O'Brien set the tack on the ground and pulled a handful of long needles from a nearby pine tree, brushed them gently against her side a couple of times, then more vigorously, rubbing down her back and flanks. The mare sighed.

"That's better, eh, lass?" She stood quietly while he stepped around to her far side. She'd a sore where the girth had rubbed under her belly. He avoided it, scratching gently all around it. The mare sidled, but stayed where she was.

O'Brien went back to search in the saddle bags. They had the Texas star stamped onto the leather. Good fortune; he'd be able to keep the mare as spoils of war. He found a length of rope and fashioned a loose halter from it. "Here now," he said, stroking her neck. "Let's have you out of that bridle, eh?" He slipped the rope onto her head with no trouble, and undid the bridle's leather straps. Freed from the bit, the mare worked her tongue, then ground her teeth and sighed once more.

"There's a stream down that hill, there," he said to her, draping the bridle over his shoulder. "You might find a blade or two of grass left. Shall we go look, cailín?"

Keeping hold of the rope, he bent down and scooped up the saddle over his left arm, got it balanced, then started to walk. The mare followed gently. He led her to the cliff, where she snorted at the battle smells, but she followed him down, picking her way among the broken rocks. Surefooted, she was. A good horse. He would sell the ill-tempered mustang he'd broke. If Miss Howland had stayed he'd have given the mare to her.

He stopped, squeezing his eyes shut. The mare nickered at his back. He turned and looked into her great, brown eyes. At least she had made him think of something besides his own aching heart for two minutes together.

He started down again, looking across the valley at his men standing about in the road. It was dusk, and the smoke from Pigeon's chimney looked inviting, but he would drive on to Kozlowski's, he decided. There was still an election to run, to fill Franklin's place, so he'd best catch up to the column quickly. Then too, he was in no particular mood to be easy on his men, and the more miles he put between himself and Santa Fé, the better.

"He offered you marriage?" said Mrs. Canby, setting down her teacup.

"I believe so." Laura glanced at her own cup, and swirled the stray tea leaves left in it.

"And did not stay for an answer."

Laura sighed. "I keep wondering what I could have done to offend him."

Mrs. Canby picked up the teapot, and Laura held out her cup to be refilled. This was the last pot of tea they would enjoy until the merchants returned to Santa Fé; Mrs. Canby's store had finally been exhausted. Laura sighed. No tea, no newspapers, no mail. It was as if New Mexico had suddenly been lifted up out of the world, to survive or fail on its own.

"Has he made overtures to you before?" asked Mrs. Canby as she poured.

"Not in words," said Laura, remembering the captain's lips on the back of her glove, just after they had buried Lieutenant Franklin. Had that been mere courtesy? She thought not, but she was beginning to mistrust her interpretation of the captain's behavior. "I believe he admires me," she said.

"My dear, he is head over heels in love with you."

Laura's heart fluttered into her throat. She took a sip of tea, savoring its fragrance, before looking up at Mrs. Canby. "Do you think so?"

"If he is not, then I am no judge of young men."

Laura let her gaze stray to the coals glowing on the hearth. "Well, I must trust your judgment before mine," she said. "I confess I don't know what to think."

"If you care to tell me, do you love him?" said Mrs. Canby gently.

"I—hardly know him," said Laura. "Do you know, it is only a week since we first met?"

"A very eventful week."

"Yes."

"War condenses a great deal of experience into a short time," said Mrs. Canby. "I remember how much older Richard's aides seemed when they returned from campaigning the winter before last."

Laura put down her cup and rubbed her forehead. She certainly felt as if more than a week had passed. She had gone from fearing the captain, to begrudgingly placing her trust in him, to relying upon his protection. She missed him, she realized. The thought of not seeing him again made her sad. "I *could* love him, I think."

"Well," said Mrs. Canby slowly, "Perhaps he is giving you time to consider your answer."

Laura smiled ruefully. "It did not seem that calculated," she said.

"Nevertheless, you have time. You need not decide right away."

"True." Laura looked into the embers again. The only trouble was, it would be rather embarrassing if she decided to accept him, only to find that the offer had been withdrawn. She drew a deep breath, which became an unexpected yawn.

"Yes, you're quite right," said Mrs. Canby. "It is time we retired." She put her cup on the tray and stood up, and Laura followed suit.

It had been a very long day. They had found places for every one of the wounded men—though they'd had to put two in the foyer and five in the shed—and had seen to their hurts as best they could. Mrs. Canby's whole house was a hospital now, saving only the parlor, the kitchen, and the occupied bedrooms.

"Would you look in on Mr. Russell?" asked Mrs. Canby, picking up the tea tray.

"Of course." Laura lit her candle from the lamp and went into the dining room, where she picked her way carefully between the sleeping men to a small door that led to Colonel Canby's study. She paused to peer down at a Texan captain—quite badly wounded—who lay close by. He was sleeping, so she opened the door slowly, not wanting to disturb either him or Mr. Russell, the young officer they had brought from Kozlowski's, who was presently in the colonel's study. Mrs. Canby had not explained how she knew him, but she apparently trusted him not to disturb her husband's room.

Not that he was in any condition to do so at the moment. He lay on a mattress on the floor beneath the window, muttering with fevered dreams. When she was sure she had not awakened him, Laura set her candle on the desk and knelt to lay a hand against his cheek, which she found was burning hot.

"I can't help it, Emma," he said, his voice cracking. "I can't stop them."

"It's all right," Laura said softly. She took up a cloth and bowl of water that Mrs. Canby had left on the windowsill, and gently bathed his face, which seemed to calm him somewhat. He sighed once, and ceased murmuring. Laura set aside the bowl and stayed watching him for a moment.

If war could wreak such drastic changes in her own fortunes in only a week, she wondered what it had done to this young man's life in the months since he'd marched out of Texas. It had worn a furrow into his forehead, for one thing, and he could not be much more than twenty.

Laura sighed, and felt his cheek again; a little better. She seemed destined to drown her own troubles in caring for the sick and wounded. Well, there was no more she could do tonight. She rose, picked up her candle, and softly slipped out of the room.

Jamie stood at the top of a cataract, only instead of water it was made of wagons in flames, drawn by teams of weary mules. Each time one approached the cliff's edge he would plead with the driver to turn, and each time he was ignored and the wagon went over the cliff to shatter on the rocks below. His sister Emmaline stood by, frowning at him and demanding to know why he allowed it to happen, why didn't he do something? But he didn't know what else to do. He feared trying to stop the wagons himself, for they would only drag him over with them.

Then Captain Martin drove up, stopped his wagon at the edge, and stared at Jamie, holding out the reins toward him. Flames silhouetted Martin, licking all around him. If Jamie took over then Martin could get down and stay with Emma, and everyone would be happy, except that Jamie didn't think he'd be able to keep the wagon from going over the cliff. Finally he jumped up on the box, but at the same instant Martin snapped the reins, and the mules went over the edge, and they fell.

Jamie woke with a start, his pulse thundering in his ears. It was daylight, and he was staring up at a roof made of solid vigas overlain with latillas, Mexican-style. He gave a shuddering sigh and closed his eyes, laying his head back down on the pillow.

Pillow?

His eyes blinked open again. He was lying on a mattress on the floor of a small room, somebody's book room, it looked like. A Mexican house, but there was calico tacked halfway up the walls over the whitewash. He'd seen that before. He frowned, trying to remember.

The door opened, and a pretty blond girl looked in. "Well, good morning!" she said, smiling. "I thought I heard you call." She came in, leaving the door open behind her, knelt beside him and felt his cheek, just as his sister would have done.

"Much better," she said. "Are you hungry?"

"Where am I?" said Jamie. His voice was rough, and he tried to clear his throat.

"Santa Fé."

The name brought back a flood of memories: Lacey evading Phillips's Brigands, himself making the Brigands bury the dead in the canyon after the first battle, the wagon train lost. My God, the train!

Battling a wave of despair, Jamie managed to smile. "I didn't know there were any sympathizers in Santa Fé," he said.

The young lady raised an eyebrow. "I doubt that there are," she said. "And if there were, they would not be in this house."

"Whose house is it?"

She looked amused. "Mrs. Canby's."

"Mrs. Canby?" Jamie struggled to sit up. "May I speak to her?" His head began to swim and he stopped, leaning back on his elbows.

"You should rest," she said, gently. "You've been very ill. I'll tell Mrs. Canby you're awake."

Jamie sank back and watched her go, closing the door softly behind her. He sighed. Santa Fé. For one blissful moment he'd thought he was back in San Antonio.

He tried to think through the past few days, but his mind was bleary. He remembered being locked in a shed with Lacey and some others—Hall, and a couple of the Brigands—and there had been a surgeon, he thought. He'd had nightmares, but he'd been having those for weeks.

The door opened again, and Mrs. Canby smiled at him as she came in. Jamie was struck anew at how much she looked like his mother. A little taller, not quite as dark, and somewhat older.

"How do you feel?" she asked.

"Wrung out," Jamie replied.

"Just rest, then. No, don't sit up." Mrs. Canby pulled a short bench away from the wall and sat down beside him.

"How did I get here?" asked Jamie.

"In a wagon full of your wounded compatriots."

"I don't remember."

"Well, you've been in a fever for two days or more."

Jamie noticed his hat sitting on a chest by the wall. The Texas star was getting tarnished. His boots were on the floor beside the chest and his jacket hung on a peg above it, but his pistol was nowhere to be seen. No, they'd taken it, that was right. The Irish captain had made him surrender it. And Cocoa, his mare, was gone too—he'd sent Sergeant Rose riding off on her to warn Scurry about the train being attacked. Jamie swallowed a sudden pang of worry.

"You said wounded?" he asked.

Mrs. Canby nodded.

"Then I owe my presence here to your generosity."

"Actually, you owe it to the generosity of a captain in the Colorado Volunteers," said Mrs. Canby, smiling.

Jamie scowled, then tried to hide it. He hoped he'd never meet any Colorado men ever again.

"There isn't a wagon in all of Santa Fé at present," she continued. "I would not have been able to fetch you from Mr. Kozlowski's. Ah, here is Miss Howland."

She went to the door to assist the young lady, who had returned carrying a steaming bowl. Jamie tried again to sit up, this time with better success, and leaned his back against the wall. He still felt light-headed.

"Miss Howland, may I introduce Mr. Russell?" said Mrs. Canby.

The young lady curtseyed, and Jamie nodded. "Ma'am."

"It's a pleasure to see you restored, sir," said Miss Howland. She flashed a brief smile, then knelt gracefully beside him.

"I had better finish my visits," said Mrs. Canby. "The men in the shed must feel they've been abandoned. I'll come back when I've seen to them." She smiled at Jamie, then slipped out the door.

"Here, now," said Miss Howland, offering him a spoonful of broth.

"You don't have to do that," said Jamie, reaching for the bowl.

She held it out of his reach. "Humor me," she said.

Jamie stifled a laugh, and obediently swallowed the soup. It was hot, and laced with red chile powder. He was suddenly ravenous. Miss Howland fed him with dextrous efficiency, and between mouthfuls he studied her. She had gentle hands—small and pretty—and a long, graceful neck, with little pale curls escaping her coiffure at the back. Her eyes were blue-gray and rather serious. Her dress was black and the fabric was wearing thin in places, which made him wonder about her circumstances. If she had been a relative of Mrs. Canby, he doubted she'd have to wear an old, worn-out dress. But so pretty a girl would never want for friends, would she?

Suddenly feeling shy, Jamie reached again for the bowl. His hand brushed Miss Howland's, and she let him take the soup and feed himself. Even half empty, the bowl was heavier than he expected, and he had to rest it on his lap between bites. He must have been very sick indeed, to be so weak still.

"How were you wounded?" asked Miss Howland.

Jamie stared at her blankly, and she nodded toward his bandaged right arm. "Oh. It's just a nick."

"Bad enough to put you into a fever. Which reminds me, I should change the dressing."

Jamie suddenly became conscious of his state of undress. He set down the bowl and tugged the sheet up over his chest. Miss Howland showed no sign of noticing; she just changed his bandage with quiet efficiency, but his skin tingled at her touch. When she was finished, she looked up at him.

"There. Are you still hungry? I think María is making tortillas. Would you like me to bring you some?"

Jamie nodded. "Yes, please. Um—do you know where my shirt might be?"

"Oh, yes, of course. We've washed it, and Mrs. Canby has it in her mending box. I expect she will finish it this evening."

Jamie nodded, feeling the heat of a blush rise up his neck. "Thank you," he managed to croak. She just smiled, picked up the empty bowl, rose in a whisper of skirts, and walked to the door.

"Miss Howland?"

She turned back, lifting her eyebrows in inquiry.

"Do you know if—by any chance, was Lacey McIntyre among the wounded brought here?"

It was as if he'd struck her a blow. Her face drained of color, her smile faded, and her eyes stabbed into him in the moment before she looked away.

"No," she said in a brittle voice. "He was not." She turned and pulled the door closed behind her, leaving Jamie bereft.

Marching was dog's work. Kip was sick of it already, after only a few days, but he was damned if he'd show any regretful feelings before Sutter or Stavers or any of the rest of them. One of the worst things about it, besides aching limbs, blisters, and lungs full of dust, was the sheer boredom of plodding along hour after hour. He would have practiced some on the fife, except that to open his mouth was to invite the desert in, and he had drunk too much out of his canteen already. He had picked up the fife pretty easily, as he'd expected to, and though its range was a bit limited, he could get some fair music out of it. There was always room for improvement of course, but not while marching through the stinking desert. Tonight, in camp, he might play a tune or two for the boys. *If* they refrained from the already-tired cracks about Whistler's whistle.

He scuffed a step, raising a small cloud of dust from the half-inch deep layer on the trail. The damn stuff got into everything, and seemed to suck moisture out of their very breath. They'd made only one stop since dawn, to swallow a few bites of dried beef and soak themselves in the river, and by now their clothes were long dry.

Hot. Hot. Hot. Kip's head was pounding so bad he almost didn't hear the order to halt.

"What is it?" he asked of no one in particular as the men around him sighed and muttered to a stop.

"Scouts coming back," said Sergeant Sutter. "Keep your ranks, boys."

Kip eased his weight from foot to foot, searching for the least painful position, and pondered whether opening a button on his shirt to let in the breeze would be worth getting a scorched neck. Stanwix Flats deserved its name; they were marching through a flat, flat valley, spotted with scrubby mesquite and here and there a lonely ocotillo. Apart from a few tufts of dried-up grass there was nothing else growing in the whole blasted valley. Kip wondered if they would halt long enough to go in the river and get wet again. The stage road they were on more or less followed the Gila River, though sometimes it swung a mile or more away.

The hooves of the scouts' horses thundered ahead, then a shout went up. Kip craned to see the cause, but the road was filled with infantrymen. He stepped out to the side to get a better view, and saw the cavalry in the van all in commotion, with one horse running seemingly mad through the ranks.

"Christ! Get out—"

But it was too late; men were scattering left and right and some falling down in the road and everyone yelling as the horse came plunging through the ranks. It was indeed a scout, and he was hauling on the reins, trying to get his mount under control. Firecracker, of course. Kip stood frozen and watched the horse skitter through the infantry, set a forefoot down on the leg of a fallen soldier, and rear, eyes rolling. The rider—Semmilrogge, he now saw—cussed, and Firecracker spun on his haunches, and suddenly over they both went sideways and backward, men leaping out of their way like popcorn out of a pan. The horse struggled up and surged forward while the scout slid unconscious from his back. With a sick feeling Kip realized he was caught with one foot hung up in the stirrup. Firecracker dragged the poor fellow away from the column, full tilt and straight toward Kip.

He didn't even think about it, he just jumped for the saddle as Firecracker came by, and hauled himself up. He clung to the mane with one hand while he searched for reins with the other, found them, hauled hard. Firecracker hitched.

"Don't you buck, you!" said Kip, low and angry, hanging

on with both knees and sitting back hard. "Whoa, Fire-cracker! Whoa!"

The gelding stumbled down to a trot. Kip tried not to think about the scout being dragged behind him. He let up on the reins and then eased them back again, saying, "Whoa, there, Firecracker. Good boy. Whoa."

It wasn't until the horse stopped still that he became aware of the shouting, though it must have been there all along. He blinked dry eyes and dared a look down at Semmilrogge. A couple of fellows were getting him untangled from the stir-rup. His eyes were closed, and there was blood all over his left arm.

Blood? The horse hadn't dragged him that far, and there were no rocks or anything in the road that might have cut him. Kip gave Firecracker's neck a pat. "Good boy. Stand."

Firecracker snorted, and Kip realized the horse was shaking. He started stroking his neck. "Easy there." Firecracker looked around at him, wild-eyed, nostrils flaring.

Something was wrong. Firecracker wasn't just being or-nery. Something had scared him but good.

The rider had been freed. Time to dismount, Kip decided. He kept talking to Firecracker as he eased himself out of the saddle and back to the road. Immediately several hands clapped his back.

"Good work, piper!"

"Well done, Kip," said Sergeant Sutter.

"Didn't know you had it in you."

Kip gave half a smile and turned away. Captain Calloway and Lieutenant Barrett had ridden down the column to see the result of the ruckus, and Kip heard his name as Sutter spoke with them. The captain was frowning as he came over, but he offered Kip his hand.

"Good job," he said as they shook. "Quick thinking." He looked at Firecracker. "I've got half a mind to shoot this beggar."

"Wasn't his fault, sir," Kip said. "Something scared him all to pieces." He nodded toward Firecracker's sweating flank. The captain glanced over his shoulder back up the road.

"Semmilrogge was on picket at the stage stop. The other boys with him said they were attacked."

Kip looked up. "By Apaches?"

"By Rebels," said the captain.

Kip met the captain's gaze, and knew this was his chance. Semmilrogge's misfortune was his own good luck. If he worked it right, the captain might just let him take the scout's place, while Semmilrogge spent the next few weeks in a wagon. Even if it meant being stuck with Firecracker, it would be worth it.

He opened his mouth to volunteer.

"No," said the captain, before Kip could speak. "The cavalry have already gone after them." The captain looked to Barrett and said, "I Company fall out by squads to fill canteens. D Company on guard."

Kip waited while the orders were shouted and the column broke up. He stood, Firecracker's reins in his hand, and watched a couple of men trying to help Semmilrogge. There was no surgeon with the advance, so they'd have to make do the best they could. Sergeant Sutter had got the scout sitting up, half-conscious, and got his shirt off, revealing a wound at the back of his shoulder.

"Ball still in there?" asked the captain.

Sutter felt around Semmilrogge's arm, making him groan. "Looks like it came out here," he said.

"Anything broken?"

"Just his leg. Johnson, find me something to use for a splint."

Calloway looked at Kip. "Can you keep that beast under control?" he said harshly.

"Yes, sir," said Kip.

"Then go fetch some water from the river. Get this man cleaned up," he said.

"Yes, sir."

"I'll help you," said one of the scouts, a round-faced fellow with dark hair that poked out in different directions under his hat. He and Kip collected canteens and slung them on their saddles, then started for the river.

"Thanks for what you did," the scout said. "Bet you saved his life."

Kip shrugged, embarrassed. The scout offered a hand. "Name's Felley," he said.

Kip shook hands. "Whistler."

"You're a pistol, Whistler," Felley said, his smile widening to a grin.

Kip felt an answering grin tugging at his own lips. "Thanks," he said as they made for the river.

4

"Yes, this one will do," said Mrs. Canby. "It only needs taking in a little. Hold still while I pin it."

"I can't thank you enough," said Laura, holding her arms out of the way while Mrs. Canby pulled at the sides of the bodice. "May I not buy the dress from you?"

"Oh, tush. I never wear it. The color doesn't suit me."

Laura stroked the soft green cotton of a sleeve, thinking it would suit her rather well. "When the merchants come back and I can buy some cloth, I'll return it."

"I wish you wouldn't worry about it, my dear. There, let me see you." Mrs. Canby stepped back, and Laura stood up straight, folding her hands before her.

"We shall have to take up the hem," said Mrs. Canby. "If we start now we can finish by this evening. I have invited Mr. Russell to sup with us."

"Oh. Very well," said Laura lightly, hoping to conceal the disturbance Mr. Russell's name caused in her feelings. She did not know how to think of him, for he was a perfect gentleman, quiet and good-natured, and an enemy of her country. Why this should trouble her in Mr. Russell more than any of the other wounded rebels she was unsure; perhaps because he was not so unwell as the rest. She had, in the last two days, avoided him as much as she could, though it was harder as he regained his strength and moved about the house and garden more. He had taken to sitting in the placita, reading a book borrowed from Colonel Canby's study, and moving his chair to follow the sun.

Mrs. Canby placed a stout stool in the center of the parlor and helped Laura onto it, then began pinning up the hem. "How do you know Mr. Russell?" Laura asked, thinking her voice sounded rather small.

"Turn, please." said Mrs. Canby. "Mr. McIntyre introduced us."

"Oh." Laura turned a step to her right.

And how did Mr. Russell know Lacey McIntyre, who had until recently been a member of Colonel Canby's staff? Laura might wonder, but that was a question she would not voice. She had been shocked to see her former suitor at Kozlowski's ranch in civilian clothes, a Confederate and a prisoner of war.

She must have frowned, for Mrs. Canby said, "Do not be too hard upon Mr. McIntyre, my dear. He had conflicts of obligation."

"I should think his oath of honor would take precedence."

"We are not all as strong as we should be."

Laura turned another step, remembering the pleading look in Lacey's eyes, and her promise to deliver his message to Colonel Canby. Once those dark eyes had made her heart quicken, but now she thought of him only with pity, and some anger.

"We had quite a long talk on the subject, when he was in town," continued Mrs. Canby. "He wants very much to do what is right. He told me he believed my husband to have been killed when he resigned his commission."

"That is no reason. . . ." Laura faltered.

"No, it isn't, of course. But you must understand, he needs friends to support him, and at the time he felt his only friends left were in Sibley's army."

A poor excuse, thought Laura, but she felt her heart softening. She knew too well what it was to feel quite alone.

"He was right in the middle of it at Valverde," continued Mrs. Canby. "He was standing with McRae when the battery was taken. Oh, don't move, dear. I want this to be even."

"If he was with McRae, then how—how did he avoid being killed?" said Laura. The cannoneers had all died at their posts, she knew, on that dreadful day.

"Some friends of his were in the Confederate advance, and they shouted to him to surrender. He did, and they took him in, and one thing led to another. He knows he has burned his bridges," said Mrs. Canby. "He cannot come back to our army. But he is thinking he may not join the Rebels."

"Has he not already done so?" said Laura. She glanced down at Mrs. Canby as she turned a little further, but all she could see was her smooth brown hair.

"Only provisionally. He said he had not sworn an oath, or not signed one at any rate."

"He told me he hopes to be exchanged," said Laura. "He asked me to tell Colonel Canby. I sent a note with Captain Nicodemus, though I doubt it will make any difference."

"It could. Perhaps we shall soon see him in Santa Fé."

That would seem very strange, Laura thought. The last time they had all been in Santa Fé—nearly six months ago now—Lacey and Nicodemus and Allen Anderson had been the best of friends, tumbling over each other to pay her the slightest courtesy. Now all was changed. How odd, how disconnected, recent events had made her feel. Laura sighed, and turned another step.

"Finished," said Mrs. Canby, offering Laura a hand. "Will you go and change, so we can stitch it up for this evening?"

Laura stepped down, and went behind the Chinese screen to put on her own dress again. Donning the worn black depressed her spirits, and she looked forward to discarding it for good. It was no use to mourn any longer. Her father was gone more than a year now, and the pain of his loss had faded to a soft sadness. She must move on, and decide what to make of her life.

Juan Carlos's gentle knock fell upon the door just as Laura was buttoning her sleeves, and she stepped out from behind the screen. Mrs. Canby glanced up at her, then said, "Yes, you may show him in." Juan backed out of the doorway, and Mrs. Canby came to join Laura by the fireplace. "We have a visitor," she said.

Before Laura could inquire who it was, the door opened again to admit a tall man with very dashing mutton-chop whiskers and a twinkle in his tired eyes. Laura had seen him once before, at Fort Union, when she had first arrived in New

Mexico Territory. On that occasion he had worn a Federal uniform; now he was dressed in splendorous gray encrusted with golden braid.

"Louisa," he said as he came through the door, reaching a hand toward Mrs. Canby. "How are you?"

"Quite well, thank you. Miss Howland, may I introduce General Henry Sibley?" said Mrs. Canby quietly.

Laura felt herself bristling, and clenched her jaw shut. She dropped her eyes to the carpet—all modesty—and made a solemn curtsey.

"We've met before, I do believe," said Sibley in a kind voice. "I'm pleased to see you looking so well, ma'am."

Glancing up at him, Laura saw that he was not looking particularly well himself; his cheeks were sunken and his forehead seemed set into a permanent furrow of pain. "Thank you," she managed to say, and was grateful when he returned his attention to Mrs. Canby.

"I've just arrived, and I came straight over to assure myself that you had not been bothered," he said.

"Not since before the battles, thank you," said Mrs. Canby. "We have a number of your wounded here. Perhaps you would care to visit them?"

"Certainly, certainly. Tomorrow, perhaps. I have a great deal to see to."

"Of course. Will you join us for dinner, Henry?" said Mrs. Canby, to Laura's alarm.

Sibley smiled. "Thank you, but I've already bespoken dinner at the Exchange. Poor Parker—did you know some idiot in my command put him in jail? As if he hadn't enough troubles."

"I did hear something about that."

"Yes, well. Hasn't got much in his pantry, but he said he'd do his best for me."

"Another day, then."

"Yes," said Sibley, nodding. He turned his hat 'round in his hands, as if feeling for something he'd tucked inside it. "It's good to see you, Louisa," he said. "I don't suppose you've heard anything from Richard?"

"Only a brief word that he was alive, and that Charley had been killed."

"Charley, that old gray he liked to ride? Now that I am sorry about. He rode that old fellow all over after the Navajos. Good, dependable mount." General Sibley sighed, staring for a long moment at nothing, then straightened his back. "Well, I should leave you. I have business to see to. Do call on me, if you are in need of anything."

"Thank you," said Mrs. Canby, walking with him to the door. "It was kind of you to visit, Henry."

"I'll give myself the pleasure again soon," he said, and with a stately bow, he was gone.

Laura looked to Mrs. Canby, barely able to contain her feelings. Mrs. Canby calmly went to fetch the green dress from behind the screen and carried it to her sewing basket.

"We can both work at once, if one does the bodice and the other the hem," said Mrs. Canby, sitting down and patting the sofa beside her.

"How can you welcome that man into your home?" Laura burst out. "He would have shown no more remorse over the death of your husband than he did over his horse!"

"You are wrong," said Mrs. Canby quietly. "Richard and Henry were friends for many years. That cannot be changed, even though they stand against each other now."

"He is the enemy commander!" said Laura. "He is the author of all this ruin and misery!"

"My dear . . ." Mrs. Canby gazed up at her, concern in her dark eyes. Laura felt panic rising in her chest, and sat down, struggling to control her breathing. Tears welled in her eyes, from what exact cause she was uncertain. She searched in vain for her handkerchief, then realized she had left it behind the screen. She wiped angrily at her eyes with the back of her hand until she felt Mrs. Canby's touch on her arm. Looking up, she saw her friend offering her own kerchief. Laura accepted it, and applied it to her face.

"War requires many unpleasant things of its participants," said Mrs. Canby softly, "but it does not require them entirely to stop being human."

Laura gave a little gulp, and nodded. Her hands were steadier now. She reached for the sewing box, and carefully threaded a needle.

Did familiarity with warfare make people callous? Would

she become so, if she married a soldier? She thought of Captain O'Brien, who most surely had blood on his hands, and yet could still be gentle and kind. With a sigh, she began sewing the hem into place, taking time to set her stitches neatly, wondering where the captain was now, and whether he thought of her.

O'Brien thought Fort Union more dreary a sight than welcome, with the late sun slanting over the mountains to the west, painting the valley grasses a dull yellow and casting shadows in the corners of the star fort. The Pet Lambs were marched to this structure, to take up their old quarters in the beetle-ridden, green log bunkers beneath the earthwork. It was cold underground, cold and damp, and it made O'Brien think of the mine and his two miserable winters at Avery.

Shaunessy had built a pokey fire in the yard outside O'Brien's quarters and set on it a pot of water for coffee. O'Brien sat on a log, wrapped in his blanket, feet stretched out to the feeble warmth. The fire smoked, and he prodded a stick with his toe. Franklin would have built up a cheery fire in no time at all, he thought glumly. He missed the lad more than he would have thought, if only for his skill with fires and cooking. Shaunessy was a slow runner at both.

A heavy boot tread, and Shaunessy himself appeared with two haversacks full to bursting. "Beef, bacon, and beans," he said, grinning as he put them on the ground. "Enough to stuff a dozen trolls!"

"So they let you draw mine," said O'Brien.

"Aye. Tappan's got me on the rolls as your striker now, all official like."

"Good."

O'Brien had never in his life had a servant, and was not about to treat Shaunessy like one. He'd taken him as a striker because he wanted the man near him. Shaunessy, Morris, and Denning were his closest friends in the company since Hall had departed. Denning was a lieutenant and Morris a sergeant already; O'Brien had tried to get Shaunessy elected as well, but the men had overlooked him and chosen others, largely due to the influence of one Hugh Ramsey, who'd bought his own rank as well as that of his friends. Ramsey, an Englishman and full of himself, had a house, wife, and child in Denver City, was a lawyer and had no business in the army as far as O'Brien was concerned. He'd been among those who'd deserted the regiment when Governor Gilpin's treasury drafts were refused. He'd come back to Camp Weld two days later, saying he'd only gone to make sure that his family was safe, and to speak with the governor to confirm the wild rumors. And it was like Ramsey, sure enough, to rub elbows with the governor and make sure that everyone knew it.

O'Brien frowned. Rice and McCraw were good men both, and would make good sergeants. He had nothing against them, but Fitzroy—who'd defeated Evans to become fifth sergeant—was an out and out toady if ever he'd seen one. What's more, he disliked the way Ramsey had spiked the election. He'd lavished around a good deal of liquor, and maybe even some of his own money, and his praises for his own favorites had been laced with subtle hints of the failings of their opponents. He'd even tried to discredit Denning. That had failed—Denning had been voted first lieutenant, as was only right—but Ramsey had garnered enough votes to become second lieutenant. It was an association too close for O'Brien's liking.

The fire spat, and O'Brien had to flick a coal from his blanket. He sighed, reached into his coat and took out the little pocket notebook that had been Franklin's. Turning a few of the leaves, he looked at the feeble scratchings he'd made, then shut up the book and put it away again.

Shaunessy got out a pan and put some beef into it, humming a tune to himself. He moved the coffee pot off the fire and set the pan on it, causing a guff of smoke that stung O'Brien's eyes. Oh, for a tripod. O'Brien had seen some of the regulars using them in camp, suspending their cook pots over hot fires. If only the army would pay them he could afford such a luxury.

"So," he said when the smoke had subsided, "any word about Slough?"

"It's true as far as I could learn," said Shaunessy. "The commissary said he'd sent his resignation. He's only waiting to hear it's accepted."

It must be true, then, that some of the men had fired on Colonel Slough during the fighting at Glorieta. O'Brien didn't love the man, but was not sure he deserved to be killed by his own soldiers. Slough was never too friendly, but he'd put much of his own time and money toward building the regiment. Poor thanks to be turned on in the heat of battle.

"So we'll have Tappan for colonel."

"Oh, maybe not." Shaunessy prodded the beef and it hissed back at him. The smell made O'Brien's stomach rumble.

"The lads are all saying they want Chivington for colonel," Shaunessy added.

"Chivington?"

"Aye. He's the great hero, then, isn't he? 'Twas he who won the battle for us."

"You were there, Egan. You saw how much fighting he did."

"But he brought us there. He found the train for us to burn."

"That Mexican colonel brought us there," said O'Brien, getting angry, "and we had to beg Chivington to let us attack the train! Don't you remember, man?"

"We never heard what you were talking about," said Shaunessy, throwing up his hands. "We just saw you go off with Chivington and Chaves and that captain from the Regulars."

O'Brien crossed his arms and stared down at his boots. So Chivington was claiming credit for wrecking the train. It was all his idea, was it?

"He led the charge brave that first day," said Shaunessy.

"Oh, aye. That he did."

"The lads all say God is on his side. He's blessed with divine inspiration."

"Divine inspiration, is it?" O'Brien stood up and tossed his blanket aside. "Is that why he made us go slaughter those horses? I seem to remember you didn't think that was so fine."

"Well, but he must have had reasons—"

"Oh, aye, they were dangerous enemies, weren't they? Don't you remember their screams, the poor beasts? How long did it take you to clean the blood off of your bayonet?"

"Stop it, Alastar."

O'Brien stared down at Shaunessy, who kept his eyes on the beef sizzling gently in the pan. The man truly admired Chivington, then. In frustration, O'Brien turned to the woodpile, caught up the ax and took out all his anger on a log, splitting it with two strokes, and splitting each half again. He added two pieces to the fire, laying them on carefully, then went back to his seat.

Chivington as colonel. O'Brien would far prefer to have Slough remain. For all of his coldness, Slough was not casually cruel, as was Chivington.

An owl cried somewhere nearby. It boded ill. O'Brien retrieved his blanket and huddled in it, suddenly feeling old.

Jamie put down his fork and leaned back in his chair, gazing at the twilit church outside the windows, at Mrs. Canby and Miss Howland, and at the wreckage on the round parlor table at which they all sat. He was blissfully stuffed with roast mutton, posole, and apple pie. He had not had such a feast since the last time he'd dined with Mrs. Canby, before the battles in Apache Canyon and Glorieta Pass, before the train was taken, ages ago. It felt almost too good to be true, or too good for what he deserved, maybe. He felt strange, dining at table in a warm, comfortable room. Like it wasn't his place to be there.

"There's some pie left," said Miss Howland. "May I give you a piece, Mr. Russell?"

"No, thank you," said Jamie. "I couldn't eat another bite. Everything was delicious," he added, knowing Miss Howland had helped prepare the meal. He let his eyes linger on a pretty curl of hair that lay along her neck. Maybe it was just that she'd taken care of him when he was sick—he heard men often fell in love with their nurses—but he was conscious of her every movement and gesture, conscious of her nearness, and of every time she turned her eyes his way. She looked beautiful in the green gown which he hadn't seen before, but she was more than just a pretty girl. She was graceful, noble, and thoroughly good. She and Mrs. Canby were a comfort to him in all this chaos of war; they were his kind of people, honorable people. The kind of people who would stick to their word, who didn't let the crazy times around them diminish their principles or tempt them to sully their virtue.

"Puedes traernos el café, María. Gracias," said Mrs. Canby. Juan Carlos came forward to clear away Jamie's plate as María left the parlor. Jamie glanced up at the quiet Mexican, whose ways were as gentle as his employer's. Juan and María Díaz were like the better Mexican families of San Antonio, good people, modest and devout.

"Would you care for some brandy, Mr. Russell?" said Mrs. Canby. "I dare not offer you one of my husband's cigars."

"Oh, no thank you, ma'am," said Jamie. "Coffee'll do just fine."

Mrs. Canby rose, and Jamie and Miss Howland joined her, abandoning the table to Juan's ministrations. The ladies' graceful hoop skirts swished gently, touching off little explosions of memory in Jamie's mind, of Sunday church mornings, ice cream socials, and laughing girls in new ribbons. He suddenly wished for dancing, and wondered what it would feel like to take Miss Howland in his arms.

What a scandalous thought, James Russell. Momma would be ashamed. Again the guilty feeling of undeservedness assailed him. He quelled it as he followed the ladies to the fire. Nights were cold here at the foot of the mountains, even in April, and Jamie was glad of the gentle glow on the hearth. Mrs. Canby sat in an armchair and Miss Howland on the sofa, leaving Jamie the choice of a chair that was obviously Colonel Canby's or sharing the sofa. Feeling both a coward and a rascal, he chose the latter. He liked how his arms tingled when Miss Howland was near.

"General Sibley arrived this afternoon," said Mrs. Canby.

"Yes," said Jamie, "I heard."

"He does not look very well. I suspect his stomach may be troubling him."

"Not his conscience?" said Miss Howland.

Mrs. Canby smiled. "I doubt it. I am sure he feels absolutely in the right."

Jamie shifted on the sofa and glanced at his hat, which he'd left on the little table by the colonel's chair. He searched his brain for a more comfortable topic of conversation.

"He remembered you very well, Miss Howland," Mrs. Canby continued.

"He is not likely to forget me," Miss Howland replied. "I had a disagreement with his driver over the treatment of a Negro. The driver would have whipped the boy for breaking a bottle of his master's wine." She turned to Jamie. "Do you punish your slaves by beating them for every small error, Mr. Russell?"

Astonished, Jamie stared at her. "We don't have any slaves," he said.

Miss Howland looked surprised, and a delicate flush of color came into her cheeks. She looked down at her hands in her lap.

"I live on a ranch," Jamie added, trying to shift the conversation. "My father and brothers and I do the work. Well, and my sister helps a lot, lately," he added, thinking of Emmaline in her ranch clothes, doing men's work and enjoying every minute of it.

"How many brothers do you have?" asked Mrs. Canby kindly.

"Three," said Jamie. "And I have two sisters, but one is married."

"Are your brothers at home?"

"Oh, no, ma'am. Well, Gabe is, but he's only twelve. No—he's thirteen now." Had he really been away so long? Gabe's birthday was in March, and Jamie hadn't even remembered it to think about it. He would have to write, as soon as he could. Lord knew when that might be. He glanced up at Mrs. Canby, who was looking at him expectantly. "The other two joined up before I did," he added.

There it was, back again. No talking about anything but it always came back to the war. There was no part of Jamie's life it hadn't touched.

Miss Howland cleared her throat. "Are your brothers in New Mexico?" she asked. Jamie thought he saw a hint of apology in her eyes, and smiled back gratefully.

"No, ma'am. One is in Virginia, and the other—well, the last I knew he was in Tennessee."

"Your family must miss all of you very much."

Jamie's throat tightened on his reply, and all he could do

was nod. María came in with the coffee tray, and for a while the conversation turned to the scarcity of flour and other travails of wartime housekeeping. Jamie sipped his coffee and listened, letting the gentle ladies' voices wash over him and gazing wistfully into the fire. So nice and cozy here, but he knew he was just avoiding the inevitable. He sighed, and when the door closed behind María and conversation paused, he looked up at his hostess.

"Mrs. Canby?"

"Yes, Mr. Russell?"

"Before I was brought here I was a prisoner."

Mrs. Canby waited, her calm eyes on his face. Jamie drew a deep breath.

"I don't recall giving my parole."

Mrs. Canby looked down. "Your situation was not discussed with me," she said.

"I don't believe they knew my position. If they had, they wouldn't have released me."

"Perhaps not."

"Ma'am . . . ?"

Mrs. Canby looked at him then, dark brown eyes sad in the candlelight. He swallowed.

"I ought to return to my duties. If you think—"

"You should not ask me, Mr. Russell. You could not wisely trust my opinion on this subject."

He knit his fingers together between his knees and stared at the cuffs of his gray jacket. It looked almost like new again since Mrs. Canby had washed and mended it. "I just want— it's not wrong, is it? They let me go without asking parole, so I'm free." He glanced up at her, anxious for her opinion however much she dissuaded him.

"So it seems," she said softly.

Jamie drew a deep breath, and nodded while his heart sank inside him. Going back to work was about the last thing he wanted, but he didn't have a choice, so it was no use to fret about it.

He stood, and picked up his hat, fingering the star Emma'd given him. Given to Martin, actually. The hat and star were the only things of Martin's he'd kept for himself after Valverde. And the watch, but he was keeping that for Emma.

"I'm very grateful for your kindness, ma'am," he said, looking up at Mrs. Canby, who nodded acknowledgment. He turned to face Miss Howland, who folded her hands in her lap and gazed frankly at him. Oh, but her eyes were bluer than a summer lake. He could get lost in them, if he let it happen. If *she* let it happen, but she never would. To her he was a Rebel, and that was the end of it all.

"Miss Howland," he said, bowing a little. "Thank you for taking care of me."

She nodded, and gave him a fleeting smile, just enough to make him doubt his conclusion. He looked away, feeling he was about to walk away from everything good.

"You will not go this instant, will you?" said Mrs. Canby. "It is late. One more night will not make any difference."

Jamie managed a crooked smile. "Thank you, ma'am, but I can't impose on you any longer. I'm quite well, now, thanks to you and Miss Howland. It would be wrong of me to stay."

And if I don't leave now, maybe I never will.

Jamie bowed to the ladies and started for the door. "Come and visit, won't you?" called Miss Howland after him.

"Yes, do," said Mrs. Canby as he turned to look back at them. "You know you are always welcome."

Jamie pressed his lips together. "Thank you," he said around the lump in his throat. With a nod, he made himself turn away and leave the room, passing through the entryway where two wounded privates lay sleeping, out though the zaguán into the cold night of Santa Fé.

Free. Free, and he'd never felt so trapped. He placed his hat on his head, and started toward the plaza and the lights of headquarters.

"That was sudden," Laura said.

"Mm." Mrs. Canby took out her sewing basket. Laura watched her arrange a sock upon her darning egg, then glanced at the door.

"I hope we did not say anything to offend Mr. Russell."

"I don't think so, my dear."

Laura picked up an issue of *Godey's* from the side table and leafed through it. She had already read every word. She put it down again, and said, "What did Mr. Russell mean, about their not releasing him if they'd known his position?"

"They would not have released him at all if he had not been so very ill," said Mrs. Canby.

"But why should his position matter? Are not officers usually exchanged?"

"Well, he is not a field officer, Laura."

"Is he not? I thought the two bars on the collar stood for a lieutenant."

"He is actually a captain." Mrs. Canby finished weaving a row of darning before she added, "He is also General Sibley's quartermaster."

Quartermaster? Laura thought of Major Donaldson, who was Colonel Canby's quartermaster, a man rather advanced in years and nothing at all like Mr. Russell.

They had been entertaining one of General Sibley's key staff officers. He knew exactly how many chickens and goats were in Mrs. Canby's domicile, and likely how many barrels of flour were in her pantry, and his army needed them all most desperately. Yet somehow Laura was sure they would be untouched. She gazed at the door through which Mr. Russell had gone, her opinion of him rapidly rising, then turned her attention to the more immediate, and safer, matter of sewing.

The men on guard outside the Spanish governor's palace were huddled over a feeble fire, but came to attention long enough to give Jamie a hasty salute. He passed into the long adobe building—twice the size of the old governor's palace in San Antonio—and sought out the office that had been Colonel Canby's and was now Confederate Headquarters. In it a man with dark hair receding from a domed pate sat at the large mahogany desk, frowning over some papers.

"Colonel Scurry?"

Scurry looked up, and Jamie saw two angry red streaks across his left cheek above the beard; battle-souvenirs, he supposed. "Russell! Where'd you spring from?"

"I've been sick," Jamie said, not wanting to mention Mrs. Canby.

"Mm? Well thank God you're here. Sit down."

Jamie pulled a straight-backed chair from the wall to the desk. "We need ordnance, rations, and blankets," Scurry continued. "And clothes—half the men are in rags."

"I don't know where I'll find them, sir."

"Well, you'll do your best. We also need stock to draw the Valverde guns. And we need to haul that spiked gun back here from Johnson's. Talk to Teel; maybe we can get it repaired before we advance again."

Jamie drew a breath. "Sir, have you considered the possibility of retreat?"

Scurry looked up, and the sharpness in his eyes faded a bit toward weariness. "General Sibley wants an advance."

"I can probably scrounge up food and clothing," Jamie said, rubbing at his sore shoulder, "and maybe some transportation, but the ordnance is a problem. The Federals have taken everything up to Fort Union."

"Union," said Scurry softly, his frown deepening. "That's what we came for, isn't it? Union, then on to San Francisco? Well, we kicked them out of Glorieta, we can kick them out of Union. The general says it's unfortified."

"Colonel, how many rounds do the men have in their cartridge boxes?" asked Jamie. "Because that's all we have to fight with."

Scurry grimaced. "The depot at Albuquerque has ammunition, doesn't it?"

"Not enough to supply the whole army, sir. Not enough for a battle."

Footsteps in the hall behind him made Jamie turn his head. He saw a familiar shock of blond hair. "Rose!" he said, breaking into a smile.

The young sergeant looked startled, then glanced at the two brimming mugs of coffee in his hands as if concerned they would spill. Jamie stood up, and Rose put the coffee on the desk and wiped his hands on his trousers. "Captain Russell. Good to see you, sir. We thought you'd been taken."

"I was, but I was too puny so they threw me back," said Jamie, laughing awkwardly and offering a hand. After a glance at Scurry, Rose shook it.

"Where's Cocoa stabled?" said Jamie. "I want to go see her."

Rose looked down and swallowed. "I lost track of her in the battle, sir, and I never could find her after. I'm sorry."

Jamie felt a stab of woe, but he forced himself to speak kindly. "It wasn't your fault. At least she wasn't slaughtered at Johnson's with the others. She wasn't hurt, was she, that you know?"

"No, sir. The last I saw her she was eating grass. I didn't have a rope to tie her—"

"It's all right," said Jamie, nodding, not wanting to speak of it any more. "Not your fault."

Rose looked down at Scurry's desk and shifted his feet. He was nineteen or so—a year younger than Jamie. Jamie wondered what his first taste of battle had done to him.

"Thanks for the coffee, son," said Colonel Scurry. "You can go now."

Rose glanced up at Scurry, then at Jamie, then left the room. Scurry pushed one of the mugs toward Jamie and waved him to his chair.

"Good boy, Rose."

"Yes, he is," said Jamie, nodding.

"You won't like it, but I've requested he be assigned to me as an escort." Scurry took a sip of coffee. Jamie stared at him, suddenly feeling hurt and betrayed. He picked up his coffee and took a long, silent pull. It was nowhere near as good as Mrs. Canby's.

"No, I don't like it," he said finally. "He's a good quartermaster sergeant."

"You can find another. It's not a hard job."

Jamie quashed a swell of resentment, and leaned back in his chair to study the colonel. Scurry had a sullen look that was new since the battle at Glorieta. With surprise, Jamie realized he was no longer intimidated by Scurry, colonel or no. Maybe because he was just so damn tired of it all.

He put his mug on the desk. "We've stretched our supply lines too far," he said.

"Hell, I know that," said Scurry.

"Our only hope of resupply is at Fort Thorn, and Fort Craig is between us and there."

"I told the general it was a bad idea to turn Craig, but he

was sure we could take the depot at Union. He still thinks so."

"Help me convince him to turn back."

"He won't listen to me," said Scurry in a low, angry voice. "Thinks he's King Arthur! Thinks the poor, oppressed Mexicans will come running to him as their savior. Well, they ain't. They're dug in. This is no way to run a campaign. That's why I'm going back to Texas and raising my own regiment."

Scurry stood up, drained his coffee, and put the empty mug on the desk. "Good night, Russell. Glad you're back safe."

Jamie listened to Scurry's retreating footsteps, thinking of the glorious visions they'd all had when they left San Antonio. They would capture Colorado's gold, and San Francisco's seaport, and all come back heroes. Instead—Lord, what a mess.

And Cocoa was gone. Jamie tried to stop frowning, but it hurt to know she was lost to him, perhaps wandering in the mountains alone, perhaps dead. She was his closest tie to home and the family, and he missed her. His eyes started stinging and he hastily rubbed the feeling away.

Scurry hadn't said anything about quarters for him. Well, he was the quartermaster. He'd figure out something.

He picked up one of the papers scattered on the desk. It was a printed copy of an address from Scurry to the men, dated the twenty-ninth of March. "You have proven your right to stand by the side of those who fought and conquered on the red field of San Jacinto." Jamie's mouth twisted into a smile. Scurry knew how to appeal to his men, however little he might privately agree with the policies he expressed.

At the bottom of the page, below Scurry's name, was a line of print that raised a hope in Jamie's heart; ELLSBERRY R. LANE, ADJUTANT.

"Ells!" Jamie said aloud. The last time he'd seen him, Lane had been among the wounded at Johnson's Ranch.

Jamie suddenly felt less weary. Grabbing his hat, he took a last swallow of bad coffee and went off in search of his friend.

5

> "... let me here record that he died the victim of whiskey, nothing else."
>
> —Ovando J. Hollister

Friday morning all of Fort Union was called to assembly to witness the death of a traitor. O'Brien had wondered if it would be this Lacey McIntyre, who he'd learned was in the fort's guard house, or—God forbid—Hall, but it was the Pet Lambs' own Sergeant Philbrook instead. One night on the march down from Denver City he'd got too much whiskey in him and shot Lieutenant Grey in the face. He'd been under arrest while the regiment was off fighting Texans, and now he'd been court-martialed, and stood up before a squad out of his own regiment on a cold, dreary morning in the middle of blessed nowhere. A bally poor way to die, thought O'Brien.

A cold wind blew off the plain east of the fort. The flat-topped hills to the north and south funneled the sharp air straight at the fort on its way into the mountains. O'Brien slapped his arms to warm them, and shifted from foot to foot as he stood before his company. The Colorado men formed two sides of a square facing east, with the Regulars making up the center and the fourth side open to the bitter wind. Philbrook was marched all round the square to the music of ominous drums. O'Brien glanced at his face as he passed; there was no life at all in it, eyes dead cold already. The guard marched him into the middle of the square and made him stand up on his coffin. The squad fired as one at the signal—sharp shooters, the Colorado boys—and the prisoner crumpled while the sound echoed off the cold hills. He was put in the box and hauled away to the death march.

"Ended it bravely, he did," said Shaunessy. "He wasn't so bad, when all's done."

"'Twas the liquor that killed him," said Morris.

"Aye," said O'Brien, thinking it could've been himself getting shot, with a little less luck and if Franklin had not been so generous. But no, he was an officer. He could be cashiered for forcing a fight on Franklin, but not likely sentenced to die. The army was kind to its gentlemen.

He would forego the whiskey, he decided, for a while. It only made him morose, and things were dreary enough in this wretched place.

The adjutant gave the dismissal, and all of the Regulars disappeared into their cozy barracks while the Volunteers slunk back to the star fort. The sky threatened rain, which would make the earthen bunkers leak. O'Brien sighed, wishing they were on the march. Better to be rained on in the open air than to have mud and bugs dripping down on one all the night long. He cocked an eye at the heavy clouds, and decided to walk down to see if the sutler might buy that Texan saddle that the mare had been wearing. It was too small for himself, and it gave him an excuse to delay going back to his gloomy, damp quarters.

"Bring it in," said the sutler. "I'll take a look at it. Can't promise much, though. Seen a lot of Texan junk lately."

O'Brien nodded, and gazed around at the sutler's stores. Dried fruit, canned oysters, and a hundred other things to set his mouth watering. He fingered Miss Howland's money in his pocket, and decided to save it against future need. He could live on his rations, dull as they were. Maybe the sutler would trade goods for the saddle.

Denning came in, gave O'Brien a smile and a nod, and set about purchasing a bottle of ink. O'Brien waited for him near the door, and together they walked back toward the star fort.

The sound of a hammer striking steel came to them as they neared the works, and O'Brien frowned, looking 'round for its source. Sergeant Rice—a black-haired sprig from Denver City, still not quite at home in his new rank—passed them in the sally port at the head of a detail whose arms were loaded with bundled gear.

"Where are you going, then, Rice?" O'Brien demanded.

The sergeant hesitated, eyes wandering to Denning. "Lieutenant Ramsey, sir—he—"

O'Brien bit back a sharp comment, and jerked his head for Rice to move on. Rice lost no time getting through the gateway. O'Brien looked at Denning beside him, who seemed as surprised as he was.

"Let's find out, then," said O'Brien, and followed the sergeant, with Denning close on his heels. They went around a corner of the earthworks and the pounding grew louder; beyond the next bastion they found I Company making a new camp, bickering and laughing in the clear air. It was Shaunessy wielding the hammer, pounding in stakes around a square of mud-stained canvas while Hugh Ramsey looked on.

"What the devil is this?" said O'Brien.

The men all looked up and fell silent. Shaunessy glanced up at O'Brien and grimaced, pushing his straw-colored hair back from his eyes.

Ramsey turned to face O'Brien, the fur collar of his overcoat turned up to his full cheeks, so that the close-trimmed beard scarcely showed at all. "The bunkers are unfit to live in, Captain," he said, black eyes watchful.

O'Brien ground his teeth. He could hardly deny it, and bitterly wished it was he who had thought of moving. It was like Ramsey, taking it on himself to give orders. Looking 'round at his men, awaiting his word, O'Brien knew he could not countermand it, nor did he want to. The men would do better out of the earthworks. But Ramsey had cost him face, and that he had trouble forgiving.

"Carry on, then, lads," he said, trying to sound friendly. "A word with you, Ramsey," he added, and strode a few paces away from the new camp, working hard to keep hold of his temper. The dry grass was stiff enough to crunch underfoot.

Ramsey strolled after him, taking his time. O'Brien folded his arms and waited, eyes fixed on the high crown of Ramsey's hat as he came up.

"Yes?" said Ramsey, arriving. Not "yes, sir." Not even "yes, Captain."

O'Brien chose his words carefully. "The next time you have an idea, best come to me first."

Ramsey laughed. "It didn't occur to me that you would disapprove—"

"I don't disapprove," O'Brien said, "but the men need to know who's in charge of this company."

Ramsey's mouth curved in an unpleasant smile. "Yes, sir."

O'Brien bridled his temper, and kept his voice low. "Suppose we'd had orders to march?" he said. "The lads would have done all this for nothing."

Ramsey worked his jaw, and seemed to be thinking. A victory, if only a small one, to have made the Denver City lawyer at a loss for words. It soothed O'Brien's feelings, and he said in a gentler tone, "Just come to me next time, that's all."

"There he is! Say, O'Brien!"

Turning, O'Brien saw Captains Wyncoop and Logan approaching. Wyncoop's face cracked into a smile.

"Fine idea, Red," he said, clapping O'Brien on the back. "I've ordered out my company, too. Logan here wanted to have a look, first."

O'Brien ignored a sly glance from Ramsey. He clamped his lips together, not trusting his temper with words.

"Are you taking your camp all the way to that bastion?" asked Logan.

O'Brien had to look to Ramsey, whose smile grew hard. "No, sir," said Ramsey. "Just as far as you see."

Logan nodded. "Excellent. Officer's Row in the lee of the works?" He looked at O'Brien and nodded again. "Good idea. I'll get my men moving." He and Wyncoop strolled off, pointing at the works, and arguing whose company should camp where.

"Shall I have your tent pitched, Captain?"

The voice mocked. O'Brien turned to glare at Ramsey, and saw Shaunessy beyond him. "See to it, Egan," he said. Shaunessy grinned, dropped the hammer on the canvas of Ramsey's tent, and loped away toward the works.

Matching gazes with Ramsey, O'Brien was not sure who'd

won the encounter, but he knew one thing for certain. Ramsey would keep pushing. He held the lawyer's black eyes briefly, then turned away, to walk through the company's new-laid camp.

"How many cases do you have?" Jamie asked, laying a hand over the box of ammunition on the counter.

Hopkins smoothed his pale mustache and glanced toward his other customers, a couple of Texas soldiers who were looking at pens and writing paper. "I can give you ten," he said, "but it's old buck and ball."

"We can use it. Are you sure you can't spare twenty or forty?" Jamie pulled a fistful of Confederate scrip from his pocket, and the old Virginian gazed at it thoughtfully.

"Have to have some for my own defense," said the merchant. "I'm none too popular in this town, especially since you fellows arrived."

"Fifty a case?" Jamie said, and without waiting for an answer began counting out bills. Might as well; Hopkins—Colonel Hopkins, as he called himself—was the only merchant in Santa Fé who'd accept Confederate paper.

"Twenty-five cases, then, and that's near all I have."

"Done," said Jamie. "Now, about the beans."

O'Brien and Denning sat before their newly pitched tents, watching the day die. The sun at their backs gave no warmth, veiled as it was by thin clouds while it slid toward the cold mountains. O'Brien held his hands out to the fire—better than the last—and watched Ramsey emerge from his own tent. Without a word he strode past them and on south, toward headquarters. O'Brien scowled into the fire.

"Ramsey's popular with the men," Denning said softly. "It might be wise to befriend him."

"It's your authority he's bypassed as well, man," said O'Brien.

"I know."

O'Brien gazed out over his company's camp, where the men were settling in. Many were miners, his own Trolls who'd followed him from Avery, friends before the war ever began. He was their leader, no question. But others he scarcely knew—Denver City boys, or lads from other mining towns who'd come late to the regiment—and they looked to Hugh Ramsey now, especially those who had known him in Denver.

I'm not easy with the men, O'Brien realized. He'd kept to himself for the most part; it was his way, even back in Avery. He threw his shoulder in with them when the work was hardest, but it was seldom he just sat and talked with them. It wasn't his nature to do so. That had been one of the differences between him and Franklin, he recalled, apart from the money and schooling. Franklin had talked with the men—with nearly anyone, in fact—and could learn whatever he needed to know, and make friends in an instant just with his smile. Now Ramsey was doing much the same thing, and it made O'Brien angry, just as Franklin had made him angry.

He gazed up at some long wisps of cloud turned salmon-pink by the sunset. "Do you like him, then, Luther?"

Denning frowned. "He's pleasant enough, I suppose. Keeps his distance." He rubbed his hands together and held them over the fire. "No, I don't particularly like him," he added. "He's ambitious."

O'Brien nodded. "You're with me, then?"

A smile softened Denning's face. "You saved my life, Alastar. Of course I'm with you."

"Bah, that. It was just a lot of nonsense."

"Nonsense with loaded pistols. Don't think I'll ever forget."

O'Brien grinned. It seemed so long ago, that foolish duel in Dooney's Tavern at Avery. That had been the first time he'd thought of joining the army.

He offered a hand, which Denning shook heartily. All at once he felt better. "We'll see what we can do," he said.

By the time he returned to the depot Jamie was bone-weary. Hopkins had loaned him the use of his own wagon to haul the new supplies, and Jamie had cajoled the two cranky mules who pulled it to take him all over the city. Most of the merchants had closed their doors and carted their wares out of town, but a few of the townspeople had been willing to sell. In addition to the few precious cases of ammunition and the dried beans and jerky Hopkins had sold him, Jamie had scraped up some clothes, a couple of sheep not worth half what he'd paid, and the promise of a quart of fresh milk a day in exchange for U.S. coin. He had enough for maybe a week's worth, which he planned to turn over to the hospitals. He felt like he'd spent the day climbing up a hill that got continually taller.

"Whoa," he said as the wagon drew up to the depot, but the mules had already slowed. With repeated sighs they expressed their disapproval of the day's work while Jamie hopped down and began hauling his scavenged goods into the building.

The depot at Fort Marcy Post had been burned by the retreating Federals before the Texans' first visit to Santa Fé. Jamie had chosen a smaller building, which had once housed the Indian Agency, for his storehouse. It was pretty well stripped even of shelving. Probably the natives had scavenged the shelves for firewood; only three sets remained, and Jamie figured they'd been left only because they were bolted to the walls. By all reports, something of a free-for-all had resulted when the Federals had abandoned the town.

Now, though, whoever possessed anything of value had it hidden or closely guarded. There had been no outright protests since Colonel Scurry had seized the newspaper office, but the town was watchful and wary. The richer inhabitants had departed long ago in their wagons and carriages, and many others had deserted the town for safer villages in the remote hills. Those remaining were here because they had nowhere else to go, and their strained faces hovered in the shadows of every door and window.

Jamie untied the two sheep, who stood bleating in the yard as if they couldn't think of anything better to do. He knew if he left them in the post's stock pens they'd be gone by morning, so he threw an armful of grass on the packed earth floor of an empty shed and shut them in with a bucket of water.

He still hadn't figured out where to make his own quarters. He'd had a vague idea of moving in with Lane, but the adjutant was just out of the hospital and Jamie hated to crowd him. Lane had set up a cot in a back office of the Governor's

Palace so he would only have to cross a hall to go to work. He'd been asleep when Jamie visited.

With a sigh Jamie stacked the last sack of beans against the depot wall. His little pile of supplies looked pretty small inside the long, echoing building. He went back for the clothes, which took three trips to bring in. He should have had some of the men unload for him, but in the time it would take to roust them out of their quarters, he'd be able to move it all twice over by himself. Besides, he hated facing them— poor cold, hungry fellows—and didn't have the heart to ask them to move the new clothes without being issued any. Tomorrow he'd round up his hands from wherever they were staying in town, and get everything organized. Have to pick a new quartermaster sergeant, he reminded himself as he stacked trousers on the shelves at the far end of the storeroom. He wondered idly why the one set of shelves had been set bang in the center of the short wall; two would have fit side by side, but maybe the goods needed to be kept out of the sun from the window hard by.

Jamie walked over to that window and sat in the deep sill; thick adobe wall cool at his back. The sun was getting golden on the mountains outside, softening their blue ridges and setting the splashes of new snow aglow. Pretty country, he thought tiredly. He put his boots up against the far side of the window. Outside he could see all the way to the end of the building, ten or fifteen feet. Inside he could almost touch the end wall with his toe.

Jamie sat up and put his feet on the floor. He was tired, but not so tired he couldn't tell that what he saw made no sense. He leaned forward and put a hand on the wall at the short end of the room, maybe half a foot past the edge of the window. Keeping his fingers on the whitewashed plaster, he leaned sideways and looked again at the outside of the building. It was longer outside than inside, by a good ten feet, and the portal extended that far as well.

A tickle of fearful excitement began in his chest. He looked up at the inside wall, the wall with one set of shelves in the middle, and that made no sense either.

Jamie ran over to the shelves and pulled down all the clothes he'd just stacked on them, then tugged at the shelves themselves. They were fastened pretty firmly to the wall by four sets of metal straps. He ran his hand along the wall behind them, feeling the plaster, which was awfully fresh, come to think of it. His fingers found a vertical ridge and his stomach did a flip-flop. He traced it down back of each shelf to the floor, reached his other arm out to the side and felt for another ridge, and found it.

A door. By God.

Jamie jumped up and headed for the yard, trying to decide where to yell first.

"Name of Oatman," said Sergeant Sutter. "Happened just a few miles east of here, back in the '50s. You'll see the grave tomorrow."

Kip stared at the antelope haunch roasting on the fire as he listened, resisting the urge to take a drink. His canteen was only half full, and it was more than a mile to the river. He didn't want to have to walk there before morning. The smell of the meat was driving him crazy.

"They were traveling to California," continued Sutter in a low voice. "Mother, father, and seven children, with everything they own in a wagon and their old ox breaks down. They tried hauling it by hand up a hill, and while they were at it some Apaches come up and offered to lend a hand."

"That was friendly," said Stavers, looking up from his bible.

"So it seemed, son," said Sutter. "So it seemed. But when they got to the top of the hill those Indians slaughtered the parents and four of the children, and took the two eldest girls and all their property."

"God damn," muttered Felley. Stavers looked back at his book without another word. The circle of dusty men shifted uncomfortably, and someone tossed a stick on the fire.

"How do you know that's what happened?" said Kip.

"One of the boys survived," said Sutter. "He lay still and they left him for dead. And one of the girls turned up five years later with a band of Mohaves, and her brother got help to purchase her freedom. She had tattoos all over her face, and Lord knows what else they did to her."

"What about the other girl?" asked Walters, I Company's drummer.

"Mohaves had her too, for a while, but she died."

Nobody seemed to have anything to say to that. Kip poked at the meat with a mesquite twig, though he knew it couldn't be done yet. After a minute Bobby Zinn came up and squattered by the fire, reaching out toward the warmth. "Captain Calloway wants to see you, Kip," he said.

Kip directed a questioning glance at Sutter, who nodded. Wrapping his blanket tighter around his shoulders, Kip got to his feet. "How's Semmilrogge?" he asked.

"Well as you can expect with your leg broke in three places," said Zinn. "They've got him liquored up good."

"Poor bastard," said Felley.

Kip looked up in time to see Stavers shoot a frown at Felley, who paid no attention. Grinning, he turned and headed for the captain's tent, making his way between camp-fires where men were cooking, talking in low tones, or already snoring. Everybody's spirits were down since the scouts were attacked. The cavalry who'd gone after the Rebels had come up empty-handed, and today's long march hadn't helped.

The captain's tent glowed in the night, lit up all golden by lamplight from inside. Since no one was on guard, Kip stood by the door and said, "Hallo? Whistler here."

"Come in," Calloway said.

Kip pushed the flap aside and stepped in. The little officer's tent was just big enough for a cot on one side and the captain's field desk on the other. Calloway sat at the desk, frowning over some papers. There wasn't another chair, so Kip stepped up to the desk and waited, shifting from one weary foot to the other.

"Good work yesterday, Whistler," said the captain without looking up.

"Thanks, sir."

"You handled that horse pretty well."

"He's not so bad, if you know how he thinks."

The captain looked up at him and raised an eyebrow, then leaned back in his chair. "I'm short an expressman," he said. "Semmilrogge won't be back for a while. Sergeant Sutter indicated to me that you might care to fill in."

Kip's heart jumped. What he wanted, right? Except riding out alone ahead of the column didn't seem so interesting just now as it had before Semmilrogge had been hurt. Maybe he was just tired, or maybe it was Sutter's damn spook stories.

Calloway was waiting, looking at him. Kip thought about saying no to him, decided the word didn't taste so good. He wanted a cavalry job, so he'd better take the chance while it was offered.

"All right," he said.

Calloway watched him a minute longer, then a tiny smile curled his mouth briefly. "You'll ride Firecracker," he said, picking up his pen again. "That means you're responsible for tending him, starting in the morning."

"Yes, sir."

"And you'll still have musician's duties."

Kip was silent, watching the captain's hand move the pen across the page. Calloway glanced up. "Dismissed," he said.

Kip pulled his arm out of the blanket to salute, then turned on his heel and went out. So Firecracker was his, now. He shook his head, laughing at himself, and made his way back to the fire.

"Harder," said Jamie.

The sledges pounded again, thumping against plaster without much effect. What they needed were pickaxes, or even shovels, but there weren't any to hand. Jamie tried not to fidget as he stood back and watched the two privates hammering at the wall. The remains of the shelves lay in a jumble at his feet. A handful of boys from C Company—compatriots of the men wielding the sledges—had wandered in to watch and Jamie let them stay, all except for one fellow he'd sent to drive Hopkin's wagon back to him.

Jamie gnawed at his thumb. There had to be a better way. Maybe Hopkins would have something they could use. He was about to tap one of the watching privates on the shoulder and send him running when a network of cracks appeared on the wall.

"Hah!" said Jamie. "Keep going!"

The wall began to crumble under the hammer blows, first

dust, then flakes, then chunks of plaster falling away. The sound of the hammering changed, getting more hollow.

"Stop a minute," shouted Jamie over the noise, and the two sweating men stood aside while he stepped up to the wall. He clawed the broken plaster away from a flat surface beneath and rubbed at it, then broke into a grin. It was wood.

"Keep going," said Jamie, stepping back. "Pete, run down to Hopkins's store and see if he'll lend us a crowbar. Make it two. Alf, round up a couple of lanterns, will you? It's getting hard to see."

Jamie made a show of going to the other shelves on the long wall, where he'd hastily tossed the clothes to keep them from getting covered in plaster dust. He folded them up, just to have something to do while the men worked away at the door. When he ran out of that he paced, watching their progress. The crowbars arrived—three of them, along with Hopkins himself—and were added to the destructive efforts. A dark rectangle was taking shape in the wall.

"Found a door, eh?" said Hopkins.

Jamie nodded.

"What do you expect's behind it?"

"Not sure," said Jamie in a tight voice.

Hopkins chawed at his tobacco and cocked his head, looking at the door. "Think they kept a carpenter's shop 'round here somewhere," he said.

Tools, thought Jamie. Nails. Wagon tires, if they were lucky. Anything at all would help.

A cry of triumph went up from the men, and Jamie and Hopkins hurried forward. A cracking of wood followed as the door was forced open,

"Stand aside," Jamie shouted, and was slightly surprised when the men obeyed him despite their excitement. The door had been mangled around the lock and handle; he pushed it wide and walked through into a dim haze of plaster dust.

The room was windowless, and Jamie stood in the center for a minute to let his eyes adjust. A friendly whiff of must reminded him of the back room at Webber's store, but he was too tense to be homesick. He was starting to see shapes: shelves lining the walls, and not empty either. He stepped toward one, reaching out, and felt good wool under his hand.

Thank you, Jesus, he thought, and pulled at the cloth, which tumbled heavily toward him, the whole stack of whatever-it-was falling into his arms. He carried it back to the main room to where he could see.

Blankets. He opened one up, letting the rest fall around his feet, and broke into a grin as the men began cheering.

Laura cautiously pulled the parlor curtain aside, just enough to peep out. The town was overrun by Texan soldiers; she saw some lounging in front of the Spanish church, and many more wandering up and down the streets. A large number of them had been quartered in some buildings belonging to Bishop Lamy, just down from Mrs. Canby's house. Another detachment had arrived last night from Albuquerque, and the newcomers were out in force, exploring the town.

Letting the curtain fall, Laura turned back to the table where Mrs. Canby was pouring coffee. "We could use some rosemary," she said, taking her seat. "Do you know anyone in town who grows it?"

"I believe the Senas do. Why?" said Mrs. Canby.

"It makes a soothing tincture."

"Ah, very good. I'll ask María to inquire." Mrs. Canby handed Laura a steaming cup. "Our patients are fortunate to have you here."

Laura shook her head. "I wish I had my father's medical books," she said. "Then I might be of some real help. I only remember little things." She sighed, and sipped her coffee. It was too hot, and she set it aside to cool a little.

Books were too heavy to be brought on the mail coach to Santa Fé. She had sold most of them to help with the funeral expenses, and given the rest away, in her sorrow, thinking she would never want them again.

She glanced toward the window, then picked up a slice of bread and began spreading jam on it. How she longed for a brisk walk! But she dared not set foot outside, except to take the air in the placita. Even there, she would likely as not be subjected to the stares of soldiers visiting their wounded friends at the house.

"Have you looked in on Captain Adair this morning?" Mrs. Canby asked.

"Yes. He's quite poorly, still." The Confederate captain had awakened briefly, but it was his men who had informed the ladies of his name. Of all the wounded in their care, Captain Adair was the worst off. Dr. Maney, who had charge of the Confederate hospital in Santa Fé, had been twice to see the captain and had begged Mrs. Canby to keep him, for fear that moving him to the hospital might do him harm.

"Perhaps your rosemary will help him," Mrs. Canby said, pouring milk into her coffee.

"Perhaps." Laura sighed. Her spirits were unsettled today. That was not surprising; her whole life was unsettled. She frowned. "Do you think the Texans will stay long?"

"Not long," Mrs. Canby said. "They cannot afford to stay idle."

"The wounded are saying there will be an exchange of prisoners."

Mrs. Canby glanced up, and smiled gently. "Perhaps there will."

And perhaps Mr. McIntyre will be set free, Laura thought. She did not think she wanted to see him. She was angry with him, and doubted she would ever feel differently. Sighing, she set aside her cup and returned to the sheet she was cutting up for bandages.

"Forty days, at best," Jamie said.

"That's nearly two months," said General Sibley, picking up an open champagne bottle from his desk. "We can make a go with that!" He emptied the remainder of the bottle into his glass and raised it to the east, where the sun was still climbing outside the palace windows. It was cold in the big room. No one had lit a fire.

Jamie glanced at Lane—mostly recovered now, though still a bit pale—who was staring between his thumbs at the floor. Colonel Scurry lounged in his chair, one arm draped over its back, and was also silent. Colonel Green would have had something to say, but he had just arrived from Albuquerque and was off meeting with his captains, getting their reports on the 2nd's condition.

"General," said Jamie, searching for words that would not

offend, "we've got food for that long, but we still don't have much ammunition."

"Wasn't there any in that cache you found?"

Jamie shook his head. "No, sir. Just blankets and food and some clothes. It was meant for the Indian Agency."

"Well, Green's fellows can share."

"Sir, even if we redistribute what's in their boxes, and pass out the rounds I just purchased, we won't have enough for a day's fighting, never mind a siege."

The general was slumped in his chair, his smile dampened by the furrow that seemed branded into his brow. He sipped his champagne and stared dully at Jamie.

Jamie glanced at the unhelpful audience again, then met Sibley's gaze. "We can get to Mesilla on forty days' rations, sir," he said slowly. "Captain Coopwood came up a trail through the mountains to avoid Fort Craig—"

"Never mind Fort Craig, dammit," said Sibley, sitting up and flashing his eyes. "We're bound for Fort Union!"

"Sir, we can't take Union. We don't have the resources—"

"Balderdash!" Sibley rose to his feet. "We took their battery away from them at Valverde! Chased them off the field! We can do the same at Union!"

"We had a supply train at the time," said Jamie bitterly, but he knew he had lost the general's attention.

"I've sent to Governor Lubbock for reinforcements," said Sibley. "Where's that map?"

"Behind you, sir," Lane said, nodding toward a heap of papers on a table. Sibley strode over to it, extracted a large map of the Territory, and frowned over it.

"We'll move the army . . . here. Manzano. We can keep an eye on Craig, and watch the roads to Union and Stanton. When our reinforcements arrive, we'll march on Union."

Jamie was silent, trying to calculate how long it would take an expressman to reach Austin, and how long for a regiment—if there happened to be one ready—to march from there to Manzano. Too long, he knew that much.

Sibley returned to the desk and picked up his glass, favoring his staff with a confident smile. "We'll win this yet, gentlemen!" he said, raising the glass toward the northwest. "On to San Francisco!" He downed it in one pull, turned, and threw it toward the fireplace. It missed, smashing against the wall and leaving a pale stain on the whitewash. Lane winced at the sound. Sibley strode out of the room, leaving silence in his wake.

Jamie gazed at the two empty champagne bottles on the desk. With a sigh, he stood up. "Thanks for your support, gentlemen," he said, picking up his hat.

Lane looked up at him. "He won't listen to any of us, Jamie."

"He might've listened to all of us," Jamie said bitterly.

At least Manzano is closer to home, he thought as he followed Sibley out and headed for his own office. Hasty footsteps scuffed the adobe floor behind him; he turned to see Lane following.

The adjutant stopped, his pale face taut with concern. "I'm sorry, Jamie," he said. "I should have backed you up. It's just—"

"Never mind," Jamie said, uncomfortable. He glanced toward Sibley, exiting the palace by the front door, and quietly added, "You were right, he wouldn't have listened."

Lane looked at the floor. "I—it hasn't been easy, coming back to work. Maybe I got up a little too soon."

A sudden pain in his chest made Jamie frown. He'd been acting like a bastard lately, and didn't know why. Yes, they had troubles, and General Sibley was not helping matters. But that was only part of it.

"I've got coffee boiling," he said roughly. "You want some?"

Lane's face lit with gratitude. "Yes," he said. "Thanks."

The Volunteers' camp was all in an uproar. Marching tonight—no, tomorrow—no, wait for new orders. O'Brien sat on a cracker box outside his tent watching Logan's company pack up the camp they had just made the night before. He kept his small glee at being proved right to himself. Ramsey had gone to the post, wearing a foul expression, when the orders first came to prepare for a march, and had not yet come back.

Captain Chapin approached from the fort with a fistful of

papers. Before he got close, O'Brien asked, "Are we marching tonight, then?"

"Not your company," said Chapin, handing him a page. "Yours and F Company will escort Clafin's battery tomorrow."

O'Brien glanced at the paper, then looked up at the adjutant. "Word from Colonel Canby?"

Chapin nodded. "He's left Fort Craig."

A cold chill poured through O'Brien's arms, making them heavy. If Canby had left his snug fort at long last, then likely they'd see some real action. Good, he decided. The lads were more cheerful on the march, and they wanted a chance to finish the job they'd begun.

"I want to ask you something," said Chapin.

O'Brien glanced up, raising his brows. Chapin looked to be in a foul mood. "Are Slough and Paul still squabbling, then?" O'Brien said, grinning. "Pull up a seat."

"Never mind them," said Chapin, folding his arms. He stayed standing. "What are your intentions toward Miss Howland?"

O'Brien was so caught off his guard that he gaped. Then he felt his face beginning to burn, and looked away.

"She may have no family," said Chapin in a low, stern voice, "but she has plenty of friends, some of whom believe you have compromised her reputation."

"I never touched her!" O'Brien looked up, angry at the accusation, the more so for how hard it had been to leave her alone. "I promised to take her to Mrs. Canby and I did!"

"She stayed in your camp, unchaperoned." Chapin took two paces toward him, and dropped his voice lower. "A gentleman would offer her his name."

"I did," said O'Brien, his throat tightening on the words. The heartache was returning, that he'd kept at bay for so long. He stared at the toes of Chapin's boots. "She'll have none of me."

"She told you that?" Chapin sounded surprised.

"She didn't have to say it." O'Brien saw again the shock in her face, before she had turned away. He squeezed his eyes shut, but the vision remained. Chapin could not know how much he had wanted to marry her.

"Well," said Chapin, in a gentler voice.

Go away, thought O'Brien. If you wanted to punish me, you've done it.

"Well, you'd best mind your step, Captain."

O'Brien looked up at him, frowning. The adjutant's tone had been milder, but it held a note of warning.

"You're being watched." Chapin lifted his hat before passing on in the direction of Wyncoop's tent.

What the devil does that mean? O'Brien wondered.

The stage station at Gila Bend was just like the others. The Rebels had burned all the hay and what little was left of the furniture. Kip poked at the smoke-blackened ceiling with a stick, to see if it would hold up. A scatter of soot came down on his head, and he coughed. Captain Calloway and the other officers would take over the building once the command came up anyway. Let them figure out if it was safe.

Kip came out of the deserted station and found Firecracker lipping at the dry grass. He led him over to greener stuff by the river, where the other scouts were already watering their mounts and setting fishing lines. The Gila River turned northward here, on its way to meander around some mountains a few miles to the north, and the wide, shallow bend attracted a host of birds. The scouts, upon heading toward the river, had flushed up thousands of quail that blackened the sky as they took wing.

Kip drew a deep breath and sighed, shaking out his stiff legs as he walked. He was saddle sore, but a herd of demons couldn't make him admit it. He had finally got on a horse and he wasn't about to give it up, even if it was Firecracker.

"There you are," said Felley. "Come on, time to draw."

Felley pulled four stems of river-grass and cut them even, then shortened one and hid them while he shuffled them up. He offered them to Kip first, which was kind of him, though it may have been because Kip had drawn short both days since he joined the scouts, and had consequently been the one to ride back to the column and report on the stage station's condition, while the rest went about making themselves at home.

Kip pulled a long straw. Aikins came up short, and with

a sigh of resignation handed his line over to Zinn. "Come on," he said to Merlin, dragging the horse's head up from the river.

"See you in an hour or so," Felley called after him as he mounted up. Aikins grunted a reply and kicked up a cloud of dust as he departed.

"Want this, Kip?" asked Zinn, offering him Aikins's fishing line.

"No, thanks," said Kip. "You won't catch anything but those god-awful hardtails."

"I'll get a trout, you watch," Zinn retorted.

Kip shook his head. "Think I'll try for some of those quail."

"Good luck," Felley said. "Don't go far."

"No, indeed," said Kip, glancing up at the mountains a few miles away. Maybe there were Indians hiding up in the rocks. Sutter told more stories every night, all manner of gruesome stories about the Apaches and what they did to unsuspecting travelers on the trail. Even the women could be brutal, according to Sutter. They'd torture a dog or a prisoner to death just for their own amusement, or so the sergeant said.

Kip stepped over to Firecracker and laid a hand on the horse's flank to keep him calm while he unlashed his rifle from the saddle. A shotgun would have been a better weapon for hunting quail—from the huge flocks they'd seen, one shot would have brought down a dozen or more—but one made do with what was at hand. And a rifle was better for other things, like shooting Indians before they got close enough to kill you. Kip checked his pistol, took a handful of cartridges from the saddlebag, and headed into the tall grass of the riverbank.

It was late, and the guardhouse was quiet. O'Brien followed a sleepy private in to where Hall was being kept behind bars. Hall, slowly pacing the limits of the room, looked up as O'Brien came in.

The air was close and smelled of unwashed bodies and things fouler yet. Men sitting with their backs against the rock walls looked up at O'Brien in silent suspicion. Others lay on the floor, sleeping. Hall came up to the bars and leaned his elbows on a crossbeam.

"Well, howdy, Red," said Hall, eyes hard. "Say, you didn't have to be in such a hurry to see me."

"We're marching tomorrow," O'Brien told him. "I came to say good-bye."

Hall looked angry, but at least it was the dull anger that he often could work his way out of. "Got any liquor?" he said.

O'Brien glanced at the guard, who seemed not to care, and handed his flask through the bars. It was the silver flask Hall had given him months ago, on his birthday. He hadn't opened it lately. Hall tipped it up and guzzled. O'Brien watched him, seeing only a ghost of his old friend, the gallant cavalier, the man who'd convinced him to join the Union army. A bitter, sad ghost, who'd been caught hand in glove with the Rebels.

"Why?" he asked.

Hall's eyes flashed anger, then he laughed. "You know me, Red. I go where the wind prevails."

"They'll be after hanging you, Joseph."

"Oh, maybe. Maybe not."

"Don't you care, then?"

"About what? Whether they hang me or shoot me?"

O'Brien frowned. "It's a joke, is it?"

Hall's face lost its laughter. "No," he said, and pulled at the flask again.

A sound came from behind him. A man had sat up, and was rubbing his face. He had dark hair all awry from sleeping, and looked twenty or so.

Hall looked 'round. "Want some, Mac?" he said, offering the flask. The man stared at it a minute, then got up and came forward, glancing at O'Brien.

"Captain O'Brien, meet Lacey McIntyre," said Hall.

O'Brien looked at the young man with sharper interest. This was the fellow who'd courted Miss Howland, and then gone over to the Texans. "So you're Lacey McIntyre," he said.

The lad's eyes grew wary. "Yes," he said. "Why?"

"I'm a friend of Miss Howland's."

McIntyre's gaze wandered down to the floor. "Oh," he said. "I hope she's well."

"She is," said O'Brien. Well away from you.

Temper, Alastar. You can't have her either, you know. He watched the lad sip from his flask, and returned his attention to Hall.

"What happened, Joseph?" he asked softly.

Hall looked impatient, and said, "Well, the boys in my company that were trying to cross the river were getting shot to hell, so I decided to stay on the safe side."

"You're no coward."

"No? Maybe I just heard Alabama calling."

"Then why did you join the Pet Lambs at all?" asked O'Brien.

"That was your idea," said Hall softly. "Remember?" A wry smile turned up one corner of his mouth. "Guess I just wasn't cut out for a soldier."

McIntyre was fitting the cap to the flask. Hall took it out of his hand, and tilted it high, draining it, then handed it back to O'Brien.

"There you go, Red. Should be able to get a few dollars for it." The laughter in his voice didn't match his bitter eyes.

"God forgive you," said O'Brien, shaking his head.

"Don't get pious all of a sudden," said Hall. "You've been listening to Chivington too much."

O'Brien could think of no answer. It seemed his friend had become more and more a stranger.

He put the flask back in his pocket, and offered his hand. Hall stared at it, and a shade of his old self came into his eyes. He clasped O'Brien's hand hard for a moment, then pulled away with a brittle smile.

"Go on and tend to your men, Red," he said. "I'm not your problem anymore."

"Good luck," O'Brien said, for there was nothing more to say. He turned toward the door.

"My best to Chas," Hall called after him lazily.

O'Brien looked back at him. "You've not heard?"

Hall's eyebrows went up. "The maître d's been bad about bringing the paper. No tip for him this week," he said.

"Franklin's dead," said O'Brien. "He was hit the first day."

Surprise went through Hall's face, then it hardened. "Too bad for you, Red," he said in the stranger's voice. "Old Chas was your best friend."

"No, Joseph," O'Brien said softly. "You were my best friend."

Hall's brow crinkled and a hungry look came into his eyes. He seemed about to say something, but instead turned his back and stalked over to the wall. O'Brien watched him for a moment, then silently turned and went out.

6

"It seems strange that man will organize war. He never would did he realize its horrors, which only come home to the soldier..."

—Ovando J. Hollister

Jamie left his office and went out into the hallway, summoned by the cacophonous racket of bells ringing all over town in the Mexican churches. He rather liked their disharmony. It reminded him of San Antonio. There wasn't a regular protestant church back home—one was being built, but construction had stopped because of the war—so the minister held meetings in whatever space he could find. Here there was a Baptist church, but Jamie hadn't been. He ought to go to a service, he supposed. He'd been spared and he ought to be thankful, but the thought of listening to a sermon didn't appeal just now.

A cool breeze blew sunlight into the main entrance, the gated door of which stood open. The passage, true to the Mexican style of the palace, was big enough to drive a wagon through. Jamie followed it out back to the large plazuela where the well was, glancing up at the sky as he stepped outside. Clear blue and cold, with the wind getting stronger. Trees were just starting to bud with the promise of spring, though the grass was still dry and brown. At home there would already be flowers blooming in Momma's garden, and green grass covering the hills. Jamie hugged his arms to his chest against the wind, went over to the well and helped himself to a ladleful of frigid water. Hanging the ladle back on its hook, he turned to face the six guns parked in the courtyard.

The cannon they'd brought with them from Texas were up at the post, in the care of their batteries. These were the

Valverde guns, trophies standing silent in the peaceful yard, gleaming in the sun. Six mismatched guns: two twelve-pound field howitzers, three six-pounders, and a twelve-pound mountain howitzer, captured at great cost and displayed here in the grounds of what had been Canby's headquarters as proof of the Army of New Mexico's superiority. The guns had been cleaned and polished since the Glorieta battle, carriages all in trim except one whose axle had been weakened by a round shot. One gun was still stained with blood where Major Lockridge and Captain McRae had fallen over it at Valverde. The tube had been hot at the time, and the blood had burned in, and Jamie figured the men cleaning it had been proud enough of that stain not to scrub it too hard. He pressed his lips together. Captain Martin—his superior officer, friend, and intended brother-in-law—had been among the many brave souls lost in the charge that had captured the guns and won the battle at Valverde. Jamie still didn't like to think about it. He put a hand out to touch the cascabel of the nearest gun—the mountain howitzer—a misfit elevated to trophy status by its capture. It was cold; the sun hadn't yet warmed the thick metal.

"Mr. Russell?"

Startled, Jamie turned to see Miss Howland coming toward him. She was dressed for church, in a worn black cloak over the green dress which was the better of the only two he'd ever seen her wearing, and a black straw bonnet over her fair hair.

"I was told I might find you here," she said. "Mrs. Canby asked me to step in and invite you and Mr. Lane to sup with us this evening."

"We'd be honored," Jamie said. "Thank you."

"It won't be anything fancy," she warned. "We are out of a number of staples, I'm afraid."

"Any meal in your company is a treat," he said shyly.

He liked her, more than any girl he'd known before. She was nothing like Emmaline, yet she somehow reminded him of his sister. Maybe it was the flash that came into her eyes when she was angry about something.

He had to write to Emmaline. Sooner or later he had to write, and tell her that Martin was gone. Maybe he could talk one of the expressmen into carrying a letter back to San Antonio.

Miss Howland's gaze strayed to the guns, and she frowned. "Have I seen these before?"

"I don't think so," Jamie said. "We brought them up from Valverde."

She looked up at him with a sticken expression, then back at the guns. "Then this was Captain McRae's battery," she murmured.

"Yes," he acknowledged uneasily.

She took a step toward the guns, pulling her cloak closer about her. Jamie watched her, concerned. She blinked a few times. Perhaps the wind was bothering her eyes.

"Forgive me," she said. "He was a friend."

Jamie's stomach twisted, and he wished himself anywhere else. The guns that his army was so proud of were a symbol of loss to Miss Howland, and were only a painful reminder to him. All that blood for six tubes of brass. Jamie frowned, his mind ringing with the echoes of the guns, turned against the Yankees as soon as they'd been captured, firing on their former owners as they scrambled into the river to get away, rifles and shotguns following up the guns and the Río Grande running brown and red—mud and blood—with the slaughter. All of a sudden his breathing was broken, and his eyes filled with unexpected tears. He squeezed them shut and swallowed, letting out a shaky sigh. He'd lost something that day, something inside of himself, he wasn't quite sure what. There was a hollowness left behind. It lingered like a wound that wouldn't heal. He didn't dare think about it too hard, but he could feel it always, a shadow on his spirit.

"Mr. Russell," Miss Howland said in an unsteady voice, "You seem such a good—an intelligent man. Why are you fighting for the Confederacy?"

He opened his eyes to find her looking at him, her face filled with sadness. "Texas is my home," was all he could say, which he knew was unsatisfactory. Texas was all very well, but it didn't explain his presence here, in New Mexico Territory. With a shock he realized that he didn't really know anymore why he was fighting, why he was still with the army.

"I'm sorry," she said, suddenly agitated. Her hand clutched her cloak near her throat, and her eyes roamed the courtyard. "That was rude of me. Please forgive me."

"No," Jamie said, "I—"

"I should go, Mrs. Canby is waiting. I'll see you this evening," she said, stepping back. "Good morning."

Jamie watched her hasten away, through the palace and out into the plaza. A single church bell tolled mournfully, calling latecomers to worship. Last chance for salvation. Jamie stood listening to the final note fade away, then slowly returned to the palace.

*   *   *

Laura walked beside Mrs. Canby with small, quick steps, suppressing an irrational desire to run. The chilly air stung her nostrils.

"What did Mr. Russell say?" Mrs. Canby asked.

"He—he said they'd be delighted to join us," Laura replied.

"Excellent," Mrs. Canby said. "Such pleasant young men, both of them."

The door to the church was closed against the cold. Laura stepped forward and pushed it open, holding the heavy wooden panel aside for Mrs. Canby to pass in. A quiet murmuring from inside told her the service had not yet begun. She did not wish to attend it. She wished to go away somewhere and think.

Mr. Russell's words—"Texas is my home"—had surprised her, not of themselves, but because they had brought a salient problem to her attention. She herself had no home, none whatsoever. She was living on sufferance, imposing on Mrs. Canby's charity and she had come to the sudden realization that this was intolerable. She must find an alternative, and soon. She had few resources, but she was not destitute, and certainly not helpless. Lieutenant Franklin's words returned to her; "A woman alone doesn't have many choices."

The minister had come in. Laura hastened to seat herself beside Mrs. Canby.

"Unless she makes her own road," Laura whispered to herself.

The sound of footsteps made Jamie look up from the list he was making. "That you, Wooster?" he called.

The new quartermaster sergeant stuck his head around the doorway. "Sir?"

Wooster's tone was less than enthusiastic, for which Jamie could hardly blame him. He suspected Wooster was blue on account of the new job, not so much because he disliked quartermaster work, but because he'd rather have remained an ordnance sergeant. Except there wasn't much ordnance to look after, which was why Jamie had claimed him.

"Go around to the storehouse and get two pounds of that sugar we confiscated yesterday." They had taken a small stockpile of stores from a back room in the abandoned shop of a Yankee merchant. It wasn't enough to ration out to the troops, which meant the officers would get it, so Jamie felt justified in claiming some. "Take it to Mrs. Canby's right away, with my compliments," he told Wooster.

The sergeant shrugged.

"Yes, sir," he said, disappearing again.

"Thank you, Wooster," Jamie called.

It was only a small gesture, but he had to do something, and it was the best he could think of. Miss Howland had mentioned they were short on supplies, and sugar was a luxury. He hoped the gift would serve to demonstrate his goodwill, since he'd been too damned tongue-tied to talk. Their conversation had left him feeling awkward and unhappy.

He frowned at his list, realizing he'd already written some of these tasks down. He shuffled through his papers without finding the one he sought. Must have carried it with him somewhere. Feeling suddenly weary, he crossed his arms on top of all the papers and laid his head down.

Why am I fighting for this army?

Annoyed with himself, he got up and went to the general's office. Sibley had roused himself and was there, along with Captain Owens, one of his aides-de-camp, who sat beside him working the cork out of a bottle of wine. Jamie avoided Owens's gaze; he had not been comfortable in the ADC's presence since Albuquerque, where Owens had tried to get him to talk about Valverde, about things he would rather forget.

The general had his feet propped up on the desk, reading the newspaper that had been captured a few days back with a small Federal supply train near Albuquerque. Jamie had already read it. The news wasn't good: Nashville taken, a battle lost on the Potomac—Jamie wondered if his brother Matthew had been in the fight—and a possible invasion of Aransas Bay. That was too close to home. Some of the 1st had been recruited not far from there in Victoria.

"Invade Texas, my foot," said the general, throwing down the paper. "They'll never invade Texas!"

"No, sir. Morning, sir," said Jamie, reaching to extract his task list from the mess of papers on the desk. "Shall I send the supplies forward to Manzano, General? I can start moving them tomorrow."

"Eager beaver?" said Owens.

"I don't suppose there's any harm in it," said the general, pushing a glass along the desktop toward the aide. "Has the surgeon given you an account of the wounded?"

"Not on paper, sir. I'll request it," Jamie said. He dug a pencil out of his pocket and leaned on a corner of the desk to make a note on his list. Owens got the cork free with a loud *pop,* just as a scatter of hoofbeats and excited voices drifted in from the plaza.

Jamie looked up in time to see an exhausted expressman duck his head to come through the low door, cross to the desk, and hand General Sibley a letter. Sibley glanced at the outside of the note, then nodded. "Thank you, son. Dismissed."

The expressman turned and clomped out, heaving a large sigh. The general opened the message and read it. Jamie watched while Sibley's frown deepened. He finished reading and stared off into space for a minute, then looked up at Owens.

"Get the staff together for a meeting," he said.

"Now?" said Owens.

"Right now."

Sibley stood up and walked over to the map spread out on a table at the side of the room. Owens looked at Jamie, then with a shrug set the open wine bottle on the desk and strode out. Jamie waited, eyes on the paper in Sibley's hand, which the general was slowly crushing as he gazed intently at the map. Finally Sibley came back to the desk, dropped the half-crumpled page and poured himself a glass of wine.

"Looks like my old friend has finally made up his mind," Sibley said.

"Sir?" said Jamie.

The general gave a sad little smile. "Canby's marching north from Fort Craig," he said, and drank deeply.

Jamie's eyes went to the map. "Will he get to Manzano before us?" Even as the words left his mouth, he realized they didn't matter.

"Never mind Manzano, son," said Sibley, echoing his thoughts. "We've got to get to Albuquerque before he does."

Jamie nodded, a cold fist gripping his guts. Albuquerque, where they'd left a small supply depot on the way up. Where his friend John Reily waited, itching for a fight. Where most of his stores within reach were guarded only by Hardeman's and Coopwood's companies and Reily's four guns.

"Go along there, cailin," O'Brien said, though the mare needed no urging. He spoke to her more to teach her the sound of his voice and remind her that he was her master. She had gone along sweetly all day, after only a slight disagreement about the saddle that morning. O'Brien had put his own saddle on her. He hadn't yet sold the one she'd had on when he caught her, though likely he would. Likely he'd sell the mustang, too, but not yet. He had loaned both to Rice, whose horse had been killed at Apache Canyon, and who might buy them, or might not. Partly he'd done it to annoy Ramsey, who considered Rice his own man.

"Good lass." O'Brien stroked the mare's dark neck, and she bobbed her head. She was only a bit tired, though they'd ridden hard all day. She'd grown used to long marches on the way up from Texas, it seemed.

The sun was just dipping toward the mountains when the column was halted and orders to pitch camp went 'round. Chivington liked to have daylight for his sermons. O'Brien grimaced as he dismounted, wishing there were some way to avoid the preaching, but he knew it would only bring him more grief from the major. He unsaddled the mare and brushed her down himself, wanting her to know his touch, then gave her over to Shaunessy to turn out for grazing.

O'Brien looked at the campsite, a spot they had used before, on their first trip down. It was near a small village the Mexicans called Bernal, a place of high hills thick with cedar and piñon, just before the trail turned west toward the Pecos. He had camped just there, beside that dying cedar, and played cards with his lady and Franklin. Turning away from the memories, he glanced at the sun tarnishing a haze of clouds over the blue mountains. It would be a cold night.

A bugle split the twilight. Time to hear God's word. With a sigh for the dull hour ahead, O'Brien sought out Morris to give the order for I Company to proceed to evening prayers. Instead he found Ramsey, Fitzroy, and Rice with their heads together. They looked up as he approached, falling silent.

"Have you seen Sergeant Morris?" he asked, trying to keep his voice pleasant.

Fitzroy jerked his head downhill, toward the spring. All three stared at O'Brien.

"My thanks to you," he said, nodding. He could feel their eyes on him all the way down the hill.

"They will be here soon," Mrs. Canby said from the kitchen doorway.

"It's almost finished."

Laura scraped the last bit of cream filling from the bowl and spread it on the bottom layer of cake, then carefully set the top layer over it. It was a Jenny Lind cake, a tribute to Mr. Russell's generous gift, the best treat they could make with the materials at hand. Their store of fruit was exhausted save for a few dried apples, but by soaking them in water María had made them fit for use in the filling. Laura regretted the absence of lemon, but hoped the cake would still be good. A small cake; sign of a hopeful future, a promise of return to civilized life. They had not thought of such frivolities as cakes in many days.

"Hurry, now," said Mrs. Canby. Laura set the cake on a shelf in María's pantry and took off her apron, brushing a bit of flour from her skirt. Through the window she saw Juan Carlos crossing the placita to the gate.

"They're here," she said. "Thank you, María!"

The housekeeper smiled and shooed her out. Laura and Mrs. Canby hurried through the dining room, still occupied by Captain Adair and two others, though most of the wounded had recovered or been moved to the hospital. They reached the parlor just in time to arrange themselves comfortably before Juan Carlos showed in their two guests.

"Welcome, Mr. Russell," said Mrs. Canby, smiling. "Mr. Lane."

"How do you do, ma'am? Miss Howland," Mr. Lane said, bowing. Laura smiled at him, and nodded. He had a kindly face, marred by a fresh scar along one temple, and was a few years older than Mr. Russell. Both men wore civilian clothes, though their shirts were identical—gray, with red threads in a crisscross pattern—so the effect was something like a uniform. Laura wondered if Mr. Russell had left off his Confederate jacket out of deference to Mrs. Canby. He looked tired, and a bit preoccupied.

"We brought you some news," he said, offering Mrs. Canby a much-creased newspaper.

"Why, thank you!" said Mrs. Canby. "We have not seen a paper in weeks! Where did you come by this?"

"Came up from Albuquerque," said Mr. Russell, with a glance at his companion.

"Well, it is most welcome," said Mrs. Canby.

María came in with a laden tray, and they moved to the parlor table for dinner. Feeling shy, Laura listened while Mrs. Canby drew out Mr. Lane, asking where he lived in Texas, and what his family was. Innocuous questions, the only kind that were safe among such a party. The illusion that all was well, that there were no dreadful conflicts behind, or indeed, before them, was fragile, like a lace curtain. It must be treated carefully, and not looked at too closely, lest one saw through to what it pretended to conceal.

Laura found herself staring at Mr. Lane's ugly scar. Looking away, she saw Mr. Russell watching her. She searched her mind for a safe question to address to him.

"Have you been to the Tesuque Pueblo, Mr. Russell?" she asked. A foolish question; he had undoubtedly been there, to buy food from the Indians, or perhaps just to take it.

He nodded. "Yes, I've visited several of the pueblos. They seem very good people, in their way."

"They are. I have learned a great deal about different cultures since I came here."

Mr. Russell smiled.

"You must already be familiar with the Spanish and their ways," Laura continued. "Is San Antonio very like Santa Fé?"

"In some ways," he said. "Different in others. Not all the houses are adobe. We have a lot of Germans living there, and they build their houses out of stone. So do the Irish."

Laura glanced up in surprise, suddenly reminded of Captain O'Brien. She felt a blush creeping into her cheek, and took up her knife and fork to cut a bite of meat. When she looked up again, Mr. Russell was gazing off into the distance.

"Have you visited the pueblos, Mr. Lane?" she asked, striving to keep the conversation alive.

"No, ma'am," said Mr. Lane, with a glance at his friend. "I haven't been able to go about much."

"Do visit Tesuque, if you have the time."

"I don't think—that is, we're pretty busy—"

"We're leaving," said Mr. Russell. The flatness in his voice surprised Laura. She glanced at Mrs. Canby, who carefully pressed her napkin to her lips, then laid it down.

"Immediately?" Mrs. Canby asked.

"Starting tomorrow," said Mr. Russell.

"Some of the men here are not fit to travel," said Mrs. Canby.

Mr. Russell nodded. "Maney is staying behind to look after the wounded. He'll try to get them all under one roof. They shouldn't be in your way much longer, ma'am."

The businesslike tone in his voice was one Laura had not heard before. His face had grown serious as well. The curtain of illusion had shifted, drawn aside by a cold draft of truth. Laura could not think of anything to say.

"Well, we shall miss your company," said Mrs. Canby.

"Thank you, ma'am. I'll miss you, too. Very much," he said, looking directly at Laura.

What could she say? Under different circumstances, they

might have gone beyond mere civilities. She liked him, she realized. She liked this man, who was an enemy of her country.

María came in, rescuing her from her struggle for words. Laura let her eyes follow the servant's warm brown hands as she cleared away the dishes and set out cups for coffee. In the center of the table she placed the cake. That cake, a pathetic attempt at normality. Made with the enemy's gift of sugar. It had become a farewell gift.

"Thank you, María," said Mrs. Canby as she accepted the coffee pot. "Do you take milk, Mr. Lane?"

María cut and served the cake while she poured, and everyone talked of nothing, of sugar and eggs, and when it might rain. When the servant left the room, they fell silent again.

Laura took a bite of her cake. It had turned out well, but she had no appetite, and put down her fork.

"Mr. Russell," said Mrs. Canby, "you need not tell me if you don't wish to—"

"We're going to Albuquerque," he said. "You'd know soon enough."

"I see." Mrs. Canby sipped her coffee, then set down her cup.

"Colonel Canby is marching north," added Mr. Russell. "You'll hear about that soon, too, I expect."

Mrs. Canby nodded, her lips slightly pursed. "Thank you," she said, smiling at Mr. Russell, but her eyes looked sadder than usual.

Laura heard echoes of battle—of cannon-fire and rifles and the screams of wounded men—and shivered. The comfortable curtain was unraveling, leaving them bereft of pleasantries.

Mr. Russell finished his coffee and rose. "I'm afraid we can't stay," he said, as Mr. Lane hastily devoured the last of his cake. "We have a lot to do getting ready."

"Of course," said Mrs. Canby. "Thank you for coming." She stood, and Laura and Mr. Lane followed suit. "And thank you so much for the sugar," added Mrs. Canby as they walked to the parlor door.

"Don't thank me," said Mr. Russell in a strangled voice.

He stopped, turning to her, and said, "Ma'am, I—I'm sorry, but I have to take your horses."

Laura caught her breath. Mr. Russell must have heard her, for he glanced her way, then looked down. "I haven't got a choice," he said.

"I see," said Mrs. Canby calmly. "Are you taking the carriage as well?"

Mr. Russell looked sidelong at Mr. Lane. "That's a pleasure vehicle," he said. "It isn't suited to heavy work."

Mrs. Canby nodded. "I'm afraid our mule is lame," she added.

"Then he's no use to me," said Mr. Russell, sounding relieved. He looked up at Mrs. Canby, unhappiness digging a frown into his brow. "I'm so sorry," he whispered. "After all your kindness—"

"Never mind," said Mrs. Canby gently. "I am used to the fortunes of war." She offered her hand, and he bent over it, then turned toward Laura, eyes seeking forgiveness.

"God be with you, sir," she said softly, curtseying.

He nodded, and bowed, and left with Mr. Lane hurrying in his wake. Laura turned to Mrs. Canby. Without a word the two ladies embraced, then moved to the sofa where a basket of bandages waited to be rolled.

Jamie rubbed at his eyes and blinked, trying to focus on his lists. The night was far from over if he were to have his wagons ready to start tomorrow. He planned to assemble the train at first light. He was anxious to get to Albuquerque.

Clothing; he'd issue it all to the men. Blankets the same. Commissary said they needed twenty wagons. He'd sent Wooster to try to talk them down to ten. The men could carry their rations. Transportation was almost impossible to come by since the battles, but he'd managed to scrape together three dozen vehicles of various shapes and sizes, and the teams to haul them. Now he was trying to figure out how to fit everything into them.

A scrape in the outer room told him he wasn't alone. His sergeant must be back. "Wooster, is there any of that coffee left?" he called. There was no reply.

"Wooster?"

A figure slumped into the doorway, much taller than Wooster, and clad in braid-encrusted gray, the coat hanging open over a sweat-stained shirt. It took Jamie a moment to recognize him as General Sibley.

"Sir!" he said, rising from the desk. "I didn't know it was you. Are you all right?"

Sibley nodded and grimaced together, and raised a half-empty bottle of champagne to his lips. He slouched to the desk and leaned a hand on it, and Jamie grabbed a chair for him. The general did not sit, but leaned heavily on the chair back.

"You make sure the guns get through," he said.

"Sir?" Jamie had gone around to his own chair, and looked up before he sat. He wondered how much Sibley had drunk. The general's face was flushed, but the eyes he turned on Jamie were clear, if fatigued.

"The guns from Valverde," said Sibley, gesturing with his bottle in the direction of the plazuela. "They come with us. Don't care if you have to leave all the rest."

"Of course," Jamie said, a little alarmed.

Sibley grimaced, putting a hand to his back, and Jamie felt a surge of pity. Clearly the general was ill. Would he hand command over to Green again?

"We're coming back," Sibley said, glaring at Jamie. "I've sent for reinforcements. They'll meet us at Mesilla, and we'll re-equip, then come back and take Fort Union."

"Fort Craig is—"

The general flung the champagne bottle at Jamie, who flinched as it brushed by his head to thud against the heavy wall behind him.

"Craig is empty, we'll smash it on the way down!" Sibley said. "Should have burned it before." He gave a sound somewhere between a moan and a growl, took a flask from his coat pocket, and pulled hard at it.

Jamie sat silent, breathing hard and fast, watching Sibley's every movement. The general was either unwilling or unable to face the truth. It would take a miracle, in Jamie's opinion, to get reinforcements where Sibley expected them, and another miracle to supply them. They had stripped the Territory on the way up, and the depot at Mesilla couldn't support a second advance northward. If they were very lucky they would have enough to get home.

Am I a coward? Jamie wondered. Is there something I don't see? Something only generals know about surviving on nothing and fighting without bullets? To him it looked like the only choice was to head home as fast as possible.

The candle guttered, spitting. Sibley stumbled toward the doorway. "You look after those guns," he said, just as the flame went out.

"Yes, sir," Jamie said. He sat in the dark, listening to the commander shuffle away down the hall. Our gallant General Sibley, he thought sadly, remembering speeches on the Military Plaza back home, with families cheering and new flags snapping in the breeze. It seemed like a dream, so distant, so unreal. He lit a fresh candle and got up to retrieve Sibley's bottle, which lay in a puddle of champagne soaking into the earthen floor. Jamie set the bottle upright against the wall, rubbed his hands over his face, and went back to the desk and his lists.

The sun was already slanting hot horizontal lances between the peaks far ahead when a glimmer of water came into view at last, and Kip knew the column had reached Maricopa Wells. He had drawn the short straw this morning, and had paused at the wells to fill his canteen and give Firecracker a drink before riding back to the tired, parched men of the column. They had marched at night from the dry camp at Desert Station—and Kip couldn't think of a more appropriate name for that spot without resorting to obscenities—in an effort to minimize the effects of thirst. Even so, the men just barely kept ranks long enough to halt and be dismissed before making a scrambling rush to the water.

A wave of heat washed over Kip as the sun cleared the mountains. He eased Firecracker away from the main camp to dismount. Firecracker didn't like being crowded, he had discovered. Kip still had the educational bruises.

He found a tallish mesquite that might offer some shade and set his saddle under it, then quickly brushed Firecracker down and tethered him to keep him from wandering to the wells until after the column had all had their fill. His own canteen was dry again and he was feeling thirsty. It wasn't the aching thirst of last night, but it wouldn't hurt to have the canteen out and ready for when the crowd at the wells thinned out. He reached for his saddlebag, but stopped when it hissed at him.

Sunlight had started to bake the dry ground. Just by the mesquite bush where he'd laid his saddle was a big, flat, sunny rock, presently occupied by an angry coil of buzzing rattlesnake. Why the reptile hadn't slithered for the hills on the column's arrival he couldn't imagine, unless it was too sleepy still, and was now rattling out of embarrassment at being caught as much as for any other reason.

Kip felt the hairs on the back of his neck rising, and even as he began slowly to pull back his hand, he knew the snake would strike. He kicked at it, reflecting at the same time that to do so was highly stupid, but as luck would have it the snake hit the side of his boot and couldn't get a bite. Kip pulled his pistol and killed it with the second shot, and a dozen men came running.

"Just a snake," he told them, and picked up the dead reptile by the tail. "Big old feller," he added, admiring the rattles.

Men crowded around to examine the trophy and exclaim over Kip's good fortune. "Gonna eat it?" asked Stavers.

"If he don't, I will," said Felley, winning a laugh from the soldiers.

"Show me how to cook it and I'll share," said Kip.

"If you're smart, you won't let him near the cookfire," said Sergeant Sutter, then added " 'ten-*shun*!" in a sharp voice.

"At ease," said Captain Calloway, stepping up to Kip through the parting crowd.

"Rattlesnake, sir," said Kip, displaying it. Maybe he'd split it three ways, and give some to the captain. Never hurt to keep your commander happy.

Calloway just stared for a minute, his face settling into a frown. "Could you have killed it without firing your pistol?"

Kip's mouth dropped open, but he shut it again. "Uh—I guess. Maybe."

The captain shot a glance around the circle of men, more of whom had gathered. "We're a long way from home, boys.

Do your hunting quietly from now on. Any man who fires without orders to do so will answer to me."

Kip watched the men who'd been admiring his kill a moment before quietly disperse. Stavers stayed a minute, staring at Kip, who gazed back, feeling a little lump of anger and shame rise up his chest. Finally Stavers, too, turned away, leaving Kip alone with his dead snake and his empty canteen.

Jamie urged the horse to a trot again, and glanced at the mountains to the east—the Sandias—a rugged range that loomed over a dozen or more villages along the Río Grande valley, of which Albuquerque was one. Their heights, which the sun hadn't yet cleared, were shrouded in snow-laden clouds. Jamie passed a Spanish church and a grove of peach trees in full bloom as he went through yet another sleeping town. He'd been riding all night, and the horse was weary. He'd have to give it a rest before long. If he could find a picket, maybe they'd trade him a fresh mount. There was no sign of an outpost in this village—Alameda, if he remembered it right—but he might have better luck in the next one.

The train, including the Valverde guns, was many miles back, plodding along under the care of a commissary sergeant and a guard of mobile wounded. Jamie had gone ahead, and outstripped even Green's mounted regiment. Lane, who had started with Jamie that morning, had given up at Algodones and gone into camp with Green's men while Jamie went on alone. Jamie couldn't sleep anyway, so he'd found a fresh horse, wrapped his blanket around himself poncho-style, and ridden on through the dawn. He wanted to get to Albuquerque and his depot, and Reily. Maybe then the gnawing ache in his gut, which had nothing to do with hunger, would go away.

Jamie let the horse drop back down to a walk, giving it a pat on the neck. He was asking too much, he knew, and he didn't want to kill the poor beast. He couldn't afford to. He thought of Cocoa and wondered where she was. Alive, he hoped. Up in some remote meadow, fattening up on the first spring grass. He was glad, actually, that she wasn't with the army. All their horses were getting worked to the bone.

He missed her, though. Missed the comfort of her warm, glossy coat and her soft nose nuzzling at his face.

Home. Home was what he really wanted. Russell's Ranch, a thousand miles away. Momma's scolding and Gabe's jabbering and Emma's tart impatience and her wonderful laughing eyes. Except she probably wouldn't laugh for a while, not after what Jamie had to tell her. He took off his hat and rubbed at the star pin, trying to shine it up a bit.

"Hola, señor!"

Jamie jumped, and his fingers closed over the star. Looking up, he saw two Mexicans, mounted, riding toward him up the Camino Real. One had a pistol in his hand.

"¿A dónde va usted, señor?" said the taller of the two, the one without a gun.

Demanding to know where he was going. They were pickets, then, Federal pickets. Jamie reined to a stop, his horse's ears twitching forward toward the newcomers. The two natives halted a few feet away.

"Buenos días," Jamie said. "Voy a Albuquerque."

"Los tejanos están allí," said the tall man.

"Yo sé, pero mi hermana está enferma." Jamie waited, resisting the urge to look at the gun. He was gripping his hat so hard the points of the star were digging into his hand, and his heart was thundering. Couldn't they hear it?

The two men exchanged a glance, and the smaller one said, "They will rob you, señor. The tejanos will take your money."

Jamie laughed. "I haven't got any." Which was the truth.

"Then they will take your horse."

Thinking of Mrs. Canby's horses, Jamie let his eyes grow hard. "They can try," he said, careful to keep the San Antonio tang out of his voice. He concentrated on speaking like Mr. Webber, who was from Maine originally and still didn't sound like a Texan.

The taller man gave a low laugh, and his companion put away his gun. "You should be careful," he said. "You are not so safe, traveling alone."

"I don't have much choice," said Jamie.

"Have you heard any news about the armies?" asked the taller man. "Any rumors?"

"Rumors?" Jamie frowned, trying to figure out what they wanted to hear.

"The tejanos. Are they coming down from Santa Fé?"

Jamie shrugged. "There are rumors like that every day. I haven't paid much attention."

The Mexicans seemed satisfied. The taller one nudged his horse past Jamie's, saying, "Buenos días, señor. Buena suerte."

"Gracias," said Jamie, nodding to them both as they passed. He clicked to his horse, and though his neck felt like pins and needles were burning in it, he made himself keep to an easy walk while he counted to a hundred.

He dared a glance back. The two men had halted and were watching him from a rise just outside the village. Jamie waved his hat at them, put it on his head, and turned southward. He looked at the star pin in his hand, which he'd removed from the hat in the meantime, and sucked in a ragged breath, letting it out in a sigh. Tucking the little star away safe in his shirt pocket under the blanket, he picked up a trot once more.

Laura rose at dawn and dressed hastily, putting on both her shawl and her cloak over her old black gown and hurrying out to the henhouse. She suspected the Texans of appropriating eggs, and had acquired the habit of rising early to get there ahead of them. Today, though, the hens most likely would not have been bothered, as those of the wounded who could walk had left the previous day with the last of Sibley's army. She could only be thankful, although Santa Fé now seemed more than ever like a ghost town, and she had begun to feel an acute loneliness.

The hens clucked softly as she entered their little domain. Only four left, poor dears. Once the Texans were all gone from the house, Mrs. Canby planned to let at least one of the birds set her clutch, so that she could begin rebuilding her flock.

Gathering the eggs was a moment's work. As Laura emerged she saw Juan Carlos crossing the placita with a pail of milk. Mrs. Canby's dairy cow had been left to her, along with the mule, thank heaven. It was hard to have anything taken, but Laura knew that had it not been for Captain Russell's kindness, they would have lost all.

She was unlikely to meet him again, she knew, which caused her a little disappointment, but mostly relief. She supposed it was foolish to have imagined all the enemy to be evil demons, bent on enslaving the Negro and dominating the free soil of the territories. Mr. Russell was none of these things. He seemed an entirely decent person, his only disagreeable characteristic being an allegiance to the wrong army. She liked him, and that made her uncomfortable.

She leaned against the adobe wall of the shed, closed her eyes and let the morning's first sunshine caress her face. She could almost imagine herself back in Glorieta, enjoying the summer's warm breezes in that peaceful valley. It would always be a special place to her; a magical place. The spot where her new life had begun.

Her eyes fluttered open, and her gaze came to rest on the snow-laden Sangre de Cristos. The change in her life was born of winter, not summer, and she knew with increasing clarity that its source was Captain O'Brien. A winter meeting: slow and cautious, sparse of comfort; yet those comforts, when found, were the more dear because of their rarity. Lately she had found herself thinking of the captain more and more, and she suspected her loneliness had something to do with his absence.

Laura glanced at the small handful of eggs in her basket. So few that they must be used sparingly, with consideration. Like her choices.

The one thing she must not do was impose upon Mrs. Canby any longer than necessary. She must therefore find means of supporting herself, and soon. Moving out of Mrs. Canby's house was unfortunately not practical. The Exchange was expensive, and her small fortune would speedily vanish if she were to remove there. She supposed she could travel back to Boston and seek employment of some kind—become a seamstress, a governess—or if she felt more daring, apply to work as a nurse in one of the many new hospitals spawned by the war. Worthy work, but it did not fill her with enthusiasm.

The thought of hospitals reminded her of poor Captain

Adair. She went into the kitchen, turned her meager harvest of eggs over to María, and passed into the dining room, where the captain lay alone now. She knelt beside him, placing a hand on his brow. It was cold.

"Oh!" she whispered. She picked up his hand and found it to be cold as well, quite cold. She felt in vain for a pulse, then sadly laid his hands across his chest and sat back, tears running down her cheeks.

Poor man. To die alone, so far from home and loved ones. He would be buried here, she knew, for the Confederates had not enough transportation to carry him to Texas. Even their revered Major Shropshire had been buried at Glorieta Pass, only his sword and uniform being taken back for his family.

Gazing at his quiet face, she wondered what Captain Adair's family had been. Had he a wife? Had children sat in his lap and pulled at his dark beard?

A wife. That was something else she could be, if she had a mind to it. She took out her handkerchief and dried her tears, not quite ready to contemplate that option. Drawing a deep breath, she rose and went to inform Mrs. Canby of her patient's demise.

Gray branches tangled overhead. Jamie listened to the noisy chatter of dozens of birds as his mount picked its way through the thick undergrowth. This bosque was the same forest of cottonwoods through which the Río Grande slunk along all the way down to Valverde and beyond. It didn't seem quite as gloomy up here. He had kept to the woods, not wanting to be caught in the open again on the main road. Couldn't make a lot of speed here, but he had to let the horse walk mostly anyway.

They came to an acequia and Jamie made his mount cross it before allowing it to drink. Almost to Albuquerque, he thought, glancing up through the grey latticework overhead. The sky was overcast, with patches of heavy cloud warning of weather, but the sun glowed weakly through them, riding past noon. Time to risk a look at the road.

Making his way slowly out of the trees, he stopped just inside the bosque and looked south. A house stood across the road and down a ways, with a trickle of smoke from the chimney, and water from the acequia glimmering into a tilled field and an apple orchard beyond it, covered in white blossoms. Farther down were rows of grapevines and more fields, some left untended, some already showing young corn. Jamie glanced north up the road and saw another house, with a corral which held a small flock of sheep. His mind instantly began calculating how many men they would feed for how long. He turned away; he could not take them now. He would come back for them, if Green's men didn't gobble them on the way in.

He nudged his weary mount forward, taking to the road once more. As he came abreast of the farm house, a voice from within shouted, "Halt!"

Jamie stopped and waited while a picket of three dusty men scrambled out of the house, rifles in hand. All of them were older than he. Not a surprise; he'd only turned twenty this year, and most of the army was older.

The first man out aimed his piece at Jamie and said, "Who goes there?"

"Captain James Russell," said Jamie, sitting tall. "You can put that away, private."

"What's the countersign?"

"That's the Q.M., dummy!" said a second soldier, pushing down the barrel of his friend's rifle. "You can pass, sir."

"Thank you."

"There's some sheep up yonder, sir," continued the second man, grinning.

"I saw that."

"Shall we capture 'em for you?"

"No," said Jamie. "Leave them be for now. Don't want to antagonize your neighbors."

The man looked disappointed. "Yes, sir," he said.

"I could use a fresh mount, though, if you've got one," said Jamie.

"Yes, sir. In the shed out back."

Jamie dismounted and gave his reins over to the second man. The third, who'd been quiet so far, shyly offered him coffee, if he would care to step inside. Jamie's stomach answered with a deep growl, and he nodded his thanks. He couldn't remember when he'd last eaten. Must have been Algodones.

The house was clean and sparsely furnished; a table, two chairs, and a mattress rolled up by the wall. A wizened, wary-looking Mexican man sat in one of the chairs by the fire. Jamie took off his hat and bowed slightly to the farmer, who watched him silently. The man was too old to manage a farm all by himself. Jamie wondered where his sons were, gone into the New Mexico Volunteers, perhaps. Down at Fort Craig, or else under the ground.

The shy soldier handed him a cup of coffee and a soft, fresh tortilla. Jamie bit into it and thought he'd never tasted anything so good. He made himself eat slowly, sipping the coffee between bites. "What's the news in Albuquerque?" he asked the pickets.

"Well," said the shy man, "they're saying we'll get attacked any day by Colonel Canby's army."

"Any idea where they are?"

"No, sir. Sorry. We've been up here since yesterday morning."

"Should've been relieved at dawn," growled the first soldier.

"Well, you won't have to wait much longer," said Jamie, setting his empty mug on the table. One way or another, he thought privately.

He dug in his shirt pocket—careful not to stab himself with Emma's star—and produced two packets of tobacco and corn husks. He handed one to the old farmer, and the other to the shy soldier, saying, "Share it with your friends, all right?"

"Thank you, Captain," the man called after him as he went out.

The second soldier had switched Jamie's tack to a bony gray that looked half asleep. "Sure this one's in better shape?" Jamie asked.

The man shrugged. "Had a day of grass and rest," he said. "Been stabled in Albuquerque before that."

"Well, all right," said Jamie, giving the horse's shoulder a pat. "Thanks."

"Sir?"

Jamie looked up as he took the reins. The soldier's brows drew together in a frown.

"It's not true, is it? That General Sibley's giving up Santa Fé?"

Jamie drew a breath. Why should he be the one to ruin this man's dreams of conquest? But he couldn't deceive him either.

"For now," said Jamie. "He's got to counter—"

A distant boom interrupted him, followed by the flapping of many wings rising from the bosque. Geese—hundreds of them, a mass of white wings flashing—taking flight at the sudden noise. A second boom rang out almost immediately. Jamie knew the sound, though he'd never heard it so far away before. Without wasting another word he was in the saddle, whistling to the horse and prodding it with his heels. The animal was livelier than it looked, and struck a canter with gratifying speed. Jamie let it have its head, while the sound of distant cannon fire continued ahead from Albuquerque.

7

"My spies from Santa Fé report that the entire Confederate force left that city and moved rapidly to Albuquerque upon the news of our appearance before that place. Their preparations indicate the intention of leaving the country."

—Ed. R. S. Canby, Colonel 19th Infantry,
Commanding Department

The artillery duel continued steadily while Jamie rode, and the sound of the guns dragged his thoughts back to Valverde and got his heart racing. He passed farm houses and new-planted fields strung out along the flat bottomland following the river. Soon he saw the towers of the village church and the Lone Star flag flying from the gigantic flagpole in the plaza—tallest in the Territory, erected by order of Major Carleton when he had commanded the post. The plaza was surrounded by shops, houses, and the buildings of the military post. To the west, a forest of cottonwoods marked the river's course. To the east, the magnificent Sandia Mountains thrust upward from the plain, making a striking backdrop worthy of any scenic artist. On this day, in the clear air, all the colors seemed stronger than normal: deep blue mountains, blinding white snow, vivid pinks and browns of the foothills, and dark greens of the nearer trees. Jamie would have liked to pause and drink in the scene, but he hadn't the time.

A cluster of civilians had gathered in the plaza, milling and watching the battle. Jamie galloped past them and through the village. At last he spotted a two-gun section under the trees near Huning's Mill, firing eastward. He reined in, waiting for the Federal cannon opposing them to fire again before he approached the guns. The horse panted, and Jamie gave its sweating neck a pat while he tried to slow his own breathing. The sun had now cleared the Sandias, casting deep blue shadows into their forbidding crags. Closer at hand, on a dark, flat ridge east of the village, a puff of smoke and a deep, distant boom were followed by a crash amid tree branches a hundred yards or so south of Jamie. He urged the gray back to a gallop and made for the guns.

"Limber up!" shouted a voice Jamie knew as his horse skittered to a stop just short of the two howitzers. The cannoneers burst into flurried action, preparing to move their guns. Jamie gave them a wide berth and rode up to their commander.

"Should've known it was you making all this racket," he said.

Lieutenant John Reily, a tall, slender youth with seemingly boundless reserves of energy, looked up at him and grinned. Before he could speak, a shrieking whine was followed by the crash of a solid shot into a tree nearby. Jamie slid from his saddle in a hurry and peered eastward, but he couldn't see much for the tall cottonwoods surrounding the mill, even though their branches were bare.

"A quarter mile south," Reily called to the drivers.

Seeing him start toward the nearest gun carriage, Jamie mounted his horse and rode it up to Reily, offering him a hand. "Want to ride with me?"

"Sure." Reily waved the artillerymen toward the south, then grabbed the back of the saddle and hauled himself up behind Jamie. "Thanks," he said. "Mine's hauling number two."

"Why are you moving? Seems like a good enough position," Jamie said over his shoulder.

"Trying to look like we've got more guns than we have," Reily answered.

Jamie nudged his mount forward, and they galloped ahead of the guns until Reily called, "Stop here."

Jamie reined in near a field of corn just sprouting. The guns came rattling up behind them and swung into battery. A muffled thump from the north made Jamie look up sharply.

"That's Charlie Raguet," Reily said. "He's got the other section east of town."

"Who's commanding the troops?" Jamie asked as they dismounted.

"Hardeman," said Reily.

"Why didn't he let the citizens evacuate?"

"Hostages against Canby's good behavior."

"Not terribly effective," said Jamie, glancing eastward toward the ridge where Canby's guns were still thumping away.

Reily shrugged. "I didn't give the order." He strode forward to consult with the gunners, and Jamie waited. He glanced up at the Federals, a dark line on the plain to the east, high enough to command the town but well below the craggy, brown and blue mountains with their powdered heights. As he watched, a puff of smoke signaled another volley, followed by the cannon's report. The shot hit in the vicinity of their former position with a crash of splintering tree branches.

The Federals didn't seem to be massing for an attack, and Jamie wondered why not. With a tingle down his neck he realized the Texans were in much the same situation they'd been in at Johnson's Ranch outside Glorieta Pass, but he had no sense of the doom he'd felt then. This time the rest of the army was on its way to support them, and so far Colonel Canby was just testing Albuquerque's defenses. With any luck, Green would get here in time to hold him off.

Reily came back to where Jamie waited between the two guns. The lanyards were stretched, and Jamie barely remembered to cover his ears before the guns fired in unison, giving a sharp kick to the soles of his feet. The horse jibbed. Jamie moved him back to the sparse shelter of a leafless cottonwood. *I'm in a battle,* he told himself, though it was so different from the others. Hard to feel one was in a battle, leaning against a tree and watching a horse pull up last year's grass.

He glanced at Reily, absorbed in watching his crews and occasionally peering through field glasses at the Federals. All of six years his senior, Colonel Reily's son seemed made for the army. He was fearless, enjoyed commanding his guns, and kept his head in combat. He had been left behind at Albuquerque during the battles in Glorieta Pass, and Jamie knew he'd been chafing for a fight ever since. The mountain howitzers that made up Reily's battery had been outranged at Valverde, so he hadn't seen much action there either, though his crew had eventually gone to man Teel's guns, and helped bring in the captured Union battery after the victory.

Jamie looked at the ground, swallowing. He himself had spent the hours after the battle searching the field until he'd found Martin, then overseeing his burial in a trench along with dozens of other casualties.

A shot screamed past; the Federals had found the range on their new location. Jamie flinched, and had to force himself not to duck behind the tree. Reily peered through his glasses as the Texan guns returned fire, then he whooped. "Hit an officer!" he shouted. "A major, I think!" The men cheered.

After one more volley, Reily ordered the guns moved again, back north, but east of the mill, by a field just sprouting a young crop. The farmer came out to stand in his doorway, watching dubiously as the cannoneers went to work.

"How many times have you changed positions?" asked Jamie as they halted.

"I've lost count." Reily slid to the ground, grinning.

Movement up on the heights attracted Jamie's attention. A cluster of cavalry was starting toward the town.

"I'd better go check the depot," he said, holding out a hand to Reily, who gave it a hard, quick shake.

"Supper tonight," Reily said. "Need a bed?"

"Probably. Good luck." Jamie paused, gazing out at the line of blue stretched along the heights. There was something appealing about the thunder of the guns and all the smoke. It set the battle at a distance, made it seem less real. No screams. No blood. You had to look through field glasses to see what you'd hit, like it was just target practice.

But it was real enough, Jamie knew, for the Federal officer who'd been struck. Or rather for those around him, as most likely he himself knew no more. And the reality of blood and bayonets and hand-to-hand battle were not so far from the artillerymen as it seemed. Valverde had proved that.

Shivering, Jamie waved to Reily before turning his horse

toward the plaza. Quartermaster work was less of a thrill, which was perfectly all right with him.

Kozlowski's Ranch looked the same as it had on the eve of battle; rows of tents pitched all down the slope to the Pecos River, with men huddled round fires in the cold. The place brought back memories of the night before Glorieta battle, and tormented O'Brien with shadows of Miss Howland.

He poured the dregs of the coffee into his cup. It was strong from sitting on the fire half the day, which suited him well enough. They had arrived at the ranch early, and gone into camp on their former camping ground. Two weeks had brought them right back where they'd started.

Colonel Slough was keeping to his tent. He'd had practically nothing to do with his men since the word of his resignation went round. O'Brien would have been angry, except that it was even worse to think of Slough's going, for the talk among the men was more and more of Chivington as colonel.

Well, he'd not make Slough's mistake himself. He'd go out among his company, speak with them, show them he cared what they thought.

He drained his cup, and set it with the dishes still dirty from dinner. Shaunessy'd wanted to get to a card game, and O'Brien had let him go. He himself had avoided bluff poker of late. The only money he had was Miss Howland's and he didn't feel right gambling with it. And beside that, he'd rather have played with his own men—his friends and old colleagues—than with the other officers, and that sort of fraternization was frowned on.

But just talking, now, that couldn't harm him. A captain must talk to his men. O'Brien pulled his overcoat tighter and strode down I Company's street.

He could hear McGuire's fiddle at the foot of the hill, and voices following in some old drinking song. Closer by, laughter drew him to a circle of men round a fire, where he found Morris shuffling cards over a blanket strewn with coins. Shaunessy looked up at him with a quick grin. O'Brien made himself remember the names of the others there: Newsom, who'd washed out in Clear Creek and come down to

Camp Weld to join up; Langston, a Denver City man—merchant, he'd been, O'Brien thought—and Tiller, a quiet fellow, also from Denver, who'd been nicked by a ball at Apache Canyon and been left here at Kozlowski's to recuperate. And Unger, one of Ramsey's recruits.

"How's the leg, Tiller?" he asked.

"Good as new, thank you, sir."

"You'll be back riding with us, then?"

"Yes, the surgeon said I might."

"Good, good," said O'Brien, nodding. He took hold of a tent pole and leaned on it, trying to think what else he could talk of.

Morris riffled his deck. "Deal you in, Red?" he said.

"Oh, no. Not tonight. I just came out to see who was winning."

"Langston," said Newsom gloomily.

"Aye, he's had half my stake in three hands," said Shaunessy. "I intend to make him work hard for the other half."

"Good for you, Langston," said O'Brien. "You can be on point the next time we're in the van."

Shaunessy chortled, and Langston looked up in mock indignation. "I don't see why I should be punished for winning at cards," he said.

"It's not punishment," said O'Brien. "If you're in luck, then we want you out front."

The men laughed. "Not to worry," said Morris as he dealt out a new hand. "We're not likely to be in the van. Haven't been since we left the fort."

That was true. The company had been the rearguard all the way down from Fort Union. Colonel Paul had his Regular cavalry in front the whole time. It was supposed to be an even rotation, but what with Paul and Slough at loggerheads, things had been less even than they should. O'Brien had said nothing, but he watched, and kept track in his head.

"Jacks to open," said Morris as he finished the deal.

The men picked up their cards, and Shaunessy sighed. "I pass, then."

"Pass," Unger said.

"Five cents," said Langston, provoking a groan from the others.

O'Brien watched, thinking he might go down and listen to McGuire for a while. Langston won the hand with kings and sixes, and collected a light pot while Shaunessy took up the cards. O'Brien was about to bid them farewell when Ramsey came up to the fire with Lieutenant Shoup, Chivington's A.D.C., in his wake.

"There you are, Captain," said Shoup, raising an eyebrow. "Lieutenant Ramsey said you might be playing cards."

"I am not," said O'Brien, trying to keep his voice light. "Only came down to check on the lads."

"I see. Well, here are your orders for tomorrow," said Shoup, handing O'Brien a paper. "We're marching early. You have the rearguard."

Shaunessy stifled a moan.

"What time did you say we're to march?" O'Brien asked Shoup.

"It's in the orders." Shoup nodded to the page in O'Brien's hand.

He was watching, O'Brien realized. Watching to see if he'd read it. Fury rose in his chest as he opened the paper. His eyes scanned the scribbling, but all he could read was the date at the top. The letters were not made of straight lines like the ones Miss Howland had taught him.

"What time, Captain?" asked Ramsey.

O'Brien looked up sharply into Ramsey's cold eyes, and handed him the page. Disappointment flickered across Ramsey's face, then he smiled thinly and glanced at the orders.

Betrayed, thought O'Brien. The rage burned in his forehead, and he longed to flatten Ramsey then and there. Instead he carefully took back the orders, folded them into his pocket, and turned to his men with a forced smile. "It's good night for me, lads," he said, stepping away. "Don't play too late."

"Only until Langston has all our money," Shaunessy said.

"Which shouldn't take long, at this rate," Morris added.

O'Brien stalked down the hill, leaving Ramsey and Shoup with the others. Anger burned in him like a smoldering coal. Ramsey knew, and had told Shoup, and God knew who else, maybe Chivington, even. Wild thoughts of resigning, or begging indulgence, or trying to explain, chased each other through O'Brien's head. Could they take away his rank? He didn't know. He supposed Chivington could do as he pleased. Even if letters were not required of a captain, they could make it a scandal and have the men vote him out. God damn Ramsey to hell, how had he known?

Ahead was the fire where McGuire had been playing. The old fiddler had stopped to retune, and sat plinking one string, grumbling softly about the cold air. The boys 'round the fire passed a bottle while they waited for the music to resume, and O'Brien was sorely tempted to reach for it, but he held back.

A little apart from the others, Luther Denning sat hugging his knees. O'Brien caught his eye, and silently summoned him with a jerk of his head. The lieutenant got up, brushed the sand from his clothes, and joined O'Brien outside the circle of firelight. Wordlessly, O'Brien led him uphill, back past the bluff game toward Officer's Row. There was no sign of Ramsey or Shoup.

In their camp the fire had died down to embers. O'Brien went so far as to poke open the door of Ramsey's tent, finding it empty. He led Denning into his own tent, and rummaged in the dark for candle and matches.

Light flared up, and O'Brien stuck the candle into the bayonet he'd been using as a holder, stabbed into the hard ground in one corner of the tent. He turned to Denning, who waited patiently, his face full of silent questions.

O'Brien took the orders out of his pocket. "I need your help," he said. It came out rough, and he coughed to clear his throat.

Denning drew a long breath. "I've been hoping you'd ask," he said softly.

"Sweet Mary and Joseph, is it that obvious?" O'Brien said, pacing to the door and hauling the canvas aside. He stared angrily out into the darkness, then let the flap fall.

"No," said Denning, "but I know you, Alastar. Lord, we've seen each other almost every day for the last two years, ever since you came to Avery. In all that time I never saw you pick up a book, or a newspaper. Not hard to guess why."

O'Brien closed his eyes, feeling the shame burn up into his face. "Hall used to help me," he said.

"I thought so," said Denning. "And then Franklin."

"Aye."

Denning's boots scraped the earth as he shifted his weight. "What can I do?" he said.

O'Brien turned to him, handed him the orders. "Read that," he said, and sat on his bedroll. "Tell me what it says."

Denning made himself comfortable on the ground and opened the page. "We're marching at dawn. Rearguard." He glanced up at O'Brien, then continued. "Chivington wants to inspect the company at five o'clock."

O'Brien reached for the page, scanning down it again. "There's no five here!"

"It's written out," said Denning softly, pointing.

"Bastards! They're trying to trap me!" O'Brien crumpled the page and hurled it against the tent wall. It bounced lightly and dropped to the ground. Denning picked it up and began smoothing it out on his knee, frowning.

"It could just be—"

"Shoup knows," said O'Brien. "Ramsey told him. Don't know how the hell he found out."

"Oh."

O'Brien met Denning's gaze. "Ramsey's after taking my place." There, he'd said it. He'd suspected, and now he was sure. "Best mind your step, Luther," he added. "You don't want to be taken down with me."

"As if I cared for that."

O'Brien stared at him, surprised at this statement. Denning gazed steadily back.

"Go on, pass the word about the inspection," O'Brien said, waving him toward the door. He buried his face in his hands, suddenly bone-weary.

Denning made no move to go, and at last O'Brien looked up at him. The lieutenant sat quietly watching. "You can beat him, Alastar," he said softly.

"Beat him into a pulp? I'd like that," said O'Brien.

Denning smiled. "You can beat him at his own game. He's made one very bad mistake already."

"And that is?"

"He's assumed you're unintelligent."

O'Brien was silent, staring down at the ground. He wasn't so sure that assumption was wrong.

"And he's forgotten that you have quite a number of friends in the company."

O'Brien sighed, and shook his head. "Chivington likes him."

"Chivington may have him, then," said Denning quietly. "But not in command of this company." He got up, and offered the battered orders back to O'Brien, who took them and held out his hand.

"Thank you, Luther."

Denning shook hands. "My pleasure," he said. "See you in the morning. Quarter to five?"

O'Brien nodded, and watched the flap fall shut behind his lieutenant. He was fighting two wars now, he realized. One that the army dictated, the other a fight for survival.

Charlie Raguet led Jamie through the rain to the door of a large casa just south of the plaza. Raguet—Reily's second in command—had appeared in the depot after dark, sent by Reily to fetch Jamie to dinner. He was Reily's age or perhaps a bit older, somewhat stockier, and usually quiet. Jamie had not spoken with him much at all.

Soft light glowed through a curtained window of the Armijo house, which had served as headquarters ever since Sibley's army had first arrived in the village. Manuel Armijo and his brother Rafael were merchants whom Jamie had met on his first visit to Albuquerque. They were staunch supporters and had given over their entire inventory to the army.

Jamie stifled a yawn as he followed Raguet in. He'd tried to nap but had been unable to sleep through the cannon-fire. The cavalry had skirmished off and on through the afternoon, and Canby was expected to attack at any time. Probably he'd wait until morning, but the small Texan force occupying Albuquerque was understandably tense. Canby was said to have a thousand men with him. Their campfires were visible—a line of orange jewels glowing dully through the rain—on the dark plain above the town.

Jamie saw Manuel Armijo standing near the door, talking

with Captain Hardeman. "Hola, señor," he said, shaking hands. "¡Qué bueno verle otra vez!"

"Vengan, vengan. ¡Bienvenidos!" said Armijo, gesturing toward the blaze of a corner fireplace, where Raguet was already warming his hands. Jamie nodded to Hardeman and hastened to join Raguet.

The room was well lit by three oil lamps hanging from the huge, round vigas of the ceiling. Jamie noticed that Raguet had tied a black kerchief around one sleeve, and silently sympathized. Major Raguet had died gallantly, leading a charge at Glorieta, and had been praised as a hero. Jamie figured that was small comfort to a man for losing his brother.

"There you are," said Reily, coming out of the kitchen to stand by a long table set for supper. "Just in time." He waved them over, and Señora Armijo appeared with heaping plates of carne adobada and fresh, soft tortillas. Everyone crowded around the table, including Armijo's two daughters and his brother Rafael. All bowed their heads for a short prayer in Spanish, then proceeded to dig in.

The meat was spicy-hot and tender, marinated in ground red chilis and cooked for hours until the spice permeated the meat. While the others regaled the Armijos with their exploits of the day, Jamie attacked his plate and listened. He couldn't remember his last real meal—no, it was at Mrs. Canby's, three days ago—seemed like forever. He ate hungrily until his stomach began to ache, whether from the chile or from being too full he wasn't sure. He put down his fork and leaned back in his chair, sipping at the rough, red native wine his host had provided.

Reily picked up his own glass and said, "Here's to Tom Green. May the wind give him wings."

"Sí, and General Sibley also," Armijo said, raising his glass. Sibley had used Armijo's house as headquarters on the way up, and it seemed the merchant hoped to welcome him again. Jamie reached for a tortilla and tore off a piece.

"How's your depot?" Reily asked.

"Safe so far, thanks to you all," Jamie said, glancing toward Captain Hardeman. "Got a good store of clothes and blankets, and the feed'll recruit our horses some. I'm just wondering how I'll move it all."

"Maybe you won't have to."

Jamie chewed a bite of tortilla and gazed at Reily. Apparently, his friend hadn't heard exactly how straitened Sibley's army was. Either that, or he was ignoring the news. Jamie thought about keeping silent, but he knew the general was still hoping to continue the campaign. If he could convince Reily of the need to retreat, he'd have an ally.

"We can't stay here, John," he said softly. "We've got to evacuate."

He hadn't expected the silence that followed this remark. Señor Armijo put down his knife. "Is this true?" he said.

"I'm afraid so," said Jamie. "We don't have enough resources for a long fight."

"We've got reinforcements coming," Hardeman said. "And you just said you've got plenty of supplies—"

"Not for an advance. If we're careful it'll get us home."

"We can hold this town!" said Reily, frustration in his voice. "I'll hold it against the devil himself!"

Jamie just shook his head. Señora Armijo uttered a soft little moan and reached a hand out to her husband, who grasped it and murmured comforts. Jamie glanced at Charlie Raguet, who looked stricken.

"It can't all be for nothing," Raguet said.

Jamie's gut suddenly tightened. All the toil, all the trouble—all the cost—Charlie was right. If it was all for nothing, why were they even there?

"It isn't," Jamie said, angry with himself for bringing up the subject.

"What's it for, if we go back?" Reily said in disgust. "We won't have accomplished a thing."

"The guns," Jamie said. "The Valverde guns. We have those."

Reily just looked at him, a frown tightening his brow. Jamie read despair in Raguet's face, and felt a fool. Six motley guns from Valverde. If that was all that three thousand men could bring out of New Mexico . . . What a waste.

No one seemed to want any more to eat. Señora Armijo vanished into her kitchen, and her daughters began clearing the table. Señor Armijo made a halfhearted offer of tobacco, which his guests politely declined.

"We'd better get going," said Reily. "We'll probably be up before dawn." He rose from the table, and Charlie followed suit. Jamie picked up his hat from a nearby shelf and turned to his host.

"Thank you for your hospitality," he said, shaking hands.

"De nada. Señor," said Armijo, "when must your army leave Albuquerque?"

Jamie hid a grimace. "Not for a couple of days, at least," he said. "We have to wait for everyone to get here from Santa Fé. The general's still on the way in."

Armijo nodded, and said quietly, "I would be grateful if you would come to me tomorrow. I would like to discuss your plans."

"I'll try," said Jamie. "Please give my thanks to your wife. The dinner was excellent."

Armijo nodded gravely. Jamie said good night, and joined his companions outside.

The rain still fell steadily. Jamie hurried to catch up to Reily and Raguet. They were silent, striding up the street toward the plaza. Jamie hugged his chest to keep warm, and wondered how badly he'd offended them. Looked like maybe he'd have to find his own accommodations for the night. Well, there was always the depot. He sighed.

All at once Reily stopped and spun around to face him. "I never took you for a coward, Russell," he shouted through the rain.

Jamie felt a flash of anger, but he held it down. He'd already thrashed out that argument with himself. If he were a coward he would have said to hell with it all and resigned, leaving the army to fend for itself.

"If I could support an advance, I'd do it," he said.

"You just want to get home safe to Mama," Reily accused him. "Didn't anybody tell you war isn't safe?"

"We lost more than half our supplies at Glorieta!" Jamie shouted, the words tearing his throat. "We're about to starve, John!"

Reily moved toward him, a menacing shadow, but Raguet

grabbed his shoulder and held him back. "It's really that bad?" he demanded.

"Yes," said Jamie. "I've been trying to tell you."

"We've got half the stores left, we can live on half rations," Reily said stubbornly.

Jamie sighed. "Fine," he said. "They're down in Mesilla. You want to go fetch them?"

That seemed to get through. Mesilla was near two hundred miles away, and Fort Craig stood between it and them. Reily fell silent, and Raguet murmured something into his ear.

"If we can get to Mesilla, we might be able to wait there for reinforcements," Jamie said, "But we can't stay in Albuquerque."

"Listen," Raguet said.

Jamie turned to him, ready to continue the argument, but Raguet wasn't looking at him. He was looking past him, to the north, and now Jamie heard it, a low, rumbling sound beneath the patter of the rain.

Horses. Many horses, coming fast. An army was riding on Albuquerque.

8

". . . there is not 10 days' rations for the Brigade above Craig . . . a march for the lower country is absolutely necessary to prevent our starving."

—Sergeant Alfred B. Peticolas,
4th Texas Mounted Volunteers

A lone rider entered the plaza from the north at a gallop. Jamie waved at him as he came up, and the rider reined to a walk, the horse blowing. "Who's that coming in?" Jamie asked.

"The 2nd." The rider circled his horse, hooves splashing in the muddy street.

Reily whooped, and cried, "Now we'll show Canby a thing or two!"

Jamie shouted to the horseman, "Is Colonel Green with the column?"

He nodded. "They've been riding at the gallop ever since they got Captain Hardeman's express. Where is he?"

"At headquarters," Jamie told him. "Thanks," he added waving a hand as the man trotted his horse across the plaza.

"Well," Reily said. "Looks like we'll get to sleep tonight after all."

"Enjoy yourselves." Jamie started after the rider. "I've got to get the 2nd into camp."

"Jamie, wait."

Jamie paused in the middle of the plaza, cold rain stinging at his cheeks. Reily caught up to him and stuck out a hand. "I'm sorry," he said roughly.

Jamie shook hands. "I'm sorry, too. Believe me."

"We'll get through it," Reily said.

Jamie nodded. He looked at Charlie Raguet, standing in

the shadows just behind Reily. Raguet gave a single nod. Somehow, yes, they'd get through.

"Get out of the rain," Jamie called to them, backing away with a wave. Relieved, he turned and headed back to the Armijos' at a jog.

It was dark and bloody cold at Kozlowski's at five in the morning. O'Brien stood stiff and resentful while Chivington inspected his company, formed up west of camp, near the picket line. Horses grunted softly and snuffled in the dirt, searching for grass roots to chew.

The lads had sat up half the night polishing, and turned out in fine trim, though there had been some grumbling. No other company had been subjected to inspection in the middle of a march. It was Chivington's spite, and the lads were beginning to notice.

The major could find little to complain of, but he did his best. A crack starting on Unger's bridle, a smudge of dirt on Ryan's boot, Flannery's coat missing a button, as if he could find a replacement out here. The men's weapons, O'Brien was proud to note, were in perfect order.

On it went, Chivington prowling slowly up and down the line, with Shoup taking notes at his elbow. Beyond them the camp was waking up, cooking breakfast. The smell of bacon frying made O'Brien's mouth water. A handful of men collected near the horses, watching the spectacle. O'Brien shot one angry glance their way, then ignored them.

Finally the major came up to the officers. Done at last, thought O'Brien.

"Your company is in satisfactory order, Captain," said Chivington.

"Thank you, sir," said O'Brien.

"You will proceed at once to scout through the pass and advance along the Galisteo road. At any sign of Confederate activity you will report back to me via courier."

Stunned, O'Brien worked his jaw until he could speak evenly. "Sir, the men have not had their breakfast," he said.

"That's what biscuits are for, Captain. You may leave a detail to pack up your camp. The rest of the column will follow you presently." Chivington saluted and turned his back at once.

O'Brien exchanged a long, speaking look with Denning, then glanced at Ramsey, who looked a sight too calm, O'Brien thought. He turned to his company.

"Sergeants," he called out. "Assign one man each to stay back and pack up. The rest form in column by twos."

The eastern sky was lightening as they rode up to the trail past a crowd of curious soldiers. O'Brien seethed, ignoring the jokes they were shouting at his men.

"Well," he heard Morris say cheerily behind him. "We finally got the van."

O'Brien stifled a laugh. God bless the man, he thought. His foul mood faded, replaced by determination. He would make this up to the lads, somehow. As they turned their backs to the rising sun, he vowed to stop at Pigeon's and let his men buy every ounce of food and drink to be had.

"They're gone," Reily said, frowning.

Jamie stood beside him in the plaza, gazing toward the ridge. Overnight the rain had turned to snow. Through Reily's field glasses he could just make out the dead ashes of the campfires Canby's men had abandoned in the night. The Federal troops had vanished. Hoofbeats nearby made him take down the glasses—scouts galloping eastward to learn where the enemy had gone.

It meant something, Jamie knew, but he had no idea what. That was what generals were for, he supposed, to figure out such puzzles. Why would Canby withdraw when he had the advantage? Before Colonel Green had come up with the 2nd, the Federals had superior numbers. So why had Canby not struck at once, before that happened?

Lane joined them, yawning and rubbing at his eyes. "Morning," he said. "Where's breakfast?"

Reily nodded. "I'm starving. Let's go."

Jamie glanced back at the ridge, questions still flitting through his head like moths. With an effort he brushed them aside, and followed his comrades in search of food.

* * *

Laura and María stood at the corner, watching hospital orderlies carry Captain Adair's body out of Mrs. Canby's house and down the street. The hospital had been set up in a nearby building owned by Bishop Lamy, in which, until lately, Confederate troops had been staying. The bishop himself was in Taos, where he had been these many months, staying clear of the trouble.

Laura felt a depression falling upon her spirits. Santa Fé seemed deserted. Except for the weary hospital men, no one within view was stirring. A trickle of smoke from a chimney was all the sign of life in evidence.

It had snowed the previous night, then melted at dawn. Snow clung in the shadows of buildings, blue-white patches on red earth dark with moisture. Laura glanced westward toward the governor's palace, whose earthen roof had borne a wild garden the previous spring. Too early for any such appearance as yet, and the clouds coming in from the west promised more snow.

Wrapping her cloak close about her, she followed María to the plaza in search of a merchant, if there might be any left to open his doors, who could sell them a few necessities. Mrs. Canby's supply of baking soda was very low, and they could do with more salt also. Her well stocked larder had not stood up to the demands of two dozen unexpected house guests.

The plaza, normally the center of activity in town, was empty. Not even a dog paced its grounds. The wine shops that stayed open day and night had barred their doors, for which Laura could not find it in herself to be sorry. But Seligman's door hung sadly from one hinge, the other having been broken, and all that was left inside was a litter of shattered glass and scattered comfits, coated in dirt, where the jar had fallen on the floor. While Laura felt certain that Captain Russell would not have been a party to such crimes, the Texans in general had proved themselves to have few scruples concerning the property of others. The same fate had visited all of the shops but one, and that belonged to Mr. Hopkins, who was a Confederate sympathizer. Had she any choice, Laura would not have given him the time of day, much less her business; however, necessity overruled preference on this occasion, and she and María made their way across the plaza and down San Francisco Street to Hopkins's store.

They found Mr. Hopkins and a native servant loading a wagon and a big-wheeled carreta with goods, in preparation to follow the Texan army. Hopkins's response to Laura's polite inquiry was a mere grunt and a nod toward the store. They went in, and found the shelves nearly bare. A tray of colored embroidery silks, a stack of broadsides, and a crate of tinned pommade, in black or brown, were among the few items the Confederate army had not deemed necessary to its survival. María found a crate half-filled with a jumble of leftover kitchen things, and began to sort through them.

Laura leafed through the music, looking for Irish tunes in the hope that she might recognize the song Captain O'Brien had sung to her. Its melody eluded her, though she sometimes felt she could have sung it if only she closed her eyes and concentrated hard enough. A haunting, sad thing.

She set aside the music, racking the shuffled papers to straighten them. In doing so she jounced the unsecured shelf, and a tin rattled down behind it to the floor. It had been resting halfway between two shelves, lodged against a brace, until Laura had disturbed it. Stooping, she retrieved the tin and found it to be seven ounces of Darjeeling tea.

A treasure! She would give it to Mrs. Canby, as thanks for her hospitality. Clutching the precious tin tightly, she stepped over to where María was digging through the kitchen box. "Have you found anything?" she asked.

"Sal de piedra." María held up a box of rock salt. "No hay bicarbonato."

"Well, the salt we can use," Laura said, and walked outside to the wagons.

Mr. Hopkins was starting to strap down his load with a long rope. As she approached, he gathered up the length in a coil and tossed it over the wagon, then went around to the far side, fed the end into a ring on the wagon's side, and began pulling the whole length of it through.

"We did not find any bicarbonate of soda within," said Laura. "Have you some in your wagon?"

Hopkins stroked his sandy-bearded chin, looking at Laura,

then peered at the wagon, squinting at it as if that would help him to remember its contents and their disposition. "Reckon so," he said. "Dollar a box."

That was very dear, almost ludicrous. Laura thought Mr. Hopkins was not likely to bargain with her, but she decided to try. "I will give you a dollar for two boxes," she said.

Hopkins stared at her briefly, then broke into a grin. "I always had a soft spot for a pretty gal," he said. He threw his rope aside and climbed up on the wagon, standing with one foot on the wheel and leaning over to reach into the middle of the load. He tossed back the tarpaulin covering the goods, pulled out a large hat box and set it aside, followed by two camp chairs and a dutch oven. After rummaging in the well thus created, he produced two dusty boxes of soda and handed them down to Laura. She waited while he repacked the wagon.

"What else?" said Hopkins, jumping down.

"María has one or two things," said Laura. "Shall we go inside?"

María had added a small jar of sad-looking dried ginger and one of anise seed to the box of rock salt sitting on the counter. She was poking through a collection of tiny cookie cutters, but left them when Laura and Mr. Hopkins came in. Hopkins took a pencil from his pocket and drew a scrap of paper to him to tally the goods. Laura set the boxes of soda on the counter, and placed the tea beside it.

Hopkins looked up, frowning. "Where'd you find that?"

"It had slipped behind a shelf," said Laura.

"It's five dollars," said Hopkins.

A ridiculous demand. Laura pursed her lips. "I will give you two dollars."

"I can sell it in an eyeblink for twice that."

"Three dollars, then," said Laura. She drew her purse, into which she'd put money for shopping, from her cloak pocket, and laid three silver dollars on the counter. Hopkins gazed at the coins, and she could see that he found the U.S. specie attractive. She laid another dollar in front of the two soda boxes, and two dimes beside the salt and spices. "That seems fair to me," she said.

"¡Es demasiado!" said María.

Hopkins's eyes flicked her way, then returned to Laura. She suspected that he understood María perfectly well, better than she, in fact. He looked about to speak, when his servant rushed in and announced, "Caballeros! Los federales vienen al paso!"

"Sold," said Hopkins, and scooped the coins into his palm, pocketing them as he hurried outside.

Los federales! That could not be misunderstood! Laura kept her joy to herself and hurried to help María tuck their purchases into her basket. María added a skein of bright red embroidery silk from the tray. When Laura gave her a questioning look, she said, "Debemos llevarlo todo. Es un ladrón."

Ladrón she knew meant thief, a word heard all too often in this uncivilized place. "But we're not. No—no estamos." Laura answered.

"No estamos, muy bien," María said, nodding. She had, at Laura's request, undertaken to teach her a little Spanish. Laura smiled gratefully, and left the red silk where it was. In truth, they might have taken all the colors, for Hopkins appeared to be abandoning them, along with the rest of the scatter. Scavengers would devour everything he left behind soon after he departed.

Hopkins ignored them as they left, Laura carefully closing the shop door behind her. The trader and his servant were tossing the rope back and forth over the wagon, hastily strapping down its load. Before Laura and María had reached the plaza the two men were whipping up the wagon horses and the mule hitched to the carreta.

Laura's first thought was to hurry home, but as they came to the plaza she spied Mr. Parker lounging in the doorway of the Exchange, and walked over to inquire whether he had any news.

"Yes," he said. "It's a troop of cavalry."

"Do you know which company?" asked Laura.

Parker shook his head. "U.S., that's all I know. It'll be good to have them back in town."

"Yes." Laura kept to herself the hope that it might be Captain O'Brien and his men. She glanced up at the flagpole in the plaza's center, from which the departing Texans had struck their colors, and hurried with María back to Mrs. Canby's.

The sky was just lightening as Calloway's command reached the Pima Villages, where the Indians, like their Maricopa neighbors, were friendly. They came out in droves to greet the column with trinkets and food to sell. Kip looked after Firecracker and got him settled, then went down to the river.

The Gila was clear and good here. The stage road left the river at this point, so it was their last chance for a good dunk, and many of the other soldiers were already splashing around. Kip left his boots on the bank and jumped in the river without bothering to take off his clothes. They could use a wash, and the sun would dry them fast enough when it came up. He swam upstream of the crowd to drink his fill, ducked his head under, tried to catch at some fish swimming by, and kicked and splashed around until he was thoroughly soaked.

Finally he climbed out and slogged over to where he'd left his saddle in the shade of a hut. Felley and some others were sitting in a circle with some Pimas, gambling hard. Kip pulled out a strip of dried beef and plopped down on a patch of grass to watch.

They had passed a couple of Maricopa settlements along the river, but this was the biggest Indian village they'd seen. Huts made of yucca leaves dotted the flats like lumps of sugar, and shade roofs on poles created gathering places where children romped and women gossiped while they wove big, cone-shaped baskets. The Pimas didn't wear much, and in fact the women weren't anything close to decently clad. Kip found it very distracting to look at them, but they didn't seem to notice. Probably they were used to white men staring at them.

Sitting here, in the middle of the first big settlement they'd seen since Yuma, with dogs wandering by and sniffing at the men walking from shelter to shelter to see what was for sale, Kip had a strange feeling. After musing about it for a while, he realized it was that he felt safe. He'd been suspicious of every rock and bush for so long, it felt odd not to have to be wary.

That was a mistake, he realized. This place was no more safe than any of their camps, and anyone who wanted proof of that could go look at Casa Blanca a few miles back. The trading post, like the nearby mill, belonged to Mr. Ammi White, who was a prisoner in Tucson at the moment, along with Captain McCleave. In fact, it was at White's that McCleave had been taken, by Captain Sherod Hunter, a Rebel masquerading as the trader. Hunter's men had ransacked the trading post and dismantled the mill, and given the Pimas all the flour White had stored up for the army's use. McCleave's company—part of Calloway's battalion— had not taken kindly to this news when they heard it from the Pimas. The mood among the men was vengeful, to put it mildly.

Kip sighed. He supposed he should do his shopping now, before all the best things got bought up. There was fresh bread for sale, he had seen: round loaves making a smell like Mother's kitchen. He got up, slung his saddlebags over his shoulder, and started to stroll through the village.

A gold-white glow over the mountains to the east—there was always another row of mountains to the east, he had learned—signaled the coming sunrise. Kip stopped, awaiting the blast of heat that never ceased to amaze him. When the sunlight spilled over the peaks and rolled across the plain, he could feel it like a blow to his face. From now until sundown, the world would get more oppressively hot every minute. The best thing a body could hope for was sleep.

He found an old woman selling bread that was still warm, and bought a loaf and a small melon. At another hut he paused to watch the basket weavers, one a girl of no more than twelve, making intricate patterns with dark and light grasses. Next to her was a man with a lot of dried gourds made into bowls, dippers, and water bottles. Kip looked them over and chose a stout one to use as a spare canteen.

"Where's your fife, Whistler?"

Kip looked up at Captain Calloway, who had come up beside him. He flipped open his satchel and revealed the instrument.

"Good," Calloway said, "I need you to settle a bet for me, when your business is done."

Kip paid the old Pima man for the gourd and a leather thong to hang it from, and followed the captain to a long, low shade. Beneath it sat three Pimas, one with a long flute carved out of wood. Kip had seen and heard some of these at a Maricopa village, and his curiosity was aroused.

Calloway took Kip's fife from him, handed it to the Pima musician, and gave the other's flute to Kip. "Can you play it?" he said.

Kip turned the instrument over in his hands. The wood was satin-smooth. He knew from seeing the Indians play that you blew into the end of the flute, but there wasn't any kind of fipple or such to direct the air, just a little notch cut near the top of the flute. He tried just blowing across, like you would a ginger pop bottle, and got a little whisper of sound. Taking a deeper breath, he blew it out long and slow, changing his mouth slightly, searching for the voice of the instrument. A gust of laughter from the Pimas made him stop. Looking up, he saw all their eyes on him. They were looking pretty smug. The musician had his fife in his lap, and Kip nodded toward it.

"Go on," he said. "You try."

The Pima man straightened his back and nodded gravely, accepting the challenge. He picked up the fife and turned it endwise up, and was astonished to find that the metal cap fitted to the end had no opening in it. The look of dismay on his face made Calloway let out a guffaw.

"Here," Kip said, holding down a grin as he reached for the fife. The player handed it over, and Kip tucked the Pima flute under his arm while he played a phrase on the fife, sharp and clear in the morning breeze. The Pimas all exclaimed, and the flute player reached out eagerly for the fife again. Kip surrendered it, showing him where to put his fingers, and tackled the Pima flute again while the other blew across the fife. After a couple of breathy minutes, Kip got a note out of the flute—low and clear, so strong it buzzed his gut—to the excitement of all the onlookers. He kept at it and found the next two notes up, played them back and forth a little bit, and got a round of applause.

"There you go," said Calloway to the Pimas. "Pay up."

While the captain collected his winnings, Kip sat down

next to the Pima musician and corrected his angle on the fife. Out came a high squeak, making all the Indians jump. They laughed, and the Pima flutist held out the fife to Kip, shaking his head.

"You're right," said Kip, giving back the flute. "To each his own."

"C'mere, Whistler," said Calloway, jerking his head toward the river. Kip got up, shook hands with his Pima counterpart, and followed the captain a few yards away.

"Here you go," said Calloway. Kip looked down and saw a half-dollar in the captain's hand. Surprised, he glanced up.

"Your share," said the captain, grinning.

"Well, thanks!" Kip tucked the money in his pocket.

A rattle of hoofbeats made them both look up. A rangy old man dressed in weather-beaten leathers halted his horse with a curse and hopped off to approach them.

"Weaver!" said Calloway. "What's your news?"

Kip eyed the scout curiously. Everyone knew about Pauline Weaver, the old mountain man who knew every rock and cactus in the Sonora. Kip had heard he was scouting for the army, but he'd never seen him before. He had the half-crazy look of a man who'd spent the better part of fifty years alone in the desert.

"You want some Rebels?" Weaver asked, accepting a chaw of tobacco from the captain.

"Where?" Calloway said, suddenly sharp.

"Up Picacho way. Them's the ones shot your man at Stanwix."

"How many?"

"More'n a dozen. Say, you got any whiskey?"

Calloway put a hand on the scout's back to lead him away. Kip couldn't stand it. "May I go, sir?" he said.

The captain looked over his shoulder. Kip made his voice as humble as he could. "I'd like to volunteer to go with the advance, sir."

"I haven't said anything about an advance," the captain replied. He led Weaver away without giving Kip another glance.

It was hot, Kip noticed. His clothes were already dry. Hot, and he was too tired to get upset about anything. With a sigh, he put away his fife and started looking for a shady place to sleep.

Laura kept close to the cauldron as she stirred it, hoarding the fire's warmth within her cloak. They had been boiling sheets all morning, and the placita was crisscrossed with lines of clean, wet linen. With the sky overcast, the laundry was not drying with quite its usual amazing speed. Laura smiled, remembering her astonishment when she had first come to this country at how quickly the sun and the dry air acted upon wet laundry. On a bright day, one could take down a sheet almost as soon as it had been hung.

Today that would not be the case. She glanced up at the clouds, hoping the snow would hold off a while longer.

A pounding at the gate made her heart quicken. Juan Carlos came out of the shed, leaned his broom against the wall and went into the passage. Laura stirred the sheets slowly and strained to hear the visitor's voice over the soft burble of the cauldron. She could not make out what was said, but she heard the creak of the gate and the sound of a horse being led in.

Mrs. Canby came out of the kitchen to greet the newcomer, smiling at Laura as she passed. Laura turned to watch her, and at the sight of a blue uniform she left the cauldron to follow. Her heart was beating rather too fast, and her feet were inclined to run, but she held herself to a brisk walk.

"Captain Howland," she heard Mrs. Canby say to the officer. "How good it is to see you!"

"Thank you, ma'am," the captain said, bowing over her hand. "I trust you are well."

Hiding her disappointment, Laura composed her face into a smile and curtseyed when the captain turned to her. She had met him only once; they were but remotely related, if at all. The captain bowed in her direction.

"I will ask María to make coffee," Laura said, and barely stayed for Mrs. Canby's thanks.

Foolish girl, she scolded herself as she crossed the placita. What must Captain Howland be thinking? You must calm yourself before rejoining them.

In the kitchen, María was already heating the kettle. Laura

hung her cloak on a peg, helped gather cups and spoons, and put some piñon nuts into a bowl to add to the tray. María then shooed her out, and she had no choice but to go to the parlor.

Juan Carlos was building up the fire as she came in. The captain rose from the sofa, and Laura nodded politely to him before taking Colonel Canby's chair.

"Good news," Mrs. Canby told her. "The troops have come back down from Fort Union."

"Will they be coming through Santa Fé?" Laura asked.

"That's unlikely, ma'am, but don't fear," Captain Howland said. "My company will remain here for the present."

Laura summoned a smile, and said, "That is good news indeed." She tried to sound cheerful, though her feelings were not so.

Captain Howland returned his attention to Mrs. Canby. "You should hear from the colonel any day, ma'am. We expect to meet up with him soon."

Laura allowed her thoughts to drift, only half attending to what was said. Stupid to have built up one's hopes. She tried to put sadness away from her, but it was hard to be required to wait quietly for news of her friends, and of one friend in particular. She would have preferred to act, but what could she do? *A woman alone doesn't have many choices.*

María brought in the coffee tray, and Laura accepted a cup. "Is Colonel Chaves with the column?" she asked.

"He has gone home," Captain Howland replied. "I understand he has had a flock of sheep stolen. He took leave to deal with it."

Laura nodded. "And Captain O'Brien?" she said carefully.

"His company is at Galisteo, I believe. You need not be concerned. He will not trouble you again."

Startled, Laura looked up at Captain Howland. "He has never troubled me," she said.

The captain looked briefly puzzled, then his face became stern. "Allow me to assure you, Miss Howland, as one who must necessarily be concerned for your well-being, that Captain O'Brien is not fit company for a lady," he said. "That you have escaped harm is a source of great relief and satisfaction to all of your friends in the army."

Laura cast a glance at Mrs. Canby, who seemed as surprised as she. With an effort, she spoke calmly. "I do not know what you mean," she said. "Captain O'Brien has been nothing but kind to me. Indeed, I am much in his debt."

"Allowances must be made," the captain began. He seemed uncomfortable, and looked at his hostess before continuing. "Allowances are a necessity in time of war. I assure you, no man in the army would dare to speak ill of your reputation, ma'am."

Untrue, Laura thought. Major Chivington would not hesitate.

"I am aware that my traveling with the army was disapproved," she said. "It was my choice, entirely." The captain opened his mouth to speak, and Laura hastened to continue. "I wish there to be no misunderstanding. Captain O'Brien was in no way ungentlemanly toward me."

Captain Howland gave her a tolerant smile. "You are very young," he said. "One day you will come to understand what you have escaped."

Laura found this offensive, and was about to tell him so when Mrs. Canby intervened. "Has the captain committed some transgression since the army left Glorieta?" she asked.

"It is not that." Captain Howland began to frown. "It is more an accumulation of things—a recognition of his character in general—in fact, there is talk of an investigation."

"Investigation!" Laura exclaimed. She was beginning to be alarmed.

"Nothing has been decided," he said hastily. "Nothing can be undertaken while we are in pursuit of the Texans. Please do not concern yourself, Miss Howland. The army will take only just action."

"Of course," Laura said faintly. She found she was gripping her coffee cup rather too strongly, and carefully set it on the table beside her.

A strained silence held for a moment. "May I fill your cup, Captain?" Mrs. Canby asked at last.

"No, thank you, ma'am. I should be getting back to my duties. I wished only to assure myself that you were well."

Laura followed the captain and Mrs. Canby to the zaguán, bade him a polite farewell, and watched him mount and ride out. As Juan closed the gate behind him, she turned a meaningful glance on Mrs. Canby, who nodded silently and led her back to the parlor.

"What can have happened?" Laura said as they sat down again.

"Who knows? Gossip goes around, especially when the troops are idle in a camp. Whatever it was, it will probably be forgotten in another week or two." Mrs. Canby lifted the coffee pot, and Laura retrieved her cup.

"I could not bear to be the cause of any trouble to Captain O'Brien. He has been so very good to me."

Mrs. Canby spoke slowly as she poured. "Well, my dear, there is little you can do at present. Do not distress yourself. The captain can look after his own interests."

Laura sipped her coffee. Mrs. Canby was right, there was nothing to be done while she was here in Santa Fé and the captain was on the march. She felt certain that, were she to accept his offer of marriage, much of the army's ill feeling toward him would be resolved. It would also be a solution to the question of her situation. But did she regard him highly enough to give him her future? To bear his children? The thoughts brought a blush to her cheek. She wished she could talk to him, become better acquainted with him, and perhaps warn him of the falsehoods—she felt sure they were falsehoods—being circulated about him. Unfortunately, she couldn't write to him, and the things she wished to discuss with him could not comfortably be entrusted to a third party. She would, she regretfully concluded, simply have to wait until they met again. There would be plenty to do in the meantime, setting the house to rights after it had been a hospital.

"The sheets! Oh, dear!" Laura put down her cup and hurried to the door.

"I'm sure María has attended to them," Mrs. Canby called after her.

Laura glanced back and waved, but continued through the entryway. She felt confined, and wanted to breathe the clear, cold air.

María had indeed attended to the sheets, and was hanging the last of them up to dry. Laura went to help her, stretching the wet linen over the lines Juan Carlos had hung. Every sheet in the house had been used, and now hung in the placita. Laura was reminded of childhood games of hide-and-seek. She gazed up at the mountains, and followed their line southward toward Galisteo.

A sharp breeze stung her wet hands, and bit at her limbs through her gown. María hustled her into the kitchen and made her sit by the stove. A pot of fragrant stew, spiced with chiles, simmered on the hearth. María reached for her big mixing bowl and began making the day's stack of tortillas, shaping each handful of dough into a flat circle. She handed a finished one to Laura, fresh and hot from the griddle.

"Gracias," Laura said, holding it between her cold hands.

María smiled, the silent, peaceful smile that Laura had come to know. How lucky I am, Laura thought, biting into the warm tortilla. I have found such good friends. I can never begin to repay them.

She wondered where exactly Galisteo was; she had not visited the town, but knew it lay upon the road that ran south from Glorieta Pass and down behind the Sandia Mountains. Wherever the captain might be, Laura was determined to keep track of him, that she might pray for his well-being, and someday find an opportunity to speak to him again.

O'Brien sat chewing a cracker in the mouth of a mine half-way up a hillside, where he had a good view of the road. Tailings spilled down the slope beneath his feet—red, black, and sulfur-yellow—a sign of the hopes that had one day bloomed here, and were now vanished. Denning hiked up to join him, holding his hat onto his head against the sharp wind. O'Brien offered his canteen.

"Thanks," Denning said. He sighed and sat down heavily, wiping the dust from it with his sleeve before opening it.

It was a dreary road, this. The Texans had raised all hell along it. All the day O'Brien's men had found signs of their passing—fences torn down for firewood, sheds and homes broken into, and carcasses of sheep and cattle stripped near to the bone. The citizenry had peered at I Company through cracked doorways as they passed. No cheers for the Pike's Peakers—the Mexicans feared them as much as they feared the damned Texans. There was no comfort to be had at any of these poor, shattered villages.

Pigeon's been devastated, too. The old Frenchman had nothing to sell—he'd lost all in the battle—and the Avery Trolls had to make do with hardtack for breakfast. O'Brien had kept an eye out as the road wound south over windswept plains and between craggy mountains. Any farmer with food to sell stood to make a profit today, but no one came forward.

At midday he had called for a halt near Cerillos. The villagers kept their doors shut tight, so the lads sheltered as well as they could in the crags of the hillsides. They ate more crackers and drank only water. Old mine shafts, abandoned, beckoned in a familiar way that O'Brien steadfastly ignored. The promise of fortune whispered by those black holes was naught but the devil's deception. There was no easy fortune in this land, where even a poor daily living must be wrested from the unyielding earth. In defiance, O'Brien sat with his back to the gaping, dark mouth of the mine.

"Rider coming," Denning said, pointing.

O'Brien followed his gaze to a wisp of dust rising between hills from the road farther south, out of sight. A moment later he heard the pickets cry, "Halt."

"Best go see," O'Brien said, getting up.

"It's probably an express," Denning said.

"Aye."

They trudged down the long hill, clouds of dust kicking up with each step, and reached the road just as the rider appeared rounding the bend. Captain's straps on his shoulders, and the form looked familiar, tall and lanky. It was not till he saw the man's face that O'Brien remembered—Captain Nico-something—Miss Howland's friend.

The man halted his horse and exchanged a salute with O'Brien. "Where's Colonel Slough?" he demanded.

"Somewhere between here and Kozlowski's," O'Brien said. "We're on scout."

The man grimaced, and glanced at O'Brien's men scattered over the hillsides. "You'd best move along," he said. "Colonel Canby is at Tijeras. You won't reach him tonight, but try to get there tomorrow. He wants to combine forces as soon as possible."

O'Brien peered up at the man, misliking his frown. "Where are the Texans?" he asked.

"Albuquerque. There was something of a ruckus there a day or two ago—Canby flung a few shells at 'em. Where are your wagons?"

"Back with the column," O'Brien said.

The Regular captain's frown deepened, and all at once he dismounted. On the ground he was scarcely taller than O'Brien. He came close, glaring, and said, "Where is Miss Howland?"

Biting down on his temper, O'Brien said, "Santa Fé. Mrs. Canby's."

"Oh." The fire died a bit in the fellow's eyes, but not altogether. He leaned toward O'Brien, one hand on his bridle, and said, "I have half a mind to call you out."

"Dueling's against regulations," O'Brien said, holding his gaze.

"Lucky for you."

"I've done nothing to harm her."

"That's not what I've heard."

"You've heard wrong, then." O'Brien cocked his head, eyeing the man—not much more than a boy, really—and sorting through the angry words that ran in his mind. He chose carefully, speaking with deadly calm. "Before you go issuing challenges you might regret, I'd suggest that you tell my accusers to bring their complaints up to me."

"Oh, they will," the man said, his mouth curling in a joyless smile. "Captain." He touched his hat, and mounted, and was gone, kicking up enough dust to make O'Brien shield his eyes.

At Oneida the well had been spoiled by the carcass of a dead horse. Kip heard grumblings among the men that Apaches had done it. Apaches got blamed for any and all calamities. Like as not the horse had been sick and stumbled into the well on its own, but it didn't matter a bit how it happened— what mattered was now Kip and Felley had been sent ahead in full daylight to scout as far as the next station and see if there was any water there. With a dozen empty canteens clanking on each saddle, they set out squinting in the morning sun.

The country was still flat, with the mountains sticking up to the east like a row of some animal's ragged old teeth. The road ran southerly, pacing the range down to Picacho Pass where it would cross and then swing southeast toward Tucson. Captain Calloway had given Kip a look at his map, and Kip had taken the opportunity to volunteer again for the advance party to hunt down the Rebels that Weaver had mentioned. The captain had said maybe, which was better than no, so Kip had to be content with that. He let Firecracker follow along after Felley's horse, and twiddled on an Indian flute he'd bought from one of the Pimas.

"That a gully over there, you think?" Felley asked, pointing to a dark line running across the desert below them.

"Could be." Kip answered. "We'll see."

"I was wondering if we might find a spring along in there. See them birds?"

Kip nodded, shading his eyes to get a better look. Two dark shapes had flown up from the gully and were winging their way eastward. Pretty big birds—raptors, maybe.

"Maybe they found a spring down there," Felley said.

"Or a rabbit," Kip said.

Firecracker snorted and tossed his head. "Easy, boy." Kip patted his neck. "We'll get you some water soon."

That gully was a good place for an ambush. Kip put away his flute and started to listen, but heard only the horses' hooves and the summer buzz of insects. He tried not to think about how far it was back to the column.

They couldn't see much until they were right on top of the gully. Running water had melted a broad crack in the sandy earth, but not a drop was there now. The road dipped down into the wash and they stopped at the bottom, looking right and left for any sign of a spring. No big clumps, but there were scrubby trees here and there with branches leafing out in bright green.

"You check east, I check west?" Felley suggested.

"No," Kip said. "We stay together."

"Aw, hell. Any scout worth his salt can take care of himself."

"We're more pickets than scouts," Kip said. That was quite in reverse of what he usually liked to feel, but being out alone in the desert had revised his view of scouting somewhat. "Let's try east first," he said, turning Firecracker.

The dry wash wound lazily side to side in the bottom of the gully and they followed it, that being the easiest footing for the horses. The sides of the gully were strewn with a variety of rocks and boulders, some calved off from the walls, some obviously washed down from the mountains, attesting to the force of the water when it was running. Kip peered down at the sandy dirt in the bottom. It was churned up with a lot of other hoofprints, which looked promising.

Rounding a curve, his first realization was that there had been a fire. A tree close by the gully wall was charred, and black streaks of smoke reached up the wall. From the tree's branches hung three blackened objects, vaguely human in form. Kip stopped Firecracker, and Felley halted, too. Firecracker snorted.

"What the hell is that?" Felley muttered.

Kip shook his head. Underneath each hanging thing was a circle of scorched earth and bits of charred wood left over from a fire. Looking up to the ropes, he realized they'd been tied up by the feet, hung upside down.

"God. Oh, God."

Kip started having trouble drawing breath. Despite Sutter's stories, he'd never imagined any human being could do such a thing as this to another person. Firecracker sensed his mood and sidled a step. A mass of flies rose from the bodies in response, unveiling glimpses of raw flesh.

"Shit!" he heard Felley say.

Firecracker reared, spun, and bolted. A rattle of fly bodies pelted Kip as they passed through the swarm. Firecracker screamed and ran harder, up the wash away from the horror and the road, canteens rattling like thunder. Kip clung on, pulling hard on the reins but the horse had his head up in the air and couldn't feel the bit. They plunged up the wash, veering right and left along the path the water had made. Kip's stomach raised a protest. Ahead there was a big log— he hoped it was a log—across the stream bed and he felt Firecracker speed up to jump it. They landed with a jolt and

Kip lost the reins and one stirrup. He grabbed a handful of mane, shouted, "Whoa, dammit!" and scrabbled for the flapping reins. The horse veered hard and Kip felt himself sliding off. He tried to hold on with his knees, but it was too late and he saw a glimpse of the sky half-blocked by a tall rock just before he hit.

9

"It was my wish to have made a junction if possible below the Confederate troops in order to cut off their retreat, but the state of our supplies and the inferiority of our force rendered this inexpedient."

—Colonel Ed. R. S. Canby, 19th Infantry, Commanding Department

Jamie scooped up another shovelful of dirt and pitched it into the hole. Sweat was trickling down his back under his shirt in spite of the cold breeze. He didn't have to help, but it felt good to be doing something real, instead of struggling with numbers and lists and insoluble problems. Beside him John Reily shoveled like a machine, his face set in a grim expression, as if he wanted to be the one whose earth covered the last of the brass showing. Eight guns—the mountain howitzers of the 1st and 2nd's batteries—had gone into the ground under Major Teel's supervision. The horses that had drawn them would go to pull Jamie's wagons. All the cannon they had left were Teel's battery and the trophy guns from Valverde.

Another shovelful, warm and smelling faintly of ancient manure. The corral where they'd chosen to bury the guns was not currently in use, though Jamie planned to run what was left of the beef herd in there tonight to obliterate the evidence of the burial.

Jamie paused to look up at the harsh mountains, snow gleaming along their pine-fringed ridges and on the faces of the pale rock cliffs below. Somewhere behind them the Federal troops were joining forces. Scouts had reported Canby's passage through Carnuel, and he was understood to be awaiting men from Fort Union—those damned Pike's Peakers—who, when joined to Canby's troops, would give him the advantage of numbers. It wasn't until that morning, in a staff meeting held at the Armijos' house, that General Sibley had admitted the necessity of retreating to Mesilla and awaiting reinforcements there. It was a decision no one liked, but there wasn't any choice.

Jamie glanced up at the men working the shovels. It reminded him of Valverde for a moment—those terrible trenches that had to be dug and filled after the battle. Suddenly he wanted to get away from the sound of the earth falling into the pit, but he had to stay. These were his only shovels, and he didn't dare leave them. He pushed the one in his hands into the dirt again, forcing his attention to the task of moving earth a bit at a time.

Reily paused to wipe his sleeve across his brow, and spat. "Leaving our batteries here and dragging those damned mismatched guns," he muttered angrily.

Jamie sighed. He knew Reily felt he'd been cheated out of the best part of the fighting, and now he had to bury his weapons and take his men on as infantry. If his father, Colonel Reily, had been here there might have been a discussion on the subject, but the colonel was still in Mexico and there wasn't time, really, for arguing.

Finally the ground was level again. Jamie had Sergeant Wooster collect up the shovels while he followed Reily to the depot nearby. Major Teel was sitting under the portal, sketching a map to the corral from the plaza. As they approached the major stood up, stuffing his notebook back into his pocket. "All right," he said, squinting as he stepped into the sun. "Let's get moving."

He started toward the plaza with Reily following. Jamie hurried to catch up. "I'll be glad to see the last of this place," he said, falling into step.

"It isn't the last." Reily frowned. "We're coming back!"

Jamie glanced across the plaza at the Valverde guns grouped around the flag pole, polished tubes gleaming in the sun. "Remember how long it took us to recruit the 1st and gear up?" he said softly. "Well, the general only sent for reinforcements two weeks ago."

Reily's eyes narrowed. "We're coming back," he repeated.

Jamie kept silent. Maybe they would be back. Sighing, he

turned back toward the depot and the task of getting the army back on the road.

O'Brien clicked his tongue and the mare, just as he had expected, broke into a trot. "Whoa, lass," he said, bringing her down to a walk again and stroking her neck. "Good lass."

Her previous owner had trained her with sounds. O'Brien had discovered it by accident the night before. He'd turned her out to graze and walked away starting to whistle an air, and she had come after him as fast as the hobble would let her. Already he'd figured out three of the commands, for trot, canter, and come.

"What's your name, then, eh lass?" O'Brien murmured. "Won't you tell me?"

"Liver Mare," Morris said from beside him.

"Ah, Thomas. You've no imagination."

"I'm saving it for supper, so I can imagine I'm eating something besides biscuit."

O'Brien cocked an eye at the massive, gently slanting mountains to their right. They were much closer than they had been all day—the company had ridden up onto the shoulder of the great slopes, and had now reached the crest of the trail. Tall pines had replaced the scrubby cedars and piñons, and the rest looked like downhill riding. The sun was just starting down toward the peaks.

"We should get in by sundown," O'Brien said. "Belike Colonel Canby will give us some meat, if we mind our manners."

"He's Regular Army, isn't he?" Morris asked. "He'll be just like the others."

"Maybe not," O'Brien said, though in his heart he held out no great hope. All the Regulars seemed to be banding against him. It was Ramsey at the bottom of it, he was sure— Ramsey and Chivington—but the Regulars were gobbling up Ramsey's lies like honey cakes, and if Canby believed it like the rest he was doomed.

He cast a glance back at Ramsey, who sat his horse idly and had said almost nothing since they'd been sent on this scout. O'Brien had taken to watching him, noting who he spoke to, who seemed friendly to him. Watching an enemy, looking for weakness. Working out where best to strike.

Putting that thought away from him, he reached down to stroke the mare's neck again. No use thinking about it. There was nothing he could do now. Thinking would only make him angry, and he had no time for that. He had to get his men into Canby's camp tonight, for tomorrow they'd not even have biscuit to eat. No supplies had been sent after them; the messengers he'd sent back to the column had returned empty-handed. Commissary would not issue rations during a march, was the answer to his request for food. He'd have gone back himself, but likely he'd get the same answer, and truth be told he'd no wish to see Chivington sooner than he must. Casting a glance back at his lads, he judged them fit for a jog now that it was downhill, and clicked the mare up to a trot.

Kip woke with a start, and blinked against the burning sun. Some sound had waked him—some hunting bird's cry, maybe. His head was throbbing, and reaching a hand up to shade his eyes made it worse. He glanced around, trying to move as little as possible. His throat was so dry it hurt to swallow, and his lips were glued shut. He left them that way, knowing if he licked them they'd just crack.

He was lying in the dry stream bed, propped up against the rock he'd hit his head on. A slight breeze stirred its fingers in his hair, enough to tease him with the idea of coolness but not enough to actually impart it. The sun was glaring at him from over the gully wall, hanging about a span above it. He'd been unconscious a while, a few hours maybe. Firecracker was nowhere in sight.

He tried to sit up, and a wave of nausea washed through him. Closing his eyes, he waited for it to pass, then gingerly reached up to investigate the lump on his head. His scalp hurt where he touched it. Sunburned. Venturing to open his eyes again, he looked for his hat, but couldn't see it anywhere. He struggled to his feet, leaned against the rock and vomited behind it, then coughed, spat, and took several deep breaths. At last he was able to stand up—dizzy, but steady enough—and look up and down the gully. His hat was nowhere in sight. Must have lost it when the horse bolted.

Firecracker, you rat. Where are you?

A sound struck him motionless; a climbing wail that rose in pitch and volume together until he thought it would pierce his battered skull, then fell away, fading into the whisper of the breeze. Animal or human? He couldn't decide. He knew, though, that this was the sound that had waked him.

He closed his eyes, trying to think. The horse was gone, and Felley hadn't found him, if he'd looked. So Felley was gone, too, either back to the column or the victim of another unlucky accident. Or—Kip's mind shied away from the charred corpses hanging in the tree, back down the gully. He couldn't face that, not yet. He started walking in the other direction, upstream instead of down toward the trail.

He had no food, no water. Only his knife and pistol. He'd walk awhile and see if he could find that spring Felley was so sure about. Trudging up the sandy wash, he realized he was following hoofprints, and thought maybe Firecracker was ahead of him. Maybe he would find the horse chewing on whatever green grew around the water that his equine nose had smelled out.

Kip stopped and stared at the sand stretching ahead, remembering that there had been a lot of hoofprints farther down the wash. Here there was only one set—running—but the dry sand didn't reveal how fresh they were or whether the horse was shod. An Indian would have been able to tell, Kip thought, disgusted with himself. The amount of sand that had fallen back into the hoofprint would have told him how old the print was, or so Sergeant Sutter had said, back around the campfire one night. It had seemed idle talk at the time, but now Kip knew his life might depend on such details.

Looking up the gully, he swallowed and started ahead again, staring at each rock big enough to hide a man, trying to move without making any noise. It was Firecracker's trail he was following. Had to be. Kip silently told his heart not to beat so damned fast.

The sound came again and this time he could tell it was up ahead. He stopped, the muscles between his shoulders tightening as the cry built; and didn't move again until it had faded. Placing each foot carefully, quietly, he made his way over to the side of the gully out of the wash, where the ground was hard and wouldn't make the soft sifting noise of sand underfoot.

That cry could be a person being tortured, he thought, except it seemed too regular. He picked his way slowly among the rocks, staying in shadow when he could, watching and listening, thinking about going back but deciding to go on. It might be Felley making that noise, though he sure hoped it wasn't.

The column would be coming and they'd send a search party out to find him. All he had to do was last the night. The smart thing would be to find a cranny somewhere to hole up in, out of sight where he could keep an eye on the gully. Or better yet, go back down to the trail and find a spot to hide in near there, where he'd be sure to hear the column approaching. That would be the sensible thing.

Kip stopped. A dark stain spread down the sandy wash just ahead. He thought at first it was blood, but the sand was red and maybe it was just wet—maybe it was water. He moved toward it, stepping slowly into the wash, trying not to make the slightest sound. Kneeling down, he reached toward the darkened sand and took a pinch, bringing it to his nose.

Water. He dug his fingers in a little, looking for the spring, but it was farther up, he guessed. The stain was spreading out from between some big rocks on the shady side of the gully up ahead. Maybe there'd be a pool.

"Aaiiiieeeeeee!"

Kip flinched at the sound—a human voice, he was pretty sure now—coming from behind the same rocks where the dampness issued. He scrambled to his feet as the weird cry died away, and stood for a minute trying to still his breathing. He moved with aching slowness toward the rocks, straining his ears for any tiny sound. One giant boulder, gray and out of place in the red sandy wash, was big enough to conceal a whole war party. Behind this rock and the smaller ones clumped around it rose a tall, green palo verde tree, its slim branches throwing lacy shadows over the boulder. The soil beneath the stones was damp; little blades of grass peeked out around their bases. With every nerve tingling, Kip stepped onto the bank and passed alongside the big rock toward the shaded gully wall, his hands brushing the cool surface. Feathery branches whispered together in the hint of a breeze.

A small scraping noise brought him to a breathless stop. His feet had not made that sound. The cry came again—shatteringly close—and Kip squeezed his eyes shut until it was over. Leaning against the rock, he slowly moved his head out to where he could see around it.

Behind the rock was a pool of clear water from a tiny, hidden spring, sunlight dappling its gently moving surface through overhanging branches. A few feet beyond the pool lay a man—an Indian—naked to the waist, with paint smeared on his face and an ugly wound in his chest. Blood had seeped onto the sand from this wound, but the bleeding seemed to have stopped some time since; what was on his body was dry. Beside him sat an Indian woman dressed in buckskins. It was she who had made that terrible sound—grieving over her dead man—and now she held in her hands a wicked bowie knife, which she raised up to the sky like some sacramental offering. The wide planes of her face were stained with tears, and her long black hair spilled over her shoulders and brushed against the dead warrior's flesh.

She had not seen Kip. He watched in silent awe while she held the knife up over the dead man's body, then grasped its hilt in her right hand and with her left drew her hair back from her neck. With a graceful motion she brought the knife point up to her ear.

"No!" Kip cried without thinking.

Her arm was already in motion; the stroke sliced through the gleaming black tresses and shifted smoothly, bringing the knife to bear on Kip. Her eyes met his, impaling him across the water, their black depths burning with a fury that seared right into his soul.

Kip raised his hands, palms outward to show they were empty, and dropped to his knees beside the rock. The smell of the water reached him and his thirst returned in full force, but he didn't dare look away from those vicious black eyes. The Indian woman stayed motionless, her knife pointed at his heart. Beyond her a pinto mustang shifted and sighed beneath the palo verde.

"I'm sorry," Kip said. "I'm sorry." As if that meant anything. Sorry for what? For disturbing her grief? For the death of her brave? For being the same color, most likely, as the men who had killed him?

Her nostrils flared and Kip realized she was breathing nearly as fast as he was. "Look, I just want a drink, all right? That's all," he said.

Slowly he reached one hand down to the water, keeping the other up in sight. The woman shifted, her eyes widening, and followed his movement with the knife. With the hair on his neck tingling, Kip dipped his hand into the water and raised it to his mouth. His lips stung at the moisture, and slurping up the few drops just made him crazy for more. He resisted the urge to plunge his head into the spring, not wanting to present the woman with so tempting a target as the back of his neck. Keeping his eye on the knife, he dipped both hands in the water this time and raised up a good drink, spilling most of it on account of trying to watch the knife instead of his hands. He did this again and got more down his throat. The third time she stood up, and Kip sat back on his heels, raising his hands up once more. He felt dizzy but the water was helping. The woman's eyes flicked to the dead man at her feet.

Kip figured if he left right now he could make it back to the trail all right. He didn't like the idea of that knife behind him instead of in front, but she probably wouldn't leave her man's body. Indians were touchy about the disposition of their mortal remains, Sergeant Sutter had said. Things had to be just so or you didn't get into the happy hunting ground, or wherever it was they went.

She glanced at the paint pony, then back at Kip, frowning. Before he'd really considered he said, "You want help getting him on the pony?"

The woman's eyes narrowed. Kip got slowly to his feet, which made his head throb some, and stood looking at her. She was kind of pretty, in a wild sort of way. Her buckskin skirt had a short fringe cut into the hem, and all the edges were rough and slanted as if the skin hadn't been trimmed, but just used in its natural shape. She was tall for an Indian, he realized. Almost as tall as himself.

"Put him on the horse?" he said, gesturing to the dead man and then the pinto.

The little pool between them was no wider than he could jump. Kip took one step toward her around the water, and the knife came back up to point at his chest.

This is a damn fool idea, Whistler. Go back to the trail.

"Tell you what," he said to the woman. "You put away that knife and I'll help you get him on the horse."

"Anah-zont-tee!" she said, brandishing the knife.

"All right, all right! I've got a better idea. You hold the knife, and I'll put him on the horse. Friends, right? Amigos?"

Her eyes narrowed, and her frown deepened. He should just go, he should go right now. She didn't want his help, and why the hell he had offered was beyond him. Hit his head harder than he thought, maybe. He was about to back away when she took a step to her left and grabbed the pony's reins, then lowered her knife.

Her frown was more sad than angry now, and as Kip watched she brushed back a tear with her knife hand. Her hair, chopped off short on the one side, gave her a forlorn look. She pointed the blade at Kip, then the warrior, then the horse.

"Right," Kip said. He came slowly forward, keeping his hands in her sight, and knelt beside the dead brave. The fellow was big—taller than himself, with wide shoulders that were all muscle. Kip's nose wrinkled at the gaping chest wound and he ducked his head so the woman wouldn't see. He got an arm under the man's knees and one behind his back, and stood with a grunt and a stab of pain to his head. He staggered back a step until he got his balance, then carried the brave over to the pinto, mindful of the bowie knife, and managed to roll the body up onto the horse's back. Leaning against the animal for a minute, he looked up at the Indian woman.

Apache, he realized. Must be. She was nothing like the village Indians he'd seen. He stared at her, breathing hard, and decided he was a complete idiot.

She gestured with the knife, indicating she wanted him to back away, so Kip retreated to the spring. Still watching him, she reached into the bushes and brought out a leather bag, slung it over the pinto's neck, and in one smooth motion leapt onto its back behind the dead warrior. She flashed a last haughty glance at Kip, and turned the horse away. In a second they were gone, down through the bushes toward the wash. Kip listened and could just hear the hiss of the pinto's hooves in the sand.

He sighed. Every muscle in his back was tight as a spring. He had just done a very stupid thing, and gotten out of it with his skin intact.

"Must be my lucky day," he said to himself. It came out as a croak, and he knelt down at the spring to lubricate his throat some more.

Something caught his eye, a black shadow on the red earth. Getting up again, Kip stepped over to where the Apache woman had been kneeling on the ground, and found a swatch of long, black hair—her hair, that she'd been cutting when he interrupted her. Kip gathered it up and smoothed the strands. It was finer than he'd expected, thick and soft and shiny. He curled it up and put it in his shirt pocket, grinning. Oh, would he have a story to tell around the next campfire!

The Federal camp filled a small meadow under the hills and spilled in among the surrounding trees. O'Brien made his way to the commander's tent and waited while an orderly informed Colonel Canby of his presence. The mare lipped at the meadow grass dry underfoot, still yellow from the winter.

At last he was let into the tent where the colonel sat working at a small field desk. Canby looked up from his papers, hard gray eyes inquiring his business. He looked nothing like what O'Brien had expected. He'd imagined him like Colonel Slough, or like Chivington—large and full-bearded—but this man was tall, somewhat gaunt, and clean-shaven. His dark hair hung lank across his brow, half concealing a frown. A large nose and ears lent the hint of a scarecrow to his looks.

O'Brien gave his report, though the colonel seemed only mildly interested. Doubtless he already knew there were no Rebels hiding on the Galisteo road. They had left Santa Fé, and were all down at Albuquerque, waiting for a fight. All he said, when O'Brien had finished, was "Very good, Captain. Dismissed."

O'Brien licked his lips. "Sir," he said, and hesitated when the sharp eyes glanced up at him. Had the colonel already been turned against him? There was no way to know. Putting worries aside, he said, "Permission to draw rations for my men, sir? We've had naught but hard biscuit for three days."

Canby looked surprised. "Why was that?" he demanded.

O'Brien studied his face, unable to tell if the frown betokened concern or displeasure. "We were sent on scout unexpectedly," he said carefully. "We didn't have time to draw anything."

The colonel's eyes narrowed. "O'Brien, is it?" he said.

"Yes, sir."

"Who gave you that order?" The gentleness of the words didn't match the hard look on the colonel's face. O'Brien suddenly had the feeling this scarecrow was made of steel.

"Major Chivington, sir," he said.

The colonel's brows rose. "Soon to be Colonel Chivington. I've just accepted Slough's resignation."

O'Brien swallowed. "Did Colonel Tappan resign, too, then?" he asked.

Canby returned his gaze evenly. "No," he said, "but he has waived his right to promotion. A wise choice, under the circumstances."

O'Brien looked at the ground, trying to hide his disappointment. The grass was starting to green up at the roots, he noticed. Tappan knew which way the wind was blowing, and so, it seemed, did Colonel Canby. Chivington was a great hero with the men, and that counted for much, if not all.

Looking back up at Canby, O'Brien fought away from the shroud of despair that was threatening him. "Please, sir," he began. The calm gray eyes met his, waiting, while he searched for the best words. His throat tightened, making his voice rough. "Don't believe all you hear of me from the ma—from Chivington," he said.

The gray eyes softened a bit, then glanced down at the papers on the desk. "You may draw your rations, Captain," Canby said. "Dismissed."

*   *   *

"Have you spoken with my husband? Is he well?" Mrs. Chapin asked anxiously.

Laura took a sip of tea as Captain Nicodemus answered. She hesitated to add her own questions, feeling uncertain—in the wake of Captain Howland's reaction—as to how he was likely to receive them.

"Yes," the captain said. "He is presently with Colonel Paul, at Kozlowski's Ranch. He is quite well, ma'am, and wished to be remembered to you."

Mrs. Chapin beamed, and gave Laura a joyous look. Laura passed a plate of empanadas to the captain, and glancing at Mrs. Canby, said, "Colonel Canby is also well, I trust?"

"Yes, very well. Sharp as ever. Won't be back here for some time, but you're not to worry, ladies. Howland's fellows will leave a detail when they go."

"Are they going?" Mrs. Canby asked. "I had not heard that."

"Yes, the colonel wants everyone together. Going to whip the Rebels out of New Mexico."

"Well, thank goodness!" Mrs. Chapin exclaimed. "It will not be too soon for us, thank you!"

Laura got up and walked to the window to look out at the parroquia. Since the removal of the Texans, Mrs. Canby's parlor curtains were once more thrown back to admit the cold light of early spring. Small buds of green leaves were beginning to show on the trees in the plaza. Across the street a neighbor was sweeping his doorstep. Slowly the city was coming to life again, now that the conflict had been carried southward. Oddly, Laura found she felt no particular joy in this. Her heart was with the army, and she chafed at having to wait patiently here while her friends were on the march, perhaps heading into battle.

Lieutenant Franklin had found a way out of that dilemma. Laura smiled to herself. She admired Franklin and marveled at her courage, but she herself had not the fortitude, she knew, to undertake such an adventure. She was not prepared to give up being a lady—she had every intention of remaining a lady, in fact—nor did she long to experience the exhilaration and the terror of battle. But the freedom of which

Franklin had spoken, that was something she did long for, most earnestly.

She ran a hand up her sleeve, remembering pleasant evenings around the campfire, playing at cards and conversing, the strains of a violin rising into the night and a pair of green eyes watching her every move. How ungrateful, after all Mrs. Canby's kindness, to be wishing herself back with the column. She wondered where they were now; away to the south somewhere.

"Did you hear that, Miss Howland?" Mrs. Canby's voice recalled her attention. "Governor Connelly is returning to Santa Fé."

Turning away from the window, Laura came back to the fire and accepted a fresh cup of tea. She did not answer.

"Won't it be good to see our old friend?" Mrs. Chapin said.

"He was my uncle's friend, not mine," Laura stated.

Mrs. Canby raised an eyebrow. "Are you sure you are being quite fair?" she asked gently.

Laura met Mrs. Canby's gaze and held it for a moment, then looked down at her cup. Perhaps she was not being fair, but she was not ready, at least not yet, to forgive Dr. Connelly. He had stood by, uttering only a feeble protest, while her uncle subjected her to the basest humiliation. Mrs. Canby knew of this; Laura had told her all the circumstances that had led to her traveling with the army back to Glorieta. If her friend judged her unkind, well. She would strive to find greater charity within herself.

"Come to think," said Captain Nicodemus, "where is your uncle? Expected to see him at the Exchange."

"I don't know where he is," Laura said. "He has gone back to the States. We have nothing more to do with each other."

"Eh?"

Laura ignored Captain Nicodemus's curious expression. "Have you any news of Captain O'Brien?" she asked abruptly, wishing to change the subject.

"Oh, that. Nothing's been settled yet. The exact charges to be brought against him are still in question."

"Charges!" Laura set aside her teacup.

The captain nodded. "It'll either be treason or murder. Don't think the major's decided."

Laura felt her heart beginning to beat rather too quickly. She cast a wild glance at Mrs. Canby, whose expression was of worried sympathy.

"What do you mean?" Laura asked, her voice sounding thin in her ears. "Has there been a fight?"

"Not lately, but there was one before the battle. O'Brien tried to kill Lieutenant Franklin at Kozlowski's, then who should turn up mortally wounded after Glorieta? There's been speculation about just how he might've been wounded."

"No," Laura whispered. She cleared her throat, and said more firmly, "No. I saw the fight at Kozlowski's. I was—I was there. It was just a disagreement."

"Well, it doesn't matter either way," said the captain. "If they can't prove murder, they'll get him for treason. He's been chummy with one of the prisoners. A turncoat, used to be his lieutenant."

"There must be some mistake," Laura said. "Lieutenant Denning would never—"

"Oh, not Denning. No, he's all right. Fellow name of Hall."

Laura shook her head, bewildered. "Hall?" She remembered the name, and believed it to be one of the men Lieutenant Franklin had helped to capture in the pass, the night before the battle. She frowned. "I don't remember anything about Mr. Hall," she said.

"Course not," said the captain. "No reason why you should. Not the sort of thing that's fit for a lady to hear." Captain Nicodemus gave her a kindly smile. "Don't you worry, Miss Howland. That fellow won't trouble you again. Chivington's determined to be rid of him, one way or another."

Silent, Laura watched the captain raise his teacup to his lips. Inside her, panic was raging. That Chivington and Captain O'Brien were at odds she knew; that the major would seek to remove her friend from his position she had never imagined. Could he indeed be a traitor? She could not believe it, and she was absolutely certain that he had not killed Lieutenant Franklin.

Mrs. Chapin was speaking again. Laura scarcely attended to the words—ponderings on when the mails might resume—for she felt herself in the midst of a nightmare. Major Chivington was determined to be rid of Captain O'Brien. To what lengths would he go to achieve his goal? Surely a preacher must have some Christian charity within him, but Laura found she could think of no constraints she was certain the major would recognize.

A stirring among the others caused her to look up. Captain Nicodemus was on his feet, taking his leave. He turned to Laura and said, "Miss Howland, would you do me the honor of accompanying me to the gate?"

Wanting nothing less, Laura made herself smile and said, "Of course."

A cold breeze struck her face as they stepped into the placita. The thyme in Mrs. Canby's garden was beginning to turn from purple to green, heralding warmer weather; crocuses were blooming around the foot of the well, and larger bulbs were reaching green shoots toward the sun. She followed the captain away from the bright garden into the shadow of the zaguán. He stopped beside the gate.

"Miss Howland, I meant to speak to your uncle, but since he's not in Santa Fé . . ."

Laura looked up at him. Beneath the new-grown whiskers and the captain's uniform, he was still the awkward, lanky youth she remembered from last summer. Just now he looked particularly young, perhaps because of the uncertainty in his expression.

"He was a bad sort anyway," the captain continued. "That's why I—well—oh, rot." He looked down at his feet, and rubbed at the dirt of the passage. "I'm not good at speeches."

"Captain—"

"I just thought you might like to marry me." He looked up again, peering anxiously at her in the shadows of the zaguán. "I could give you a home and a name."

Laura felt a hollowness inside, which she strove to conceal. "That's very kind of you," she said, "but I assure you I am in no need of charity."

"Not charity," he said. "I like you. Always have. Just never thought I had any chance."

Laura felt anger rising. She had liked him, too, once, but she could not care for anyone who abused Captain O'Brien. "I am sorry to disappoint you, but I already have an understanding with another gentleman." She was glad of the shadows, for she felt herself blushing.

"Oh. Well, that's no surprise." He laughed, and his teeth flashed white in the dim passage. "Anyone I know?"

"I don't believe you know him," she said softly.

"Ah. Well. All happiness to you, then."

"Thank you."

Laura shook hands with him, and opened the door in the gate. "Thank you for visiting us," she managed to say.

"Always a pleasure," he said. "I'll come again."

Laura nodded, and did her best to smile as he stepped out into the street. When he was gone she closed the door and leaned against it, staring at the gentle garden.

So, she had an understanding with Captain O'Brien, had she? She knew her cheeks must be flaming. Well, even if he had changed his mind, she expected she would have no trouble finding another suitor in New Mexico, where there were very few American women. This thought, which should have comforted her, produced unexpected pain. She did not want another suitor, she realized. She preferred Captain O'Brien to any other officer of her acquaintance.

"Oh," she said aloud.

Was marriage indeed the solution to her problems? If so, it seemed her choice of a partner had already been made.

Frowning, she stood away from the door and pressed her hands to her cheeks. She had time yet to consider that question, but she must, she absolutely must prevent the disaster that threatened her friend. She could not write to him directly, and dared not send a message to him through Mr. Denning, not knowing his opinion of the scandalous accusations. She might write to Colonel Canby, but she could not expect him to be concerned with such matters while he was engaged in a military campaign. She knew few of her army friends well enough to enlist their aid—Captain Chapin, perhaps, or Colonel Chaves—and those she felt she might call upon were not with the column to the best of her knowledge. Colonel Chaves was at home attending to his personal affairs, and Captain Chapin was still dancing attendance on Colonel Paul.

It appeared the only way she could help Captain O'Brien was by her direct testimony. If she were present at whatever trial or hearing commenced to judge him, she could explain to the officers exactly what had happened at Kozlowski's Ranch and exonerate him from any accusations concerning the death of Lieutenant Franklin. Moreover—and her heart quickened at this thought—she could speak to him privately and resolve to their mutual understanding and satisfaction what their future association was to be.

Laura felt as if she stood at a precipice, pondering whether to leap. To seek out the army again, to leave Mrs. Canby's protection for the uncertainties of the highway, was rather a desperate step. *Her* circumstances alone did not seem to warrant it, but with the addition of the captain's apparent danger . . .

She must go to him. At once, for she dared not wait until the army returned. It might all be over by then. Captain O'Brien might have been subjected to an unfair trial, and convicted unfairly, only because she was unable to speak in his defense.

The decision made, a great weight of worry fell away, and she straightened her shoulders. She had no idea how she would reach the captain, but reach him she would. She had faced seeming impossibilities before. Far from daunting her, the challenge gave her new energy, and she smiled, happier than she had been for many days. Lieutenant Franklin had not allowed society's objections to stop her. Laura would not take such extreme measures as Franklin had, but she would stop at nothing that was decently possible to achieve her object.

At dusk the rest of the Pet Lambs came into camp, and O'Brien watched their arrival with mixed feelings. His men flocked to the company's wagon, anxious to retrieve their gear, and he could only be glad that they had it, for the nights were cold up in these heights, and the last two they'd spent without even a blanket. Chivington came in mounted on a mule, with a private on foot leading his last gray, which had near given out from the long march. That sight was less satisfying. In all, O'Brien would rather have learned of the major's unfortunate demise along the way.

He himself had marched all of six miles on that day; an easy ride down the canyon to Carnuel, where the pass widened and offered more room for Canby's enlarged command. Canby's acting adjutant had invited O'Brien's company to camp on a bare, rocky hillside, far from the little stream that trickled through the valley. O'Brien had made no protest, though he made sure to have his men lead their horses right through the main camp when they took them to water.

The hill offered a splendid view, at least. It sat at the southern end of the mountains they'd come down behind, across from a lesser range that rolled away southward, and from its summit O'Brien could see that the west face of those mountains was sharply different from the side he had already seen. On the east they sloped long and gentle, covered with pines, to end in cedar-dotted hills much like this one. On the west, they rose up from the plain in steep cliffs of pink rock that turned red in the sunset, only their heights and the deep, creviced valleys adorned with a dark blue fringe of distant trees. Their very crest was bare rock, and just now it was dusted with snow that glowed pink in the sun's last rays. West of the range the ground sloped long and level down to a gray swath of leafless trees that marked a river valley. Signs of cultivation and small villages followed the river southward, staying close to the life-giving water in this dry, wasted land. Beyond them, the ground rose again toward a long, flat horizon broken by a handful of small peaks. It was vast, this land, and vastly empty. To O'Brien, it made even the bleak Colorado mountains look rich. His eyes roved the valley, vainly seeking some green other than the drab cedars that grew on the hills. Perhaps daybreak would bring some sign of life—some pale little grasses, or flowers hiding in the shade of the shrubs—but now the dark fell on a cold, empty land.

Someone gave a wolf's howl down below, and O'Brien glanced eastward to see the moon rising, round and bright, over the hills of the pass. Laughter rose up from the camp, and Shaunessy's voice floated into the night, singing some nonsense about digging gold in California, as if he hadn't learned enough in Colorado of the folly of chasing after gold. O'Brien laughed wryly, and started to pick his way down the slope toward the welcoming camp fires, his stomach growling. Time for more of the beef Canby'd been kind enough to dispense.

It was falling dark quickly, and he had to keep his eyes on his feet. There were cactuses hiding among the rocks, and the footing was loose and uncertain. With his mind thus distracted, he was caught by surprise by a blow falling on his shoulders from behind.

Knocked off balance, he stumbled and ran a few steps down the hillside before he regained his feet and slid to a stop. Uphill a dark shape loomed—large, with a hat pulled low—rocks crunching underfoot as it came toward him. O'Brien thought of Hambleton at first, and this man was much like that giant, but Hambleton was still rotting in a Colorado jail for all he knew. It was the last thought he had time for before his attacker leapt at him again.

O'Brien tried to sidestep, but the other was quick and grabbed hold of his coat. They slid downhill, loose rock shifting beneath them, arms grappling. O'Brien tried to throw his weight against the fellow, but his heels slipped on the scrabble and he couldn't find a steady footing. A sharp stab through the side of his right boot made him cry out. He moved his foot, but the pain stayed on—cactus, piercing the side of his foot, aching more with the pressure he had to keep on it. His opponent tried to knock him off his feet completely as the pair of them slid along the slope and westward. O'Brien caught a heart-stopping glimpse of a steep drop to his left, down a tumble of moonlit boulders that looked anything but inviting. Toward this his opponent pressed him. O'Brien's good foot slipped, then came down again on solid rock just short of the drop.

10

---

*"Oh, mother! says Pat, it's a shame for to see
Brothers fighting in such a queer manner,
But I'll fight till I die, (if I shouldn't be killed)
For America's bright Starry Banner."*

—*Pat Murphy of Meagher's Brigade,* Anonymous

Straining to resist the weight bearing down on him, O'Brien felt his left leg start to shake as he pressed with all his might against the rock beneath it. His attacker's hands gripped his shoulders, and O'Brien strained against the grip but couldn't break it. He was being pressed toward the rocky fall, and knew in a moment his leg would buckle and he'd go over. He had one hope, and one only. He sucked a deep breath, then dropped suddenly to his knees, striking upward at his attacker's arms and ducking his head. For a moment they were both sliding downhill; O'Brien heaved upward against the other's chest and sideways, and with a wild, surprised cry the man went over the edge, nearly dragging O'Brien with him. The cry was cut off sharply; a patter of small rocks followed, then silence.

O'Brien lay panting, his chin in the dirt and his feet hanging over the edge, limbs shaking and his heart going like a steam engine. His right foot was starting to throb. He scrambled back onto the hillside and got to his knees, then to his feet, squinting up and down the hill to be sure his attacker had no friends along. It appeared he did not.

O'Brien turned to the edge of the drop and peered down. A dark form lay still on the rocks below. No, not quite still— it moved, and then groaned.

"Who are you?" O'Brien called, short of breath. "Name and rank!"

The only reply was a slow, steady panting. The man

moved again, and this time gave a sharp cry, quickly stifled.

"Tell me your name and I'll get you out," O'Brien demanded. "Otherwise you can rot there."

The panting continued, a bit faster, then a strained voice said, "Private Unger."

Unger. One of Ramsey's lot. Bitter fury welled up in O'Brien's gut. He resisted the urge to spit over the edge, and instead sat down and commenced pulling cactus spines out of his boot.

"What's the matter with you, Unger?" he asked, tossing a spine over the drop.

"Leg's broke," Unger answered. A shifting of rocks followed, then a stifled grunt.

"Is it then? Well that's less than you planned for me, isn't it?" O'Brien listened a while, pulling spine after spine from his foot. One stubborn needle refused to come out; he hissed at the pain and tried for a better grip on it. "Who set you on to me, Unger?"

Silence. Then, "No one."

"No one? What have I done to you, then, eh? Speak up."

The reluctant spine still wouldn't come. O'Brien shifted his grip, pulled again, and felt it break. "Hell and damn," he muttered. He felt for the end, but it had broken off inside the boot. His groping fingers found two more spines, which he pulled and tossed over the edge. He got to his feet once again, and gingerly put his weight on his right. The broken spine bit, but he could walk on it.

"Who set you on to me, Unger?" he repeated.

"No one. I thought you was a Rebel spy."

O'Brien laughed. "There're no Rebels in twenty miles of us! They're all down at the river, having fandangos. Come on, Unger. Who sent you?"

"No one."

"Ah, well. Good night, then." O'Brien started away, gravel crunching underfoot.

"Wait!" Unger cried. "Don't leave me here!"

O'Brien stopped. "Come clean, then," he called softly.

Unger made a frightened sound, almost a whimper. "Please, sir. No one sent me, I swear. I thought you was a Rebel. I'm sorry."

"Sorry?" O'Brien said. "Aye, that you are."

"Please, Captain! Please." The man was weeping now, O'Brien could hear it in his broken voice. "I didn't have a choice. Please, sir, don't leave me."

A cold hardness settled in O'Brien's stomach. He was sure now that Unger had been sent by Ramsey, but from the fear in his voice the man would rather lie in pain all night than admit it. Whispering a curse, O'Brien stepped back to the edge. Unger was a bulging shadow among the boulders, twenty feet down. O'Brien stared at him.

"I'll send someone to fetch you," he said at last. "Can't carry you myself. You've a good two or three stone on me, haven't you Unger?"

"Aye, sir," came the feeble reply.

"Aye. You can think about that, while you're waiting."

Turning away, O'Brien limped down the hill, hissing now and then when a bad step pushed the spine sharper into his foot. He passed the men's fires, glancing at the faces around each, ignoring the occasional curious look. It was one fire he wanted, a fire that would have Sergeant Fitzroy at it, and Sergeant Rice, and Ramsey. When he found it he stood at the edge of the firelight, watching until Fitzroy's gaze fell upon him. The sergeant looked surprised, and nudged Ramsey next to him, who rose, looking more than surprised.

O'Brien stepped up to his lieutenant, holding his gaze, and suddenly seized the front of his jacket. The flash of fear that came into Ramsey's dark eyes pleased him; he gazed at it a long while, enjoying the liquid roving of Ramsey's eyes. It was true fear this. He'd not seen it in Ramsey before.

"Unger's broke his leg," he said at last, almost growling. "He thought he saw a Rebel, and fell down the hill trying to catch it. Go take a dozen men and fetch him back." On the last word he released Ramsey, pushing him away, almost into the fire. Ramsey stumbled a step and glanced at his companions, who rose without a word and followed him away. Left alone at the fire, O'Brien watched them out of sight, then limped down the hill to his own camp, thinking how curious it was that Ramsey hadn't asked for directions to where Unger lay.

*   *   *

Kip woke with a start and saw that it was nearly dark. His head still ached from the bruises, and his legs were stiff and sore. He groped for his canteen and drank what was left in it, then sat up and brushed the sand off his face.

Most of the camp was asleep. The few who were up and about were at the wells, where the water was blissfully good, thank God. When he'd come in that morning, Kip had fallen on his knees and drunk until he sloshed inside with each little movement. The vedettes who'd found him on the road and brought him in had laughed, but he didn't care, not a whit. They'd shut up when Calloway called him into his tent to report.

Kip thought about that, wondering if maybe he shouldn't have told the captain about the Apache girl. Calloway had sat silent through the whole story, listening with a serious face, and then told Kip to go get some sleep. Yes, Firecracker had been found—Felley had brought him in and he was fine—Kip wasn't to worry about it now but just rest. A detail had been sent to take care of the hanging bodies. No, the captain hadn't decided whether to send anyone after the Apaches. The trail was pretty cold.

Kip hoped Calloway wouldn't send a party out. He didn't want that girl to get hurt. It made no sense at all, of course. Most likely she'd be happy to hurt any of them. But it had seemed like, just for a minute, he and she had stepped outside all of that and just seen each other as people.

Kip sighed, reached for his hat—he'd found it back by the ghastly hanging bodies on the way out of the gully—and got up to go relieve himself, then carried his canteen and his gourd bottle to the wells to fill them. Blue Water was a good place. The station house had been abandoned, but not burned. Kip ducked his head under the low doorsill and stepped inside, walking to the back wall and then turning so the light from outside was in his favor. The building was empty except for a few old bent nails and a scrap of cloth in one corner. Dust hung in the air. Kip gazed out the doorway at the desert outside. They were a long way from anything like civilization. He was lucky to have made it back to the column alive.

Voices reached him, and he looked out and saw that the

camp was stirring. He left the building, intending to find
Felley and get his fife, but Sergeant Sutter found him first
and sent him back to the captain's tent. Calloway's striker
was cooking a rabbit over a fire out front, sweating in the
heat. Kip skirted the fire and went into the tent, where the
captain looked up from his desk.

"Feel better?" he asked.

"Yes, sir," Kip said.

"Good. I want you back in the saddle. You're getting your
wish, Whistler. I'm sending you out with the advance."

Kip swallowed. "After the Apaches?"

"No," Calloway said, gazing down at the map under his
hands. "After those Rebels at Picacho Pass. Report to Lieutenant Barrett, he'll give you further orders."

"Yes, sir."

Calloway glanced up at him. "Sure you feel all right? You
were banged up pretty badly."

"I'm fine, sir," Kip said. Excitement was taking hold of
him, and the hint of a smile the captain gave him made it
stronger.

Calloway nodded. "Keep your eyes open," he said. "Dismissed."

Kip went out and asked the striker which tent was Lieutenant Barrett's. The flap was shut, and Kip hesitated to call
out in case the lieutenant was asleep still. He was about to
head for the horses, grazing by the edge of the camp, when
he saw Barrett walking up.

"Reporting for duty, sir." Kip said, saluting.

"You're fit, Whistler?" said Barrett, looking him up and
down with a sharp blue eye. "Draw three days rations and
report to me by the wells in an hour, ready to ride." He
ducked into his tent without waiting for an answer.

"Yes, sir," Kip said. His belly rumbled at the mention of
rations, but he wanted to check on Firecracker first, so he
headed toward the herd.

Three guards watched over the grazing horses, keeping
them together and close to the camp. Kip walked into the
herd and toward a familiar coppery form. Firecracker raised
his head and snorted, and the horses nearby moved away.

"Don't give me that," Kip said softly. "You're the one

who panicked." He held out his hand, and after staring at him for a second, Firecracker came up and nuzzled his palm.

"You are a pain in the neck," Kip told him, scratching between the horse's ears just above the pale forelock. Firecracker blew out a sigh, spattering his other hand with grassy foam. "Thank you," Kip said, laughing.

Damned if he wasn't starting to like the bugger.

O'Brien peered at the lights of the house not so very far off, and listened to the low voices of the other company commanders. The officers had gathered on a slight rise under a stand of trees, close enough to hear the music from the Texans' fandango. The Rebels had taken over Governor Connelly's house, and all their officers were inside it raising a royal racket while their infantry slept. Chivington and Tappan stood with Colonel Canby, who had a pair of field glasses trained on the enemy camp.

O'Brien rubbed at his eyes and paced a few steps, trying to keep alert. His right foot was still sore, but by dangling it out of the stirrup all day and night he'd been able to rest it, and no longer limped when he walked. Pulling out Franklin's watch, he stepped into a patch of moonlight—near bright as day, riding full as she was in the cold sky—and had no trouble at all reading it. Past two, and they'd been on the march since dawn and had not had a meal since midday. Back among the ranks behind them O'Brien could hear the men shifting and murmuring while they waited for orders. They wanted a fight, that he knew. He himself wanted sleep more than anything else.

"We can surprise them!" Chivington's voice cut through the dark, and O'Brien glanced toward the house, though he knew it was too far for them to have heard. He moved closer to Chivington, the better to hear the debate, and saw him take the glasses from the commander.

"Their position is too strong," Colonel Canby was saying, his voice calm and low-pitched. "Do you see all those walls? Each one is a breastwork, and there are ditches between. Any attack on them would mean severe losses."

"But we outnumber them," Chivington said, returning the glasses. "Half their force is across the river!"

"I am aware of that, Colonel."

"Sir, allow me to attack with my own regiment. We will carry the town, I promise you."

"No. I'm sorry. Wait until daybreak, and you will see what I mean. Have your men make camp."

A fast, heavy tread told of Chivington's approach, and O'Brien stepped back as he passed. Tappan followed him, and in the moonlight O'Brien glimpsed his face, looking grim.

"Damnation," said Wyncoop nearby. "Just when we've got them where we want them."

O'Brien bit down on a sharp answer. Wyncoop had been promoted to major, filling Chivington's old place in the regiment. It was said that the honor was given him because of his valor at Johnson's Ranch, where his sharpshooters had played havoc with the Rebel cannoneers. All Chivington's praises had gone to Wyncoop and Captain Lewis, with none for O'Brien and his poor Trolls, though they'd done their share of work on that day while Chivington had watched from safety.

"At this rate we'll never attack them!" Downing complained.

"I guess outnumbering them doesn't mean anything to old Colonel Canby," Sanborn said.

"No, he's right," said O'Brien. "If we can't attack them without heavy losses, we shouldn't attack them at all."

The silence that met this caused O'Brien's skin to crawl. All at once he wished he could see his fellow officers' faces. He waited, listening, straining to see their shadowed forms in the darkness beneath the trees.

"There's such a thing as being too cautious," came a low voice nearby.

Ramsey. Damn the man.

"Better cautious than reckless," O'Brien said, keeping his voice even.

"I hear Canby and Sibley were comrades of old," Ramsey said.

No one answered, and O'Brien could think of nothing to say that would not dig him worse into trouble. The others began drifting away, murmuring of duties, of errands, of wine to be drunk. No one spoke to O'Brien, and at last he was alone among the trees, regretting his unguarded tongue.

"I think you should reconsider," Mrs. Canby said softly. "Would it not be better to wait here until things are more settled?"

It was quite late. The fire had burned down to embers, and Laura felt her eyelids growing heavy, but she knew she needed Mrs. Canby's advice. She looked up at her hostess, who sat reclining in her velvet chair, the orange glow of the coals casting deep shadows in the hollows of her face.

"That is what I have been telling myself for some time," Laura said, "but I am worried. Does it not seem to you that everything our friends have said about Captain O'Brien lately has been malicious gossip? He cannot have deserved it."

"How can you be certain of that? Remember, you have scarcely known him a month."

"I know him well enough to be sure he would never become a traitor." Laura said. "I know he did not compromise me—he was at great pains not to do so, in fact. And I know he did not kill Lieutenant Franklin."

"You were not present at the battle," Mrs. Canby said.

"The lieutenant told me—described to me—how h-he received his wound. It was a Texan who shot him, not Captain O'Brien."

"Very well, you have a strong case of support for him. Can you not wait to present it formally?"

"Chivington won't wait," Laura said bitterly. "He hates him."

"Oh, my dear." Mrs. Canby sighed. "I do understand your feelings. Naturally you want to help him, but going to him now—in the midst of this conflict—I do not see what good it will do."

"It will at least lay to rest any accusations that he has behaved dishonorably toward me. If he still wants to marry me, that is." Laura looked down at the coffee cup in her lap, and realized she was gripping the saucer rather tightly. She forced herself to relax.

"I am afraid I do not like to see you rushing headlong into

marriage," Mrs. Canby said gently. "You may feel you have no choice—"

"No, it is not that," Laura said. She raised her head and met Mrs. Canby's gaze. "We—understand each other. It is not something I can easily put into words." She set the empty cup on the table between them, her heart quickening with remembered feeling. "Do you remember the letter General Sibley sent to your husband at Christmastime?"

Mrs. Canby frowned. "Yes."

"Colonel Canby was going to burn it, and you stopped him. You stopped him without saying anything. You understood each other." Laura sat back against the sofa cushions. "That is how it is between the captain and myself."

"Oh."

Juan Carlos came in with an armload of cut piñón logs. Mrs. Canby picked up her sewing, her forehead creased in thought. Laura watched Juan stack the wood, then carefully set three logs in the beehive fireplace, leaning them against the back wall so that they formed half of a teepee shape. His hands, weathered by years of hard work, glowed a golden brown in the soft light cast by the embers.

Laura shifted on the sofa. She felt less confident than her words had implied. So many things were uncertain. Would the captain feel that by traveling to warn him she was trying to force his hand? That was not her desire.

"We are not even sure where the army is at present," Mrs. Canby said.

"We know they have gone south," Laura said. "I have a little money. I had thought perhaps I could buy a horse, and accompany the next courier who stops here."

"That will not do," Mrs. Canby said firmly. "I am sorry, but if you wish to preserve your reputation you must not ride about the country escorted by unmarried gentlemen. Or married ones, for that matter."

Laura laughed softly. "Oh, dear. I'm afraid I deserved that."

"I do not mean to be harsh. If you wish to help your captain, it is important to give his enemies no reason to criticize you."

"Yes, of course. They will criticize me anyway, I fear. Chivington thinks me no better than a—a—"

"Well, you will prove him wrong by your good behavior."

Juan blew gently on the coals and a yellow flame leapt up between the new logs. Laura sighed and stretched a hand out to the warmth. "I was thinking I might hire a chaperon. I wonder if Lupe Bachicha is still in town. She used to go about with me for a penny, when I needed to leave the hotel and my uncle couldn't be bothered to escort me."

"She has gone to Mora with her family," Juan said, getting up and dusting his knees.

"She would be terrified in any case," Mrs. Canby said. "You need more than a poor little maid for chaperon if you're heading toward the army."

Laura glanced up. Apparently Mrs. Canby had decided it was useless to try to dissuade her. It gave her a measure of comfort, however slight.

Juan faced them, his back to the fire, and folded his hands. "Perdón señora, señorita," he said quietly. "I do not mean to intrude, but I think perhaps I can be of help to the señorita."

Mrs. Canby tied off her thread and trimmed it with the little silver scissors from her sewing basket, then looked up inquiringly. "Yes, Juan?"

"The señorita wishes to travel south?" he asked Laura, raising his silver eyebrows at Laura, who nodded. "María and I have a daughter who lives in Lemitar."

"Is that Angelina?" Mrs. Canby asked.

"Angelina, sí. Her husband is in the New Mexico Volunteers, at Fort Craig. She is expecting a baby soon."

"Juan! I did not know," Mrs. Canby said. "My congratulations."

"Gracias, Señora," Juan said, smiling. "It is our first grandchild."

"How delightful," Laura said. "Congratulations indeed!"

Juan nodded his thanks. "María would like to be with Angelina when her time comes. We have been meaning to ask you, señora, for permission to visit her."

Mrs. Canby set her work aside and glanced at Laura. "I do not see why not. Are you offering to escort Miss Howland in that direction?"

"If that would please her," he said, with a slight bow to Laura.

"Oh!" Laura's sudden delight faded quickly. "Oh, I couldn't," she said to Mrs. Canby. "You would be all alone."

"No, for Mrs. Chapin is still in town. And I'm sure Mrs. Williams would be willing to come and help me. She's a good soul, don't you think? There is not very much to do any longer, thank goodness."

"I do not wish to inconvenience you," Laura said, feeling a rather painful hope.

Mrs. Canby smiled, and rose. "We really should retire. Tomorrow will be busy. The mule can draw my carriage, but the harness will have to be adjusted for him. I think we can get you on the road before noon."

"But the mule is lame!" Laura exclaimed.

Mrs. Canby exchanged a glance with Juan, whose expression remained unreadable. "He is much better lately," she said. "My only worry is that he will not be able draw the carriage fast enough to catch up to the army."

"I'll buy another mule, then, if one is to be had." Laura tried not to let her rising hopes carry her away. It would be a difficult journey, she knew. Difficult, but now possible, thanks to Mrs. Canby and to Juan.

"If the señorita permits, I will make inquiries," Juan offered. "I do not know if a mule can be purchased, but perhaps one can be leased."

"Thank you, Juan!" Laura said. "You are much too kind to me, both of you," she added, jumping up to grasp Mrs. Canby's hand. "May I at least pay you for the use of your carriage?"

"Hush. Go to bed. We have been talking much too late. Good night, my dear." Mrs. Canby embraced Laura. "I shall retire presently. I have something to ask María. Good night, Juan."

"Good night," Laura called after her. She turned to Juan, who had picked up the poker and was pulling apart the fire he'd just built.

"I cannot thank you enough, Juan," she said.

He straightened, a smile deepening the creases in his face. "You are welcome, señorita," he said kindly. "We will do our best to make you comfortable on the journey."

On impulse, she reached out a hand to him, which he gravely clasped. "Thank you," she said again. Smiling, she left the room, thanking God for her great good fortune.

O'Brien sat as close to the tiny fire as he could without hindering Shaunessy from stirring the coffeepot. They ought not to have a fire at all, but with himself and Shaunessy and Denning around it, the little flame wouldn't be seen by the enemy. The coffee smelled good. O'Brien was tired, having got little sleep in the few weary hours since they'd come here. The sky was lightening behind them, the Texans' camp-fires had all burned down to ashes, and the hacienda had fallen silent and dark. Doubtless the Rebel officers had made free with the governor's wine cellar until it was empty, and were now sleeping off the effects.

"The war trump has sounded, our rights are in danger; shall the brave sons of Erin be deaf to the call?" Shaunessy sang softly, barely above a whisper. "When freedom demands of both native and stranger, their aid, lest the greatest of nations should fall?"

He stopped stirring and leaned forward to peer into the pot. "Not quite ready," he said.

A blast of cannon-fire split the quiet morning. O'Brien glanced up. "There goes Chivington's surprise attack," he murmured.

Denning, huddled in his great coat across the fire, looked up. "We haven't received any orders, have we?" he asked.

"No. It'll be the Regulars, most like. No glory for us poor Trolls today."

Shaunessy took up the song again.

"Need we fear for our cause, when true hearts uphold it?
See, the men of all nations now march to the wars!
And shall Erin's stout hearts stand by and behold it,
Nor strike in their might for the Banner of Stars?"

O'Brien stood up and climbed the small hill behind which they'd hidden the fire. Streaks of cloud to the west were tinged red by the coming dawn. Night lingered among the trees around the house and along the river, softening the woods with a dusky haze. Canby had his two big guns from Fort Craig trained on the house where the Texans had danced through the night. A line of infantry stood ready to advance. As O'Brien watched the guns fired again, belching flame and smoke. The Texans, thus rudely awakened, had begun to scramble up and reach for their arms.

From the hilltop O'Brien could see a good distance around. To the south some three miles was the town of Peralta, also full of Texans. His gaze followed the gray swath of cottonwoods northward toward Albuquerque, and encountered movement.

Wishing for field glasses, O'Brien squinted, trying to make out the travelers. More than one vehicle, he knew, from the amount of dust raised. They were coming down the road from Albuquerque, and looked to be heading toward the hacienda. O'Brien's pulse quickened.

"Get the lads up," he called to Denning, scrambling back down the hill. "Boots and saddles!"

Without question Denning rose and went to it while Shaunessy pulled the coffee back from the flames. O'Brien glanced at the pot, but his stomach had tightened down. Instead he went to where the horses were picketed and began saddling his mare.

Shaunessy scrambled after him. "What is it, then?" he asked, taking up the bridle and slipping the bit into the mare's mouth.

"Wagons, I think," O'Brien said, tightening the girth. "Could be a supply train. Get your own saddled up. I'll be back."

O'Brien left him to finish and jogged uphill toward headquarters. He paused to glance again at the little column. There was less dust now, and he could see that it was indeed wagons, with an infantry guard and a handful of cavalry.

Colonel Canby was standing with the guns, dressed in a gray shirt and an old dusty black coat, with a cold cigar clamped in his teeth and his field glasses trained on the approaching column. A handful of officers stood with him. O'Brien arrived at the same time as Chivington, who cast him a dark look before turning to the commander.

"Permission to capture that train, sir," Chivington said crisply.

"Yes," said Canby slowly, lowering the glasses. "Be cautious, Colonel. They have a field howitzer. Take your cavalry, and a company or two of infantry in support."

"My men are saddled up by now, sir," O'Brien offered.

Canby raised an eyebrow. "Very good, captain."

Chivington glowered, then turned to Shoup hovering at his elbow. "Companies E and H, on the double," he said sharply. "They'll support Company F." His eyes flicked to Canby, who stood watching in silence. Chivington's teeth bared as he continued. "And Company I. Assemble north of camp in five minutes." He at once turned away and followed his aide toward the camp, as if not to receive O'Brien's salute, but O'Brien gave it anyway. As he started back toward the horses, his eye caught the colonel's, and Canby gave him a nod.

Thank sweet Mary and Joseph for this chance to make good, O'Brien thought as he broke into a run.

Jamie rode at a gallop to meet the small supply train. Its escort, a company of infantry from the 2nd, parted to let him through. The road was deep in sand, and as he came up with the wagons, he saw that one had foundered, slid partway off the road and stuck at an angle, axle-deep in sand. The drivers had double-teamed it with mules borrowed from another wagon and both teams were straining at the tresses, but the wagon showed no sign of budging.

"Damn it!" Jamie said under his breath. He looked back at the enemy camp, poised north of Connelly's house ready to pounce. They had to have seen the train.

"Get the rest of the wagons together up there," he shouted, waving toward the crest of the road. He urged his mount forward again, to where Charlie Raguet stood leaning against the carriage of one of Major Teel's six-pounders. "You'd better unlimber that gun," Jamie called. "We're going to have company."

As if in answer, the Federal guns fired again. The sound carried clearly through the dry air. Raguet began calling orders to his men, and Jamie turned to Lieutenant Darby, in command of the infantry escort. "I need your men to help free that wagon," he said.

"Not all of them," said Darby, gesturing toward the Federal camp. Horsemen had begun to gather in a milling mass at the near end.

"A dozen, then," Jamie said. "We've got to get that wagon moving." His heart was beating fast as he returned to the trapped vehicle. Better to abandon it and save the others? Except they couldn't afford to lose even one.

A shout from behind him told him it was too late anyway. Turning, he saw a wave of cavalry coming up from the enemy camp.

"Never mind!" he called to the teamsters. "Get your shotguns!" With a muttered curse, he rode back to join Raguet at the gun.

11

"As we galloped across the bottom towards them they fluttered like birds in a snare, and I think had they consulted wisdom would have left the miserable overloaded train and proceeded leisurely to their command."

—Ovando J. Hollister

O'Brien rode hard, with music ringing in his ears, one of Shaunessy's wild tunes. Up the slope toward the train he galloped, and Lieutenant Nelson, in command of F Company, kept pace. Nelson was well enough, if a bit grim. At least he wasn't openly hostile, like some of the others. F and I were the only two mounted companies in the Colorado Volunteers, and they naturally kept somewhat apart from the foot soldiers.

O'Brien found himself edging ahead. The mare ran well—sure, he'd like to race her, if he could find some weightless lad to mount her. Such thoughts flicked through his mind as he stared at the train ahead, until they were shattered by the blast of the cannon.

The mare hitched, but ran on. Other horses behaved not so well. O'Brien turned, and saw his company faltering. "Come on, lads!" he cried. "You've ridden at a cannon before!"

Not uphill, his mind answered. The horses are tired.

Nelson's fellows were faring no better. Another blast and a volley of rifle fire from the train's guard brought them to a standstill. Nothing for it but to finish it on foot.

"Dismount!" O'Brien shouted, and led the way by getting off his mare. She snorted and stood trembling, but allowed him to lead her out of the road. He handed her reins to McGuire and waited while the lads lined themselves up, muskets ready. Nelson followed suit, and O'Brien stepped over to him.

"Once we're up to that tree we can charge them. They'll have to surrender," he said.

Nelson nodded. "Unless they drive off."

"They'd have to turn all their wagons, and there isn't room in the road. No, we've got them. Let's get to it."

The snap of a rifle was chased by a minié ball's whine. "We're too tempting a target," O'Brien said, and moved away from the lieutenant. He gave out his orders, drew his saber, and signaled for the line to advance. As he strode steadily uphill, Shaunessy's voice rose up in song down the line:

"God prosper the bold hearts on both land and ocean,
Who go in defiance of danger and scars,
And send them safe home to their wives and their
sweethearts,
With the Harp of old Erin and Banner of Stars!"

O'Brien grinned. He kept his eyes on the cannon, and when he saw it flash, shouted, "Down!" The lads dropped to the ground to let the shot fly over them. Once, twice more they lay down, for the gun or the volleys of the escort. The smell of powder burned in O'Brien's nostrils. When they rose again, one of Nelson's men didn't get up.

They were close now. With a glance toward Nelson, O'Brien held his saber aloft. "Company, halt!" he ordered. "Ready, aim, fire!"

The muskets sounded as one, and the crack of the volley echoed off the hills. As the smoke cleared, O'Brien saw that some of the wagon guard had run. "Charge!" he shouted, swinging the saber 'round his head, and the lads roared behind him and ran up the slope toward the wagons.

"No," Jamie whispered as he watched the mass of men surge toward them. There were too many. The teamsters broke and ran; Jamie got behind them, whipping at the ones he could reach, but it was too late. Half of them had already disappeared into the sand hills. He saw one of the infantry guards sheltering beneath a wagon, tying a dirty handkerchief to his ramrod. Some of the artillerymen had fled, too. Raguet was loading the gun with his own hands.

"Charlie!" Jamie called, but Raguet didn't hear.

The Yankees were almost on them. Jamie saw the captain's saber glint in the first rays of sunlight spilling over the mountains, and in that same moment he recognized the man—it was the Irishman, the one who'd captured him at Cañoncito and burned the train. Shock washed through him, followed by rage.

"No, God damn it!" Jamie said under his breath. "Not again!" He would not be taken again, especially by that one. "Hyah!" he called to his horse, whipping it forward with the reins, into the melee.

Raguet was down to two men on his crew and was sponging the gun when Jamie reached him. "Charlie! It's too late," Jamie called, reaching a hand down to him.

Raguet raised his head, frowning furiously. He glanced over his shoulder, and with a bitter look he dropped the sponge and grabbed Jamie's hand, catching hold of the saddle to haul himself up. A shot whined toward them and the horse screamed, the two sounds uniting into a hellish shriek that made Jamie flinch before they were absorbed in the roaring crash of collision between the two small forces. Jamie glimpsed Lieutenant Darby out of the corner of his eye, aiming a pistol point-blank at the attackers, then disappearing behind a wave of blue.

Raguet was up. On their right a Yankee was trying to grab Jamie's reins. Jamie kicked at him and backed the horse away, hooves scrambling in the sand. As they turned, Jamie's glance found the Irishman's. Hate poured through his eyes toward the enemy in the instant before he spurred away toward the river.

The animal was worn down, and Jamie knew it shouldn't be carrying two. He had to keep whipping it to make it run. The hair prickled on the back of his neck and he hoped to God he was not being pursued.

Not a prisoner. Not again. Please, Jesus God.

He wove in and out of the hills, angling away from the road and keeping out of sight as much as he could so as not to provide any Yankee guns with a target. He let the horse drop to a trot when he came into the bosque, and realized he was out of breath. He inhaled deeply and blew it out in a long sigh, trying to slow his thundering heart.

"Anyone behind us?" he asked Raguet.

"No. I've been watching."

A few flakes of snow drifted among the naked branches. They were too far away to hear the noise up at the train; here it was strangely quiet, almost peaceful. The Río glided silently by, a water road urging them ever homeward, flecks of white floating on its muddy surface.

Governor Connelly's residence was visible up ahead through the woods. Jamie rode toward the house, tallying up the losses in his head. Seven wagons and their contents—commissary and quartermaster stores—eighty mules, the cannon, and who knew how many casualties. A couple killed, at least, and Lord knew how many prisoners. A minor disaster, brought about by that damned Irishman. Next time he saw him, he'd kill him.

That was a cold-blooded thought. Surprised at himself, Jamie realized he meant it. Out of all this confusion, an enemy had emerged whom he could truly hate. He didn't recall ever wanting to hate someone before.

They reached the fields around the house, and since the horse couldn't jump the adobe walls carrying two, Jamie let it walk and mused about the anger that was so strong in him. It hadn't been that way when he'd left San Antonio. He hadn't been angry at all, just excited, and maybe a little nervous. Where had this fury come from? Valverde? Cañoncito? Friends lost, supplies lost, wounds to his person and his vanity, or was it all of that together? Sometimes he felt so black inside it was like he'd never be good for anything but getting even. And that Irishman was the one he most wanted to get even with.

Past the house he could see a group of cavalry—no uniforms, but they came from the Yankee camp—heading toward the village. The Federal guns kept up their thumping, and occasionally a line of infantry would fire a harmless volley toward the men of the 2nd entrenched behind the adobe walls around the hacienda and the fields surrounding the town.

Jamie reined to a halt in front of the house, and Colonel Green came out of it as he and Raguet dismounted. The horse stood with its nose to the ground, shaking.

"Anything saved?" Green asked.

"No, sir," Jamie said. "The guard ran."

"Well, can't blame them, I guess. Abs sent a goddamn battalion after them," Green said, stepping off the porch. "Your horse is bleeding," he added, and strolled toward the garden wall.

Jamie turned and found Raguet examining a bullet wound high in the horse's right foreleg. The blood had soaked the whole leg and was still flowing. God knew how much it had lost. The horse coughed, and Jamie frowned.

Raguet glanced up at him. "Thank you for getting me out of there."

"You're welcome."

"It wasn't wrong of us to leave, was it?"

Jamie's frown deepened. "No."

A distant boom of cannon sounded to the south. Jamie glanced up, but the village was out of sight, hidden by the trees.

"That's John," Raguet said.

Jamie nodded. Maybe Reily would get his fill of fighting today.

The horse gave a shuddering grunt and collapsed, sprawling on the ground at Jamie's feet. Too far gone to be saved, Jamie knew. He closed his eyes, wishing for the thousandth time that he was home and done with all this.

"Will this do?" Mrs. Canby asked, coming into Laura's room with a small carpetbag.

"Yes, thank you," said Laura. "I haven't much to pack."

"Would you mind taking this to my husband?" Mrs. Canby asked, holding out a letter.

"Of course not," Laura said, accepting it.

"And these are for you. To help allay the tediousness of the journey." Mrs. Canby proffered a small tin. Laura opened it, and found it filled with lemon drops.

"Thank you," she said, smiling, and was surprised by a tear that escaped to slide down her cheek. "Oh, I shall miss you," she said, wiping it away.

"I shall miss you too. I do hope you will come back soon."

"I will." Laura opened the carpetbag to busy back the tears, and laid her few things inside it. She had donned her old black gown again after mending it to the best of her ability, thinking that the less affluent she appeared, the less likely she would be bothered. Beneath her petticoat she also wore the trousers Lieutenant Franklin had procured for her on the march from Las Vegas. They would help keep her warm in the open carriage, and she felt better wearing them, somehow. The green dress she folded carefully and placed in the bag. She kept only a few coins in her purse; the rest of her fortune was hidden in her bodice. She packed the bag with her brushes, a small folio of writing paper, pen and ink, her father's portrait, and her little knife. Finally she placed her pistol carefully along the side, ready to hand. She had not been able to secure any more cartridges, but she had what remained of Lieutenant Franklin's, some dozen rounds, which she tucked into the bottom of the bag.

The clasp closed with a click. Laura put on her cloak, then picked up a large, triangular black shawl like those the native women wore. She had purchased the shawl the previous morning from a native merchant who had just returned to Santa Fé. The shawl would probably be warmer than her bonnet today. Despite hints of approaching spring, the days were still quite chilly, and traveling in Mrs. Canby's open carriage was bound to be somewhat uncomfortable. She draped the shawl over her head—heavy but soft—and wrapped the ends about her throat.

"Well, I suppose I am ready." Laura looked up at Mrs. Canby.

With a smile the lady embraced her tightly. "God be with you, my dear."

"And with you," Laura said. "Thank you for all your kindness."

"You are more than welcome," Mrs. Canby said. "You have been a great help to me, and such good company. I am afraid we shall be very dull and lonely here without you."

The sound of the zaguán gate came through the open window. Laura stepped to it and saw Juan Carlos leading a gray donkey into the placita. "He found one!" she cried, and the two ladies hurried outside.

In the placita Juan Carlos and another native were introducing the donkey to Mrs. Canby's mule. The stranger, a younger man with shining black hair cut in a bowl shape around his head, looked up and flashed Laura a shy smile.

"Señora, señorita," Juan Carlos said, coming forward, "this is Esteban Gutiérrez. The donkey is his."

"Are you willing to sell it?" Laura asked the young man.

Esteban looked to Juan Carlos, who said, "His English is not so good, señorita. He will not sell, but he will lease it as long as he can come along to make sure it isn't taken by the tejanos."

"Do you know him, Juan?" Mrs. Canby asked gently. "Is he trustworthy?"

"He is the son of my brother-in-law's cousin. He is a good boy, un buen hombre. He can help with the driving."

"Excellent," Mrs. Canby said. "When you are ready, Miss Howland's bag is in her room."

"Oh, I will fetch it," Laura said. She smiled awkwardly at Juan Carlos. "It is so kind of you to accompany me, Juan—you need not wait on me as well."

A small smile curved Mrs. Canby's mouth. "Nevertheless, I expect you to look after her as if she were my own daughter," she said to him. "Keep her safe."

Laura felt so near to overflowing she could only smile her thanks, and hastened inside to collect her things.

Hall should have been here, O'Brien thought as he made his way through the mass of frightened mules. The infantry were unhitching them from the wagons, and Nelson's fellows had fallen on the gun and were making the prisoners haul it back to the camp. His own lads had done well—Private Vogel was the company's only real casualty, with a ball that had passed through the meat of his leg, just missing the bone. His mates were carrying him to the surgeon.

O'Brien saw Shaunessy wrapping a bandage around Morris's shoulder. "Are you hit, Thomas?" he called out.

"Just clipped," Morris answered, waving a hand. "I'll do."

O'Brien nodded and turned his attention to where Denning had the lads going through the wagons, pulling out their contents to see what might be worth saving. "Anything good?" he asked, coming up to them.

"Tack and furniture, mostly," Denning said. "Some soap and candles."

"Looks like they unloaded a fair bit before we got to them," Sergeant Rice said, joining them. "Sir," he added belatedly.

O'Brien gave him a sharp look, but detected no insolence. "Well, sort out what's useful and then fire the rest," he ordered.

"Keep the wagons?" Denning asked.

"No. Too much work to dig them out, and we've wagons enough. Keep one or two to haul with, and burn the rest where they stand."

A half-strangled yelp came hard on these words, and O'Brien raised his head. "What was that?"

"Dog?" Rice suggested.

O'Brien shook his head. It had come from the wagons, he thought. Frowning, he stepped over to the nearest, and began poking about among a jumble of saddles, blankets, and furniture. It was all tossed in willy-nilly, and he was about to give it up when he noticed a blanket shaking in one corner of the wagon bed. Stepping closer, he reached in and flicked it aside.

"Hoh!" cried a voice from beneath it, and in spite of himself O'Brien jumped. He leveled his pistol at the form curled in amongst the gear. The face that looked up at him was a Negro's, set in a mask of fear.

"Don't shoot!" the man cried. "For God Amity's sake don't shoot! I'm just Massa's nigger, I can't help what they doin'!"

O'Brien frowned, blinking. "Get out of there," he ordered, holding his weapon steady.

"Yessir! Yessir, I get out. Here I come. Don't be shootin', now!"

The figure that climbed out of the wagon was tall and thin, with eyes that stared like a frightened deer's. He stood trembling, holding his large, pale-palmed hands in the air. He looked much the same as the Negroes O'Brien had seen in New York, only thinner and dirtier from campaigning. O'Brien had lost a good job as a teamster to a Negro who'd work for half the pay.

"What have we here?" Denning said, grinning. "Looks like you've captured some contraband, Captain."

O'Brien holstered his pistol. "Get your things and get out of the way," he said to the slave.

A smile broke across the man's face. "Lord bless you, Cap'n sir, I ain't got no things!"

"Then move away, boyo!" Annoyed, O'Brien made a show of searching in the wagon for anything else that might be of use. Tucked down into one corner was an oddly shaped block of polished wood. He reached for it, and found himself holding a clock, shaped like a pointed arch, with a round, white face behind a little glass door. Its numbers were made of letters the Roman way, as they were on the fine watch that Franklin had given him. Miss Howland had taught him how to read them. The clock's hands had stopped at twenty past five.

Swallowing the sudden tightness in his throat, he tucked the clock under his arm. Such a thing shouldn't be burnt. It was a gentleman's thing, clearly.

He turned to Denning. "Finish up here and get the lads back to camp. I'm off to report."

Denning nodded. O'Brien's gaze fell on the Negro, who had climbed up the hill a short way and sat watching, his hands clasped together between his knees. Maybe the fellow would run off, O'Brien hoped. He turned away and sought out Morris, still standing with Shaunessy.

"Best have the surgeon take a look at that, Thomas."

"It's the merest scratch," Morris said.

"If you don't they'll be saying I don't take good care of my men. I'll go with you."

"Damned gossipy bastards," Shaunessy said. "You should pay them no heed!"

"I don't. Take this to my tent," he added, handing the clock to Shaunessy. Something inside it clanked softly. "Be careful with it," O'Brien added.

"Pretty," Shaunessy said, then he grinned. "Finders keepers, eh? It'll bring a good price."

The three of them returned to where the holders were waiting with the horses, and O'Brien swung into his saddle, paused for the others to mount, then started for the camp at a trot. He felt no great elation, which he considered a bit of a puzzle, seeing as how he'd just helped capture a wagon train and perhaps cleared a bit of the mud from his name. He frowned. It was that Texan, the scrap of a fellow he'd noticed, the same one he'd caught at Cañoncito. Seemed the lad didn't care to be captured today. O'Brien was surprised to find him alive, for he'd left him half dead at Mrs Canby's doorstep—and now he realized the cause of his dissatisfaction. The last time he'd seen that fellow was the last time he'd seen Miss Howland. He'd taken them both to Santa Fé in a wagon and left them both there.

He found he was clenching his teeth, and with an effort forced himself to relax. No use mooning over what could never have been anyway. She'd been kind to him and he'd misunderstood her kindness, and made a great fool of himself. Now it was over and best to move on.

As they came into the camp they were greeted by the sound of an infantry volley. O'Brien spied Colonel Canby in the middle of a cluster of officers, watching the house from behind a mud wall. He had a couple of companies firing at it, in between rounds from the big twenty-four pounders. The Texans fired back in the same lackadaisical way. There was time, O'Brien judged, to visit the surgeon before he must go to report. He and Morris dismounted.

"Give her some water." O'Brien told Shaunessy, handing him the mare's reins. "I'll see you back at camp."

He hurried Morris to the surgeon's tent where they found Vogel waiting to be tended, sitting on the ground outside, sheltered from the sun by the canvas fly. A few of Nelson's fellows were there as well. Inside the tent the surgeon was busy over the worst hurt of them.

O'Brien stepped over to Vogel, a small, dark-haired fellow, who lay propped against a knapsack, looking pale. Some friend had tied a tourniquet 'round his leg just above the wound. He looked up at O'Brien with a shaky smile.

"Well, you'll have a story to tell the Denver ladies," O'Brien said, squatting beside him.

Vogel laughed, then winced. He was one of the younger men in the company, not much over twenty.

"How bad is it, lad?" O'Brien asked softly.

"Oh, it doesn't hurt so much," Vogel said. "I feel pretty light-headed, though."

O'Brien thought of his silver flask—Hall's gift—empty for days now, lying uselessly in his breast pocket. "Thomas," he said, glancing up. "Have you got any liquor?"

"I have." Morris reached into his pocket and handed a small bottle down to Vogel, who took one deep pull at it, then offered it back.

"Thanks, Sarge," Vogel said.

"Keep it. You need it more than I do. Especially when that bone-cracker gets hold of you."

Vogel gave a broken laugh, said "Thanks" again, and rubbed at his face.

He's afraid, O'Brien realized. Not knowing what to say to ease him, he reached out a hand and gripped the lad's shoulder. The eyes Vogel turned to him seemed very young, very lost.

"You'll be fine," O'Brien told him. "Just sore for a while."

Vogel nodded, and a smile flashed across his face. It faded too quickly.

"Captain! There you are! I've been searching all over."

O'Brien looked up to see Ramsey standing outside, peering under the tent fly. "Colonel Chivington wants your report," Ramsey added. "On the double, he said."

O'Brien bit back a sharp response and stood. "Stay with him," he said softly to Morris, who nodded.

"Thank you, Captain," Vogel said, reaching up.

O'Brien looked down at him, squeezed his hand and nodded, then followed Ramsey off toward the cluster of officers around Colonel Canby.

"Late, Mr. O'Brien," Chivington said as he came up.

"I was on my way, sir. Just stopped to look in on the wounded."

Lieutenant Nelson, standing nearby, looked up sharply at this. O'Brien gave him a nod. "The surgeon's working on your man Hawley," he said. Nelson's gaze flicked toward the surgeon's tent, then to the ground at his feet.

"I am waiting on your report, Captain," Chivington said. "We have orders to advance."

"To flank," Colonel Canby corrected quietly, without taking the field glasses from his eyes.

"Sorry, sir," O'Brien said. "I've lost one man wounded, and one with a flesh wound. None missing."

"Very well. Bring your company up in the rear of that column," Chivington said, pointing northward to where they'd assembled before attacking the train. Most of the Pet Lambs were already there, O'Brien saw.

"Remember, Colonel," Canby said, "you are not to attack. Force them out of the house and grounds, but do not bring on an engagement."

Chivington's brows drew together. "I urge you to reconsider, sir," he said. "We can take them!"

"I've no doubt you can. What do you propose I do with them once they are taken?" Canby handed his field glasses to an aide and turned to face Chivington, his gray eyes cool and hard. "I cannot feed two thousand prisoners. Fort Craig is on half-rations already."

"Because the Texans are between us and them!" Chivington said. "Once we crush them, we can get supplies through."

"Let me disabuse you of the notion that we have endless supplies, Colonel Chivington. This campaign has severely depleted our stores, and disrupted the planting season as well. This Territory is in for a difficult year."

"You cannot intend simply to let them go back to Texas!"

"What would you have me do? Slay them all?"

Chivington stared at the commander, his brow furrowed in a frown of frustration. O'Brien looked from one to the other, their gazes locked in a silent test of will. Canby was the smaller, less passionate, less imposing—and immovable as stone. If anyone could break Chivington, O'Brien decided, it was he.

"Colonel Paul," Canby said, without shifting his gaze, "you will lead your column around to the north of the hacienda. Colonel Chivington's column will follow through the woods and toward the river. Force the Texans out of the town, and prevent their being reinforced."

"Yes, sir," said Paul. He cast a glare at Chivington, his pointed beard moving as he worked his jaw, then he stalked away.

"If you let them go," Chivington said, his deep voice vibrant with passion, "they will return to haunt us. Here, or in Virginia. They will not stop until they are made to stop!"

"That is a risk we shall have to endure," Canby said.

O'Brien nodded. The movement attracted Chivington's attention, who turned on him, furious.

"What are you waiting for?" Chivington snapped. "Get your men in the column! You've delayed us already!"

O'Brien clamped his jaw shut and saluted before turning away. Ramsey was right behind him—had seen and heard all, no doubt. O'Brien set off at a jog, leapt a ditch filled with water and a low adobe wall bordering a cornfield, then increased to a run indulging a hope that the short-legged lawyer would have trouble keeping up.

"Can you see anything?" Raguet called from the street.

Jamie squinted beneath his hat brim and peered at the trees north of town. The view from Peralta's church tower was good; he didn't need to borrow the lookout's glass to see there was some kind of movement to the north, beyond Connelly's hacienda, screened by the swath of cottonwoods beyond the bordered fields. On the hillside above, the wagons they had lost that morning were on fire, wraiths of Cañoncito rising in the smoke. Jamie looked away, swallowing the bitter taste in his mouth. He scrambled down the narrow stairs and emerged onto the town's main street, where Raguet was waiting with Lieutenant Fulcrod, who commanded a battery attached to Green's regiment.

"They're moving through the woods," Jamie said. "To the left."

"That's where I'm headed," Fulcrod said, nodding. "Care to join me?"

Raguet looked at Jamie with an eyebrow cocked. "Might as well."

Jamie felt uneasy, but said, "For a little while."

They strode along beside Fulcrod's guns, into the bosque west of town. The Yankees were trying to cut them off from the river, but Colonel Green had anticipated them thanks to the lookouts in the church tower. Major Pyron already had skirmishers in among the trees, waiting for targets. Jamie watched Fulcrod choose the best ground for his battery, with Raguet making suggestions.

A distant sound—a rattling, rumbling, crunching of many men passing through the woods—told of the enemy's approach. The back of Jamie's neck began to tingle. A dull report echoed among the woods and a cannonball bounced past to the left of the battery. Fulcrod's men fired an answering round, and the smell of powder rose up to cling among the tree branches. They were bare like the branches at Valverde had been. Suddenly Jamie felt an urge to run— back to the town, down the river—anything to get away from the closeness under the trees and the approaching enemy. Instead he stood where he was, just behind the battery, and checked his pistol with hands that wouldn't stop shaking.

He could go, he realized. He had not been ordered here. He could go with impunity, back down to Los Lunas to check on the train. He *should* go, in fact, but his feet were rooted to the ground and he couldn't take his eyes from the artillerymen. *They* had no choice but to stay and face the ordeal. He squinted through the smoke in an effort to see the coming enemy, but saw only shadows. His gaze flicked to the cannoneers smoothly loading their guns, no time to be worried or afraid. The tubes gleamed dully through the smoke. Jamie crossed a dozen paces of ground to stand with Fulcrod and Raguet, right between the two guns, where he could watch both crews and keep an eye on the enemy. Raguet greeted him with a fleeting smile, which he returned. This felt different, he realized, faintly surprised. At Valverde, he had been among the foot soldiers charging the cannon. Now he was on the other side.

A distant crunching of feet through the forest heralded the coming of the bluecoats. The gun to his right let forth a blast of orange flame and smoke, making Jamie's heart lurch, then thump wildly. He stood his ground, grip tightening on the hilt of his pistol as the Yankees came on.

*   *   *

It was past midday, the sun riding high in a hot blue sky, and most of O'Brien's men still hadn't eaten. Company F had caught and killed some of the Texans' beeves the night before and a few of the Trolls had got some of the meat, but most hadn't had but the coffee they'd brewed around dawn. O'Brien's stomach grumbled at the reminder as they moved slowly toward the woods. The companies ahead were deploying to either side of the artillery battery, which had stopped to fire at the Texans. Rebel guns answered, and the infantry seemed to be anxious for the shelter of tree trunks.

A sharp breeze picked up out of the west, drying O'Brien's mouth. He took a pull from his half-empty canteen and glanced up at the sky, where long, high streaks of thin clouds ran toward the mountains.

Shaunessy sidled his horse up to O'Brien's. "Think we'll have a fight?" he asked.

"No." O'Brien shook his head. "Not today."

"Canby doesn't want to fight," Ramsey said from nearby.

O'Brien turned in the saddle to glare at the lieutenant. "He never said that. Only that he wanted no prisoners."

"He wants to let them go back to Texas," Ramsey said.

"And you heard his reasons."

"His excuses, you mean. He's a coward."

O'Brien took one deep breath and let it out before answering. "How long have you been in the army, Hugh Ramsey?" he asked. "Colonel Canby has served since before the Mexican War. I wonder if he might know just a wee bit more about soldiering than ourselves."

"Cowards can come from anywhere," Ramsey said. "Even West Point."

Ahead of them, F Company began to advance again, putting an end to discussion. They moved westward, with both sun and wind in their eyes. O'Brien squinted to keep out the worst of the dust. There was plenty of it, with themselves in the rear of the column. He found himself thinking more fondly of Irish mud than he ever remembered doing before.

At last they were into the trees and sheltered somewhat from the wind. Chivington had the two mounted companies draw up in support of the battery. Standing in line, mounted, was not quite the most comfortable spot when the enemy was flinging cannonballs. A spent round shot rolled past, at which the mare expressed her dissatisfaction. O'Brien stroked her neck.

"There, lass. It won't hurt you."

"Alastar?" Shaunessy said softly beside him.

O'Brien glanced up.

"Is Canby really a coward?"

"I don't think so," O'Brien said. "He's cautious. Doesn't want to waste lives."

"Well, thank God for that!" Shaunessy grinned. "I don't want my life wasted."

"Ah, you'll waste it yourself in some tavern."

"Some tavern with women," Shaunessy agreed, and sighed dreamily.

O'Brien laughed and shook his head. A horseman galloped toward them and skittered to a stop. "Colonel Chivington's orders are to countermarch and advance eastward in column," he said breathlessly.

"Thank you," O'Brien said, and the aide wheeled and sped off.

The artillery had limbered up and were already moving, with half the infantry ahead and the other half falling in behind them. The Texan guns still spat at them while the mounted troops waited to move. At least it was solid shot, O'Brien thought. They must have run out of shells. If this was all it was to be today, it might almost be pleasant.

At last F Company went into the column, and O'Brien signaled to his men to fall in. Shaunessy hummed "Molly Durkin" as they moved into place.

One more crash of the guns was followed by a shriek that grew louder. O'Brien glanced up but couldn't see the coming shot. His grip tightened on the mare's reins, then a horrid smack sounded beside him and Shaunessy flew from his horse.

12

"Egan!" O'Brien cried.

Shaunessy's mount reared and whinnied, then ran off through the woods. Shaunessy lay still on the ground, his blood slowly darkening the earth beneath his left shoulder, or what remained of it, crushed by the shot.

A scramble of hoofbeats, and Morris was there, staring down at their friend in disbelief. Others started to draw near, and Morris made to dismount.

"No!" O'Brien shouted. His throat was so tight he could barely draw breath to give the orders. "Keep your ranks! Move along!"

Morris cast him an accusing look, then returned to his place in the column. O'Brien turned the mare away, back to the head of the company, leading them on. His eyes stung. He had to keep blinking to stop them from spilling over. He kept seeing Shaunessy lying there, silenced. Someone would see to him, but his own duty was clear; those who fell in the ranks were to be left. Sound men could not be spared to tend the wounded. It was policy. Policy dictated he must turn his back on his friend.

The wind increased to spin howling and moaning among the trees, carrying with it a stinging flail of sand. O'Brien hunched in his saddle, trying to protect his face from the onslaught. A heavy ache filled his chest; he coughed, but could not clear it off. The column advanced at a slow walk, and the air became so filled with dust that he could scarcely see F Company's horses before him. He silently cursed the wind, the dust, and the army with all of its rules.

My friend is back there, alone. Dying.

The fighting had shifted again. The column that had been advancing toward Fulcrod moved elsewhere, leaving the guns to exchange compliments with the Yankee artillery. Jamie was oddly disappointed at the aversion of a head-on conflict. It made him feel restless, as if he had unfinished business.

"I'd better go check on the train," he told Raguet, who nodded.

"I'll stay," Raguet said. "If you see John, let him know where I am."

Jamie scrounged a mule and rode into Peralta, where lookouts had been stationed in the church tower to observe the enemy troop movements. He found the tower abandoned, marred by a dent where a Yankee cannonball had struck it. He didn't bother to climb up, but stood in the street at the church door and watched the brown billows of dust wash across the river from the west. Even as he looked they obscured his view of Connelly's hacienda, turning the world into a swirling brown cloud. There could be no serious fighting in this. Relief and disappointment went through him, followed by a tickling worry over the train. He paused to tie his bandanna over his nose and mouth, then managed to goad his unenthusiastic mule into a trot, and reached Los Lunas within half an hour. Nervous pickets challenged him but let him pass when he showed his face. He found the supply train secure, and hurried to Sibley's headquarters, which he'd set up the day before in the parlor of the Luna home, the largest house in the village.

"News?" General Sibley demanded, before Jamie had a chance to shut the door against the howling wind. The general sat at a heavy, round table on which lay a map and a scatter of papers. With him was Major Teel, the artillery commander, smoking his pipe. Owens lounged on the banco, eating pecans. A scatter of broken shells lay at his feet.

A fire crackled on the hearth. Jamie sighed, and pulled

down his bandanna. "I think we'll have to quit, sir. It's blowing dust like nobody's business."

General Sibley looked up from the papers, his forehead creased with a frown. "Scurry got through, didn't he?"

"I don't know," Jamie said. "I think so."

"We tried to cross over, but their damned pickets fired on us." The general glared down at his map.

"We lost the train from Albuquerque," Jamie said.

"Yes, I know. Doesn't matter, we need to lighten our load anyway. Come look at this."

Jamie joined him and peered at the map. His eyes were still adjusting to the dimness of the room. He rubbed at them to clear the dust away.

"What do you think?" the general asked.

Think? I'm too tired to think.

Jamie stared at the map, trying to figure out what the general wanted him to say. They were eighty miles or so above Fort Craig, perhaps fifty above Socorro, where they'd left a makeshift hospital full of wounded from Valverde. He wondered wistfully if anything remained of the stores of flour he'd left for the hospital.

"You see?" Sibley said, poking Teel in the shoulder. "We'll make it through."

"You haven't given him a chance to answer," Teel said.

Jamie glanced at the major, who raised an eyebrow at him and continued to puff on his pipe. He felt as if he were in school, being quizzed by the teacher over something everyone else thought was obvious. He looked back at the map, searching for the answer to the puzzle.

The Río was high with runoff from the snow melting in the mountains, so the ford at Valverde would be hard to cross. Jamie frowned. They might not want to get that close to Fort Craig anyway.

"How many men are in Fort Craig?" he asked.

"Exactly!" Teel slapped a hand down on the table. "It's a trap, I tell you!" he said to the general.

Sibley straightened, his lips pressed together in displeasure. "We can make it," he insisted. "They won't come out of the fort."

"Oh, they won't? Not even when Canby has us bottled up in that narrows?"

Jamie looked harder at the map and began to see what Teel meant; north of Soccoro the mountains closed in toward the road and the river, making a bottleneck around about Polvadera, where the army had camped on the way up. If Canby continued to pursue them, he might easily capture them there. The only way to avoid the trap was to leave the road.

Jamie closed his eyes. He was so tired. He didn't want to think about trying to move the army through open desert.

"Canby didn't attack us here," Sibley said. "He won't do it there either." The general ended the discussion by rolling up the map, and turned to Jamie. "Cross all the troops to this side of the river, and bring Green's men down here. I want us all together."

"Yes, sir."

"Have the men keep their blankets and cooking gear and a spare suit of clothes. Destroy all the rest."

Jamie glanced up. The general was still frowning, half worried, half determined. "We'll get through there before Canby knows we've left camp," he said.

Jamie nodded, concealing a sigh as he turned to face the dust again. He pushed his hair back from his forehead and put on his hat. Glancing back from the doorway, he saw Owens watching him, chewing a pecan. He turned away, and drew a deep breath before stepping back into the storm.

The fighting had been called off on account of the blowing dust. O'Brien kept his back to the wind as he and Morris dug out a grave at the foot of a hill. The storm had settled in for a long stay, and the Pike's Peakers had gone into camp, finally getting their breakfast along with a generous helping of sand. The wind seemed to sap the strength from O'Brien's limbs. It taunted him, blowing sand back into the grave near as fast as he scraped it out.

Shaunessy had died before they could get him to the surgeon. Maybe he'd died right away. O'Brien hoped so. He hated to think of poor Egan lying on the ground, helpless while his life's blood flowed out of him and his friends rode away. It made him angry, and he silently cursed as he stabbed at the ground with his shovel.

"Here they come," Morris said, pausing to look toward the camp. Through the dust a small party appeared, led by Denning, and bearing a litter. O'Brien looked away.

"Damn this wind," he said, wiping the back of his hand across his eyes. He went back to digging. The grave must be deep, so that every cursed wild animal in this godforsaken country wouldn't try to get at it.

"May I take a turn, Captain?" Kimmick asked as he came up.

O'Brien looked up at the sergeant, one of the original Trolls from Avery, an old friend of Shaunessy's. His eyes were dark with sorrow. With a nod O'Brien handed him the shovel and stepped up out of the grave, standing back to watch. He was weary all of a sudden. His shoulders ached.

Others came up the hill to join them: Evans, Carter, McCraw, Ryan and Quinn, and McGuire with his fiddle— all old friends—and a few of the newer lads. Sergeant Rice had come, and immediately wrested the shovel from Morris. Newsom and Langston were there also. It was good of them, O'Brien thought, to leave what small comfort there was in the camp and trudge up here to pay last respects. Ramsey was absent, to no one's surprise, and none of his cronies save Rice had bestirred themselves. Good, O'Brien thought. Better it should be only true friends.

At last the grave was finished, and the lads gently lowered Shaunessy in. He'd an army blanket for his shroud, and only McGuire's mournful violin to play him up to heaven. The fiddle sounded thin in the wind, and ceased altogether when the body lay at rest. The lads turned as one to O'Brien.

They're expecting me to pray, he realized, gazing over their faces. How can I pray, when instead I'd like to curse heaven itself for taking my friend from me?

He looked down at the poor, bundled body, and swallowed, trying to moisten his throat. "Dear God," he began, but his voice cracked upon the words, and he cast a beseeching glance at Denning, who gave a nod and stepped forward.

"Dear Lord," Denning said. "Receive our brother Egan Shaunessy into your kingdom this day with all blessings. Let him sit at your right hand, and know that he is remembered by his friends and comrades here gathered. As he gave his life in the service of his country, so his name shall be written in the glory rolls and honored henceforward forever. Amen."

"Amen," O'Brien murmured along with the others.

McCraw and Newsom took up the shovels, and the rest stood 'round while they filled in the grave. McGuire played the "Parting Glass," and O'Brien and the lads sang softly along:

> *"Oh, all the comrades that e'er I had,*
> *They're sorry for my going away,*
> *And all the sweethearts that e'er I had,*
> *They'd wish me one more day to stay.*
> *But since it falls unto my lot*
> *That I should rise and you should not,*
> *I'll gently rise, and softly call,*
> *Good night, and joy be with you all."*

Denning had somehow acquired a bottle of Mexican brandy, which the lads passed around until it was gone. The last drop was poured over the grave, and Carter set up a board onto which he'd scratched Egan's name and the date and a little cross. O'Brien stood staring at it, thinking how soon it would be gone in this hard country. First the wind would blast the letters from it, then the sun would crack it and a winter or two would melt it into splinters. After that there would be nothing left of poor Egan, nothing but memories of his laughing face and his wild songs.

One by one the lads drifted away, back to camp. Rice took up the shovels and carried them off. Morris and Denning remained, standing silently with O'Brien until the others were all gone away. Morris spoke up, his voice rough from the wind.

"Don't be blaming yourself, Alastar. I know you. It's none of your fault."

"Damn you, Thomas," O'Brien said, wiping away the tear that had escaped to run down his cheek. "We should never have come here."

"If we hadn't the Texans would be in Fort Union by now," Denning said.

"I must have been mad," O'Brien said, shaking his head. "I was thinking it was all a grand adventure. What a bur-raidh."

"No," Morris said. "We all thought so. We came of our own free will. Egan as much as the others."

"Damn the gunner that sent that ball into him!" O'Brien's voice cracked again. He squatted by the grave and covered his face with his hands. After a moment Morris knelt beside him and threw an arm across his shoulder.

"Come away, Alastar. Come to the wake."

O'Brien looked up at him. The sun had broken through the dust and set the air afire, slanting red-gold across the hills, casting long shadows over the fresh-made grave.

"Aye," O'Brien said. He stood, and gazed down at Shaunessy's name on the board. With a nod of farewell, he followed the others away.

It was dusk by the time Laura's party reached the rancho in La Cienega where Juan Carlos had said they would spend the first night. Laura sighed as she stepped down from the carriage. The ride had been somewhat dull but, despite the sharp air, not nearly so uncomfortable as her journey to New Mexico by mail coach a year ago. Mrs. Canby's carriage, though open, had a stout leather top and a wide, comfortable seat which was more than enough room for herself and María. Laura silently blessed Mrs. Canby again for her generosity.

The rancho, called "Las Golondrinas" which María informed Laura meant "the swallows," was hidden away in a tiny valley shaded by cottonwoods overhanging a whispering stream. The house was on level ground, but a short distance to the south the ground sloped gently, then fell away down to fields just showing green with new crops. Laura strolled toward them to ease the cramps out of her legs. Gazing downhill toward the field, she saw a silvery glimmer spreading through the furrows, setting the whole field magically alight. As she watched, the silver turned to gold in the sunset, and Laura realized it was water. She followed a cart track down the hill a few paces, and spied a ditch—an acequia, as María had called similar ditches they had crossed—which was the source of the water flooding the field. The acequia burbled across the slope to feed a little mill tucked against the hillside. Evening wrapped the building in shadows, blurring its lines into masses of blue-gray and pale, glowing white.

"Señorita," Juan Carlos called from behind her. "Please come in now. The supper is ready."

Laura turned and saw him standing atop the hill. Behind him light glowed golden through the windows of the ranch house. It was already dark beneath the trees.

"Thank you," she said, and followed him into the house. Their host, a small, stocky man with immensely strong arms, came up to her and bowed.

"Señorita Howland, this is Señor Baca," Juan told her.

"How do you do?" Laura said, curtseying slightly.

"¡Bienvenidos, welcome! You are family of el Capitán Howland?" Baca asked.

"A cousin," Laura replied. In these troubled times she was not above claiming the captain as such, however distant their true relationship might be. She doubted he would object.

"Bien, bien," said their host. "We will take good care of you, eh? El capitán, he has been here many times."

He led her to a table where Esteban and a couple of other native men were already seated. Juan joined them, and María emerged from the kitchen with Señora Baca, carrying plates heaped with food. The supper was simple: mutton stewed with red chiles and onions, fresh tortillas, and a rough red wine that had been made in Bernalillo, a town farther south on the old Camino Real. The chiles were so hot they made Laura's eyes water, but by taking bites of tortilla between bites of stew she was able to eat most of her portion. The men at the table talked quietly in Spanish, and she listened, catching a word here and there but not really enough to understand their conversation. After a time Señor Baca gave her a sidelong glance, and addressed Juan Carlos in English.

"How far are you going, Señor Díaz?"

"To Lemitar," Juan replied.

"Eh, you will run into the tejanos! They left Albuquerque

only a few days ago." Señor Baca raised an eyebrow as he said this, and glanced again toward Laura. Perhaps he was trying to frighten her, she thought with amusement.

"I am already acquainted with the tejanos, señor," she replied. "I helped care for their wounded in Santa Fé."

"Eh, but you have not seen them in a battle, I think?"

She had, in fact, but she remained silent. She did not care to discuss her presence in Pigeon's Ranch, the eye of the storm, during the Battle of Glorieta Pass.

"They were in a battle at Albuquerque a few days ago," Señor Baca continued.

"They were?" Laura glanced up sharply at their host. "How many casualties? Was the Colorado regiment involved?"

"I don't know very much about it," he said. "Some cannons fired into the plaza, and the tejanos fired their cannons back. One of the balls hit the wall of my nephew's house. The next day the tejanos packed up and left."

"I see," Laura said, trying to hide her frustration. She looked at Juan Carlos. "Where is our next stop?"

"Algodones," he said.

"How far is that?"

"Twenty miles."

Laura frowned slightly. "Can we drive a little farther than that? We came fifteen miles today, did we not? And we didn't leave until past noon."

Juan looked at her soberly, then spoke to Esteban in Spanish. Esteban, who was seated across the table, glanced up at her with his fine, dark eyes, and shyly looked away. He exchanged a few words with Juan Carlos, then returned his attention to his plate.

"We might be able to reach Bernalillo," Juan said. "It is thirty miles. We will have to see how tired the animals are when we get to Algodones."

"Very well," Laura said, nodding.

"The señorita is in a hurry, sí?" Señor Baca said.

Laura gazed at him, searching for a hint of mockery in his face, but detected none. "Señora Díaz would like to reach her daughter before her baby is born," she replied.

He seemed satisfied with that, and offered to refill her

glass. She accepted, hoping the wine would help her to sleep, for she'd had little rest the night before. The conversation drifted back into Spanish, and Laura listened, trying to catch at least the gist of the words. Señor Baca seemed to be asking Juan Carlos a great many questions, presumably about the battles near Santa Fé and the Texan occupation of the capital. The word "tejanos" figured strongly in their discussion, as did the words "los federales" and "batalla."

At length they rose from the table, and the men took out their tobacco and corn husks, and started toward the door. Laura stopped Juan Carlos on his way outdoors. "May I look at your map?" she asked.

He gazed at her in surprise. "I do not have a map, señorita. I know the way."

"Oh," Laura said, feeling foolish. "I see."

"I have a map," Baca offered. "It is not very new, but you are welcome to look at it."

"Thank you," Laura said, favoring her host with a smile.

Señor Baca went to a small chest that stood against the wall, opened it, and carefully removed an old cigar box, a leather pouch, and a stack of newspapers before producing a yellowed roll of paper. He handed this to Laura and repacked the rest into the chest.

"Thank you, señor," she repeated. She carried the map to the table, which María and Señora Baca had already cleared, and spread it out carefully, holding the edges to keep it from curling up again.

It was not new at all, for it had been made in 1846, the same year that General Kearney had conquered New Mexico. She was startled to see that, on this map, New Mexico was a tiny strip of land running north from Mexico, with the Río Grande as its eastern border. All of the land to the west was designated California, and Texas extended eastward from the river, with Santa Fé shown well within its limits. She found this mildly offensive; however, it was her route down the Río Grande that interested her more than obsolete political boundaries. There were a number of villages marked along the river, but Algodones was not among them, nor was Albuquerque, nor Lemitar. "S. Bernilla," she assumed, was Bernalillo. From La Cienega to Soccoro was about one hundred and fifty miles, a journey of five or six days at the least. The mail coach had traveled as much as forty miles in a day, but it had a team of eight mules. Laura knew they would have to be careful not to overwork their two animals, for replacing them would be next to impossible.

"I would like to make a copy of this, if I may," she said. Looking up, she saw that Señor Baca had left the room, and she was alone. No, not quite alone—for Esteban sat on the banco beside the beehive fireplace. He had been watching her, she thought, but he glanced away when their eyes met.

"¿Tu no avez los cigarillos?" she asked, in what she knew was a mish-mosh of Spanish and French.

Esteban looked up, surprised, and flashed a sudden smile. "No, no me gusta fumar," he said.

Laura smiled, and shook her head. "No entiendo."

"No cigarillos," Esteban said. "Saben mal. Bad," he added, making a face.

"Ah." Laura nodded. "I agree."

She went to her carpetbag, which had been set against the wall, and took out a piece of writing paper. She wished she had thought to acquire a pencil, but pen and ink would do. She carried them to the table and sat down to copy Señor Baca's map.

The map was uncooperative, resisting her attempts to flatten it. Her inkwell was not heavy enough to hold down a corner; also, she feared upsetting the ink onto the map. Nor did she want to use Señora Baca's candlestick as a weight, for fear of dripping wax onto it. She tried holding it down with her left forearm while she drew, with only partial success. She was about to fetch her bag for a weight, when Esteban slid onto the banco opposite her and took hold of the map's top corners.

"Gracias," she said, smiling up at him.

Esteban ducked his head, but she noticed a shy smile. What a nice boy he was. The girl who married him would get a good husband.

She began by sketching the Río Grande, and soon realized she was a poor mapmaker. She had traced the major contours accurately enough, but the lesser ones defeated her. She became lost in the endless small meanderings of the river, and at last she gave up. They might well be important, but Juan Carlos knew the way, and she settled for marking the names of the villages as near to where they should be as she could. Lemitar was just upstream from Soccoro, she knew, so she added that, and drew a question mark south of Soccoro where she thought Fort Craig might be. She straightened, and looked at her handiwork.

How far would she have to travel to reach the army? They had left Albuquerque, and that was all she knew. They did not, as a rule, travel quickly, but if forced marches were called for it would take her some time to catch up to them. Then, too, they might leave the main road and march off across country.

She sighed. She would go to Lemitar, and if they had not yet encountered the army she would see what she could learn there. She glanced up at Esteban, who looked hastily down at the map. Was it foolish of her to make this journey? Was she needlessly inconveniencing these good people?

No, for María truly did wish to see her daughter, and Esteban would be compensated by the money she paid him for the use of his donkey. So she must not kill the donkey by driving it too hard, she thought, smiling to herself.

"Gracias," she said to Esteban, closing her inkwell and setting aside her copy of the map.

"De nada," he answered.

She laid her hands on the map, and after a moment he released it. She smiled up at him as he stood. He nodded, then went away to the fireplace again.

Laura looked over the map, to make sure she had not left out any detail that might be important. She had not sketched the river past "Passo del Norte," but she trusted she would not have to venture so far south.

The map had been made in Philadelphia, Lieutenant Franklin's home. Seeing the name reminded her of the letter she had insisted on writing to Franklin's family. It was still in her cloak pocket, waiting for the day when some semblance of order returned, and the mails began running again. It would be unhappily received, she knew, for it gave no explanation of their young relative's death. She had written only the barest of notes to cover it. Perhaps she should write at greater length—but no, Franklin had asked Laura not to contact her family. And how could she explain? To tell them that their cousin, their daughter, had died as a soldier in the Federal army would only increase their pain.

She sighed, and stood up to stretch her tired shoulders. María and Señora Baca came in from the back of the house. "Your room is ready, señorita," María said.

"Thank you."

Laura picked up her copied map, blew on the last wet spots to dry them, and put it and her writing things away in her bag. Outside the men's voices murmured softly. Feeling sleepy, Laura picked up her bag, and handed Señor Baca's map to Señora Baca. With a last glance at Esteban, watching her once more from his spot beside the fireplace, she followed María back to her room.

It was four in the morning by the time the last of Green's men slogged into Los Lunas, wet from crossing the river and practically asleep on their feet. Clouds of dust swirled around them, caught up from their footsteps by the relentless wind and settling on their wet clothes. Jamie sat a sulky cart horse that was slightly better than the mule he'd had earlier, and watched the weary men march into the campsite he had picked for them. At times like this he missed Cocoa, who would have patiently accepted the extra work, no matter how tired she was. No use thinking of that, though.

It had been a long night, what with sorting out essentials from the company wagons and making great bonfires of the nonessentials. The exhausted teams didn't show much improvement, but the lighter loads would make a difference tomorrow. Later today, rather.

At last Jamie judged his work done and rode back to the Luna place, where he'd stashed his gear. General Sibley and the others had long since gone to bed. In the parlor, Owens and some others of the staff snored softly on mattresses by the glowing remains of the fire. Jamie took out his bedroll and laid his blankets out under the table, which was the only space left on the floor. He righted an empty wine bottle that lay on the table, so it wouldn't roll off and fall on his head if he happened to bump one of the legs. With a sigh, he crawled under the table, lay down and instantly slept.

The wind howled, and McGuire's fiddle moaned back at it. O'Brien sat propped against somebody's knapsack, staring dully into the fire. The flames danced and spat as the wind beat them about, and occasionally a gust of smoke in his direction would force O'Brien to close his eyes. Every time this happened it got harder to open them, but he didn't want to go to bed. He owed Egan one sleepless night, if naught else.

The lads had found liquor—saints knew where—and O'Brien was right and properly drunk, as befitted a wake. "Another song," he called out, though they'd sung all of Egan's favorites already. Never hurt to sing them again, after all. He sat up a bit, took a deep draught at the whiskey as it passed, and sang,

> *"When Pat came over the hill, his colleen fair to see,*
> *His whistle low but shrill the signal was to be,"*

McGuire took it up, and soon the lads were all clapping and singing along. It was a foolish song, and Egan had sung it often, never failing to lighten the mood at the worst of times. O'Brien found himself grinning as they sang, and it ended in a jumble of laughter and calls for the bottle. He leaned back and watched Morris toss some more sticks onto the fire. There were not many left at this hour. A while back Quinn and Carter had gone to fetch more wood and never returned. Asleep in a ditch somewhere, most like.

O'Brien glanced around the circle. Just a few left awake. Denning had gone to bed hours ago, apologizing all the way. Kimmick, propped against his saddle, had dropped his hat over his eyes and was snoring softly. Newsom lay stretched out with his head under a shrub and his feet to the fire. Someone had decorated his boots with tufts of wheat grass, so that he looked like a wee sheaf of barley standing there. He'd catch fire if a spark fell just so, O'Brien thought, and chuckled.

Ryan and Langston began arguing over the bottle, until

McCraw cuffed them both and took it away. Beside O'Brien, Sergeant Rice sat with his arms wrapped around his knees, watching. He'd been silent mostly, young Rice, and O'Brien wasn't sure why he'd stayed. He had never been that close to Shaunessy and the other original Avery Trolls—had been one of Ramsey's boys, in fact—but here he sat, staring into the fire, listening to the songs. He accepted the bottle from McCraw and took only a sip before passing it on to O'Brien.

"That's no way to drink a man's memory," O'Brien said, handing it back. "Take a real drink, if you'd honor him."

Rice gazed at him for a moment, a slight crease in his wide forehead, then took a respectable pull. He winced a little as he handed on the bottle. Sure, it was bad enough whiskey, O'Brien thought as he helped himself to another mouthful and passed it along.

"How long did you know him, sir?" Rice asked.

"I?" O'Brien frowned. "Oh, I met him up Clear Creek, scrabbling for gold like the rest of the Trolls. It's Morris who knew him best. You knew him at home, did you not, Thomas?"

Morris glanced up from the fire. He'd been stirring the coals with a twig, which he now held aloft. A coal glowed on its end, brightened by the wind. "Aye," he said. "We came over together."

"From Derry?" O'Brien asked.

"From Donegal. I found him there, going from tavern to tavern trying to find passage, and getting relieved of his money by every pretty-faced wench in the town."

They all laughed. "That's our Egan," said McGuire. He set his bow to the strings and slowly drew "Lark in the Clear Air" out of them, playing softly while Morris went on.

"We had to work for our passage, shoveling coal in the belly of a steamer, but we got across. Egan wanted to start for San Francisco the minute we were ashore. He'd have walked all the way, if I'd let him."

Ryan laughed, and Newsom stirred beside him, knocking loose some of the wheat grass. Ryan carefully restored it to its place among Newsom's bootlaces.

"Did you ever get there?" Rice asked.

"San Francisco? No." Morris examined his twig, which

had gone out. He stuck it back into the coals. "No, we hired on to drive wagons for a party going to Oregon, but they had a big row at Fort Laramie and broke up, and they had no more need of us. We spent half of our pay in the tavern, then we heard of the gold on Cherry Creek, so we followed the Platte down to Denver."

"And on to unimaginable riches," muttered Langston.

"As you can see," Morris said, spreading his empty hands. "But it was a good life."

"Aye. It was." Regrets crept into O'Brien's heart, darkening it, making it cold. "I should never have brought him away."

"He'd have come away anyway," Morris replied. "He'd have joined up with Hambleton's lot. He was much better off with you."

O'Brien sighed. McGuire's fiddle filled the silence, and O'Brien picked up the tune, humming softly along. A gentle tune. Fair enough for his mood.

Beside him, Rice sat up. "Sir, I think you'd better go," he whispered.

"Eh?" O'Brien frowned at him. "It's not morning yet."

"Go, sir! Now!" Rice's eyes were sharp and he jerked his head toward the darkness beyond the row of tents.

They'd assembled the wake at the foot of I Company's street, so as not to disturb Officer's Row, but now someone was coming down from that direction. O'Brien got to his feet, but by the time he'd done so it was too late, for Ramsey stepped into the firelight, with Chivington's sour-faced aide at his elbow.

"There you are, Mr. Shoup," Ramsey said. "The captain is here, just as I thought."

"Good of you to come pay your respects, Ramsey," O'Brien said to him. Ramsey ignored him.

The darkness and the cool air made O'Brien just a bit dizzy. He spread his stance to improve his balance.

"Fraternization, Captain?" Shoup said. "I'm afraid this will go on report."

O'Brien wanted to damn his eyes, but he held back. "It's a wake," he said softly. "Am I not to honor one of my own men?"

"At the appropriate time and place," Shoup replied primly.
He cast a glance around the circle, and wrinkled his bulbous
nose at the bottle Ryan held out toward him. "Drunkenness,
too," he said. "You are not setting much of an example,
Captain O'Brien."

"He's all the example we need!" Ryan cried. O'Brien
caught his eye and gave a little shake of his head. No use
arguing with Shoup. He and Ramsey would find some way
to twist it, and would pass it to Chivington, and he would
then enter it as another black mark on the tally he was keeping.

"Oh, yes, a fine example," Ramsey said. "It is not every
captain who manages to get one of his men killed in a battle
as harmless as today's."

For a second all was still; then O'Brien lunged for Ramsey. In a flash Rice leapt up and got in between them. Everyone shouted at once, and O'Brien could make no sense of
the words. Rice was shorter than he, but he'd dug in his heels
and was stubbornly holding him back. After a moment
O'Brien gave up trying to get to Ramsey, realizing through
the whiskey haze that nothing would please the bastard more.
Strike Ramsey, and he'd be court-martialed before he could
draw breath. He settled for staring his hatred, and wondered,
if he stared hard enough, could he melt him right down
where he stood?

The shouting subsided. Newsom sat up, bumping his head
on the bush, which sent a shower of little dry seeds down
onto him to match the wheat grass. "What is it?" he asked.
"Is it morning already?"

"Almost." Sergeant Rice nodded toward the mountains,
where the sky had just started to glow a shade brighter than
black. "The captain was just going," he said to Ramsey, then
turned to O'Brien. "Would you like me to walk with you
sir?"

O'Brien looked down at Rice's young, anxious face. He
must want something of me, he thought. With a shrug, he
turned uphill toward Officer's Row. He could do with a rest,
and if morning was just over the mountain's shoulder, it was
fair enough to end the wake. He'd have Egan call him in an
hour or so and make coffee.

O'Brien stopped, and Rice nearly ran into him from behind. Hell and the devil, he thought, trying to swallow the lump that had risen in his throat. He stood clenching his fists, cursing the many ways in which he'd miss his friend.

He'd no striker now. Doubtless his tent hadn't even been pitched. Hell and damn.

"Sir?" Rice said. "Would you like to lean on me?"

"No, I'm fine, lad." O'Brien started walking again. His limbs were heavy and the gentle slope was just enough to make it slow going. He glanced over his shoulder. Shoup and Ramsey had gone.

He would sleep on his blankets, and choose a new striker tomorrow. Must remember to get up and look to the mare. Denning had taken charge of her after the fight—after he'd gone back and found Shaunessy. That hurt to think of, and he swallowed.

"Were you wanting to ask something?" he said to Rice.

"Sir?"

"Or are you just here for the pleasure of my company?" O'Brien paused again, and turned to look the young sergeant square in the face. Rice glanced down, then met his eyes.

"Just, please don't get relieved of command, sir," he said softly.

O'Brien cocked an eyebrow. "Thought you liked Ramsey," he said. "Didn't he recruit you?"

A frown creased Rice's forehead. "Yes . . . he was friendlier back in Denver City."

"And didn't he get you elected sergeant?" O'Brien asked softly.

"Yes," Rice replied. He glanced furtively behind him. "And I don't like the way he did it. And I don't like what he expects of me in return." Eyes of worry looked up at O'Brien. "He sent me to watch you tonight," Rice whispered. "To get evidence that you're irresponsible."

O'Brien drew a long breath. "And what will you tell him?"

"I'm not going to tell him anything," Rice said, a stubborn set to his young jaw.

"You'd better be careful, lad," O'Brien said. "It isn't a game he's playing."

"I went to see Vogel after dinner," Rice continued. "He

couldn't stop talking about how kind you'd been to him. Sir, Mr. Ramsey is telling everyone that you hate your men, except for the ones who came with you from Avery. It isn't true!"

"Of course not." O'Brien wondered what other tall tales Ramsey'd been telling about him. That he ate little children, no doubt. He felt a sad little smile creeping onto his face. "Thank you for telling me," he said. "And thank you for keeping me from getting into worse trouble than Ramsey's already made for me. But you'd best stay clear now, or he'll try to tar you with the same brush."

"It isn't fair!"

"No, it isn't. There's your camp, lad. Good night."

O'Brien walked on a few paces, then glanced back. Rice stood watching him, frowning still.

Don't turn your back, Alastar. The lad wants to like you.

He retraced his steps to where Rice stood waiting. "There is a favor you can do me, if you care to," he said.

Rice straightened his shoulders. "Sir?"

"Keep your ears open," O'Brien said softly. "I'll not ask you to spy, as I think that's ungentlemanly, and you must choose for yourself who you'll follow. But if you hear anything said against me that you feel I should know of, come tell me."

Rice looked pleased. "Yes, sir," he said. His jaw took on a determined firmness.

"Thank you," O'Brien said, and it was heartfelt. He offered his hand, and Rice shook it, then gave him a nod and turned toward his camp.

O'Brien went back up I Company's street toward Officer's Row. He could see the embers of a fire glowing at the top of the street. Denning must have built it up before going to bed.

The sky over the mountains had begun glowing a deep, jewel blue. To the west the last star hung silent over the plain. The wind had gone down some, but it still moaned among the restless trees, and blew gusts of dust over the company street.

Reaching camp, O'Brien saw that his tent had been pitched after all. Denning had seen to it, no doubt. The orange coals beckoned, and O'Brien squatted to reach his hands out to them.

Something moved across the fire. O'Brien jumped up, heart in mouth, hand to pistol. What he'd taken for a roll of bedding uncurled itself into a man.

"Jeesus, lordy, don't shoot, Cap'n! It's just me, old George!"

O'Brien frowned, squinting into the shadows beyond the coals. The scared face turned toward him looked familiar. "Sit up!" he commanded.

"I'se sitting up, yes, sir! I been sitting up all night, I only just must have fell down asleep for a minute. Been keeping the fire for you, Cap'n. I done made your camp all nice—"

"Shut up," O'Brien ordered.

"Oh, yes, sir," said the fellow, and fell to glancing back and forth from O'Brien's face to his gun.

It was the Negro he'd found in a Texan wagon—had it just been that morning? It seemed ages ago. O'Brien's frown deepened. "What are you doing here?" he demanded.

"Well, I'm yours now, ain't I? You done captured me."

13

"No, you're not mine!" O'Brien said in disgust. "Go away."

"Oh, please don't send me off, Cap'n! Ain't no way a poor old nigger gonna live in this here desert all by hisself! It's all full of snakes and Mexicans!"

O'Brien closed his eyes. He was too tired to deal with this now. He holstered his pistol, at which the Negro relaxed and put down his hands. O'Brien gazed at him dully, then turned and without a word went into his tent.

His bed had been laid out, his saddlebags lay neatly beside the tent wall, and a blockish shape in one corner proved to be the clock he'd dug out of a wagon that same morning. Too long a day. Much too long, and one he'd prefer to forget. He crawled under his blankets, and knew no more.

Picacho Pass looked to Kip to be more of a break in the mountains than a climb to a true mountain pass. The red peaks that rose up out of the plain were gigantic crags of rugged rock, beaten by wind and weather into weird shapes. Picacho itself looked like some wizard's tower, rising up to scratch at the sky with its sharp spires. The lower slopes were covered with the pale green fingers of saguaros and a golden-orange fuzz; as they came nearer, Kip realized it was poppies—millions of poppies—their bright faces turned to the sun.

Lieutenant Barrett called a halt and ordered the squad to check their weapons. Kip had his pistol and rifle ready, having sat up during their last halt cleaning and loading them, more because he was too excited to sleep than because he needed something to do. After marching two days and nights, right through the awful desert heat, they were finally going to get a shot at some Rebels.

Lieutenant Barrett moved over to confer with John Jones, the civilian guide Captain Calloway had sent with them, who had seen the Rebels in Tucson and come out alive to carry the tale to Colonel Carleton. After a month in the saddle he looked not quite so wild as Pauline Weaver, but along the way to being so.

Next to Kip, Billy Leonard stood up in his stirrups, peering eastward. "Think Lieutenant Baldwin's made it around the other side yet?"

"Maybe not," Kip answered. "He's got farther to go."

Baldwin's squad was the same size as Barrett's—a dozen cavalry and a guide. Calloway's orders were for the two squads to come at the pass from either side and trap the Rebels between them. The captain wanted information, so they were to capture rather than destroy the enemy, and hold them in the pass until he came up from the Pima Villages with the rest of the advance.

Jones trotted off to scout ahead, and Barrett started the squad forward again at a walk. They were off the main road now, and moving through a sea of swaying poppies. Occasionally a spike of some other plant, covered with blue flowers, would rise above the orange-gold mass. Firecracker bent his head but Kip wouldn't let him eat more than a mouthful of the flowers. They needed to be ready for action any second.

It was hideously hot. Midday, and the sun pounding down like a hammer on an anvil. Kip took a sip from his canteen and resisted the urge to take more. He could feel the sweat evaporating on his skin. He'd got used to the sensation of being in an oven, but with the added excitement of a possible fight, he felt prickly all over. He wriggled in the saddle in a useless attempt to get comfortable. Firecracker responded with a snort.

"Easy boy," Kip said, reaching down to pat his neck.

"Wants to eat some Rebels, does he?" Leonard asked, grinning.

"No, just some poppies."

"You're pretty damn good with that bastard. I had to ride him on a scout once, when Blue here was lame. Couldn't hardly stay on him."

"He's like that. He gets excited."

"He's insane if you ask me," said Leonard. "Puts his head up in the air, and his brains drain right out his ears."

Kip laughed. It was all too true. There was never any telling what Firecracker would do. He hadn't been in a real fight that Kip knew of, except for when the pickets got shot up at Stanwick's, and he hadn't behaved too well then. Kip rubbed absently at his shoulder, still sore from landing on the boulder up in that dry stream bed. He'd just have to watch the horse closely, and be ready to hold on like a buckleburr when the time came.

They were riding along a little depression where maybe the water ran when it rained. Here the mesquites and palo verde trees were taller. As they wound their way through them, Kip stared hard at each one big enough to hide a man, looking for a shadow or any sign of movement. He did not like the fact that there were so many, but at least there were only a few Rebels. All the trees in this place could have hidden a battalion.

Lieutenant Barrett halted again. Up ahead was a dense thicket of mesquite. Jones was trotting back to them.

"They're in there," Kip heard him say to Barrett, pointing toward the shrubs. "Playing poker. They haven't seen us. I'd go in single file—less chance of them hearing us."

"They must know we are here," Barrett said, holding a field glass to his eye. "I don't see anything."

"Can't see them from here, but they're there," Jones said. "About thirty yards into the mesquite."

Barrett shut the glass with a snap that made his horse sidle. "Perhaps we should go in on foot."

Jones shook his head. "You've got a better chance of catching them if you're mounted. Go quietly, and you should be able to take them without a shot."

"Is there a trail through that?"

"No. No trail except the main road."

Barrett frowned. "I want us kept together. A column of twos—"

"Single file's better," Jones said. "It gets thicker up ahead. Not really room for two abreast."

The lieutenant sat staring at the mesquite, tapping his field glass against the saddle. Kip looked at the forest, too, not very happy about going into it.

"Very well," Barrett said at last. He turned his horse to face the squad. "In column, single file. March," he ordered, and led the way with Jones close behind.

Kip fell in behind Leonard. His shoulders itched. Jones has been right about the woods—after a short distance they entered a dense thicket that was hard to pass through even in single file. Kip clenched his teeth as the black mesquite closed in around them. The open branches and feathery leaves were deceptive—they seemed insubstantial, but were thick enough to hide snipers. Kip's skin crawled.

"Where's Lieutenant Baldwin?" he asked softly of no one in particular.

"Don't know," Leonard whispered over his shoulder.

"Hot in here," Kip muttered.

The horses plodded slowly along. It seemed every snapping twig and every creak of leather must be audible a mile away. The Rebels must be deep into their game not to hear. Kip wondered how long it would take to find the Rebels— it seemed like an age had passed already. Finally Jones angled his horse uphill a bit, and the file followed. Thorny branches grabbed at Kip's clothes and reached toward his face. He blocked them with his right arm, pistol in hand. He was just bending aside to get around a thick, low branch when he heard a clicking sound that could only be the cocking of many pistols.

A gunshot split the air, ringing in the heat, and suddenly everyone was firing at once. Leonard's horse reared, tipping him off. Firecracker whinnied, but Kip had a hard hand on the reins and managed to keep the horse's head down, though he bucked and tried to jump sideways. Men were screaming and shouting all around.

"After them!" he heard Barrett cry. Leonard's horse bolted into the woods, and all of a sudden Kip's way was clear again. He plunged after the lieutenant, passing a man scrambling to get back into his saddle and a litter of cards flung all over a small clearing. Firecracker's hooves scattered the coals of a campfire as they crashed through the open space and back into the mesquite. Kip could see Jones up ahead, and followed him, urging Firecracker on and cursing under his breath.

Gunfire snapped all around. The woods were choked with the sulfurous smell of powder. Kip's heart thundered; he held his pistol ready but couldn't see anything to shoot at. The ground was rough, and the mesquite so thick it was hard to get through it at all. Up ahead he heard a pistol crack once, twice. Kip peered through the black thorny branches, looking for a target. The lieutenant had paused in a little gap, with Jones and Private Johnson halted beside him. As Kip caught up, he reined in. Behind him Private Swingler did the same.

"They've retreated," Barrett said, squinting into the thicket. "How far does this go?" he asked Jones.

"Quite a ways."

Barrett glanced over the handful of men still with him. "Let's go get them," he said.

Oh, hell, Kip thought, and followed.

Every second he expected to be shot from the saddle. He most decidedly did not like riding through this rat's nest of mesquite. Now and then a ball would sing past, and once out of sheer frustration he fired his pistol back at the endless green-black tangle.

Straight ahead, a half-dozen shots went off at once. Lieutenant Barrett fell forward, then slid from his saddle.

"No!" Johnson cried, just ahead of Kip. A second volley shot the private to pieces. Kip shuddered and flinched back as blood spattered onto him. Firecracker jibbed, and Kip gripped the reins so hard he thought his fingers would freeze together.

Jones's horse reared and peeled off to the left, away from the rifle fire. Firecracker tried to follow but Kip held him and brought up his pistol, firing three rounds at the shapes moving beyond the nearest bushes—the merest man-shaped shadows—without hitting a thing. His breath was ragged all of a sudden. It was hard to breathe at all in the thicket, no air among the dense branches and the smoke from the rifles hanging in a heavy haze. He coughed, and fired again at a fleeing shadow.

Barrett's horse broke away, crashing through the brush, and two of the mounted men followed it. Firecracker let out a piercing whinny and started after them. Kip let him, half ashamed, half scared out of his mind. He kept low over Firecracker's neck as the branches whipped at his face. Musket balls sang after them; the hidden Rebels had loaded again.

They cleared the mesquite after what seemed only a short time, and Firecracker broke into a gallop. Kip kept enough pressure on the reins to remind the horse he was there, but let him run as hard as he wanted, praying there were no gopher holes hidden by the poppies. The ground was an orange blur; they descended a slope and heard no more firing. Firecracker showed no inclination to slow down. Kip let him go along until they reached the stage road, then pulled up.

"Whoa, there," he cried, pressing Firecracker left with both the reins and his knees. The horse neighed a protest, but swung around and fell to a loping canter, blowing now, heading back west along the road. Kip scanned Picacho, but except for a few wisps of smoke he saw no sign of the Rebels. Nor could he see any of the others from the scout. The mountain looked peaceful, serene, covered in golden flowers.

Kip slowed down to a trot and finally to a walk, catching his breath. Firecracker heaved a great, slobbery sigh, and Kip gave him a reassuring pat.

The question was, should he try to find the rest of his squad, try to go back for the wounded, or ride on to meet up with the column? The third idea appealed, as it would get him away from the Rebels the fastest. However, he didn't think Captain Calloway would be too happy at the news he'd be bringing, or more especially, the fact that it was incomplete news. Better to find out who was left alive. Kip shivered. He did not want to go back into that thicket of death, not alone. Not at all. He should at least try to find some of the other survivors, though. Maybe Lieutenant Baldwin's squad was nearby. With an unsteady swallow, he turned Firecracker around and headed back into the pass.

* * *

The mare plodded along in the blasted eternal wind. She held her head low, and O'Brien was inclined to agree with her. The dust and sand battered them constantly, making life a misery whether moving or halted.

The troops were in no very good mood. They'd arisen that morning to find Peralta deserted; the Texans had fled in the night. Chivington was mad enough to chew horseshoe nails, and the mutterings of the men were largely in agreement with him. They'd been robbed yet again of a chance to conquer the Rebels. Canby was a coward, or possibly even a traitor in league with the enemy. O'Brien kept silent, knowing that speaking his disagreement would only bring abuse down upon him.

The column had mounted up soon after breakfast and moved forward down the river. At Los Lunas they'd passed the remains of a couple of bonfires, still smoking. The Texans were west of the river and a few miles to the south, so the scouts told, and O'Brien could imagine a thickness in the dust clouds a ways downstream.

Behind him the Negro rode the mustang, and kept up a litany of "good boy" and "whoa boy" and other such nonsense.

"Lucky he's tired," O'Brien called over his shoulder. "If he weren't, he would throw you off."

"You hear that, Lucky?" said the Negro. "Your massa says you's tired. You be good and don't throw Old George off, and the next time we stop he'll go find you some corn."

O'Brien shook his head. Witless, the fellow was. He'd gone 'round and 'round in his mind over what the devil to do with the man. Oh, it was pleasant, he had to admit, to wake to a cup of hot coffee and the soft hiss and spit of bacon over the fire. And it was helpful to have his traps and his horses attended to, but all that could be done—should be done—by a striker, for very little cost and much less annoyance. Old George never ceased talking, except when threatened with physical harm, and then kept still but a short while. O'Brien had tried again to send him away, but the fool begged and pleaded so hard that at last O'Brien had relented and agreed to keep charge of him for the present. He had put him on the mustang, half hoping the beast's bad temper would change his mind, but no such good fortune had blessed him. Old George was a competent rider, or so it appeared. Of all the many things that terrified him, horses were not one.

Ah, well. It would do for now, until they got into some town, or a fort even, where O'Brien could be rid of him. Until then he'd at least have his meals cooked. Old George was handy at that, he admitted. His breakfast that morning had been better than anything Shaunessy had produced.

The reminder made him sigh, and close his eyes. They were so sore and tired from the wind that at once they began to water. He kept them closed, the dust being a reasonable excuse, and half-dozed in the saddle while the column plodded relentlessly on through the storm.

Kip stared at the mesquite from the same spot where the squad had stood an hour or so before. He hadn't wanted to go in there in the first place, and he wanted even less to go back. He hadn't seen a sign of anybody—Jones, or any of the squad, or any of Baldwin's squad. He could have been alone in the pass, but he knew he wasn't.

He sighed and dismounted, toying with the idea of tying Firecracker and going in on foot. Quieter that way, but the horse might be stolen. Better to lead him, and hope he didn't do anything crazy. Clenching his teeth, he pulled gently on the reins, and Firecracker followed him into the woods.

Going slowly, every tiny snap of a twig or branch sounded like a gunshot. Broken branches and a trail of crushed poppies made it easy enough to follow their previous route. Kip listened as he went, and kept an eye out for any movement.

It seemed a very long time before he finally reached the spot where they'd first been shot at. He paused before entering the clearing. A man lay on his side up ahead, not moving. Looked to be Private Leonard. After straining his ears for a full minute and hearing only the twittering of birds, Kip left Firecracker to graze and went forward to kneel beside him.

It was Leonard, sure enough, shot through the neck and barely breathing. Kip turned him on his back.

"Billy?" he said, but Leonard didn't answer.

He stood up, wondering if he should tie something around Leonard's neck before trying to move him. Looked like he'd bled a lot—his kerchief was soaked. Kip was about to untie his own when he heard a crunching noise, somebody walking, coming from up ahead.

He crouched, not moving his feet for fear of making a noise, and carefully drew and cocked his pistol. The steps were definitely getting louder; one man, walking briskly. Kip stared through the mesquite, looking for the intruder through the spiderweb tangle of black branches. Finally he discerned a solitary figure coming along the path they had forced through the brush.

"Halt!" Kip commanded. "Put your hands up over your head!"

The figure halted. Kip thought he saw it move a hand toward its hip.

"Hands up now or I'll shoot!" Kip shouted, his voice cracking on the words.

Slowly the hands went up. Kip squinted, trying to see the man's face, but there were too many leaves and branches in the way. No sound of anyone else approaching.

"Come on down here," he said. "Nice and slow."

As the figure approached, Kip made out more details: black civilian coat, dusty black leathers, a hat slung back off the shoulders ranchero-style, and finally the face.

"Mr. Jones," Kip said, sighing. He uncocked his pistol and stood up.

Jones stood at the edge of the clearing and folded his arms. "You're the musician, aren't you? You can take it easy now, there's no one left in the pass but us."

"I didn't know that. You're the first one I've seen since—up there."

Jones glanced over his shoulder. "Barrett's dead, if you're wondering. So's Johnson."

Kip swallowed. "Leonard here's still alive," he said. "I was about to put him up on my horse and take him down to the road."

"I'll help."

They got Leonard over the saddle without too much trouble, and Jones led the way out of the mesquite. They turned east when they got clear of it, skirting the woods. After a bit the ground began to slope gently downhill. Kip saw the rest of the squad assembled up ahead, together with Baldwin's squad. Men hurried forward to help as they approached, including Felley, who'd been assigned to Baldwin. They tenderly lifted Leonard from Firecracker's back, set him on the ground in the shade of a big saguaro, and bathed his face with water from their canteens.

Jones went over to where Lieutenant Baldwin stood. Before him three men sat on the ground, their hands tied behind them. The lieutenant appeared to be questioning them.

"Rebs," Felley said, following Kip's gaze. "Caught 'em heading toward Tucson after the fight. Say, you want some coffee?"

"Sure."

Felley led him to where some of the others were nursing a small fire, feeding it with dead branches. "We were pushing our way through that damned mesquite when we heard the firing," Felley told him. "Tried to get to you, but we were too far away. Never even found where you were. We were still searching when Jones came along and told us what happened."

Kip couldn't find anything to say, so he just nodded and stared at the fire. It looked like Lieutenant Baldwin meant to stay in the pass until the captain arrived. He sat down beside Felley and watched the men watching their pot of coffee, waiting for it to boil. The burning mesquite smelled good.

A rattle of hoofbeats made him look up. It was Jones, riding off to the captain, no doubt. Kip glanced to where Leonard lay.

"He doesn't look too good," Felley said. "Good thing the captain's on his way."

Kip nodded, and looked out toward the stage road. Beyond it on the north side of the pass the tall spires of rock were beginning to cast long shadows in the latening sun. He thought he saw something move, and raised a hand to shield his eyes.

A lone figure on horseback stood on a ridge between two crags. It stayed still for a moment, only its black hair, brushing the shoulders, floating a bit in the wind. Kip felt an odd tingle of fear as the figure turned and disappeared into the rocks north of Picacho.

Laura paced beneath the graceful, drooping branches of an old cottonwood tree while the mule and donkey drank from a nearby acequia. They had made good time to Algodones, and she was anxious to continue to Bernalillo. Juan Carlos had not yet voiced an opinion of the animals' fitness to go on, and she did not wish to press him, so she concealed her impatience with brisk walking, and fought against the weariness that now threatened to overcome her spirits.

It had been a day of disappointments. Her first glimpse of the Río Grande, to which she had long looked forward, was a sad shock. The mightiest river in New Mexico Territory had proved to be merely a muddy snake that twined back and forth between banks much too wide for its stream. Even the rivers here are brown, she had thought to herself.

The wind had grown stronger as they continued southward. Gusts of blowing dust had assailed her and María, the carriage's top proving inadequate protection from the shifting winds. Laura had tried unsuccessfully to sleep through the weary miles. That failing, she had asked María to teach her some Spanish. She now knew the names and colors of every object that could be found inside Mrs. Canby's traveling carriage, a short but potentially useful catalogue. To set them in her memory, she began reciting them to herself.

"El cojín negro, la puerta, el banco—"

"Señorita?"

Laura paused, looking up to find Esteban nearby. He bobbed his head in a little, polite bow, and pointed to the carriage. Evidently he wished her to reenter it.

"Señor Díaz dice que debe regresar al coche ahora. Vienen unos hombres." He gestured toward the carriage, then southward.

A cloud of dust on the road ahead told of a party on horseback. Squinting, Laura could count perhaps half a dozen, riding quickly toward the village.

"Yes," she said slowly. "Sí."

Juan was already leading the donkey and mule back to the carriage. Esteban hurried ahead to help hitch them up, while

Laura hastened to the steps. María was already inside. Laura joined her, and watched the approaching riders. A faint hope that they might be Federal soldiers soon faded; they were natives, five in number, badly clothed and rather heavily armed. Laura leaned farther back into the shadow of the carriage top. She saw Esteban climb onto the driver's seat with Juan and reach underneath it, producing a shotgun which he laid across his lap. She had not known they had such a weapon, but she was glad to see it. Quietly she placed her carpetbag on the seat beside her, opened it, and slid her hand inside it to close around the reassuring butt of her pistol.

The strangers spoke to Juan in rapid Spanish. Laura couldn't follow the conversation at all. She watched María, who listened intently but showed no sign of alarm. Juan said something brief and started the animals forward.

The next moments would tell. Laura listened for the sound of pursuing hoofbeats. The carriage rolled along smartly, and they were soon past the trees and houses of the village. Shortly thereafter the cultivated fields gave way to wild grasses. The road never strayed far from the gray forest of bare cottonwoods that marked the Río Grande's course. Laura could discern no sound other than that of the carriage. She leaned forward to speak to Juan Carlos.

"Are they following?"

"No, señorita," he said. "They said they were going to Santa Fé."

Sighing, she leaned back and looked at María, who gave a brief smile. Laura closed up her bag again and set it on the floor.

It appeared they were continuing to Bernalillo. She was glad, for the sooner this journey was over the better. Doubts and worries assailed her; she tried to repress them. She had known there were risks all along. For herself she did not care so much as for the others—if anything were to happen to them, she would feel responsible. She could almost wish that they were driving in a wagon rather than Mrs. Canby's carriage, for the American vehicle attracted attention. Well, there was no help for it, and before long the carriage would be so covered in dust as to make its appearance less smart.

"María, what is 'carriage' in Spanish?"

"Pregunte en español."

"¿Cómo se dice 'carriage'?" Laura asked obediently.

"El coche."

"¿Cómo se dice 'pistol'?"

María raised an eyebrow. "La pistola," she said.

"Gracias." Laura sighed, and gazed out at the ribbon of cottonwoods curving along beside the road.

Thank the Lord for la pistola, she thought.

Kip looked up at the darkening bulk of Picacho and shivered. He wasn't cold, particularly, but he'd gotten to disliking the peak. Now that Captain Calloway was here with the rest of the command it was unlikely that they'd be attacked, but still his eyes roved the lower slopes, and the rocky ridges across the road, for any sign of movement.

The captain had questioned the captured Rebels for hours. Kip had lingered close enough to hear most of it. The news wasn't good. McCleave was being held prisoner in Tucson, guarded by a large force of Rebels under Captain Sherod Hunter. Their number wasn't exactly clear, but there were enough of them to make Calloway cautious, which meant there wouldn't be a battle. The captain had no surgeon, and didn't want to have to deal with a lot of casualties without one. Kip could understand this—poor Billy Leonard wasn't doing so well. They'd washed out his wound and bound it up, and the captain had even given him some of his own brandy, but there wasn't much more they could do for him. Calloway had finally sent the prisoners away and was now talking with Lieutenant Baldwin about getting the command back to the Pima Villages.

Kip sighed. Back up to Pima. They'd be by the river again, which was good, but no closer to getting out of the desert. It sounded like Calloway was planning to wait in Pima until Colonel Carleton came up with the main column. Just exactly the opposite of what Kip wanted to hear. The thought of weeks spent cooling their heels made him crazy.

He heard a crunch of boots on gravel and looked up. Felley loomed out of the darkness. "Got us some jackrabbits roasting," he said. "You want some?"

"Sure." Kip stood up, legs a little stiff from sitting so long, and followed Felley back down toward B Company's tiny campfire. The captain had allowed only one fire per company, and ordered them to be kept small and smoke-free. Hard to do when green mesquite was the main source of wood, but the boys were managing. They'd found some dry branches, and now that it was dark the smoke didn't matter quite so much.

Felley led Kip past a big palo verde. A ring of dark lumps blocked the flames from view; men huddled as close as they could get, even though it wasn't all that cold. Huddled for comfort, and also for safety. Kip hunched down outside the ring while Felley stepped in to check the rabbits—three of them—roasting over the small pit, sharing the coals with a coffeepot.

"Almost done," Felley said, returning. He squatted down and wrapped his arms around his legs. "Wonder if the captain means to spend the night."

"I doubt it," Kip said. "Sounded like he wanted to ride for Pima as soon as he could."

"Can't say I mind. I don't like this place." Felley looked around at the black cliffs against blue-black sky. "Feels like we're being watched."

"We probably are."

Felley laid his head on his knees and gazed sideways at Kip. "Were you scared today, in the fight?"

Kip hesitated, wondering if his courage was being called in question. At least he'd been in the fight, which was more than Felley could say. "Yes," he said. "I was scared, but it was half because of wondering what Firecracker would do."

Felley laughed, and so did a couple of the others.

"You shoot anybody?" someone asked.

"I shot at them. I don't think I hit anyone."

"Were you with the lieutenant?"

That was a grim question. It brought back the confusion in the tangled woods, the balls whining by much too close, the shriek of frightened horses. All these things were stamped on Kip's memory, but he didn't know how to begin to describe them. Finally he just said, "Yes."

"He was a brave man, the lieutenant."

Too brave, thought Kip. He should never have gone into that thicket.

"I think they're done," Felley said. He got up and went to check the rabbits, pulled one off its improvised spit. Someone immediately replaced it with another, freshly skinned. Felley divided up the hare and brought back a leg for Kip. The meat was stringy but it tasted good. Kip made himself chew it slowly, even though it was the first thing he'd eaten since breakfast. He hadn't realized he was hungry.

Bootsteps approaching. "Whistler down here?" called Aikins.

"Mm," Kip said through a mouthful of meat.

"Captain Calloway wants to see you," Aikins said.

Kip swallowed, and turned to Felley. "Thanks for the rabbit," he said with a wave.

He followed Aikins, gnawing the last of the meat from the bone. Someone had built a tiny fire for the captain, and Calloway was sitting by it on the ground, writing something, using his saddlebag for a table. He looked up at Kip.

"There you are. Is Firecracker sound?"

"Yes sir," Kip said. "He did fine today."

"Good. And are you fit to ride?"

"Yes, sir."

"All right, then. You'll leave right away, soon as I finish writing this."

Kip's heart lifted a little. "Dispatch for Colonel Carleton, sir?" He wouldn't mind a hard ride back to the main column. Better than a slow march to the Pimas.

"No. For Colonel Canby."

Kip looked down at the paper and blinked. Colonel Canby? In Santa Fé? To carry a message there would mean getting past Tucson, getting to the Río Grande without being killed by Captain Hunter or Cochise and his innumerable in-laws, and getting through or around the Texan army. Kip's stomach did a slow roll. He threw the rabbit leg away into the bushes.

"Where's Muñoz?" Calloway demanded.

"At his devotions, I believe," Aikins said.

"Hm. Well, as soon as he's ready, you'll go." Calloway signed his page with a flourish, took out a fresh sheet of paper and began writing again. "Where's that map, Aikins? Show Whistler here the route."

Aikins stepped to a pair of saddlebags propped against a rock and extracted a much-creased map of New Mexico Territory, which he brought to the fire and spread out on the ground. Kip crouched beside him, peering at the yellowed paper.

Aikins ran a finger along a thin road. "We'll follow the stage road. We can stay off it and out of sight except in the passes."

We? Kip thought. So it isn't just me. He was part disappointed, but mostly relieved.

"What about Mesilla?" Calloway asked. "Isn't Baylor still there?"

"We'll turn north before we get there," Aikins said. "At Mimbres. There's a trail that runs up through the mountains. We should be able to get to Fort Craig."

Kip stared at the map. It was a long way to Fort Craig, nearly as far as they'd come from Fort Yuma. A long way for two riders to go.

"Is it just you and me?" he said, looking up at Aikins.

"And Muñóz," Aikins said, gesturing toward the bushes. "He's our guide."

Three. Three, against long odds. Kip swallowed.

Calloway stood up. He had put away his writing things in the saddlebag, and left it on the ground while he stepped around the fire toward Kip and Aikins. He handed each of them a folded page, sealed with wax that was still warm. Kip peered down at his, noticing the imperfect impression of the captain's ring, and the black in the wax that came from melting it over an open flame.

"One of you has to get through," the captain said.

Kip glanced up at him, and his eyes were stern in the firelight. One must get through. Was that his purpose here? To be the one who falls behind, gets snapped up by the enemy, to make sure the others get through?

Aikins folded up his map and tucked it back in his saddlebag, then slipped his copy of the letter inside his shirt. Slowly Kip did the same.

"Better saddle up," Calloway said.

Kip stood up, and found the captain's hand held out to him.

"Good luck," he said.

Kip shook hands. "Thank you sir, but—"

Calloway raised an eyebrow. "Yes?"

"I guess I—I'm surprised you chose me," Kip said.

The captain gazed at him for a moment. "You kept your head today, Whistler. You've turned out pretty tough. For this mission I need men I know won't quit."

"Thank you, Captain." *I think.*

Calloway gave a single nod and turned away. Kip drew a deep breath, and went off to find Firecracker.

14

". . . everyone detests the country so much that they are really glad to go, for they think that our operations here will all be lost in history, when such great struggles are going on nearer home . . ."

—Sgt. James F. Starr, 5th Texas Mounted Volunteers

"Tell the general I'll be there in five minutes," Jamie said to the waiting orderly, and poked at the sizzling strips of beef in his pan. The orderly made a pained face, but saluted and took himself off.

Sibley had halted the column at noon after crossing the Río Puerco where it met the Río Grande, and called for a staff meeting. Jamie was late, but he didn't give a damn. He was exhausted after two days of coaxing the weary army through merciless wind, and by God he was going to eat two bites of dinner before he went to the meeting.

The brigade had made the best possible time down the Río, but the men and horses were so broken down they couldn't travel as fast as the general had hoped. The Yankees had shadowed them, following a few miles back and across the river, their pickets harassing the column but keeping just out of range. It made for nervous traveling. Now, since they'd stopped, the blue column had passed them and headed on down the river, toward Polvadera. There was no longer any chance of getting through the narrows ahead of the Federals.

The hot, sizzling beef made Jamie's mouth water. He decided it was done and took the pan off the fire, then scrabbled in his haversack for the piece of cornbread he'd saved from breakfast. He pried it in two and stuffed most of the meat into it, popping a small strip of beef into his mouth—burning his tongue but it tasted so good—and took a swig from his canteen.

"You're a bad boy, Mr. Russell."

Jamie looked up into Lane's grinning face. Jamie grinned back.

"Sibley send you?"

"Yep. He's waiting. None too patiently, either. He's run out of champagne."

"Poor general. Want a bite?"

"Don't mind if I do."

Jamie handed Lane two strips of beef, took the last one from the pan and bit off half of it, and stood up. He followed Lane to Sibley's tent, munching as they picked their way through the camp. Men sat huddled in half-circles around fitful campfires, their backs to the wind, talking in low voices.

Jamie got a sour look from Sibley's orderly as he entered the tent. He stuffed the last bit of cornbread into his mouth and hung back near the door while he chewed, glancing around to see who all was there. Company commanders lounged around the walls of the big Sibley tent, complaining softly about the weather and the Yankees. Sibley had his map spread out on top of a camp desk—one of the ones Sergeant Rose had built, the last one the army still had—and Scurry, Green, and Teel were leaning over it. Owens stood nearby with Captain Coopwood, commander of the San Elizario Spies. The other spy company, the Brigands, were represented by their second in command, Lieutenant Madison, Captain Phillips having disappeared shortly after the battle in Glorieta Pass, at which no one was especially disappointed.

Lane went over to Reily, who was sitting on one of Sibley's several trunks. Jamie followed. Major Teel had given Reily charge of two field guns after his own battery was buried in Albuquerque, which had cheered his spirits somewhat, but the unspectacular duel at Peralta had left him dissatisfied.

"What's the matter?" Jamie asked softly, sitting beside him.

Reily sighed. "Lost two horses today. I don't have enough left to haul my section."

Jamie nodded in sympathy; the horses had been giving out all along the road. He nodded toward the general and his colonels, their heads together over the map. "What's the discussion about?"

"Polvadera," Reily said. "Sibley still wants to make a stand there."

"There's Russell!" Sibley called. "Captain Russell, didn't you tell me we could get through at Polvadera?"

Jamie glanced at Lane, and slowly stood up. "Sir, at the time we thought we'd be well ahead of the Federals. As it is—"

"As it is, we'd be walking into a trap," Scurry said.

Captain Coopwood stepped forward. "General Sibley, may I make a suggestion?"

Sibley straightened, and pushed a damp curl back from his forehead. "Certainly, Captain."

Coopwood came to the desk, a tall, bearded and weathered man who knew the Territory like the back of his hand. He'd been a frontiersman, a prospector, and a lawyer, among other things. Jamie was a little in awe of him, and also liked him. He was soft-spoken, much less flamboyant than most of the commanders, and fiercely loyal to his men.

"On our way up we came through the mountains to avoid Fort Craig," Coopwood said. "Along here." He bent to point at the map.

Sibley frowned. "Come here, Russell. Tell me if you can get the wagons down this."

"Oh, you can't," Coopwood said. "It's the merest trace. You'd have to pack everything on mules."

"Then it's out of the question," Sibley said.

Jamie joined the senior officers at the desk. Green made room for him, and leaned over the map. "We can do this," the colonel said. "It'll get us past Craig. They won't be expecting us to leave the road."

Jamie looked at the map. Coopwood ran a finger down the route he had taken, striking west-southwest of the narrows from their present position at the mouth of the Rio Puerco, skirting the feet of craggy Ladron Peak, and passing between the Magdalena and San Mateo mountain ranges, then picking up a creek called Cuchillo Negro and following it back to the Río Grande, well below Fort Craig. There was no trail marked on the map, but Jamie knew Captain Coopwood had led his men safely around Craig by this route on their way up to join the army—was it only two weeks ago? A flicker of hope, followed by one of apprehension, fluttered inside his chest.

"Yes," he said slowly. "I think we could get through." He looked up at Captain Coopwood. "How's the terrain?" he asked.

"Pretty rough," Coopwood admitted. "You'll have to cross some arroyos."

Jamie nodded, and leaned a hand on the desk, using his thumbnail to measure the miles they'd have to travel. His head was busy with calculations: fodder times animals times days, and how many animals to carry the fodder? They were leaving the river, and there might not be any grass to speak of along the way. Rations times men times days, versus how many pounds a man can carry. Take some off of that, because the men are sick, a lot of them, and all of them tired. It would not be an easy march.

"Can you point out where there's water?" Jamie asked Coopwood.

"Yes," Coopwood said. "There are springs here, and here. . . ."

Sibley stood up. "I am not convinced that this is our best course of action," he announced.

Scurry rose, too, a hint of annoyance in his face. "Our only other choice," he said, "is to make a stand at Polvadera, surrender to Canby, and pine away in a Northern prison!"

"Unless we break through—"

"In which case Carson brings his regiment out of Craig and mops up what's left of us! It's hopeless," Scurry said. "Coopwood's route is our only chance."

"I agree," Green said.

"You are underestimating the men of Texas," Sibley said. "The heroes of Valverde can whip Carson's Mexicans any day of the year."

"It's not just Mexicans in Craig, begging your pardon, sir,"

Coopwood said. "That's the 1st New Mexico, and they're sound. They're the ones that didn't run at Valverde."

Sibley's eyes narrowed as he frowned. "We are not whipped yet, gentlemen! By God, I'll see this through!"

"General, if it's your reputation you're concerned about, you shouldn't worry," said Captain Thurmond, an old Ranger. "If the mountain trail doesn't work, everyone'll blame it on Coopwood here."

A laugh, quickly stifled. Sibley turned molten eyes on Thurmond. "You are insubordinate, sir! I might have you arrested!"

"Oh, for God's sake!" Scurry exclaimed.

"General," said Colonel Green, drawing himself up to his full height, "we are all behind you, of course, but I ask you to consider what's best for your army. We can't hold New Mexico unless we get reinforcements and resupply. You have already determined that we must retire to Mesilla. That being the case, should we not preserve as much of our army as possible, rather than waste it in a fight that would gain us nothing?"

The tent was silent. Sibley stood straight as a rod, frowning as he looked Green in the eye. "Captain Russell," he said, without shifting his gaze. "How many days will it take us to get through on Coopwood's trail?"

"At least a week, sir."

"At least," Coopwood murmured.

"Food and water?" the general demanded.

"We'll take as much food as we can carry," Jamie said. "For water, we'll have to make do on what we can find in the mountains."

Green shot a concerned glance at him, and Jamie gave a helpless shrug. If he could have done better, he would.

"Seven days across country in the condition we're in?" Sibley said. "We'll lose half our horses."

"We'd lose them anyway, in a fight!" Scurry insisted. "Better horses than men!"

Voices were raised in agreement, others in dissent. A heated discussion began, to which Jamie paid little attention. He stared down at the map, not wanting to undertake this journey, but wanting even less to face another fight, and what looked like a hopeless one at that.

Captain Coopwood stalked out of the tent, and Jamie looked up. The argument was still raging. Sibley had a few supporters, but it sounded like most of the commanders wanted to take their chances in the mountains. Green sat silent, his enthusiasm damped. Jamie caught his eye, and Green returned a weary smile. It disappeared as quickly as it had come, leaving the colonel's face grim.

"Russell," Sibley said, turning his gaze on Jamie across the desk, "you haven't given us your opinion. Which plan would you choose?"

"Death in the mountains?" Green said softly, "or death in a Northern prison?"

Jamie licked his lips. "Sir, to be honest, I think the men have already decided. Sergeant Davidson told me he saw the 2nd strapping extra rations and cartridges to their saddles. If we fight and lose at Polvadera, they're planning to go off through the mountains anyway, back to Texas."

Scurry gave Sibley a meaningful glance. The general looked cross, and suddenly tired. "Camp rumors," he said. "Shouldn't heed 'em."

"It's not just the rumors, sir," Jamie said. "I've got to agree with Colonel Scurry. A chance in the mountains is better than no chance at all."

Sibley looked slowly around the tent at his commanders. No one advanced any more arguments. The general's eyes seemed sunk deep in his head, and his voice was dull as he said, "Very well. We shall take Coopwood's route."

Jamie heard a couple of the men near him sigh. He bent over the map again and checked his watch—Martin's watch, with the portrait of Emma hidden in the fob. He'd send a foraging team out at once to cut as much grass as they could find along the riverbank. They'd pack what they could, enough for a day or two. After that, the stock would have to make do on whatever they could nibble off the ungenerous desert.

Jamie gnawed on the back of his thumb, and he looked up at General Sibley, who had sunk into a chair by the desk. "Sir," he said, "what about the wounded?"

Sibley rubbed a hand over his forehead. "How many are they?"

"Sick and wounded together, about a hundred, I'd say. They won't make it down this trail, sir," Jamie added softly.

"We'll have to leave them. You've got a hospital flag?"

"Yes, sir," Jamie said, his voice barely above a whisper.

Sibley's eyes peered at him out of their dark sockets. A great weariness, and an even deeper despair, filled them. "We'll leave by night. Let the Yanks think we're camped. It'll give us a head start."

Jamie nodded, then left the meeting and began to prepare for the march. He put Wooster in charge of packing the train, with orders to bring essentials only. Colonel Green wanted to bring all his wagons, and after a brief, hot dispute Jamie gave up trying to dissuade him, though he expected they would run into trouble. There were the company wagons, the officers' wagons, one full of ammunition, one of commissary stores that would be useless on the trail they were taking, and a couple more to bring the convalescents who were near enough well to be walking in a day or two.

After consulting the commissary sergeant, Jamie determined it would be best to slaughter the remaining beeves and divide the meat among the men. It would last maybe two days, then the brigade would be down to bread and coffee. All afternoon the howling wind carried the sounds of slaughter into the camp, and all evening it bore the smell of roasting beef and baking bread.

Jamie went to work getting the sick and wounded together and making them as comfortable as he could. The wind was relentless, and Jamie made a little bit of a shelter by drawing up the empty wagons around a slight depression where the men would not be battered quite so badly by the blowing dust. He and a couple of hands built fires for them and, once it was dark, hung the yellow hospital flags so they'd be conspicuous in the morning. A stream of men flowed through the little encampment, come to say farewell to their unfortunate comrades. It was hard, after all they had gone through to avoid capture, to be leaving them to fall into the enemy's hands at last.

Slowly the column assembled in the darkness, the men

silent and grim. Jamie sent a reminder down the column to fill every available container with water, and to leave everything nonessential behind. Even so, men and beasts alike were burdened with heavy packs. He ordered all the campfires to be built up full, so that the Federal pickets across the river wouldn't suspect they were gone until they had a good head start. The fires crackled merrily, feeding on old papers, old clothes, lost hopes.

Reily and his artillerymen stood ready with their guns. Sibley's ambulance rolled into place at the head of the column, followed by the Armijos' private coach, Judge Baird's carriage, several other light vehicles, and a number of civilians on horseback. Most of the refugees had kept up with the army pretty well, and with good reason. Having supported the Texans, their fate, should they remain behind, would be grim. They knew it; fear showed in their eyes, men and women with haunted faces. Sibley had offered some of them room in his carriage. Jamie heard mutterings in the column. The men didn't like the fact that these civilians—a much kinder name than the soldiers were using—rode in comfort while the half-crippled army must walk. There was nothing Jamie could do, though; Sibley's private vehicle was his private business.

Colonel Scurry rode up to where Jamie waited. "All ready?" he asked.

Jamie nodded, and Scurry gave the order to advance. The column slowly moved forward, southwest along a gently rising road that led up onto the desert plain. Ladron Peak loomed in the darkness, a jagged pile on their right. Farther south were the mountains they'd have to pass through—tall, dark shadows, their crags delineated by silvery moonlight between the gusts of blowing dust—a silent, grim barrier. Jamie rubbed at his ears, which were getting cold. He'd given his scarf to one of the wounded men they were leaving behind. He glanced back toward the river, where the glimmering fires seemed to beckon. Turning away from comfort, he nudged his tired horse, and started slowly forward.

Kip lay on his back, staring up at the moon, too tired to sleep. They had got past Tucson without any difficulty, skirt-

ing the feet of the mountains and giving the town a wide
berth. Muñoz, the guide, seemed to know the country pretty
well, and they'd gotten water from the rivers they'd crossed,
so in all they were pretty comfortable. Kip wanted to take
out his Indian flute and play a while, but he didn't dare. They
were too few, the three of them, to take any chances of being
noticed. They made no fires, and even spoke in whispers,
when they spoke at all. Aikins kept to himself mostly, and
the others followed his lead.

Kip sighed. Past Tucson, but not out of danger. The Rebels
held the whole southern part of the Territory, so much as it
could be said to be held. The party was coming into Cochise's country now, and not even Captain Hunter in Tucson
could claim to be in control of that. Though they weren't
traveling on the stage road, they kept it in sight, and every
station Kip had seen had been destroyed.

"Aikins?" Kip whispered.

A grunt came back.

"You awake?"

"Hm."

"What was it set Cochise off, again?"

"Hanged his brother-in-law, I think."

"Oh."

Kip supposed that would make him angry, too, but the
things Cochise and his warriors had done—he shivered, remembering the bodies hanging in the gully. A rustle in the
grass made him raise his head to listen, heart beating a shade
faster, until the muted grinding of large teeth told him it was
one of the horses, picketed nearby. He laid his head back
down and shut his eyes. If he couldn't sleep he should at
least rest. They'd be up and riding well before dawn.

A melody was running through the back of his mind, and
he hunted it down, trying to identify it. Something in a minor
key, with long, drawn out notes. He let it lift him up, drifting
on the tune like a leaf on a flowing river. At last he dreamily
remembered where he'd heard it—in the Pima Villages,
played by the young Indian he'd had a contest with. Smiling,
he slipped gently into sleep.

*   *   *

All night the wind had beaten against the tent, robbing O'Brien of sleep. Dawn came, and it showed no sign of diminishing. At last he gave up, and came out to blink at the dust-covered camp. Old George, engaged in coaxing the fire back to life, looked up at him warily. O'Brien ignored him and after a moment the Negro said, "No coffee left. I can make up some breakfast."

O'Brien nodded, and walked up to the road to have a look at the river. He was not the first. A half-dozen officers stood clumped together beneath a tree, staring westward. Through the woods on the opposite shore he could see the remains of the Texan's campfires, wisps of smoke drifting with the wind. They had gone, slipped away again in the night, as they'd done at Peralta. O'Brien's stomach tightened. Chivington would not like this.

Captain Downing glanced toward him, then looked away again. O'Brien made no move to join the group. They were Colorado men, and so favored him more than the Regulars did, but not much more. That Chivington hated him was well understood. No one wanted to be cast in the same light as himself, so they kept apart, even old friends. It should have made him angry, but he was far too weary to care. His own lads, his oldest friends, still stood by him.

He went back to camp, where Old George had bacon frying. Its smell was not grand; the bacon was old and beginning to rot, but it was near all they had. Old George had managed some flat cakes, sweetened with molasses, and somehow had even got hold of some milk. O'Brien's mood rose a little as he ate.

"We marching today, Massa?" George asked.

"Don't call me that. I'm not your master."

"Yes, sir, Cap'n."

O'Brien munched his last bite of bacon. Old George sat eating a flat cake, chewing each bite slowly, as if savoring some rare treat instead of a plain pancake of flour.

"Yes, we'll probably march," O'Brien said, relenting a little. "It's a question of where."

George nodded, as if it made no difference to him which way they went, and O'Brien supposed it didn't. The Negro would face neither enemy guns nor Chivington's wrath. He cared only for his pots and pans, and for whether they'd move or stay camped.

O'Brien glanced toward Denning's tent, pitched a few feet from his own. Luther wasn't up yet. O'Brien sighed. He wanted someone to talk to. Shaunessy might not have made flat cakes for breakfast, but he was an old friend, a trusted comrade, always ready to listen. His loss was like a wound in O'Brien's gut.

A figure approached, head lowered against the wind. O'Brien watched the man trudge toward his camp, and realized it was Shoup. The lieutenant stopped by the fire and glanced up at O'Brien, as if to be sure of who he was speaking to, before bending his head down again so his hat sheltered his face. "Captain O'Brien, you are to report to Colonel Chaves immediately." He turned without awaiting an answer, hunching his shoulders.

"Blast." O'Brien dove into his tent to retrieve his hat and hurried to headquarters. Colonel Chaves was a stiff-necked Spaniard and a friend of Miss Howland's. No doubt he was planning some hell for O'Brien, like all of the others. O'Brien had taken to avoiding Miss Howland's friends.

Reveille sounded as he trudged up the hill to headquarters. He searched for Chaves's slight form among the few men moving about, and at last found him seated in front of a tent while an orderly strapped spurs onto his boots. Chaves was smaller than most, but strong as granite, with a face to make the ladies swoon and gray eyes that could flash thunder and lightning. He looked up at O'Brien without smiling, and raised his chin. O'Brien saluted.

"Captain," Chaves said, nodding. "Your company has been detailed to me. We are ordered to collect some wagons and supplies that the tejanos have left behind and take them to Sabinal."

O'Brien said nothing, trying to figure out where was the trap; or the insult. He supposed it was Chivington seeking to demean him by giving him a work detail. The rest of the army would follow the Texans, and fight them maybe, and earn laurels. Well, O'Brien was too tired to care for that, and maybe he didn't want any laurels at the cost of the lives of his men.

Chaves said something in Spanish to the orderly, who nodded and went away. "Get your company ready to march," he said to O'Brien. "As soon as they've eaten and struck camp, we go."

O'Brien nodded. "Yes, sir."

Chaves continued to gaze at him steadily. O'Brien waited for dismissal, but instead the colonel said, "I have been hearing some things that surprise me."

O'Brien raised his chin. "Does the colonel believe all that he hears?"

"No," Chaves said softly. "But if I find that what I hear is true, it will go hard with you, my friend."

A chill ran across O'Brien's shoulders. Somehow, coming from this little scrap of a man, the threat that he'd heard so often in the last weeks gave him greater pause. Colonel Chaves, who'd suffered and nearly been killed by Indians at a tender age, knew what hardship was, and O'Brien did not want to receive any lessons from him. He respected Chaves, and cared for his good opinion. He wanted to tell him to ask Miss Howland for the truth. He wanted to beg Chaves to plead his suit for him with her, but all that was useless. She was far away, and likely he'd not see her again. Maybe by now she had heard some of the lies that were being told about him, and believed them, and thought herself lucky to be rid of him. The thought made a slow, heavy anger boil up in his gut.

So he'd go collect wagons, and try to forget her. There was naught else he could do.

"You may go," Chaves said.

Roused from his gloom, O'Brien saluted and turned to leave. He nearly stumbled into Chivington, coming out of a nearby tent. O'Brien saluted again and kept his gaze down. If he looked at Chivington's great, round face, the temptation to punch it just might get the better of him.

Chivington walked past with slow deliberation. O'Brien found that his teeth were clenched so hard together as to make his jaw ache. He rubbed at it, forcing himself to relax, and headed back to his company's camp.

*   *   *

Laura sat silently, leaning against the cushioned seat while the carriage rattled its way down the Camino Real. Juan was not driving very fast. So far they had been making close to thirty miles a day, but today they would be lucky to make twenty. The animals were tired, and good grass was scarce. The armies had devoured everything on their way down the river from Albuquerque. At that village, so denuded by the Confederates' stay there, Laura had first heard of the battle that had taken place at Peralta. The news made her more anxious than ever to catch up to the army.

Now they were nearing Peralta, and Laura leaned forward to look for signs of the conflict, but saw only sandy hills and a few squares of farmland crisscrossed by acequias. She sat back, clasping her hands together in her lap. Juan would surely stop at the village to water the animals and ask for news.

At last they pulled up, and Laura left the carriage. They had stopped in the center of the village, on its tiny plaza, drawn up outside of a church whose bell tower bore the marks of cannonballs. To the east, blue mountains jumbled their way southward down the plain, ever softening as they descended parallel to the river valley. Westward the wind-scoured plain rose to the distant horizon, marred here and there by small crags. A picturesque landscape, but rather lonely, Laura thought.

Esteban hopped down to attend to the animals, while Juan Carlos strolled toward a house where an elderly man sat on the ground in the shade of a wall, and struck up a conversation. Laura gazed about the silent, dusty town. She could see only one building that looked like a merchant's, and its door was firmly closed. No one was abroad.

"Señorita, if you do not mind, I would like to visit la iglesia," María said.

"By all means," Laura agreed, and followed her companion to the door. She glanced inside the modest church, watching María kneel before an altar covered in a cloth coarsely woven and embroidered with flowers stitched in brightly colored wool. Saints looked out from nichos in the walls, their bodies roughly carved out of wood, their faces and clothes painted in broad strokes. A similarly carved figure of Christ crucified, his wounds depicted rather too realistically for Laura's taste, hung upon the wall behind the altar, and the Virgin of Guadalupe, her form wreathed in rays of light, stood watch nearby.

Laura smiled. La Guadalupana had become a friend to her recently, a familiar, comforting figure. Be he ever so poor, no native lacked the means to obtain an image or a statue of this lady. She was met with everywhere—the natives loved her, and considered her their guardian. To Laura she had become a talisman of hope, though she knew it was a papist custom to revere the Virgin.

Perhaps she would have to get used to papist customs. Captain O'Brien was an Irishman, after all. Presumably he was a Catholic, as the Protestant Irish had not been in the habit of migrating to America.

Suddenly feeling restless, Laura glanced once more about the church to satisfy herself that no one else was there, then walked down the road to join Juan Carlos. The old man began to struggle to his feet as she approached.

"No, no," she said. "Please don't get up."

"No se levante, señor," Juan said, but the man had already risen.

"Buenos días," he said, bowing to Laura.

"Buenos días, señor," Laura replied. "Juan, could you ask him if he knows anything about the battle?"

"He has already been telling me about it. The soldiers trampled his cornfield, and now he will have no crop."

Laura looked at him, and found him watching her, dark eyes looking out from deep sockets, wrinkled skin stretched too tautly over sharp cheekbones. The loss of a crop would be a great tragedy to his family. "I'm so sorry," she said. She conjured the Spanish word for corn. "El maíz. Lo siento."

The old man gave a little smile. "Gracias. Voy a plantar frijoles. Por lo menos, tendré algo."

"He says he will try some beans," Juan translated. "That way they will at least have something to eat."

Laura nodded. "Does he know anyone who could tell us about the casualties?"

Juan translated the question, and the man responded by

shouting into the house. He spoke rapidly to Juan for a minute, gazing all the while at Laura. By the time he had finished, a younger man, perhaps thirty, appeared in the doorway.

"This is his son," Juan told her. "He watched the whole fight. ¿Sabes algo de las pérdidas?" he added, addressing the son.

"Sí, sí. Vi los entierros."

"¿Nos muestras dónde están?"

The man gave a wary look. "Los tejanos o los federales?"

"Los federales," Laura said promptly, understanding this question at least.

"Cuatro de sus entierros están en las afueras del pueblo," the man said, gesturing toward the north, "y uno está pa'allá. Se los muestro dónde están."

"He'll show us," Juan said.

"Excellent. Thank you," Laura said, turning to the old man. "Gracias."

"De nada," he replied, nodding.

María had come out of the church, and together they followed the native to the edge of town, where wooden markers stood in a row over four fresh graves. Laura's heart quickened as she came close enough to read them: Long, Thompson, Wilson, and the fourth grave, which looked very new, marked Hawley. He was from F Company of the 1st Colorado, Captain Cook's company. The others were also Colorado men. The regiment had been in the thick of the battle, it appeared.

"There is one other, señorita," Juan said. "Up on the hill. Do you wish to walk?"

"Yes," Laura said. "We could use the exercise."

Their guide led them along the road a short distance, pointing out Governor Connelly's ravaged hacienda to the west, then led them off into the hilly terrain above the village. The sandy ground made walking slow. Laura restrained her impatience, and offered María her arm in support. At last they reached a hilltop upon which they found a solitary grave. Laura bent to read the marker: EGAN SHAUNESSY, BORN IN IRELAND, DIED APRIL 15, 1862. I COMPANY, 1ST COLORADO VOLS.

Shaunessy. One of Captain O'Brien's men. Laura frowned, remembering the jovial private, who seemed always to be singing. A soft sadness filled her. "Rest in peace," she whispered, her fingers tracing the roughly carved letters of his name. She was sorry for Shaunessy's fate, but she could not help being glad that the captain had apparently been spared.

She straightened, and brushed a bit of dust from her skirt. Reaching into her pocket, she took out her purse and extracted a silver half-dime.

"Gracias, señor," she said, holding it out to their guide.

"No, no," he protested, but Laura pressed it into his palm.

"Tell him it's for his father," Laura said. "To make up for the corn."

Juan translated, and the man frowned. Hard times made it difficult to be proud.

"Tell him its a gift in honor of my friend," she added, gesturing at the grave.

The native responded to this with a deep bow, and crossed himself, clutching the coin to his chest. "Gracias," he said. "Muchas gracias. Dios le bendiga, señorita."

I am learning, Laura thought. She permitted herself a small smile as they walked back down the hill to the village.

O'Brien stared at the cluster of wagons, his spirits sinking. No mules or horses, but that wasn't the worst of it. A hundred or so Rebels, wounded and sick, looked up at them from within the circle, sitting around the ashes of their fires. The huddled men were hunched together, some draped with blankets, some lying down, protected from the wind by their comrades' bodies. Surgeons walked among them, sent by Canby, trying to make them a bit less miserable. O'Brien rode up to Colonel Chaves, who sat astride his big black, frowning in thought.

"Did the colonel say anything about these fellows, then?" O'Brien asked.

"They are to be given a hospital," Chaves said, gesturing northward, and O'Brien frowned, chewing at his lip. Northward was where the wagons were to go as well, to Sabinal. They were parked to the south of a river—Puerco, Chaves had called it—that emptied into the Río Grande. O'Brien already knew what Chaves's orders would be: hitch your men's mounts to the wagons to haul them.

"I don't like crossing here, sir," he said. "Most of my horses have never been in harness."

"Then they will learn." Chaves frowned at the river, then gestured toward the Rebels. "Get the ones who can't walk into wagons."

O'Brien nodded, and turned to the task, detailing a squad of men under Denning to sort out the Texans. He himself set to putting teams of horses together to haul the wagons, and allowed himself the pleasure of personally dismounting Ramsey. His own mare he kept—she was too small to match well with most of the others, and he needed to stay in the saddle—but the mustang he gave over to the teams, which set Old George to grumbling.

"Lucky don't want to pull no wagon," the Negro said. "He a saddle horse. Don't do no good hitching a saddle horse to wagon."

"Shut your noise and get in," O'Brien told him, "unless you want to walk." He knew full well the trouble before him. It was difficult getting some of the animals to accept harness, and the raw teams would be the devil to drive, but at last he'd assembled enough to draw all the vehicles. He chose from his company the men best suited for driving—who'd been teamsters, or at least had some experience. The rest he assigned to guard the prisoners, giving Ramsey command of the task.

The sun was starting westward by the time they were ready to march. O'Brien joined Chaves, who stood by the Puerco while his horse drank. All the grass had been chewed to the ground, and the black lipped idly at the stubble.

"Ready to march, sir," O'Brien said, saluting. Chaves nodded, but said nothing, frowning northward across where the two rivers met. O'Brien slid from the mare's back and let her join the black by the water.

"We won't reach Sabinal before dark," Chaves said. "Not with those wounded prisoners, and not with those teams."

O'Brien waited in silence. At last Chaves heaved a great sigh.

"We'll go to La Joya," he said. "It is closer. We'll have to cross the Río Grande, but there is a good ford."

O'Brien nodded, but felt some misgiving. A black crow flew across the river before them, cawing harshly. O'Brien watched it shrink to a speck. "Will Colonel Canby object, sir?" he asked.

"I doubt it. Certainly not when he has heard my reasons. Start the wagons south along this bank. You will find a ford about two miles down the river."

Chaves turned to his horse and mounted. O'Brien followed suit, and clicked the mare up to a canter, reining in at the head of the train, where Denning sat on the box of the lead wagon.

"Turn it 'round," O'Brien told him. "We're going south."

Ramsey, afoot with his guards, frowned and stepped up beside him. The mare sidled, and O'Brien laid a hand to her neck.

"South?" Ramsey said. "I thought we were going to Sabinal."

"Now it's south," O'Brien said. "To La Joya. It's closer."

"Who made that decision?"

"I have orders to set up a hospital," the chief surgeon protested, coming to join them. He was an older fellow, crusty, and crossed his arms as he stood next to Ramsey.

O'Brien looked down at the two of them. "Colonel Chaves's orders," he said, and glanced at Denning, who nodded. With a jerk of his head, O'Brien summoned the train into motion. Denning drove his wagon slowly forward, turning in a wide arc around some scrub and back into the woods. O'Brien rode just outside the leaders, helping to guide them in the turn. With the sun casting shadows through the branches of the trees, they made their way southward along the river.

Jamie's mount tried to drop to a walk, and he urged it back up to a trot. He rode alone, back along the tracks left in the sand by the army, back toward Green and his foundering wagons, and the poor, tired men of the 2nd. Everyone else had halted at a brackish trickle that Coopwood's guides called the Rió Salado; they'd camp there tonight, waiting for

Green to come up. Sibley's ambulance had come through all right, as had the civilians' carriages and the artillery, but Green's heavily laden wagons were hopeless. The colonel had finally admitted it, and had promised to abandon his train if the rest of the army would wait for him.

The sunlight was getting tinged with gold; it would set in an hour. Jamie wanted to get back to Green before then, so he kept his horse going at a steady pace. Along the way he saw various things the men had dropped beside the trail—an Indian doll, a patch of black and white rug, a little tin box—souvenirs, now discarded. With each one left behind some small dream had died, of a happy reunion, a presentation of gifts to loved ones long missed. Gifts weren't essential, said the quartermaster's conscience. It was home, only home, that mattered now.

Something moved, off to the left. Jamie gasped in surprise, drawing his pistol, and wheeled the horse so hard it grunted and sat back on its haunches.

A mule, running away through the brush. Little scrawny thing; it must have escaped from some farm, or maybe it was wild. Jamie holstered his gun and unlashed a coil of rope from his saddle, quickly tying it into a lariat.

"Hyah!" he cried, slapping his horse, and galloped after the mule. Anything on four legs was useful to him. As he caught up to it, he swung the lariat and let it fly, snagging the mule on the first try. It squealed in protest, but Jamie already had the rope tight around its neck. He slowed to a trot, circling the frightened animal and then gently pulling it back toward the trail. It fell into step with the horse after only a little struggle. Probably too tired and hungry to fight him. He felt sorry for it, the more because he couldn't feed it any better than it had fed itself, but he needed it.

The sun was nearing the mountains off to the west when he came up with Green's rearguard. They had halted to transfer as much as they could from wagons to mules and horses. Jamie saw most of them parked close together, and a much reduced train, still laden with ammunition, company gear and so on, waiting to start. He sighed; Green wouldn't part with everything, but at least he had lightened his load. A little way off a group of convalescents sat on the ground, huddled in their blankets. They had not wanted to stay behind and be taken prisoner, but they hadn't counted on having to walk. Jamie felt both sorry for them and annoyed with them for insisting on coming along.

He gave his horse and the mule over to an orderly, and walked up to Green, whom he found staring at the parked wagons. More than half of them were still full of goods. The mules that had drawn them stood waiting, easing their weight from foot to foot under heavy packs.

Jamie saluted, and waited for Green to say something. The colonel looked glum. Sayers, Green's adjutant, was nearby, and Jamie caught his eye. He was a sharp-eyed fellow, about Jamie's age, who had somehow found the energy to shave that morning.

"Have you finished unloading?" Jamie asked him.

Sayers nodded. "The men couldn't carry another coffee bean. Half of them will have to walk, they've packed their horses so heavy."

Jamie glanced back at Green, who still stood silently brooding, then looked to where a couple of sergeants stood near the wagons, waiting with lit torches. "Go ahead, then," he said.

Sayers strode off toward the wagons, calling out orders, and in a minute flames leapt up. Jamie stood watching Green watching the fire.

"I'm sorry, sir," he said softly.

Green glanced up at him, then looked back at the burning wagons. A worried frown had settled onto his forehead. At last he turned his back on the fire, and called out to Sayers. "Let's get these men moving. Got a long way to camp."

Jamie started back toward his horse, but his attention was caught by the knot of wounded men. A sergeant was getting them to their feet. One or two could barely stand, and leaned heavily against their companions. All at once Jamie's chest felt like a giant hand had wrapped around it, squeezing him tight, so hard he had trouble taking breath. They wouldn't all make it, he knew, and there wasn't a damn thing he could do about it.

Or maybe there was one thing. A little thing. He jogged back to the orderly and took the mule's lead rope, then hurried to the wounded. The sergeant looked up at him as he approached.

"One of them can ride this," he said.

The sergeant nodded. "Nettles," he said, gesturing to a soldier, pale as death, one foot swathed in bandages and his arm around a comrade's shoulders. "Give us your blanket."

Jamie cut a length off the rope and they tied Nettles's blanket to the mule's back for a saddle. It took both the sergeant and his friend to lift the wounded man onto the animal. Nettles looked down at Jamie, his brow crinkled up with emotion.

"Thank you, Captain," he said hoarsely.

Jamie nodded, not trusting himself to speak. He wanted to ride off and hunt down more mules, until every wounded man had a mount. He wanted to throw Green's baggage down in the road. He wanted to give up his own horse, but he couldn't—he couldn't do that—he had duties. With a wave, he turned away from the wounded, hurrying off before his feelings got the better of him. He didn't dare look back.

Please, God, look after them. I've done what I can.

"Can we not reach Belen?" Laura asked. She had left the carriage and commenced walking up and down the riverbank to revive her numbed limbs, while Esteban took the mule and his donkey down to drink. They stood on a tiny bank of sand, heads to the water, and Laura could see every swallow travel their extended necks.

Juan Carlos shook his head. "The animals are too tired, señorita. They must rest."

Laura bit the inside of her lip. It was late, true, and everyone was tired. María had stayed in the carriage, closing her eyes and leaning back to catch a little sleep.

Laura glanced westward at the sinking sun, its light dazzling her as it glinted between gray branches in the bosque. Juan was right, they must stop soon in any case. She looked back toward the carriage sitting in the road. They had passed one or two very humble farm houses, but nothing more.

"Where are we?" she asked.

"Close to Tomé."

"Tomé? Colonel Chaves lives there, does he not?"

"He lives at Ojuelos," Juan answered. "It is east of Tomé, about ten miles."

"Oh." A brief hope of staying at the colonel's home faded. Belén was closer than Ojuelos. She sighed. "Do you know anyone in Tomé?"

"Esteban has a brother there, he tells me. He may not be able to speak to him, though."

Laura glanced up at him. "Why not?"

Juan nodded to a large, brown hill east of the road, the most commanding landmark nearby. "Do you see the crosses?" he asked.

"Yes, I noticed them earlier—oh!"

A procession was winding its way up the steep hillside, a dark line of figures moving slowly, some dragging heavy wooden crosses, taller than themselves. Atop the hill were several more crosses, standing black against the distant mountains, which Laura had noted earlier. The late sunlight cast a red-golden color on the earth, and set the white trousers of some of the marchers aglow.

"Los Hermanos Penitentes," Juan said. "It is Good Friday. Esteban's brother is with them."

"Good Friday." Laura felt her cheeks tingle with shame. She had not kept track of the days. She no longer even possessed a bible; hers had been lost with her trunk at Las Vegas. Gazing at the procession, she felt an urge to match their devotion, to spend the sunset in prayer. As she watched, one of the cross-bearers stumbled, then recovered and continued slowly up the hill. It must be very hard, Laura thought. "Who did you say they were?"

"The Penitentes. They kept God's word for us when we had no priests. Now the new priests do not like them so much, but they still keep God's word."

"Why do they carry the crosses?"

"It is penance. They do it to honor Jesus. They are very holy men."

Laura stared at them, fascinated. Such a thing would never be seen back in proper New England. It was like something out of a medieval story. It spoke of a depth of faith that came close to fanaticism; strong feeling that commanded respect, however one might disagree with the Penitentes' practices.

The sound of hooves distracted her; Esteban was leading the animals back to the carriage. He spoke to Juan Carlos as they hitched up the mule and the donkey. At length, Juan turned to Laura.

"We will go to Tomé," he said. "Esteban thinks his brother's neighbor will help us."

Laura nodded, and looked once more toward the hill. The head of the procession had just reached its top. Beyond them the mountains glowed red in the sunset, like the Sangre de Cristo east of Santa Fé. It was as if God's gaze had illuminated the landscape, casting the penitents upon the hilltop into strong relief. She would not soon forget the sight. With a small sigh, she stepped into the carriage, and sat watching the procession until it was out of view.

Kip was dreaming, a dream of endless riding, racing a faceless enemy who was certain to win. He knew it was a dream, but he was not yet strong enough to break out of it. He could feel the horse under him—not Firecracker—and the sun's dreadful heat, and the invisible enemy breathing down his neck, and these things kept him in the dream. He rode past burned buildings, where flaming people waved at him. Past a forest of trees laden with dangling corpses. Past men walking, with arms or heads missing, or bleeding from many gunshot wounds, and one man so stuck full of arrows he looked like a porcupine, trudging along the road. They were all headed east, like himself, to the promised land. They all wanted him to help them, to take them up with him, but he couldn't stop, just as he couldn't escape.

A hand clamped down hard over his mouth, and suddenly Kip was awake. His body jerked once as his eyes flew open, and then he was still, obedient to the pressure of a knife point at his throat. He breathed through his nose in short, quick inhalations, and blinked at the figure looming over him, silhouetted by moonlight. Dark hair brushed the shoulders. The figure leaned back, turning face to moonlight, and Kip inhaled sharply.

It was the Apache girl. The one from the gully. How the hell had she snuck into their camp? Kip looked to his right, trying to see his companions without moving his head. Were they dead? Their throats cut? Was he next?

She reclaimed his attention with a jerk of her hand on his mouth. He blinked up at her, his heart beating furiously. Beautiful, terrible. Dark eyes glinting in moonlight. She withdrew the knife from his throat and held a finger to her lips.

She wanted him to be quiet. Kip nodded, and slowly she removed her hand from his mouth and backed away to let him up. She held the knife ready, and Kip kept a nervous eye on it as he slowly sat up. He glanced over at the others. They were unharmed, sleeping; Kip could hear Muñoz snoring softly.

The young woman stood in a single, silent movement, and gestured to him to follow her away from the camp. He hesitated, then put aside his blanket and got to his feet. The Apache took a few steps toward a hill that stood between the camp and a view of the stage road. Kip followed, conscious of the small sounds made by his boots and of the fact he was still breathing too fast. She could be luring him away so as to kill him, but why would she bother? She could have slit his throat as he slept.

She went around the hill, putting it between them and Kip's comrades. A mile to the north lay the stage road, a pale line through the desert. Kip's glance swept the hilltops, looking for figures on horseback, or afoot. He saw nothing, but there could have been dozens in the shadows of rocks and trees. He turned to the Apache woman, who stood watching him. Her buckskin dress glowed in the moonlight. Why had she come?

The woman stepped closer, and Kip was conscious of his heart racing. She had put away her knife, he noticed. That was comforting. She looked at him, frowning, as if making up her mind about something. In a voice he could barely hear, she said, "You will be attacked tomorrow."

Kip's mouth dropped open. "You speak English!"

The Apache pressed her lips together. "White men are like

dogs," she said in the same low voice. "You have to tell them something ten times before they understand."

"How—I mean, why . . . ?" Kip couldn't even form a question.

"You and your friends have been observed," she told him. "In Apache Pass, you will be attacked."

Kip gazed at her face. She was frowning, but he didn't think she was angry at him. "Why are you telling me?"

She looked away, down at the ground, or at something far distant. "You helped me," she said softly. "Now the debt is paid."

"You mean, with—your husband?" Kip whispered.

"My brother." She looked up at him, dark eyes glistening under brows drawn tautly together.

"I'm sorry," Kip said softly. She stood still for a moment, and Kip thought he could stand there all night looking into those eyes, so proud, so sad.

"He was the last of my family," she said in an angry whisper. The eyes hardened, like two chips of flint in the moonlight.

"All I have is a brother," Kip said softly. "I'd be mighty sore if someone killed him." That was true, even if Elijah did drive him mad sometimes. "I'm sorry," he repeated.

"You go back tomorrow," she said, jerking her head toward the northwest.

"I—we can't," Kip told her. "We're carrying a message—"

"This is our land," she said. "Not yours."

Oh, hell, Kip thought. "Look, we don't want to fight your people," he said. "We're just passing through—"

"If you go into Apache Pass, you will not come out," she said flatly. "I have seen what Cochise does to his enemies." She stood staring hard at him, and Kip remained silent.

"I don't want that to happen to you," she hissed, and abruptly turned away.

"What?" Kip whispered, but she was gone, gliding downhill like a leaf on the breeze. As he watched she disappeared behind a tree, then reappeared on horseback—the same damned pinto from the gully. It made him think of Firecracker, and he glanced up toward the camp, thinking he'd better check on the horses. Maybe she'd stolen them, but somehow he didn't think so. By the time he looked back, she was gone.

15

"Some talk of spiking the artillery and leaving it ... but it was not done. Scurry undertakes to take them through and will not consent to leave behind us the only trophies we have been able to keep of our victories."

—Alfred B. Peticolas

Jamie reined in beside Major Teel's carriage, which had foundered in the boggy ground. The Salt Creek—aptly named, as the water was practically unfit even for making coffee—meandered down a narrow, steep-walled canyon, sometimes sinking, sometimes trickling from side to side, leaving no firm ground for wagons or men. The army bore it with only a few grumbles, being promised fresh water from a spring five miles up the canyon, but the vehicles were having trouble.

Teel looked up from supervising the transfer of his baggage to the backs of the carriage's team. "Good morning, Russell," he said. "Have you got any shovels?"

"Six," Jamie said. "That's all I could keep." He had almost left them behind, but a grim realization that they would likely be needed had changed his mind.

"Six will do, then," said Teel. "Bring them down here."

"We can probably pull this free, sir."

Teel glanced at the vehicle. "No, I don't need it. Just get me the shovels. I'm lightening my load." He gestured to his three field guns standing nearby. They had been removed from their carriages, which were now laden with wounded. Jamie met Teel's gaze, and found the major's eyes steady and unemotional. A practical man, Major Teel. He faced necessities squarely. Jamie was glad that Teel had found a way to provide transportation for the wounded, and also glad that

Reily wasn't present to witness the burial of more guns. He
doubted his friend would have taken it well.

With a hasty salute, he urged his horse forward. The shovels were up with the pack train, ahead of the 2nd. Jamie
splashed through the creek, passing men and horses trudging
along through the muck. He glanced at each soldier, a habit
he'd acquired of late, looking for those who seemed about
to give out. To his great relief, quite a few more wild mules
had been found, and many who had been afoot were now
riding with improvised saddles and rope bridles.

He caught up with the train at the head of the creek, where
men clustered around the spring, drinking and filling canteens. Fill them full, Jamie thought. According to Coopwood,
it was twenty miles to the next water.

"Wooster," he called as he came up with the train. "Where
are those shovels?"

"Up here." Wooster looked tired, and Jamie, who had intended to send the sergeant back to Teel, changed his mind
and decided to take the shovels himself. He had the quartermaster's hands pack them on a mule, took its lead rope, and
turned east again.

Going back down the creek, he could see the men's faces,
a parade of expressions from sullen to woeful, all weary.
He'd have liked to let them camp up at the spring, but rations
were short—already down to coffee and bread, the meat
having gone the first day—and they had only begun the journey. As he watched, a soldier on foot with his arm in a sling
stopped, took two books out of his pack, stared long and
hard at them, and finally tucked them into a crevice in the
steep canyon wall, then marched onward.

Twenty miles, Jamie thought. You can make it.

By the time he got back to Teel, the major had his horses
packed and stood waiting by the three guns. Nearby, Green
had parked several more wagons and was once again packing
their teams with goods. The boggy creek bottom had made
the colonel face facts, it appeared. Green glanced up at Jamie, who gave him a nod and a salute, and dismounted beside the guns.

"Thank you," Teel said as Jamie handed out shovels to

the waiting artillerymen. "We'll bring them up with us. You needn't wait."

"I'll leave you the mule," Jamie offered.

Teel nodded, and began putting his men to work digging in the wet ground. Jamie walked toward Green's wagons. Two were full of powder barrels, and Green had parked these in the middle and piled up dry brush around the wagon wheels. The artillery caissons and the extra ammunition chests they carried were to be burned as well. It seemed to Jamie that he was always burning things he would rather have kept.

"Do you need any help, Colonel?" he asked.

"No." Green squinted up at the sun, close to midday. "How far to the spring?"

"About a mile," Jamie said.

"And to camp?"

"Twenty."

Green gave him a hard look, then nodded.

"Are there many stragglers?" Jamie asked gently.

"Not so far, but there will be." He glanced back down the canyon. The rearguard had passed them on the way up to the spring. Far off, a solitary man on horseback stood atop the cliff. As Jamie caught sight of him, he wheeled his horse and galloped away.

Spies. The Yankees were watching them. Well, let them watch. Jamie went back to his horse, and stood beside Major Teel as the artillerymen lowered the first tube into the ground with ropes.

"That leaves how many?" Jamie asked.

"Nine, altogether," Teel said. "We can drop the last three field guns if we must, but I'd prefer not."

Jamie nodded. With Teel, as with Scurry, there was no question of leaving the other six guns, the ones that had been taken at Valverde. If they left everything else behind them, those guns would be saved.

"I'd better get back," Jamie said.

Teel nodded, watching his men. They had already placed the first gun, and were now tying the second tube into a sling. Jamie glanced at the jumble of wagons. Quite a nice bonfire they'd make. With a sigh, he got in the saddle and headed back up the canyon.

"Why can't we swing north of the mountains?" Kip asked, gesturing to the Dos Cabezas looming up ahead. "Isn't there an easier pass up north?"

"Because there's no water," Aikins said. "You know that."

"Well, how far is the next water after that?"

"Too far."

"I still think we should find another way."

"Whistler, it was a dream."

"No, it wasn't. I know when I'm dreaming."

Aikins didn't deign to answer that, and Muñoz kept silent, as was his habit. Kip thought he saw the Mexican frowning, but failed to catch his eye.

All Kip's persuasions had only half convinced them of the Apache woman's existence, even after he showed them the lock of her hair, and neither of them could understand why any savage would want to help them. Kip wasn't sure he understood it himself. She'd taken a big risk, sneaking into the camp like that. She must have done it alone, because he couldn't imagine any Apache warrior helping her to warn away their enemies. Every time he thought about her face in the moonlight, he got an unsettled feeling down in his gut.

He stared up at the mountains, the two rounded peaks that gave them their name looking for all the world like a couple of heads, but too close together. Like they were heads stuck on stakes, to warn away unwary travelers. To the south of them a rough mountain range—the Chiricahuas, named for the Apache tribe that made their home among the rocky heights—ran away down to Mexico. Kip shivered, even though the sun was broiling. He did not want to ride into that pass, but the others were determined, and he couldn't figure out a way to convince them. And Aikins was right, anyway—they couldn't get on without water. The horses were suffering already as they crossed the alkaline plain, and Kip's canteen was only half full even though he'd been miserly with it.

So they'd go in, though they rode toward certain death. Kip kept thinking of Calloway's words: one of you must get through. If he was a brave, adventurous sort, he would have taken off around the mountains himself, but he guessed he wasn't that brave, or that stupid. He wasn't a mountain man—he was no Pauline Weaver, able to live off the desert. His best chance at survival, even if it was a slim one, was if there were two other targets around.

"Maybe we should lie up a spell, and go in after dark," he suggested.

"Maybe we should grow some wings and fly over the mountains," Aikins retorted. He urged his horse back to a trot, and with a sigh, Kip nudged Firecracker. The horse gave a small grunt of protest but picked up his gait, and Kip kept a wary eye on the two-headed mountains before them.

"I insist that the colonel come here and see for himself," said the surgeon. "This will not do!"

O'Brien nodded agreement. The little barn, which was half fallen down anyway, was stuffed full of wounded Texans, and more outside, lying in the hot sun. "I'll tell him," O'Brien said.

"Do so," said the surgeon, who looked fit to burst at the seams.

O'Brien went out and saw Ramsey lounging in the shade of a nearby house with Sergeant Fitzroy and Sergeant Rice. The latter glanced up at O'Brien, then away. Denning and Morris were helping to move the wounded to the shady side of the barn. When the column had come in the evening before, the Texans had just been set down anyplace round the building, the sickest ones inside. One had died overnight, and O'Brien had borrowed two shovels—which were all that were in La Joya—because no one had thought to bring any.

O'Brien traversed the tiny village in fifty steps, and found Colonel Chaves talking to a native in rapid Spanish. Nearby, the wagons, some still loaded with goods left behind by the Texans, stood where they'd stopped the previous evening. The horses were being grazed down by the river; here the grass hadn't been touched by the Texan army, so the poor beasts were at last getting their fill.

O'Brien waited for the colonel to notice him. Finally Chaves glanced up, and nodded, then said a few more words to the native, who hurried away. "Good morning, Captain," Chaves said in answer to O'Brien's salute.

"Sir, the surgeon requests that you come have a look at the hospital."

Chaves gave a small sigh. "I'm aware of the problem."

"Beg pardon, sir, but he'd like you to look at it anyway."

"Very well." Chaves gazed over the houses. "While I am doing that, you will go through the village and find somewhere to put the rest of the wounded."

"Yes, sir."

O'Brien grimaced as he turned to the task. The village was full of nothing but poor, grimy Mexicans, and none of them spoke any English to signify, and him with but two words of Spanish. He wanted Franklin, blast the lad. He ran down the names of his company, trying to think if any others of them spoke Spanish. Denning, he knew, did not. If Ramsey did he didn't want him. He paced the street, looking at the houses. Hovels, all of them, but he'd lived in worse himself. Glancing up, he saw Old George approaching, leading the mare and the mustang up from the river.

"Brush 'em down, Mas—uh, Cap'n?" the Negro said.

"Yes." O'Brien took the mare's lead and stroked her neck. He was getting fond of her. She bumped her soft muzzle against his chin, and he couldn't help smiling.

A piercing squeal made him look up. Two Mexican children stood pointing at Old George and shrieking, "El Diablo! El Diablo y su caballo negro!" A woman draped in shawls ran out of a house, and hurried the children inside, crossing herself.

"¡Así soy! ¡Y te voy a comer!" Old George shouted after them, grinning.

O'Brien stared. "How the devil did you learn that gabble?" he demanded.

Old George blinked in surprise. "I done grew up in Victoria, sir. Lot of greasers there. I was only jess a little thing when Massa bought me—"

"Get those horses picketed and come back here at once," O'Brien ordered. Old George's eyes widened, and he hurried to obey.

O'Brien paced the street, silently fuming. How dared a

slave speak Spanish when he himself could not! God or the devil was laughing at him, sure it must be. Well, he'd not be so daft as to pass by this gift, however it might amuse the Almighty Powers.

The Negro returned in short order, and O'Brien at once set him to asking at each house whether there was room for wounded. A couple of the villagers agreed, reluctantly, to house a tejano or two, but before they were through half the town O'Brien realized it wouldn't do. They needed a whole house—or two, even three—if they were to get the rest of the prisoners under shelter. He went on, now observing the houses and the families that dwelt in them, trying to decide which of them to evict. A family could stay with their neighbors, and their house be given over to hospital. No one would like it, but it could be done. He would get the colonel's approval first. Likely if Chaves spoke to the villagers himself, they'd agree to it more readily.

They had reached the end of the cluster of houses that marked the village proper. As in most towns they'd seen along the river, other homes dotted the landscape nearby amid fields green with young crops. O'Brien fixed his eye on one not far off—a small, sorry-looking house, its adjacent field fallow, its mud walls eroding under the influence of rain and wind. He observed two of his own men emerge from it, laughing together as they returned to the town and to whatever duty they'd been neglecting.

Frowning, O'Brien started toward the house with Old George at his heels. If some Mexican had a still set up in there, he would have to close it down, more's the pity. The Texans were not so far off that he could afford to let whiskey flow free to his company. He glared at the two men—who hurried past him toward the village—and strode up to the door. It stood open, the top hinge sagging and a corner resting on the unswept earthen floor. O'Brien peered into the dimness, knocked once on the door, and went in.

There was no still inside. In fact, there was no furniture, not even a table. The far end of the single room was closed off by an old blanket tacked to the roofbeams for a curtain. Nearer by a woman sat on the bench built into one wall. She looked up at O'Brien and grinned, revealing a tooth missing, though she was not so very old.

"Buenos días, señor."

"Buenos días," O'Brien said. "Get in here," he called to the Negro. "Ask her if it's her house."

Old George did so, and the woman laughed. "No, sólo la tenemos prestada. La cama es muy cómoda. ¿Le gustaría probarla?" These last words she addressed to O'Brien, glancing up at him slyly.

"Lord a-mercy," Old George muttered, looking unhappy.

"What?" O'Brien demanded. "Is it her house or not?"

"N-no," the Negro said. "They's jess borrowing it, she said. They likes the bed."

"Bed?" O'Brien frowned, and looked to the curtain. He started toward it, but the woman jumped up before him.

"No, no, espere, espere." She smiled, and her fingers ran across the buttons of his coat. "Pero no por mucho tiempo, señor—"

O'Brien put her aside, and deaf to her further protests, he reached the curtain in two strides and tore it down. A feminine squeal and a flurry of motion told him all he suspected was true. A Mexican woman—younger than the other—scrambled to the far corner of a dirty wool mattress, clutching a blanket to cover herself, while her partner grabbed at pieces of his uniform and gazed up apprehensively at O'Brien.

"Oh, Lordy!" Old George exclaimed.

O'Brien clenched his teeth together and took two breaths through his nostrils before he dared speak. "Get your clothes on, Dougal," he said roughly, "and get out."

He turned his back on the scene. The air seemed foul all at once, and he made for the door and the sunlight. The older whore followed, railing at him in Spanish. Old George, already at the door, stared like a frightened deer.

"She says—"

"I don't give a damn what she says," O'Brien snapped. "Tell her to get the other one dressed and clear out of here. We're taking the house for the hospital."

Outside, he inhaled deeply and leaned against the crumbling wall of the building, listening to the Negro and the woman argue in Spanish. There were definite disadvantages to being a captain, he reflected. Had he been a private soldier, he'd likely have visited this house in an altogether different manner.

He closed his eyes. It had been a very long time. Long enough to make even a Mexican whore look appealing.

At a scrape of bootheels, he looked up. Dougal emerged from the house looking sheepish, and glanced warily at him. O'Brien dismissed him with a jerk of his head toward the village, and the private hastened away.

"¡Pero él no pagó! ¡Y ahora usted me debe el dinero!" the older woman burst from the house, angrily gesturing after Dougal.

O'Brien gazed at her, then casually took out his pistol and began to examine it. It needed cleaning, he decided, rubbing a finger along the barrel. The woman's angry chatter ceased, and she flounced back into the house, passing Old George in the doorway. The Negro hastened to put a safe distance between them. O'Brien hid a smile.

A few minutes later both women emerged, the younger looking sullen and disheveled, the older ready to scratch someone's eyes out. Between them they had but two blankets and a dusty old satchel.

"Tell them to go to Sabinal," O'Brien said. "If I catch them following the army, I'll have them arrested as spies."

Old George swallowed, and translated. The older slut flashed her eyes, and spat in the dust at O'Brien's feet, then stalked off. The younger followed unhurriedly, casting a lazy glance over her shoulder. O'Brien watched them pass through the village. Once they'd turned north, he went back into the house, gesturing to Old George to follow.

It would hold eight, perhaps ten wounded. There was only the one mattress, with a window above it covered by a scrap of cloth. O'Brien stepped over to pull it aside and let more light in. Something rustled beneath his heel, and he glanced hastily down, expecting a scorpion or some other vermin. Instead he spied a crumpled bit of paper, half hid by the mattress. He picked it up and smoothed it out flat. It was printed all over with pictures and letters in brown ink.

"Now where'd they get that?" Old George said.

O'Brien turned it over—more pictures, including a man's portrait. "What is it, then?"

"Money," Old George told him. "Confederate money."

"Paper money?" O'Brien asked in surprise. "Have they no mints, then?"

Old George shrugged. "No gold. That's why we come up here, to get the gold in Colorado."

O'Brien gave a bitter laugh. That was why he had gone to Colorado, too, for all the good it had done him. "It doesn't just lie on the ground, you know," he said.

The Negro shrugged again, clearly uninterested. O'Brien turned the note over in his hand, gazing down at it. Paper money. Absolutely useless money.

So the whores had catered to both armies. Well, saints grant that they don't have the pox. Stuffing the note in his pocket, he led Old George back toward the village.

It was getting late, and the hills rising up all around Apache Pass would soon cut off the sun. Shadows lengthened from scrubby juniper trees dotting the hillsides. Kip's eyes roamed ceaselessly, looking for movement. The muscles between his shoulders were tight. The attack was coming, he felt sure. It was only a question of when.

The mountains surrounding them were not as rugged as Picacho, and not as red. Instead of saguaros, the slopes were covered with yuccas and chollas. The road had meandered its way into the pass and now led up a gentle rise into a deepening cleft. They reached the stage station—abandoned, like all the others—a long, dark structure built of rock.

"There you go, Whistler," Aikins said. "If there were Apaches after us, they would never have let us get this far. This place is too defensible."

"We still have to get to the water," Kip said.

With a shrug, Aikins moved on, turning off the stage road onto a smaller trail that led up toward a defile, gradually getting steeper. They passed low-growing oaks and manzanitas, and one scraggy willow overhanging a dry wash. The hills closed in around them, and ahead Kip saw some tall, green trees filling the valley where the spring must be. His heart rose a little. Maybe they would make it. If one drank while the other two stood guard—

A flash of red among the trees to his right made him jump. Pulling his pistol, he pointed it toward the movement, reining Firecracker to a halt. A shock of excitement ran down his arm.

"What is it?" Aikins said, halting beside him.

"Not sure," Kip whispered. He couldn't see anything more. Up ahead Muñoz stopped, and Kip strained eyes and ears. A high chirp came through the clear air, a rustle of leaves followed, and a cardinal hopped into view on a tree branch. Sighing, Kip uncocked the gun.

"Didn't know those got down this far south," Aikins said.

Almost as the words left his mouth, a scatter of rifle shots rang out from the hillside to their left, and Aikins's shoulder erupted in a plume of blood. Kip cried out in dismay and brought up his pistol. There were puffs of smoke all over the hills—twenty, at least—but no targets. The rocks themselves seemed to be firing on them, though Kip knew it was Apaches hidden behind them. He saw a movement and fired even though his chance of hitting anything was poor. Muñoz was shouting something, trying to get his plunging horse under control. Aikins had collapsed over Merlin's neck. Muñoz galloped up the road toward the spring, but even as Kip glanced his way the Mexican was shot from the saddle. A ball sang past Kip's ear, so close he flinched from the heat. Suddenly he could feel his heart pounding, and the sounds of rifle fire seemed muffled in the stillness of the pass. He turned Firecracker and sped downhill, heavy hoofbeats thumping on the hard road, back toward the station.

The shooting fell off behind him. The Apaches were on foot, and it would take them precious seconds to mount and ride after him. Hope flickered, but he didn't dare pause. He leaned low over Firecracker's neck like a jockey, like he had during that race against Merlin who would now be taken by the Apaches, and why the hell had he taken it into his head he had to have a horse? If he hadn't been mounted he wouldn't now be about to die here a thousand miles from anything. He prayed he wouldn't be hit, or if he was, that it would kill him. The Apache girl's words returned to haunt him. He did not want to gain personal knowledge of what Cochise did to his enemies.

"Come on, get up!"

The horse needed no urging; wind whined in Kip's ears as they flew down the trail. A rifle shot kicked up dust in the road before them and Firecracker reared, shrieking. Kip clamped his knees to the horse's sides, hauled his head down and started him forward again. Another shot struck the trail and he knew that it could have—should have—hit him. The horse jumped sideways, but Kip managed to cling on, and looked up, searching the hillsides while the sound of the rifle echoed away. Atop a low hill a figure rose up from the brush. Kip aimed at it, then dropped his arm as a surge of fear washed through him. It was the Apache girl, holding a rifle. She pointed it toward the station and shook her head, then swung it toward Kip, making him jump, but the barrel moved past to point eastward beyond his shoulder. He glanced that way, out of the pass; he could see the stage road curving around the foot of a mountain. When he looked back she was out of sight.

Kip stared down at the station, maybe a hundred yards ahead, walls of pale rock that seemed oh, so inviting; the only real shelter in the valley. He was out of breath, which seemed odd as it was the horse who'd been running. Back up the canyon, two rifle shots sounded in quick succession. Firecracker grunted and shifted, wanting to flee. Kip agreed with him and started forward at a trot. He could last a while in that station, but how long? One against twenty or more?

And she had shaken her head, with her hair all ragged around her shoulders, a savage wild thing. Why on earth was she giving him advice in the middle of a fight? Was she trying to trick him? He couldn't think it through, the horse was striving to break into a canter, all he could think was how beautiful her sad eyes had been in the moonlight. Abruptly, and suffering a pang of true regret for the solid walls of the station, he turned Firecracker off the trail, away from the structure, climbing a short rise to the east. As he did so, a volley of shots came from the station straight at him, tearing at his clothes, blowing the hat from his head, and one thumping into the saddle just before his leg.

"Jesus!" he shouted, and whipped Firecracker on up the hill.

16

"Patriotism has a good sound, but soldiering as a private requires the genuine article."

—Ovando J. Hollister

In less than a minute Firecracker was scrambling down the far side of the hill, sheltered from fire by its bulk. Kip heard yelling and whooping, and dug his heels into the horse's flanks as he leapt from the hill into a sandy wash. Firecracker's hooves tore up the loose dirt. The wash was only three or four feet deep—not enough to protect them from being seen—and the sand slowed them some. Kip hoped the Apaches wouldn't be able to get ahead of him and cut him off. He kept his eyes forward, down the long, straight stretch of the wash. No motion amidst the scrub on either side, but that meant nothing. All at once a bright slash in the wooded banks flashed by, and Kip wheeled Firecracker around. The stage road! The pale sandy cut dipped into the wash and continued eastward. Kip turned the horse onto it, sparing a glance back up the road toward the station. A gunshot answered him, and as Firecracker surged up onto the hard-packed trail Kip bent low over his withers so as to be less of a target.

Firecracker strained at the bit, and Kip gave him his head. Too busy running to go crazy, the horse was like an arrow shot from a powerful bow. Kip concentrated on keeping his balance and scanning the rocky hills for movement. He saw none. The road passed into the shadow of a tall hill, and he realized it must be running almost due north. He could see ahead down through a wide canyon. Green trees marked the course of the wash to his left; the road seemed to be following it out of the pass. The trees' presence told of water, but there was none there today, nor any hint of cloud to fill the ghost river with rainwater. Kip pressed his lips together and tried to get a swallow down his dry throat. There was only a drop left in his canteen.

Best not to think about that. Instead he thought about his friends. The first of these who came to mind was the Apache woman—he wished he knew her name. She had now definitely proved herself a friend. She'd saved his life, and he thanked her in his heart, and hoped to hell she hadn't been caught. Why she had done it he wasn't sure—out of loneliness, maybe, remembering her dead brother—but he would be eternally grateful, assuming he survived.

That was not at all a sure thing. Aikins was certainly dead by now, or at least Kip hoped so. Muñoz, too. The Apaches hated the Mexicans; those two peoples had been at war long before white men came into the country.

So he was alone. No guide. No map. No water, and not much food, and he had to get to Colonel Canby, because he was the only one left. Laughter welled up inside him, but he kept it down. It was the laughter of desperation, and he couldn't afford to be distracted by it.

The road swung east for maybe half a mile, then north, east, and north again, following the wash around the foot of a mountain and descending toward a flat plain. Firecracker slowed up a bit, and Kip sat up in the saddle. It looked like they'd got away clean. He didn't dare look back, but kept on, letting the horse set his own pace. Staying on the stage road was risky, but he couldn't see that leaving it would be any less so. Slower going off the road, and this was not a good country to be lost in.

He wished he had copied Calloway's map, and cussed himself for ever wanting adventure. What a lot of fun this had been, to be sure. If he ever made it back to California, he would crawl back to his brother on hands and knees for a job in a nice, safe, countinghouse.

Firecracker ran on. He'd been running a long time—it must have been an hour at least. The setting sun sent long streamers of light across the plain through the gaps in the mountains. Dust lit up the beams, and it looked as if God was reaching across the desert, stretching his arms toward the east. A glint showed up ahead where the golden light struck the plain.

"Water!" Kip almost laughed with joy. "See that, Firecracker? Just a little farther!"

The horse must have smelled it, because he picked up speed again. Kip had never seen anything like it—Firecracker had been running since they quit the pass and didn't seem about to stop. Admiration and gratitude, mixed with fading terror, made a symphony of feelings inside Kip's chest. He ran his fingers along Firecracker's neck under the pale mane. The horse's body was hot.

"Don't kill yourself, now," Kip murmured. The last thing he needed was to be stranded afoot in this desert.

The glint grew into a winding creek—San something—he remembered Aikins talking about it but hadn't paid enough attention. Firecracker turned off the road, dropped to a trot and splashed right into the water, standing with all four feet in the creek bed and bending his head down without waiting for Kip to dismount. Kip managed not to tumble off, and got down in the stream, not minding the wetting of his boots. It wasn't deep enough to get inside them. He stepped upstream and squatted down to drink the heavenly water, but fear soon made him stand up and cast his gaze westward.

Would they follow? Or would they be preoccupied with the spoils of their victory? Kip climbed up on the creek bank to get a better view. The sun was down, only scattered fragments left to brighten the sky. The mountains, cast in shadow, yielded little detail, but after squinting a while he was sure of what he'd seen. A plume of dust—a small one—along the road back a few miles. He was being followed.

Firecracker had finished drinking and was now cropping grass along the creek bank. Kip took out his canteen and filled it, then drank some more and ate a strip of dried beef from his satchel, all the while watching the little plume of dust.

A small party, not the whole band of twenty or fifty or however many there'd been in the pass. It wouldn't take the whole band to catch and kill him.

He was tired, and he wanted nothing more than to go to sleep by the murmuring creek, but if he did he knew it would be his final sleep. He looked eastward, where the last shards of sunlight lay broken on the plain. Across it ran the stage road, a bright scar leading off into night. That road was his lifeline, he knew. Somewhere along it, many miles distant, civilization lay waiting to welcome him back.

Firecracker's head rose and he snorted, then bent to the grass again. Wanting to let him eat a little longer, Kip took down his saddlebags and made a quick inventory of his resources. Thirty-two cartridges for his pistol, about two day's worth of jerked meat, bedroll, his fife and the Pima flute—silent a long time now, both of them—a length of rope, Firecracker's halter, a small box of matches, his sketchbook, and his uniform. It was brand new, never worn. Calloway had been saving them for the triumphant march into Tucson. In his pockets, a few coins, two pencils, and Calloway's letter to Canby.

He took out his pistol and replaced the round he had fired in the pass. Thirty-seven rounds between him and death. He peered at the darkening desert, but the dust plume was no longer visible.

"Time to go, boy," he said softly. Taking Firecracker's reins, he hauled his sore body into the saddle and coaxed the horse back onto the road, setting an easy pace for the long night ahead.

"How far is it to the water?" a soldier asked, clinging to Jamie's stirrup.

"Not far," Jamie said. "Keep going."

The man stumbled back, his face a twist of pain and anger, and slowly turned to march on. Jamie wished he had some water left to give the poor fellow, but the six canteens he'd brought back along the line were already empty.

Through a long, hot, dreadful day the column had dissolved into a straggling line of thirsty, weary men. Their route was littered with gear: broken tack, cookpans—the ones Jamie'd ordered back in San Antonio—that he knew they'd regret losing later, improvised packs that had slid from mules and been left to lie by the trail. Some of the mules had refused to go on, and some of the men also had just quit, sitting down by the wayside to rest before struggling a little farther.

They had reached the summit around sundown, and started down the other side into a deepening valley filled with pines. Now that it had fallen dark the men had begun to gather in groups and make fires, too exhausted to press on to water. Jamie knew he had no chance of getting them organized tonight. He had been up at the pass when the head of the column had reached the spring at Ojo del Pueblo, six miles down the valley, and had thus not been present to lay out the camp. When he got to the spring himself he found the advance had camped without regard to order, so that men as they came in had to wander from fire to fire in search of their own companies. It was just an awful mess, but there wasn't anything he could do about it.

Up the shadowed valley the line of march was picked out with campfires, stretching back a mile or more and ahead to the spring, flickering through the pines like so many clusters of fireflies. He could fetch more water and bring it back, but it would only help a few. A lot of the men were already asleep. And he was tired, so tired. Giving up, he turned toward camp, resolving to come back early in the morning.

His weary horse plodded along slowly, now and then passing a man or a few who were still afoot, making doggedly for the spring. Jamie murmured words of encouragement. No, not that next fire, but it's not far, keep going. It was partly a lie, because not far could mean anything at all, but every man who made it to water tonight was a man less likely to fall out tomorrow.

"Jamie."

Turning his head, Jamie peered at the two men he'd just passed, one helping the other along with an arm around his shoulder. "Ells?"

"Thought that was you," Lane said with a weary chuckle. "No one else would be mad enough to ride back at this hour."

Jamie stopped and dismounted. Lane's companion, a convalescent, looked about ready to drop. With Lane's help Jamie got him up into his saddle. Lane was carrying his saddlebags and blanket, and Jamie strapped them on top of his own gear. Taking the reins, he walked with his friend down the valley.

"What happened to your horse?"

"Gave out around sunset," Lane said. "Just stopped, and when I got off, he lay down and wouldn't get up again. I left him there, and he cried after me for half an hour."

Jamie sighed. "I'm sorry."

"It's all right. Does the men good to see a staff member walking. Makes them feel like it's not just them suffering. Is it very far to camp?"

Jamie laughed under his breath. "Probably about a mile," he said softly.

"Oh. Well, all right. Wish I had better boots."

"Want mine?"

Lane laughed. "No, stupid! I'd never fit into 'em." He trudged along for a minute, steps in rhythm with the horse behind them, then asked, "Seen Reily?"

"He's in camp," Jamie said. "He and some others shot a bear earlier, up at the pass. You never saw a carcass stripped and butchered so fast."

"Don't suppose there's anything left," Lane said wistfully.

"Sorry, no. I didn't get any either."

"I saw them shoot those three antelope that tried to cross the head of the column. Sat right down to cook 'em."

"I just saw the bones."

Lane sighed. "You know, I haven't the faintest idea where we are."

"Coming into the Magdalena Mountains," Jamie told him.

"Still north of Craig?"

"Still north of Socorro."

Lane was silent for a while, then said, "This is going to be a long march, isn't it?"

Jamie swallowed, for he'd just referred to Coopwood's map earlier in the evening, and the distance yet to travel was disheartening. "Yes, it is," he said, not wanting to burden Lane any further than that.

Up ahead was a campfire. Not the camp, Jamie knew, but he noticed Lane's steps quicken, and lengthened his stride to keep up. The fire snapped and crackled at them, being made of green wood. All around it men lay sleeping, some muttering in their dreams.

Lane paused, and squatted to warm his hands. "Maybe we should stop here a while," he said, glancing up at Jamie.

Jamie shook his head. "It's not much farther," he said softly, "let's keep going." He glanced up at the man on his horse, whose chin was on his chest. Asleep in the saddle. Jamie tugged on the reins to get the horse to quit eating weeds, threw an arm around Lane's shoulder and gently urged his friend back to the march.

"Do you think maybe you could find a bumpier road to drive us over?"

O'Brien ignored the prisoner, though he was tempted to say if he disliked the ride he might get out and walk with the others. Two thirds of the Texans were on foot already; Chaves had given him wagons enough only to take the worst off, and one for I Company's tack and the weapons confiscated from the prisoners.

Even with the house O'Brien had cleared out, and the few beds he had wheedled from the villagers, there was nowhere near enough room in La Joya for all the wounded Texans, and Chaves had finally yielded to the surgeon's wishes so far as to send them away. He did not send them to Sabinal, but south to Socorro, though it was five miles farther. In Socorro a large hospital already tended to Confederates wounded in the Battle of Valverde, and Chaves had reasoned that it would be easier to watch over them all in one place. So he'd sent O'Brien to escort the prisoners with half of his company, keeping the other half back while he figured out how to dispose of the wagons. It meant O'Brien had only thirty men to guard a hundred prisoners, and he didn't much care for the odds. Half his own men were on foot, their horses drawing the wagons. He himself rode up and down the little column, keeping a sharp eye on all of the Texans.

"Here comes Paddy again," hollered the same wounded man from his wagon. "Can't decide whether to ride in front or in back."

"Well, if he rides in front he might meet some greasers," said another, "and if he rides in back he might meet . . ."

"More greasers," said the first, and both laughed.

O'Brien kept his eyes away from the wagon, for if he looked at the noisy fellow he might be inspired to murder him on the spot. His glance fell on Ramsey, walking at the head of the guard, who smirked back at him. O'Brien looked away again and faced straight ahead.

At the front of the train was the tack wagon, with Old George perched among the saddles, looking resigned to his discomfort. A wagon of wounded followed, then the prisoners on foot flanked by guards, then two more wagons, with a dozen mounted men bringing up the rear. Denning was back with Chaves and the rest of the company, as was Morris. O'Brien felt strangely alone.

Ramsey called up to O'Brien, "Colonel Chaves seems to be taking a long time getting those wagons where they ought to go."

O'Brien shrugged. It was none of his concern.

"Is he sending them on up to Sabinal?" Ramsey asked.

"I don't know."

"He didn't tell you anything about it?"

"No."

"Hm." Ramsey tilted his head up to look at O'Brien. "May I see the written orders?"

"There are none," O'Brien told him.

"None? Colonel Chaves didn't give you a written order? I wonder why."

It was said in the kindest of tones, like a father concerned at some slight to his son. It made O'Brien hate Ramsey all the more. Ramsey knew damned well that no written order was necessary for such a case. It was a simple task; take the prisoners to Soccoro and leave them there. Ramsey made an everyday occurrence sound like an oddity, only to torment him.

O'Brien gave no answer, staring instead at the road below. Every step of the horses' hooves raised a tiny cloud of dust. He wanted to throw Ramsey down and see how big a cloud he'd make.

"If I were you, Captain, I'd be very concerned," Ramsey continued. "Colonel Chaves's handling of this admittedly minor operation seems—inefficient, at best. Has he not disobeyed Colonel Canby's orders?"

"Colonel Chaves is a gallant officer," O'Brien said roughly. "If he's disobeyed orders, he had good reason."

Ramsey said no more, but smiled half a smile and moved off. O'Brien's mood sank, borne down by the feeling that he'd given Ramsey exactly what he wanted.

Firecracker dropped to a trot, which brought Kip's wandering mind back to the road. He had let the horse go as fast or as slow as he liked for the most part, and he seemed to like to go pretty fast. That was good, because it would have been a chore to have to constantly whip a horse to keep him running.

Kip glanced over his shoulder. The dust cloud was still there. He had gained a good lead on it by traveling through the night, and in fact he had thought it was gone when he stopped at dawn to let Firecracker drink from a spring out back of a stage station. Within half an hour, though, the cloud had reappeared, spurring him to ride on through the heat of the day.

He gazed around him, feeling a little bit dizzy from the heat and lack of sleep. He wished he hadn't lost his hat—his scalp was sore from sunburn, and he had finally resorted to tying his kerchief over it, which helped a little but didn't shade his eyes from the sun. The countryside had changed some; the ground rose steadily as he continued eastward. The road was starting to get hilly, too, which made it harder on Firecracker to keep running.

Kip leaned forward to stroke the horse's neck, and Firecracker responded with a toss of the head and a low nicker. He had shown reserves of strength that Kip hadn't even dreamed of. The animal was like a steam engine.

"Good boy, Firecracker," Kip said, his voice a croak. "When we get to Fort Craig I'm going to give you the best grass there is, and the cleanest water, and a big steak. I'd offer you a pretty mare, too, but you wouldn't be interested."

Getting to Fort Craig would be the trick. Kip didn't know the country, and had no map. Unless he happened on a friendly native who'd be willing to guide him, he was strictly on his own. The stage road led to Mesilla, he knew. Once he saw the first sign of the town, he would have to leave the road and strike northeast for the Río Grande, because Mesilla would be full of secessionists. If he got to the river safely, he could follow it north to Fort Craig. It was a pretty simple plan, he knew, made riskier because there were Texans all over that part of the country. He would have to trust to luck to see him through.

He glanced back at the dust cloud again. No nearer, no farther. He wondered when the damn Apaches would give up and go home. Sighing, he returned his attention to the road ahead.

Hoofbeats startled Laura out of her reverie. The afternoon's warmth had made her sleepy, and at first she thought it must be Juan Carlos and Esteban returning from watering the animals at the river's edge. But they would not have been galloping. Standing up from her seat beneath a gnarled and failing cottonwood, its branches bare save for one skyward-clawing limb struggling to leaf itself out in green, she rubbed her stiff neck and peered down the roadway.

It was a party of men on horseback. Her first impulse was to reach for her bag and get out her pistol, but as they came closer she saw that they wore dark coats—army uniforms— and one of them rode a black horse. Excitement welled up inside Laura, but she quickly damped it. The black was much bigger than Captain O'Brien's scrawny mustang. In fact, it looked familiar—quite familiar.

"Colonel Chaves!"

Smiling and waving, Laura ran the few steps to the roadway, reaching it just as the party reined in.

"Miss Howland!" the colonel exclaimed, and immediately dismounted and bowed over Laura's hand. He glanced toward María, who had risen to greet him, and looked inquiringly at Laura.

"Colonel Chaves, perhaps you remember Señora Díaz," Laura said promptly. "She is in Mrs. Canby's employ."

"Ah, yes," he said, bowing. "A pleasure to see you again, señora."

"Gracias," María replied, gracing him with a dignified curtsey.

Laura smiled. "I am so glad to see you, Colonel! Do you know, I have not played at whist since we last played together."

"There have been other matters to attend to," he said lightly, but his eyes became serious. "What brings you into this country, Miss Howland? This is not a safe place for you."

"I—the Díazes wanted to see their daughter, who lives in Lemitar, and I accompanied them—because—" Laura stopped, and laughed softly at herself. "I have a letter for Colonel Canby," she said.

Colonel Chaves accepted this calmly, though one eyebrow climbed a little. "Would you like me to deliver it to him?"

"No, thank you. I promised to deliver it myself." Knowing that she owed him more explanation than this, Laura drew up her courage. "Have you seen anything of Captain O'Brien?"

The colonel's eyebrow climbed higher. "I have just sent him to Socorro," he said.

Laura's heart beat against her ribs like a bird trying to escape its cage. She blinked, and took two careful breaths before speaking again. "Is he well, Colonel?" she asked.

"Perfectly well, I believe."

"Oh." She looked up at the colonel, and saw concern writ on his handsome face. "I—have heard rumors," she said. "Please tell me, Colonel. Is all well with the captain?"

The colonel's eyes narrowed. "Has he wronged you, Miss Howland? Because if he has done anything to harm you—"

"No, no," Laura hastened to say. "Not at all. He has always treated me kindly, and with the greatest respect. In fact, I fear I may have harmed him, imposing on him as I did."

His eyes softened. "You are very innocent, mi amiga."

"But not ignorant, Colonel," she replied. "Captain O'Brien has enemies, does he not?" The colonel nodded. "And they are seeking to damage him. They accuse him of wronging me."

"Perhaps," he acknowledged. "But there is nothing you can do about that."

"I can set matters straight. And I can warn him."

"I assure you, he is well aware."

Laura pressed her lips together. "I wish to speak to him, Colonel Chaves. Will you help me?"

The colonel regarded her thoughtfully. Laura waited, chin high, blinking as the dappled shade of the dying tree wavered over her face.

"I am at your service, of course," he replied at last. "But, Miss Howland, I doubt very much that your seeking him out can help him."

"He is my friend," Laura said. "He asked me a question the last time we met, and I have not given him an answer." That was all she dared say, for to allude more explicitly to the captain's proposal when she was not sure it was still open could only embarass them both.

The colonel gazed at her in silence, his gray eyes half-hidden by seemingly lazy lids. Laura was not fooled, for she knew he was always alert, never more so than when he appeared not to be. At last, with a gracious bow, he said, "Miss Howland, would you do me the honor of accompanying me to the river? I would like to look at the water. I believe it is beginning to rise."

Taking the arm he offered, Laura fell into step with him, feeling some misgiving as they strolled away from María. They made their way to the river in silence and strolled along it until they were out of earshot, both of María and of Juan Carlos and Esteban, still tending the animals upstream. They stopped and stood together on the bank, a few feet beneath which the brown water glided southward. Like chocolate, Laura thought inconsequentially. A river of chocolate.

"Miss Howland," the colonel began, "I hope I do not offend you. Our acquaintance is not of long standing, but— knowing that you do not have your parents to advise you—"

Laura turned to face him, removing her hand from his arm. "You think I am wrong to seek out Captain O'Brien?" she challenged.

Colonel Chaves's eyes seemed to search hers, and he said quietly, "It does present a very particular appearance."

Of course it did. Laura looked away, toward the water, and frowned. Yes, certainly it presented a particular appearance. Why should that trouble her? Was she not on the point of accepting the captain's offer of marriage?

The river seemed wider than it had a few days ago. The colonel must be right; the water had risen. What had seemed a sluggish stream was now a respectable flow, and judging by the drop of the bank beneath her feet, would yet grow further into a formidable torrent.

What am I doing?

Panic assailed her. She did not really know Captain O'Brien, not really. On the strength of an extremely short acquaintance, made under the distressing circumstance of having left her uncle's protection, and in the midst of all the turmoil accompanying a campaign of war—how could she possibly trust her feelings in such a situation? She could not. Indeed, Mrs. Canby was right. She was rushing toward an alliance with a man she scarcely knew, whose class and upbringing were vastly different than her own, and whose temperament was, to her own knowledge, volatile to say the least.

Laura took a step back from the riverbank, pressing fingertips to a suddenly aching temple. She liked Captain O'Brien. Loved him, perhaps. But was she prepared to join her life to his irrevocably? It was not a small step to contemplate. It represented the end of freedom, the obligation to submit to his will, to rely on his judgment. A man who could not even read or write.

"That is not fair," she whispered to herself. He was trying—he was willing to learn. She must not judge him for what chance had denied to him, not when he was able and eager to better himself. And while marriage might be the end of some freedoms, it would be the beginning of others.

She gazed unhappily at the muddy water swirling in eddies near the shore. She felt confused and frightened, so lost in her own thoughts that when Colonel Chaves spoke again she was startled.

"Forgive me," he said gently. "I did not mean to distress you."

"No, no, I . . ."

"It is not my place to criticize you. I only wish you to know that as a friend, I am concerned for your well being."

At this Laura smiled ruefully, and met his gaze. "Thank you, Colonel. I am most grateful for your friendship."

"But not for my interference. No." He raised a hand to still her protest. "I have overstepped my authority. I ask your pardon."

"Your intentions are unimpeachable," she replied. "I—I know my traveling toward the army presents a particular appearance. I am willing to risk that."

"To help your friend?" Colonel Chaves murmured. "Bien," he said. "Only remember that you have other friends as well." He looked across the river, then turned a sudden smile upon her. "So. What do you require of me? Shall I give you an escort?"

"No, thank you. I am well cared for." Laura gestured toward Juan Carlos and Esteban, who were returning to the carriage with the animals. "I only need to know where I may find—the captain."

"He is escorting some prisoners to Socorro," he replied, "then he will continue to Fort Craig."

"Thank you," Laura said. "Thank you for—for everything."

"It is always my pleasure to serve you, Miss Howland," the colonel said, offering his arm once again.

When they reached the carriage Colonel Chaves carried Laura's carpetbag to the vehicle, placed it inside, and handed first María, then Laura up the two steps. "May I invite you to take supper with me at La Joya?" he said.

"Thank you," Laura said, "but I'm afraid we must press on. We are hoping to make Lemitar tonight."

The colonel glanced at the sun, which was well westward already, glinting through the branches of the old tree. "You will have to drive into the night," he said.

"Well, there is still half a moon," Laura replied. "We shall manage."

"Good luck, then, Miss Howland," he said, closing the carriage door. "You have my very best wishes."

Laura reached out to shake his hand. "And you have mine, Colonel. Thank you again."

With a smile and a nod, he turned away toward his waiting escort. Laura looked at the soldiers, thinking they seemed familiar. Suddenly she realized they were members of Captain O'Brien's company. One, a brown-haired youth, glanced up at her and gravely acknowledged her gaze with a nod. Feeling her cheeks begin to flame, Laura leaned back against the cushions as the vehicle started forward once more.

17

"Every man knew the table mountain and could distinguish the glistening waters of the river away down in the valley 10 miles from where we were crawling along the side of the mountain."

—Alfred B. Peticolas

O'Brien led his little column into Socorro just as the sun was rising. His men were weary after standing guard in shifts all night, though the prisoners showed no inclination to break for their freedom. It had been their exhaustion that prevented the column from reaching Socorro the evening before; O'Brien had wanted to press through, but he'd at last taken pity on the Texans and camped three miles from the town, in a spot where, from the looks of the place, Canby had been a day earlier. The best wood had gone to a hundred or more campfires, of which all that was left were dead, black circles on the hard ground.

Socorro was bigger than any other village they had seen since Belén. It had a large church, and a mill, and a hospital full of all the wounded Rebels from Valverde, a number of whom had recovered and got up to help nurse the rest. O'Brien left his prisoners in their tender care, and turned over the wagons to the guard. With his men mounted again and freed of their burdens, he struck south toward Fort Craig and put the town behind him with all possible speed, his spirits much higher than they had been for days.

He was not far behind the main column, and the sooner he reached it, the better. Behind, he could hear Ramsey and Fitzroy murmuring together. It made his skin crawl. He disliked being alone with Ramsey, which was what it amounted to, with Morris and Denning back with the rest of the company. Sure, he had other friends among the lads, but the barrier of rank was between them, and he didn't dare fraternize, not with Ramsey watching. He kept silent, because it was safest, and hoped to high heaven that Chaves would hurry to join them.

Glancing back, he saw Old George plodding along on the mustang, and beckoned him forward for want of a better distraction. "You came up with the Texans, didn't you?" he asked.

"Yes, sir," said the Negro.

"Were you at Valverde, then?"

A furtive glance, then the Negro faced forward again, as if frightened to look O'Brien in the eye. "I was back with the wagons," he said.

"Well, you must have heard somewhat about it. Tell me what you know of the battle."

Old George shook his head. "Alls I know is it took near the whole day, and there was a lot of noise and smoke, and a powerful lot of horses got killed."

"Horses?" O'Brien's mind went back to Apache Canyon, and the Rebel horses that Chivington had ordered him to slay. The sound of their screaming still haunted him.

"Men, too," the Negro went on. "But the horses—those Yankees shot so many of them in the morning, Colonel Scurry, he had to give up the rest of his horses, and his regiment went on foot after that. They still on foot."

"Hm." O'Brien made no answer. The dull clop of hooves on the hardened dirt roadway was all that he heard for a moment.

"They's mighty proud of them guns they took, though," Old George added.

"What guns would those be?"

"Cap'n McRae's guns. Didn't you know about that?"

McRae. Yes, he'd heard that name, spoken in grieving tones among the Regulars. McRae had gone down by his guns, and was sorely missed. O'Brien had never met the man—had arrived in the Territory after the battle at Valverde—but he felt the faint tug of loss for a fellow Irishman, sharpened by Shaunessy's recent passing.

"Cap'n McRae he had six guns, he did. Colonel Green

ordered them took, and took they was. Then the boys chased the Yankees into the river."

The Negro stopped abruptly, and shot another wary glance O'Brien's way. Fool, to think he'd be punished for such. He might flap his jaws all the day long, for all O'Brien cared. Many words, little meaning. He reached down to stroke the mare's neck, and gazed at the road ahead, squinting for a sign of Canby's forces.

Laura paced along Lemitar's single street, to the church, and back to the house. Overhead a great flock of birds wheeled and circled, finally settling down into the rushes near the river. Laura wished she could fly with them, but that was foolish, and she turned away from such idle thoughts.

María would not leave this place today. Angelina was near her confinement, and Juan Carlos had gone to negotiate with a woman whose husband was at Fort Craig, hoping to hire her as a chaperon for the journey to the fort. Laura stifled a sigh of impatience, and occupied herself with attempting to count the black-and-white geese that flew by. She had reached two hundred and twenty-seven before Juan returned.

"She will come with us for two dollars," he said.

Laura raised an eyebrow. Two dollars was a great deal of money, especially for someone in this tiny village, but beggars could not be choosers, and it was quite possible the journey would take more than one day. "How soon can she be ready to depart?"

"She is preparing now. I will go and find Esteban."

"Thank you," Laura said. "Thank you very much."

She stepped into Angelina's house, which had but one room, and crossed to the curtain that concealed the bed. "María?" she called softly.

"Sí." A rustle of clothing, then María pulled the curtain a little aside.

"Will you mind if we go on to the fort? I will send Juan Carlos back as soon as possible." Laura asked.

"Oh, Señorita Howland, I am so sorry—"

"No, no, please don't be. You cannot leave your daughter at this time." Laura smiled. "Perhaps by the time I return you will have a new grandchild."

María glanced over her shoulder. "Vaya con Dios, Miss Howland," she said, grasping Laura's hand.

"Gracias," Laura murmured, and the curtain fell between them.

A quarter of an hour later she and her new chaperon were in the carriage, rolling at a smart clip toward Socorro. Señora Sánchez was younger than Laura had expected—about five and thirty, by her looks, or possibly less. She had large black eyes, even teeth, and a shy, pretty smile. She spoke no English, of course, and responded warily to Laura's awkward attempts to make conversation in Spanish. At last Laura gave up and turned her attention to the scenery outside her window, leaving the señora to her own thoughts. The sand hills here were devoid of the scrubby cedars that grew further north, supporting only thin grasses and a few sparse shrubs. The mountains were barren as well. Laura found herself longing for Santa Fé.

By midday she was beginning to be very hungry, and was glad when they began to pass houses on the outskirts of what proved to be Socorro. Juan Carlos halted the carriage in a small dirt plaza. No gentle cottonwoods here to lend a bit of shade, but there was still a good deal of activity in the town's center. The remains of what appeared to have been a fairly large market did desultory business in the hot, dusty square.

Laura stepped down and pressed a few coins into Juan's hand, asking him to buy them something to eat, then stood gazing about her uncertainly. There was no sign of Captain O'Brien or his company. A number of white men were lounging around the front of a building on one side of the square. They wore no uniforms, but she knew with a stomach-churning certainly that they were Texans. She stayed close to the carriage, searching the crowd for a Federal uniform. She was near giving up when she spied a soldier crossing the plaza; a native man in infantry dress, with a corporal's stripe on his arm.

"Señor!" she called, waving to him. "Corporal!"

The man paused, then came to her. "I'm looking for Captain O'Brien," Laura told him. "Is he here?"

"No habla inglés," he said, shaking his head. "Lo siento."

"El capitán, Irish," Laura said.

"Ah, sí," said the soldier, brightening. "Él está en los corrales." He gestured down a street. "Los corrales."

"Thank you," Laura said, nodding. "Muchas gracias."

Her heart was beating rather quickly, she noticed. Juan returned with bread and half of a cold roasted goose, which he divided among the party. Laura made herself eat, though she no longer felt hungry.

"Does 'corrales' mean corrals?" she asked Juan, who nodded. "Then I think I know where to find Captain O'Brien. I believe he is at some corrals down that way."

"Bien," said Juan Carlos, following her gesture. "Maybe we can water the animals there. If not, we'll go on to the river."

Hurry, she thought, as the others finished their meal. It was difficult to restrain her impulse to walk briskly down that street, but she waited, and climbed back into the carriage to ride the short distance cloaked in unassailable respectability. The street was narrow; two vehicles could not have passed in it. It was not long, however, and soon opened into a wider path between two large, rudely fenced corrals. A number of empty wagons were parked around one. Juan Carlos drove into the other through a gate opened by a native, and halted the carriage inside. Esteban unhitched the animals and led them to a large trough in one corner. Several mules and a couple of horses were gathered around the water, and others stood about the sunny corral, twitching their ears to shoo away the occasional fly.

Laura got down again. She saw no soldiers, only a couple of natives watching over the animals. Thrusting away disappointment, she stepped over to Juan, who was inspecting the harness.

"This rein will need replacing soon," he said, showing her the worn leather.

"Juan, please would you ask one of these men—"

"No! No me llamo Juan Ramón!" It was Esteban's voice, and confusion of shouting ensued. Juan Carlos hurried toward the trough, and Laura followed.

"I've a great mind to shoot you for desertion!" growled a white man in a dusty, dark coat that Laura suddenly realized was a cavalry jacket. "Calla la boca, chavato." He placed one hand on Esteban's shoulder, the other gripping his right arm behind his back, and began marching the youth toward a building.

"Sir!" Laura cried. "Sir, you've made a mistake!" She ran to intercept them, and placed herself between them and the door. The captain, for so he was, though the bars on his shoulders were nearly indistinguishable, blinked sharp blue eyes at her in surprise.

"No me llamo Juan Ramón! No me llamo Juan Ramón," Esteban gasped.

"This man's name is Esteban Gutiérrez, and he is in my employ," Laura said. "Please release him at once."

The eyes narrowed, and with a grimace the man let Esteban go. Juan Carlos had come up behind Laura. "Regresa al coche," he said to Esteban, who nodded and hastened away, rubbing his wrist.

"Sorry, Miss," said the captain, who did not look sorry at all. "Thought he was a deserter." A certain lilt in his voice caught Laura's attention.

"Are you Irish?" she asked, her spirits sinking.

"Yes, I am. Paddy Graydon, ma'am, if you was wanting to remember who let your man go. I'm surprised he's stayed out of the army this long."

Laura sighed. "I don't suppose you've seen Captain O'Brien?"

Captain Graydon nodded. "He was here this morning. Dropped off a lot of prisoners, and those wagons, which the devil knows how they'll get to Fort Craig, begging your pardon miss. Few enough beasts in the district. I've got trouble enough just to keep my men mounted." His eyes followed Juan Carlos, who had gone to the trough to retrieve the team. "Don't suppose you'd like to sell one of yours," the captain added.

"I'm afraid not," Laura said. "Can you tell me how long ago Captain O'Brien left?"

"Oh, three or four hours since." The blue eyes turned on her, filling with curiosity. "Begging your pardon, but what business do you have with O'Brien?"

Laura felt herself coloring, but said calmly, "It is a private matter. Thank you for your assistance."

She strode back to the carriage, her posture erect, though she was greatly disappointed. That there should be two Irish captains under Colonel Canby's command seemed at that moment to be most unfair. She stifled a sigh as she set her foot on the step of the carriage. Esteban was sitting on the driver's seat, looking frightened still, while Juan Carlos hitched up the animals.

"Don't worry, Esteban," she said. "You're safe now. Tó estás seguro."

Esteban glanced over his shoulder at her, a sudden smile breaking across his face. "Seguro," he said.

"Seguro," Laura repeated. "Perdón."

Esteban grinned, his fear apparently forgotten. Juan Carlos climbed into the seat beside him, clapping him on the back, and said, "It is not the first time someone has tried to force him into the army."

A little chill tickled Laura's shoulders. She shook it off; no sense indulging in trivial worries. Señora Sánchez seemed to have enough of them for all the party, and Laura could not afford to waste time. "Should we replace that rein now?" she asked.

Juan Carlos shook his head. "It will hold for a while, and if it breaks we can get by without it for a short time."

"Very well," Laura said. "Let us go on, then. We are only a few hours behind them."

She stepped into the carriage, which was already in motion as she pulled the door shut behind her. Señora Sánchez peered at her, eyes large, from the depths of the seat. Laura spared her a kindly smile, and settled herself to watching the road.

It was hot, and Jamie fiddled with his hat, trying to get the most shade out of it. In the morning they had climbed out of a valley into a hot, dry, cactus-covered plain that ran between two mountain ranges. Now the army was crossing along the feet of the San Mateos, having passed the Magdalenas, which opened up a view eastward. All eyes were turned in that direction, where a flat plain was broken by a brown cluster of buildings that was Fort Craig. Beyond it the black mesa loomed—a threat; a reminder. At the north end of that mesa lay Valverde, where the graves of the Texan battle-dead were still fresh. Two months ago. Two months this day, Jamie realized. He could almost smell the powder, even now.

He was trembling, he noticed. He took a shaky breath, willing himself to be calm. He still had nightmares, when he wasn't so dead tired he slept without dreaming. He'd have liked nothing better than to blot that dreadful day out of his memory, but so far it stayed with him.

The charge on the guns. His hands shaking as he clutched the shotgun, borrowed from a teamster, and Martin smiling at him as they walked on together, into the face of the guns blasting canister at them, cutting down men on either side, and Martin falling—

Jamie squeezed his eyes shut, but the memory only came clearer. He opened them again, feeling waves of terror as he looked at the rocky hill ahead, its base covered in golden grass scattered with chollas and the weary men marching toward it, their heads turned toward the battleground, lost in their own memories.

Ride ahead, he decided, and kicked his horse into a trot. He could put Valverde behind him, out of sight at least, by going forward along the trail. Coopwood had said the water would be difficult tonight, and Jamie used that as an excuse to put foothills between him and the view of the battleground.

The head of the column was already working its way into steeper ground. Captain Coopwood hailed him, and Jamie joined him and Colonel Scurry. Sibley's ambulance, its windows shrouded, rolled along drawn by weary mules, with Judge Baird's carriage close behind.

"Russell, you'll want to pick out a campsite," Coopwood said. "Dry camp—no way the vehicles can get close to the water."

"Can the animals be led to it, at least?" Jamie asked.

"Yes, but it won't be easy. Got to lead them up over a cliff. Shall I show you?"

"Please."

Coopwood turned his horse out of the column toward the

west, and glanced back at Jamie. "You all right, son?" he asked.

Jamie nodded. "Just tired."

Coopwood's gaze flicked from Jamie's face to something beyond him. He nodded and started toward the San Mateos. With a last glance over his shoulder toward Valverde, Jamie followed the scout into the hills.

Kip gazed dully around him, slowly coming to an awareness of his surroundings. He'd been dozing, he supposed. Firecracker was walking, pausing now and again to crop the dry grass by the roadside. It had been hours since they'd seen any water. Firecracker would have gone to it if there'd been any. It was coming on to evening now; the sun was behind them, casting long shadows ahead on the road. Kip twisted in the saddle and shaded his eyes. Little dust cloud, back in the distance, still there. He silently cursed the Apaches. Didn't they have anything better to do?

He felt dizzy, and faced forward again, gripping the saddle so as not to fall off. Got to rest sometime soon. His legs ached, and his feet were getting numb. He should find a hiding place and sleep for an hour or two. He'd ridden pretty much straight through the night, and hadn't been on the ground since the last water, just before dawn. He shook his canteen, and decided he could afford a sip.

Firecracker nickered, and Kip patted his neck. I know, old man. You'd like a drink too. Soon as we find a spring or something.

There should be a river somewhere along here. Mimbres? Madres? He'd heard Aikins talking about it with Captain Calloway, but he hadn't been listening. Should have listened. He'd crossed any number of dry streambeds. He could dig in one of those, he supposed, if he got desperate for water.

He squinted at the hills ahead. In the distance a little ripple of brown mountains broke the horizon. Mesilla was this side of the mountains, he was pretty sure. So he should be turning north soon. North-northwest, and eventually he'd strike the Río Grande. But how long? How long could he keep going?

This was bad, he decided. He was hungry, but all he had left was jerky and that would make him thirstier. He'd like to hunt down a rabbit or something—he'd seen a lot of cottontails bounding away from the road as he passed—but the gunshots would attract attention, and he shouldn't waste the ammunition. Couldn't afford the time, either, not with that dust cloud bearing down on him. He blinked, frowning, slowly realizing that the dust cloud he'd been watching the last couple of minutes was ahead of him, not behind.

Oh, hell.

"Come on, boy," he said, turning Firecracker off the road and nudging him to a trot. The brow of the next hill hid the dust for a minute, and Kip hurried Firecracker up a little valley—really just a dip between hills—to a cluster of trees. Not the best hiding place, but Kip dismounted, stifling a groan, and stood behind the screen of junipers, watching the road. Maybe the party he'd seen would ride on by. Maybe they'd go meet the Apaches and have a row, he thought with wicked satisfaction.

That hope died soon after they crested the hill into view. There were six—no, seven—in the party, and they pulled up at the bottom of the hill, near where he'd left the road. They looked at the ground, and talked a bit, and then started up toward him. Following his tracks.

"Shit."

Kip hurled himself back into the saddle and flicked the reins against Firecracker's neck. "Hyah!" he shouted, and the horse burst out running from the shelter of the trees, hooves digging at the sandy hillside. Up and over, and Kip could hear shouting behind him. At least they weren't shooting at him, he thought, leaning low over Firecracker's withers.

Dust adhered to the back of his throat. He coughed, and pressed Firecracker for more speed. The horse responded, but not with the fire Kip had hoped for. He was tired; no rest in the last twenty-four hours, and there wasn't much left in him.

Over another hill; at its foot a dry wash which gave better footing. Kip hesitated, then struck upstream—northwest—rather than doubling back toward the road.

"C'mon, get up," he croaked, and Firecracker lunged up the hard-baked wash. Kip spared a glance behind and saw his pursuers gaining. Were there fewer in the party than before? Couldn't keep watching to make sure. He was feeling sick to his stomach already.

Rocks in the wash. Firecracker sailed over one, and Kip let out a grunt as they landed. There were more up ahead, and Kip stared at them, keeping himself gathered for another jump.

Three horsemen poured down a hillside ahead to the left, into the wash to cut him off. The bank had risen to five feet or so—just enough to keep him from jumping out the other side. No breaks, either, to scramble up. Clenching his teeth, Kip bore down on the threesome, hoping they'd part and let him through.

Their horses did part, but one of the men grabbed at Firecracker's rein as they went by, jerking the horse's head around. Firecracker let out a shriek, and Kip clung on for dear life as he swerved and then reared. Hooves lashed out; somebody yelled, and everybody cussed. A clear spot opened ahead, and it looked like they would break through, then something whacked Kip under his left arm and he doubled over, lost the reins, and felt himself falling. He kicked out of the stirrup just in time to keep from being dragged like Semilrogge had. Firecracker's hooves pounded away up the wash, and Kip's head began to pound along in time. He curled up around the pain in his ribs, spat sand, squeezed his eyes shut and prayed for unconsciousness.

18

Someone pushed Kip over onto his back. He was surprised he didn't scream—the vicious pain in his side sent lightning bolts through his body, but all that came out of his mouth was a grunt.

"What's your hurry, friend?" drawled a voice.

Kip didn't answer, nor even bother to open his eyes. Someone started searching through his pockets, and he stifled a gasp at the pain of being handled. Must have cracked a rib, to hurt so bad. He hoped that was all it was.

"Oho, what have we here?"

Crinkle of paper; Calloway's letter. Kip felt his stomach twisting into a knot.

"Looks like our friend here's on his way to see old Canby."

"That so?" said another, then spat. It hit the ground near Kip's face, and he flinched.

"Well, we can give him an escort as far as Mesilla," said the first voice. "I bet Colonel Steele would like to meet him. Get him up."

Rough hands hauled Kip to his feet. He bit down on his lip to keep from crying out, wrapped his arms around his chest, and managed to stay standing. Blinking dust out of his eyes, he looked at his captors, who seemed to be just a bunch of toughs. No uniforms. Armed to the teeth. They must be Rebels, or else bandits working for the Rebels. He thought feebly of trying to break away, but they'd probably just shoot him down.

Hooves pounded toward them from behind Kip. The leader, a thin-faced, mustachioed fellow, glanced up.

"Couldn't get him," said an out-of-breath voice.

"What, you couldn't catch up to that nag?" the leader demanded.

Kip heard the newcomer slide to the ground behind him. "We caught up to him, all right, but he wouldn't let us near him. Bastard kicked like all get out, and gave Banjo here a cut on the knee."

Good for you, Firecracker, Kip thought, resisting a smile.

The leader glared. "I told you to catch him, goddammit! How the hell am I supposed to get this Yank spy to Mesilla?"

"Tie him up and make him walk behind us," suggested one of the Rebels, a tall fellow chewing at a wad of tobacco. His eyes were invisible in the shadow of his wide-brimmed hat. He spat, and a black gobbet landed on Kip's boot.

"Too slow," said the leader. "And he wouldn't make it, looks half dead already. No, you can carry him over your saddle, Bobby, since you couldn't manage to catch one goddamn horse. Tie him up."

Kip closed his eyes, taking short breaths while his arms were forced away from his ribs and his hands lashed behind him. Someone else tied his ankles together at the same time, then two of them picked him up like a sack of meal. Kip let out a yelp, and clenched his teeth as he was flung ungently over a saddlebow. Tears leaked out the corners of his eyes. He kept them squeezed shut. The sounds of the party preparing for departure penetrated to his dazed mind, then the horse started moving, bringing jolts of pain with each step, making Kip wish for merciful death.

No such good fortune came to him. His world was filled with the endless, pounding agony of motion. He could hold no thought, no idea. In an effort to focus his mind on something other than the pain he tried to remember the words or even just the tune to a song, any song, but to no avail. The most he could do was to count—one, two, three, four—and every so often he would lose track and find himself groaning a long, low, stifled groan. Whenever he became aware of this he began counting again. He had no idea how long the journey went on. He seemed to be at the bottom of a dark well to which only occasional sounds could penetrate. It was days or years later when an increase of noise finally got his attention, then the motion suddenly stopped.

He cried out in pain and surprise as he was pulled down from the horse. Someone untied the rope binding his ankles, but his legs wouldn't support him and he half-sprawled in the dust while his captors cussed and yanked him up again by his arms. They hauled him under an archway and into a building, sudden dark shutting out the hot sun. Kip's eyes wouldn't focus on anything, only shapes as they passed through another doorway. Voices pummeled him, making no sense, the words meaningless sounds. They paused, moved forward into yet another room, and stopped again, two men holding him up between them by his arms, sustaining the pain in his side. He wondered idly if he was bleeding. He became aware that he was gazing at a dirt floor in need of sweeping and the boots of his captors—nearly as dusty as his own—then the legs of a table and another pair of boots beneath it, these shiny, as if they'd just been oiled. The pain was receding a little, and he realized that the various voices were discussing him, describing his capture, the letter—

God, the letter!

Kip dared to raise his head enough to look at the man behind the desk. He was standing, wearing a gray coat with gold braid on it of a style Kip had never seen before. It must be a Confederate uniform. The man was forty or so, with dark hair starting to go gray and brows very close to his eyes, curved in a frown as if he spent too much time squinting at the sun. He stood reading the letter Kip had carried, the frown deepening as he stroked his bushy mustache with one long-fingered hand.

"Are you aware of the contents of this letter?" he demanded.

"No," Kip said, his voice a mere croak.

The leader of his captors kicked him sharply and his legs buckled, sending him to his knees. "No, *sir,*" the man said.

"That isn't necessary, Miller," the officer said quietly. "Why don't you fetch a chair for our guest."

Miller grumbled something, but obeyed, pulling a chair away from the wall and thrusting Kip into it. The hands that had been holding him up released him. He tried to keep still, breathing in short, shallow gasps, his lips pressed shut.

"You're injured?" the officer asked.

"Yes," Kip whispered. "Sir."

"Fetch the surgeon," the man ordered Miller, who left, casting a glare in Kip's direction.

The man in gray came around to the front of the desk and leaned against it, perusing the letter once more. At last he looked up at Kip. "I am Colonel William Steele," he said. "And you are?"

"Whistler," Kip said. "Christopher. Private, Company I, 1st California Volunteers." That was all he was obliged to say, he thought.

"Where's your company, Whistler?"

"I don't know, sir. I left them at Picacho Pass." They would know about Picacho by now. Some of the Rebels there had got away. Kip closed his eyes, trying not to think about anything. He'd pretend ignorance. Hell, he was ignorant, mostly. Except he wasn't sure what the Rebels would want to know, and whether anything he knew would interest them.

This isn't good, he decided.

"Do you know where you are?" Colonel Steele demanded.

Kip tried shaking his head, and discovered it was a bad idea. "No, sir," he said instead.

"You're in Mesilla, capital of the Territory of Arizona."

Arizona? Kip frowned, but kept silent. No such thing as a Territory of Arizona, never mind what the damned Rebels thought. He was in New Mexico. He knew that much for sure. New Mexico.

"Who's your commander?" Steele asked.

That would be in the letter. "Captain Calloway," Kip said.

"Commanding Company B?"

Kip gave a single nod.

"And who else?"

"Sir?"

Steele's dark eyes remained steady on him. "What other units are under his command?" he said quietly.

Kip swallowed and looked at the floor. He was pretty sure Calloway would want him to shut up about now.

"Don't, son." Steele's voice was very gentle. "Don't make it hard on yourself. We'll find out anyway."

Kip closed his eyes. Someone behind him moved, boots scraping on the packed earth, and Kip jumped at the sound. He was lonely all of a sudden. He wished he were back with the column, sitting around a fire, listening to one of Sergeant Sutter's bullshit stories. A firm step made him look up at Steele, now standing right before him. Steele was tall, he realized. Real tall.

"What other units are under his command?" Steele repeated. His eyes were hard but they didn't look unkind. Not yet at least. Kip couldn't think of any way to answer. He just shook his head and looked down again, waiting for the blow.

Instead, Steele retreated. Other footsteps were coming from outside, hurrying. Kip looked up and saw Miller return with the surgeon, a grizzled fellow who came over to Kip and put a hand on his shoulder, causing him to yelp. The surgeon shot him a glance and proceeded to squeeze his collarbone.

"Not broken," he said, and moved on to prod him in the chest. Kip bit the inside of his lip, but he couldn't help gasping when the old coot poked him and a flash of pain shot through his side.

"Aha," the surgeon said. "Broken rib." He kept mauling at him and Kip wanted to smack him a good one, but his hands were still tied. He kept still, and finally the bastard let him alone.

"Two ribs broken," the surgeon declared, brushing his hands as he straightened. "Doesn't seem to be bleeding inside. We'll find out in a day or two."

"Thank you, Dr. Cupples," Steele said.

"Shall I bind him up?"

"Not yet. I'll send for you."

Kip swallowed again as he listened to the surgeon's footsteps departing. He kept his eyes on the floor.

"You're sure you don't know what's in this letter?" Steele said in a conversational tone. "It's very interesting. It says there's an army column preparing to march here from California. Is that true?"

Kip didn't move, except to breathe. For a long pause there was silence. Without warning Miller stepped up behind him and grabbed his wrists, yanking them back and up. Kip caught his breath at the pain.

"Answer the question," Miller growled.

"I don't know," Kip gasped.

A jab at his side sent stars whirling across his vision. He wanted to curl up but couldn't; Miller still had his wrists in the air. Kip had trouble even breathing in; his throat seemed to want to close. At last he sucked a trickle of air past the pain, wheezing like an old man.

"Who's in command of the column?" Steele asked quietly.

Kip glanced up at him, saw pity in the fine, dark eyes, and gulped a couple more breaths. He felt Miller shift his grip and braced himself, but Steele raised a hand.

"It's in the letter, son. I just want you to confirm it. Who's in command of the column?"

"C-Carleton," Kip heard himself say.

"James Carleton?"

Kip nodded.

Steele frowned. "And what sort of troops does he have? Infantry?"

Another nod.

"Cavalry?"

"Yes," Kip whispered.

"Artillery?"

Hating himself, Kip nodded again. Steele's frown deepened and he glanced up at someone behind Kip, then his gaze shifted to Miller.

"Let him go."

Kip's arms dropped to his back, causing another wave of anguish. He leaned forward, feeling sick to his stomach. The room seemed to be getting darker, maybe he would rest his head on his knees a while, only he was falling now, falling into oblivion.

Laura was awakened by a babel of shouting in Spanish. The carriage was slowing. She sat up, blinking, surprised that she should have fallen asleep. It was sunset; red-gold light streamed across the river valley. She glanced at Señora Sánchez, who blinked back at her. The vehicle halted, and Laura opened the door and stepped out.

"¿Crees que se puede reparar?" Juan Carlos said. "The rein has broken," he added, glancing at Laura.

"No, dos partes se rompieron." Esteban held up two frayed ends of leather, one dangling a foot-long section nearly severed. The donkey sighed noisily, and tossed its head, jerking at the broken rein in Esteban's hand.

Juan Carlos frowned, got down from the seat, and strode to the back of the carriage where he proceeded to rummage in the tool box. Laura followed him.

"May I be of any help?" she asked.

"No, no. Do not worry, we can still continue, señorita. I am only trying to find if we have some extra leather."

Feeling useless, Laura paced a few steps to shake the stiffness from her limbs. The setting sun was quite warm. They were still west of the river, with no trees to screen them from the sharp rays. Laura gazed wistfully toward the bosque. A little way ahead a thin column of smoke rose up through the tree branches. She squinted, trying to see whose fire it was, hoping to glimpse a blue uniform, but the undergrowth was too dense. And only one fire, she reluctantly concluded, meant it wasn't the army. Travelers like themselves, most likely. Camped for the night beside the river.

Stifling a yawn, she climbed back into the carriage and opened her bag, poking through it until she found the tin of lemon drops Mrs. Canby had pressed upon her at her departure. She offered one to Señora Sánchez, who peered at it uncertainly.

"Dulce," Laura said. "Avec—I mean, con limón."

The señora took it, sniffed it, then popped it into her mouth. Her face was shadowed, but Laura could see her smile.

"Gracias," said the señora around the sweet.

"De nada," Laura answered, smiling back. She took a drop herself, savoring its sweet tang, then returned the tin to her bag and leaned back to wait.

Hoofbeats made her look up. Four mounted men were approaching from the direction of the river. It must have been their campfire she'd seen. Frowning, she leaned back under the shelter of the carriage top.

Juan Carlos closed the box at the back of the carriage with a snap. Laura heard his hurried footsteps coming around, just as the horsemen reined in. They were Anglos, and appeared to have been camping for some time, as both they and their horses were rather dirty. She pulled her shawl over her face, and watched through the open weave of its fabric.

"Hola, amigos," called one of the strangers. "Need some assistance?"

"No, thank you," Juan Carlos answered. "We are all right."

"That's not how it looks to me," the man said. He moved his horse closer, gazing speculatively at the carriage. His eyes were pale blue and contrasted strongly with his burnt and dirty face. Laura shrank back as he passed.

"We have a broken rein," Juan Carlos said. "It is nothing."

"Oh, a broken rein," said the stranger. "Well, that's a nuisance."

Another rider came forward. They were circling the carriage, which Laura disliked. The men looked like ruffians to her. Of course, one must make allowances for the exigencies of travel, but there was a glint in the second man's eye that displeased her.

"Why don't you come on down to our camp?" he said. "Maybe we can fix it up for you."

"No, thank you," Juan Carlos replied. "We can manage."

"Now, that's not very friendly, is it?"

The carriage leaned slightly as Juan Carlos climbed into the driver's seat. Laura reached for her carpetbag, drawing it silently toward her.

"Here we are, just offering to help, and you won't even come say howdy," the second man continued. "Maybe we ought to ask your wife, eh?" He leaned toward the carriage, peering beneath the top.

"Back away, please," Laura said in her frostiest tone.

"Well, well!" The stranger grinned, and did not back away. "Why don't you show us your face, sweetheart?"

"No," Laura said. Beside her she heard Señora Sánchez stifle a whimper. She pressed her lips together, annoyed at the sound, which might tempt the unwanted visitors to intrude further.

"Come on, now, ma'am. You and your friend just step out here," the stranger persisted. "We'll fix your reins for you."

The voice was all kindness, and Laura's determination wavered. But no; a gentleman would not insist. "No," she said firmly. "Go away."

The man dismounted, and reached for the carriage door. Laura brought out her pistol and aimed it at the stranger's head. She cocked it, making sure he had heard, and said, "Put your hands over your head and back away."

The man's eyes widened briefly, then he frowned and stepped back.

"Juan Carlos," she called, "¡Vámnos!"

Shots rang out from their left, and a piercing thump struck the cushioned seat back between Laura and her chaperon. Señora Sánchez squealed. Juan brought his shotgun up, and a blast shook the carriage. The animals were shrieking, and Laura's heart pounded dreadfully. The shotgun roared again, then Laura's attention was drawn to the pale-eyed stranger, who had leapt onto the carriage steps and reached an arm in, trying to grab her pistol. Fear sang in her ears. She placed the muzzle against his elbow and fired. The explosion rocked her back against the seat, and at the same time the carriage lurched forward. Blinded and deafened, she heard only a whisper of screaming—the man's and Señora Sánchez's— as she fumbled to recock her gun. She blinked and squinted at the steps; there was no one on them, she realized with pleasure. The door itself was flapping with the motion of the carriage, and she scooped up her carpetbag to keep it from sliding out.

"Hold this," she said to Señora Sánchez, shoving the bag into her arms. Bracing her feet against the floor and her shoulder against the seat back, she reached for the door handle as it swung toward her. On the second try she managed to catch it and pull it to. It was sticky and wet.

There were more shots behind them. Laura counted five— two of which thumped into the body of the carriage while another pierced the top—then three more, then they ceased. Her heart was thundering, and gradually she realized that the señora was weeping uncontrollably. Laura carefully uncocked the pistol and laid it on the seat beside her, wiped her gloved hands on her skirt, then put an arm around her shivering chaperon.

"It's all right now," she murmured. "Estamos seguras. Seguras. Let me take that." Gently she removed the carpetbag from the señora's grasp.

Juan Carlos was alone on the driver's seat, she noticed. A horrid fear gripped her; she leaned forward and was relieved to see Esteban mounted on the donkey, holding its broken reins together as the two animals galloped along the highway. Like a postilion, she thought, and couldn't help but smile. Now we are indeed traveling in style!

A chuckle grew into a fit of laughter. Laura tried to stifle it, without much success. Señora Sánchez frowned reproachfully at her from the shadows. It was getting dark, Laura realized, looking at her companion. She wondered how long Juan Carlos would continue to drive. How long until they were truly safe?

Her laughter ended abruptly in a hiccup. Tears threatened, but she held them back. What a dreadful thing to have happened, and whatever would Mrs. Canby say about the damage to her carriage? No, I will not laugh; it is not the least bit funny.

The carriage rocked gently on its springs. Señora Sánchez had subsided to whimpering. With hands that shook only slightly, Laura took her pistol into her lap, which comforted her somewhat. She had never fired it before, she realized. She did not even know how to clean it, and she would certainly have to do so, after this. A sob rose in her throat and escaped her lips. She caught the second one back. Time for that when they knew they were safe. Thank you for sparing us, dear Lord, she thought over and over.

At last Juan slowed the animals to a trot, then stopped the carriage altogether. He turned round on the seat to peer at her. "Are you all right, señorita?"

"Yes," Laura answered. "We're all right." She looked up and was surprised to find that it was not completely dark yet; the sun was down, leaving behind a swath of ruddy red in the east, and the rest of the sky glowed a deep, intense blue.

There were buildings nearby—small houses—a village. Laura sighed with relief.

Juan Carlos got down and came to open the door, offering Laura a hand as she stepped down. His eyes widened.

"¡Madre de Dios! Are you hurt?"

"No," Laura said, shaking her head.

"You are covered in blood!"

Laura glanced at her dress. Even in the twilight she could see a large splatter of dark stains upon the black fabric. Sudden revulsion filled her; she felt ill, and struggled not to be sick. Her hand came up to cover her mouth, but the black glove was sticky and smelled of blood. With a cry of disgust she flung it down again. Before her the carriage door hung open, also slick with the dark stains. She stumbled a few steps away.

I've shot a man. Dear Lord, I may have killed him.

That he deserved to have been shot mattered not at all. The horror of her deed came home to her fully, and tears flowed down her cheeks while she struggled for breath in great, gasping sobs.

Juan Carlos, who was helping Señora Sánchez out the other side of the carriage, looked up at her in concern and called out something in Spanish. Esteban appeared at her side and spoke, but Laura did not understand the words. Mastering her tears, she drew a shuddering breath and tried to smile at him.

"I'm all right," she said. "Está bien." Glancing toward the awful carriage she noticed the donkey sidling in his harness, and saw a dark line of blood running down from a deep gash in his rump.

"Oh, dear!"

Esteban followed her to the donkey's side. "Miguel está lastimado," he said. He ran a hand along the animal's rump, and the donkey grunted. Its sides were heaving, as were the mule's; they had given their all in the flight. Laura looked at the donkey's wound. A bullet had glanced along the hip, and from the angle of its path, she thought it must have just missed striking Esteban. She met his eyes, and saw that he must be thinking the same thing.

"Lo siento," she said, which was entirely inadequate, but

she had no adequate words in any language. Esteban nodded acceptance, and began to unhitch the animals.

"Señorita," Juan Carlos said, hurrying up to her with one of the villagers, a tall, older man. "This is Señor Aragón. His family will give you shelter for the night. Come, please."

"Oh, gracias! No, don't touch me, I'm a dreadful mess."

A bar of soft, golden light spilled from the foot of the doorway to which Señor Aragón led her. Shrouded women peeped and whispered behind it, then opened it wide, spilling the welcoming light into the street. The women—two younger, one older who must be their mother—were clearly shocked at the condition of Laura's person and repeatedly crossed themselves, but beckoned her inside.

The house was warm, lit by a corner fireplace and two lamps hung from the ceiling. Laura realized she was shaking quite badly; her teeth chattered, and she wanted to go to the fire but feared to drip blood on the jerga rug. The younger girl let out a squeak at the sight of Laura's pistol, which she'd forgotten she still carried. "Lo siento," Laura said, showing that it was uncocked, then setting it down on the table.

"Pobrecita," said the older woman, shaking her head. She beckoned Laura through a curtained doorway and into what proved to be a small kitchen. A pot of water was heating on the coals of the fire, and a smaller pot hung from a hook, emitting a savory smell. The woman filled a small basin with steaming water and gestured to her to undress. Laura stripped off her horrid gloves and emptied her pockets of her handkerchief and the few coins she carried there. She offered the latter to her hostess, who shook her head vehemently.

"No, no," the woman said. "¿Tiró a los ladrones, no?"

This was too much for Laura, who shook her head apologetically, saying, "No entiendo."

"Los hombres malos," said her hostess, then made a gesture of shooting a gun, and pointed to Laura, who nodded.

"I shot the bad men, yes." Laura closed her eyes briefly, suppressing a shudder.

"Bien. Ya basta," said the woman with a grim smile, and firmly pushed Laura's hand away.

Laura put the coins down and stripped off her stained and

battered dress. The blood had soaked through to her under-things, which looked even more shocking, great splotches of brown-red on their whiteness. She took all off and proceeded to sponge herself with a soft, cotton cloth provided by her hostess, who disappeared with the soiled clothes, shaking her head and tut-tutting. Laura had not had any sort of bath since leaving Santa Fé, and the luxury of warm water against her skin filled her so much with relief that she found herself crying again. She scrubbed vigorously at her face, then worked her way down the rest of her tired body. By the time she had finished, the water in the basin was alarmingly red.

Her hostess returned with a blanket of soft, scratchy wool. Laura wrapped herself in this and sat on a stool by the hearth. "¿Cómo se llama usted?" she asked shyly, watching as the woman set a skillet on the fire and began dishing up a bowl of fragrant stew.

"Señora Aragón," said her hostess, smiling as she handed Laura the bowl and a spoon. "¿Y usted?"

"Señorita Howland," said Laura. "Gracias."

"De nada." The woman then took down a larger bowl and put corn meal into it, and a dash of salt. The gestures were very familiar; making tortillas, Laura thought with a trembling smile. Like María in Mrs. Canby's kitchen.

She did not think she would be able to eat, but she tried a bite of stew, and for the next few minutes thought of little else. The broth was thick and rich with onions and chili peppers—making her eyes water, as usual—and the meat was tender from long simmering. She had emptied the bowl by the time the first tortilla was ready, and gratefully traded.

"¿Más?" asked her hostess, lifting the bowl.

"No, gracias," said Laura. She could have eaten more, but she did not want to be greedy, and she suspected the stew was the family's dinner. Instead she warmed her hands with the tortilla, and took a bite of it, warm and grainy.

A small commotion in the outer room was followed by voices; Señora Sánchez had come in and begun talking rapidly with the daughters, relating her woes, from the tone of her voice. Poor woman, Laura thought, smiling. She'd been through much more than she had bargained for, even for two dollars.

One of the daughters came into the kitchen, gingerly hold-ing Laura's carpetbag, which had also been spattered with blood. Laura jumped up to receive it. She could hear Juan Carlos and Señora Aragón conversing in the next room, and hastened to dress herself. She had only one corset, which Señora Aragón had taken away, but she had another shift, and her green dress. Luckily, no blood had gotten on them. She dressed quickly, combed her hair, wrapped her shawl about her, and considered herself presentable. Señora Aragón seemed to agree, for she nodded approvingly.

Juan Carlos paused in his conversation as she entered the room. "Are you feeling better?"

"Yes, thank you. Please tell Señor Aragón I am exceed-ingly grateful."

Juan translated, and Señor Aragón bowed.

"Those men we saw have been bothering the village for a few days," Juan told her. "They stole a sheep, and beat a farmer who lives near here."

"W-well, I trust they will cause no more trouble tonight," Laura said. "Did you hit any of them, by the way?"

Juan Carlos nodded gravely and crossed himself. "Two," he said, and would vouchsafe no more.

"Have they seen or heard anything of the army?" Laura asked. She glanced toward Señor Aragón. "Los federales?"

"Sí, sí," he said, nodding, and spoke rapidly to Juan Car-los.

"They are camped a few miles south of here," Juan said.

"Oh!" Laura said, but her joy quickly faded. They would not be traveling to the army's camp this evening. The reins needed mending, the carriage was a frightful mess, and she could scarcely present herself to Captain O'Brien as she was. The proximity of the army made her feel safer, at least.

"I will go now," Juan said. "Esteban and I are staying with another family. I will come back in the morning."

"Will Miguel be all right?" Laura asked.

"Sí. The wound is not bad." Juan Carlos smiled at her. "You are a brave lady, señorita. Goodnight."

Señor Aragón gestured toward the fire, and Laura grate-fully sat beside it until Señora Aragón and her daughters appeared carrying food out to the table. Laura declined to take a plate, which was just as well, as there seemed to be only four. The two daughters shared, staring curiously at Laura with eyes rather wide. Señora Sánchez ate in stately dignity. Laura sensed that her chaperon was displeased with her, for which she could hardly fault her. She sipped a cup of water while the others ate, and listened to their conversation, growing sleepier by the minute.

Tomorrow early she would rise, and cajole her companions to take her to the army's camp. It would be worth all the trouble they had been through to see Captain O'Brien at last. A shiver went through her, whether of fear or of cold she was uncertain. She pulled her shawl closer and closed her eyes, silently giving thanks that she and her companions had escaped harm.

Kip was in a deep, dark valley, and high above him his mother was singing to him. He kept trying to call to her, but he couldn't seem to speak, and he had been forbidden to move. He didn't know why, but he knew it had been forbidden. There was no one nearby, though, so if he moved, who could accuse him of doing anything wrong? He decided to try turning over.

Pain brought him immediately to his senses. He froze, then slowly relaxed his muscles and opened his eyes. He was lying on his back in a dark room. Someone was playing a flute nearby; that must be what he'd thought was singing, in his dream. Carefully he sat up, taking short, shallow breaths. His chest had been strapped with bandages, which helped the pain in his side some, but it still hurt with just about every little movement.

He was in a jail cell, he realized. There were bars on the door, and bars in the tiny window high on the stone wall behind him. Moonlight trickled in between the window bars, casting stripes of bluish gray into the room. A plate of food had been left by the door: bread, and what looked like a hunk of meat. His mouth watered, but he didn't know if he could walk over there and get it.

He was a prisoner. Memories began to flood back, of his capture, and of Colonel Steele asking him questions. He did not know how much information he had given. It was like a bad dream; only some of the details remained with him. He closed his eyes, fighting back despair. No great secrets had been entrusted to him. His worst problem was not whatever he'd told the Rebels, but that he had failed to get his message to Colonel Canby.

He wished whoever had that flute would pipe down. What the hell was somebody playing a flute in the middle of the night for, anyway? Sounded like one of those Pima flutes, but he'd bet money there wasn't a Pima within a hundred miles.

Kip frowned on that for a minute, then looked up at the window. The flute music was coming from outside. It was pretty soft, to be fair. He doubted anyone else would be able to hear it, and that struck him as a mite strange.

Clutching his arms around his chest, he stifled a grunt as he got to his feet and turned around to look up at the window. He put a foot on the bed to test it, concluded it would take his weight, and carefully got up on it to peer out.

The music stopped, and he found himself looking down at the Apache girl. She was seated on her paint pony just under the window, and had a flute in her hands. *His* flute.

"You sleep too hard," she whispered. "Someone could cut your throat."

"What are you doing here?" Kip had to bite it back from a yell to a harsh whisper.

"I followed you," she said simply.

"That was you?"

She nodded. "Your horse is very good. Runs fast, runs far. He's mean, though."

"He's just spooky. Is he all right? Where is he?"

"In a safe place," she said. "Why are you in jail?"

Kip was glad of the bars at that moment, because he wanted to shake her, and he knew she wouldn't like it, and anyway it would probably hurt. "Because we're at war," he said. "You saw the fight at Picacho."

She nodded. "Your enemies made you a prisoner?"

"Yes."

She gazed speculatively at the window. "Shall I get you out?"

Kip stared at her, his feelings boiling up in a mixture of

wonder, delight, and disbelief. "No," he whispered, imagining her fate at the hands of the Rebels if she was caught trying to break him out of jail. "I couldn't go very far. I'm hurt."

She frowned. "They hurt you? Shall I kill one of them?"

"No," Kip said, laughing. It quickly turned to a gasp of pain and he stopped, and just smiled like a silly fool instead. He couldn't help liking this fierce little maiden. For a moment he savored the thought of telling her to kill the one called Miller, but he refrained from voicing it. She would probably take him seriously, and he didn't want to be the cause of her getting hurt.

"Why did you follow me?" he whispered.

She looked down, and Kip thought he glimpsed sadness in her face, but then she raised her chin proudly, her eyes cold in the moonlight. "I left that war party," she said. "They saw me warn you away. I told them it was to pay a debt, but they didn't think about that. They're too stupid. So I left. My brother was dead anyway. I only went with them because of him."

"Why did he take you with a war party?" Kip asked.

"Because I speak your language. The Indian agent said I should go to school, so I did. I left school, though."

Because it was stupid? Kip wondered. The grin had taken up permanent residence on his face. "What's your name?" he asked softly.

The Apache gave him a long, measuring look. "I am called Rain Weaver," she said finally.

"I'm Kip," he told her. "Kip Whistler."

"Kip Whistler," she repeated.

"Listen, you shouldn't hang around here. There are bad men in this town. I don't want them to catch you talking to me."

"I will wait for you outside town, then. North, by the river. I will take care of your horse. He's very tired."

"You've paid your debt, you know. You don't have to keep helping me." Which was a stupid thing to say to a woman who had possession of his horse and all his belongings, Kip reflected.

She shot him a contemptuous glance. "You need a lot of help," she said.

"All right." Kip smiled down at her. She just made him smile, that was all. He was feeling light-headed. He ought to go eat something, but an idea was coming to him. "If you really want to help me, there is something you could do," he said.

She waited. Kip glanced behind him to make sure no one was listening at the door. He dropped his voice as low as he could. "Follow the river north to an army fort—"

"There is an army fort here, across the river," she said promptly.

"Not that one. My enemies have control of that one. Further north, two or three days. It's called Fort Craig."

"Fort Craig."

"Take Firecracker with you. My horse. My uniform is in his saddlebags. Show the soldiers my uniform, and ask to speak to Colonel Canby."

"Canby."

"Yes. He's the commander there. Tell him—" Kip paused, wishing he knew what Calloway had written in his letter. "Tell him there are soldiers coming to help him from California. Many soldiers. An army."

"Why should I tell Canby this?"

"It's what I was trying to do before I got caught."

She frowned. "This will help you?"

"Yes. Yes, it's the best thing you could do for me. Tell Canby I'm a prisoner here. He'll get me out." *I hope.*

She gazed at him long and hard, her forehead creased. Finally she gave a short nod, and picked up her reins.

"Rain Weaver?" Kip whispered.

She looked up.

"Thank you," Kip said, reaching a hand through the bars. It was awkward; he had to reach up to get his arm out the high window, then dangle his hand down. She looked at it for a moment, then solemnly clasped it with strong, slender fingers. Kip stared into her dark eyes. He thought he saw something warm there, past the hard silver moonlight on their surface. Her hand slipped from his and she rode silently off into the night. His arm was tingling, and he brought it back inside the cell, gripping the bars with both hands and watching Rain Weaver until she faded into the shadows.

19

"We could see nothing of the Texans today. They have taken an old trail through the mountains, passing twenty miles back of Craig and striking the river thirty miles below the Post."

—Ovando J. Hollister

"Colonel Canby wants to see you," Ramsey said.

O'Brien blinked, still half asleep. The previous day had been long, despite his early arrival at the army's camp. Chivington had found some imperative work for O'Brien's depleted company: firewood detail for the entire regiment. Distinctly unfair, but O'Brien had been so glad to get back to the column that he'd borne it without complaint.

He took a long pull at the coffee Old George had made for his breakfast—first coffee in three days, it was. A commissary train had arrived at the main column in his absence, received with cheers by men who were weary of short rations. Old George's coffee was a lot better than Shaunessy's, and O'Brien drained the cup, handing it to the Negro to refill, before he favored Ramsey with an answer.

"Kind of the colonel to send my own lieutenant for me," he said.

Ramsey gave no response, but he looked a bit smug. Brewing mischief, O'Brien concluded. "Very well, I'll come to him," he said, dismissively.

Ramsey didn't budge. O'Brien sighed, and took back his cup from Old George, who glowered in Ramsey's direction. That cheered O'Brien somewhat, and he winked at the Negro, then got to his feet, sipped the hot coffee, and started toward the commander's camp, with Ramsey tagging along at his heels like an unlovely terrier.

Colonel Canby had his headquarters on a little hillock

overlooking the camp. From it, O'Brien could see the smoke from dozens of breakfast fires rising in thin lines to join a high pall over the river valley. The sight warmed his heart; it was home to him now, this army. A much better home, despite all its privations, than a freezing, taunting mine in Colorado. He smiled, amused at himself, and took a long sip of his coffee. He wished Denning were back, for he'd no one to read for him, but soon he'd return and all would be as near well as it could be.

"The colonel's waiting," Ramsey said behind him.

"Oh, Ramsey," O'Brien said lightly. "I'd almost forgot you were there." Not favoring the lieutenant with so much as a glance, he turned and went into the tent.

Colonel Canby was waiting indeed, seated behind his camp desk, and beside him was Chivington. O'Brien forced down a scowl. Ramsey followed him in, and took a chair to one side, where Fitzroy was already sitting. All at once it looked less like Canby wanting to speak to one of his captains, and more like an inquisition.

No one offered O'Brien a chair. He stood, holding his coffee cup, looking a fool and feeling his anger starting to rise. He quelled it, knowing it would serve him no good, and to make the best of things he snapped to attention.

"Good morning, Captain," Canby said mildly, looking at some papers on his desk. "I have a few questions for you."

"Sir," O'Brien said.

"I understand you left some army property in Socorro."

O'Brien blinked, puzzled. "Oh, the wagons? Yes, sir, I left them at the depot."

"Why did you not bring them on?"

"They were for taking the prisoners to Socorro," O'Brien said, surprised. "Colonel Chaves told me to leave them there."

"Those were Chaves's direct orders?" Canby said, glancing up with his steady, gray eyes.

"Yes, sir."

Canby nodded, and made a note on one of his papers. Next to him, Chivington shifted, and the camp chair creaked under him.

"How many wagons were placed in your charge?" Canby asked.

"Four."

"And how many did Colonel Chaves retain?"

O'Brien frowned. "I think, twenty or so," he said.

"Did he tell you how he planned to dispose of them?"

"No, sir. They were still full of gear, a lot of them, from the Texans."

"Did Colonel Chaves give you any instructions for the disposal of those goods?"

"No, sir. The wagons I took away were already empty."

Canby paused to write again. O'Brien heard Ramsey mutter something to Fitzroy.

"Colonel Chaves retained half your company, correct?" the colonel continued.

"Yes, sir. To help with the wagons."

"Did he give you any indication of his intentions regarding those wagons or the goods they held?"

"No, sir."

"I see. Thank you, Captain."

Chivington sighed heavily, and there was a general shifting among the others, while Canby continued to write. For a few moments there was no sound in the tent save for the scratching of his pen. At last Chivington leaned toward him. "There's the other matter, sir," he said.

"I am getting to that, Colonel." Canby glanced up at O'Brien again. "Captain, I understand you have taken a Negro into your service."

"Well—yes," O'Brien said.

"A Negro slave!" Fitzroy burst out.

"Sergeant, you will refrain from speaking unless I address a question to you," Canby said sharply.

O'Brien cast a glance over at Fitzroy and Ramsey, who sat glowering in their chairs. Ramsey seemed less smug, but no less determined. Bloody bastards, O'Brien thought.

"He *was* a slave, sir," he said, turning back to Canby. "We captured him from the Rebels back at Peralta."

"And you retained him?"

"I tried telling him to go away, sir, but he begged to stay."

"So you kept him as a servant."

"An unpaid servant," Chivington said heavily.

"I pay him in rations," O'Brien protested. He looked at Canby. "It's all I can do, sir! We haven't been paid for—"

"Yes, I know, Captain," Canby said. "That isn't the issue. Have you made it clear to this man that he is not your property?"

"Yes, I have, sir," O'Brien said, glancing at Chivington, whose small eyes glared back at him. O'Brien held them a moment, to show he was not afraid.

"That is well," said Canby. "Since he was confiscated from a force in rebellion against the United States, he is now free. You will explain this to him, Captain."

"If he is free then O'Brien should not have kept him!" Chivington protested.

"I see no harm in the captain's looking after him," Canby said. "He's providing for him out of his own rations, and it keeps the fellow out of the way." The colonel leaned back in his chair, his gaze thoughtful. "I understand you recently lost your striker," he said softly.

A stab of heartache surprised O'Brien. He nodded. "At Peralta," he said.

"So you are in need of a servant. I see no reason why you should not continue to employ this Negro, with the understanding that he is free to leave your service at any time."

O'Brien swallowed. "Thank you, sir," he said.

Canby nodded, and held O'Brien's gaze for a long moment. Was he trying to judge him? Or warn him? "Dismissed," he said quietly.

O'Brien blinked, then saluted and hastily left. Outside the tent he paused to gulp a deep breath of morning air. It tasted like woodsmoke and bacon. He let it out in a great sigh, feeling as if he'd just narrowly missed stepping off a cliff.

He looked down at the cup in his hand. The coffee had gone cold, a film of oil swirling on its surface. He strode away from headquarters, tossing the liquid onto the dirt and resolving to be rid of Ramsey the first opportunity he found.

It was several hours into the morning, certainly past ten o'clock, and Laura was beginning to find it difficult to restrain her impatience. She was dressed in her green gown, because the black was still damp from Señora Aragón's washing. So was her corset, and the dampness crept through her shift to make her itchy and cold, which did nothing to improve her mood. She sat by the fire in the Aragóns' house, waiting while Juan Carlos and Esteban finished cleaning up the carriage. She had offered to help, but Juan would not let her near it. Señora Sánchez had expressed a desire never to enter the carriage again, and had to be cajoled with the prospect of soon seeing her husband, and with Laura's solemn promise not to shoot any more men in the carriage while the señora was her companion.

Their hostess had loaned Laura a rag and a dish of water with which to clean the spatters of blood from her carpetbag and her bonnet. It had helped her to pass the time. She had made them as presentable as they could be, and now held the bonnet at arm's length, examining it. The black straw looked dull to her. She really must get another, when opportunity allowed, and trim it up prettily. She had bought this but lately in Santa Fé, to replace the one she'd lost in Las Vegas. The plain black of mourning no longer suited her mood, however. She had, in fact, been out of black gloves since Christmas. Sighing, she set the hat aside, and retrieved her pistol from the shelf where Señor Aragón had set it the evening before. A small sound of alarm escaped Señora Sánchez, who sat at the opposite corner of the fire, as Laura approached with the weapon.

"Don't worry," she said, keeping her voice pleasant. "I only wish to clean it."

She sat down, trying to remember the night she had watched Lieutenant Franklin clean the pistol after nearly being drowned in the Pecos by Captain O'Brien. Dear God, what that woman had risked! A little episode with a handful of ruffians had set Laura to shivering; Franklin had gone willingly to war, shoulder to shoulder with the rough frontiersmen of Colorado. She herself could not have faced such dangers with anything approaching equanimity, much less with the enthusiasm Franklin had shown.

I am so sorry I did not know her better.

Suddenly Laura's face was wet with tears. She let them flow silently, breathing deep and even. All the cares of the past days rained out of her, and a coolness flowed through her limbs. She took out her handkerchief and dabbed at her face—the handkerchief given her by Franklin. The handkerchief, the pistol, trousers. Laura smiled through her tears. If only the lieutenant had also given her some of her extraordinary courage.

She sat up, frowning in thought. In a sense, Lieutenant Franklin had taught her courage. She could not imagine herself even handling a pistol a year ago, much less firing it. Nor would she have undertaken to journey through a war-torn country in this manner.

I am not who I was, she concluded.

Feeling as if released from fetters she had been unaware of, Laura drew a deep breath. Her fortune, her friends, all the circumstances of her life had changed. She was a very different person indeed, less afraid, despite having become aware that she had more to fear.

Unbidden, a memory of Franklin came to her; smiling up at her from her deathbed, telling her that Captain O'Brien would be a good protector, if she should happen to need one. Franklin, she realized with a shock, had been in love with the captain.

Astonishment washed through her. Yes, it must be true. Franklin had been so very fond of the captain, despite his unkindness and jealousy. Laura was certain Captain O'Brien had never learned Franklin's secret, which meant that she had kept her feelings to herself. Oh, how lonely, how agonizing her life must have been, so close to the man she loved and yet unable to reach out to him!

It will not happen to me.

Laura bit her lip. Franklin, among all her other gifts, had bequeathed Captain O'Brien to her as well. She let out a surprised cough of laughter. Clearly, she must strive to deserve her friend's generosity.

And Franklin, a woman alone and in a dangerous situation, had trusted the captain. That remembrance quieted all Laura's doubts. Wiping away a stray tear, she smiled. She now knew for certain what her answer to him would be, assuming she ever managed to catch up with him. Feeling unutterable relief, she set about figuring out how to clean the pistol.

Jamie rode back along the column to see how the guns were managing going over the hills. That morning before they'd started, Colonel Scurry had made a speech, saying he was committed to the Valverde guns, would bring them home no matter what, and assigning a company or two to each gun to help it along, so they wouldn't have to halt so often. It made sense to Jamie, and he'd helped get the guns distributed, with the artillerymen scattered among the 1st regiment, some with each gun, to oversee them. Colonel Green hadn't said much about it, but he hadn't protested. General Sibley had not been there at all.

Now one of the guns had stopped moving, and Jamie trotted his horse over that way to see what was the trouble. The column broke around the obstacle—one of the six-pounders—like a stream around a rock, weary soldiers scarcely sparing a glance for it. All their efforts were focused on continuing to place one foot in front of another.

As he came near, Jamie saw that one of the artillery horses had fallen. The drivers were working to remove the harness from the dead animal, while the men of B Company, to which the gun had been assigned, stood to one side and watched. Captain Scarborough stood talking with Reily, who glanced up to give Jamie a nod and a grimacing smile. Jamie dismounted and led his horse forward.

"Want him?" he asked.

Reily straightened. "If you can spare him."

"Have to bring the guns home," Jamie said with a shrug. He handed the reins to a soldier and pulled off his saddle-bags, then reached for the girth. Reily joined him.

"We can stow your gear on the limber," he said, taking the bags. "Do you care about the saddle?"

Jamie shook his head. His own saddle was long gone—lost at Glorieta, along with Cocoa. The thought stopped him short; he stood holding the military issue saddle, realizing it had been days since he'd remembered about Cocoa. He missed her as much as ever, but there'd been so much to do. He pushed away the sadness, dropped it with the saddle beside the trail, like everything else he didn't have time to worry about. Slinging his canteen over his shoulder, he helped get the horse into harness and then took up the march with Reily.

He would be less in touch on foot, but he didn't know that he minded. Any more, his duties mostly consisted of picking up what could and should be saved out of the broken leavings along the army's trail—men and gear alike. He'd stationed Sergeant Wooster and three hands at the very end of the column, with a dozen extra canteens and the six shovels, to make what they could of the stragglers, and to deal with the less fortunate. Jamie had lost count of the graves they'd left scattered along the route. At first they'd piled rocks and cactus on them to keep off wild animals. Lately there hadn't been time or energy to do more than dig a dirt grave and wish the fallen comrade godspeed.

The day was warm, and each hill seemed taller than the last one. Reily was disinclined to talk, and Jamie walked on beside him in silence. There wasn't much to say, anyway. On the hills, Jamie pitched in to help push the gun carriage up. It was weary work, and he began to have a new appreciation of what the foot soldiers had been going through for the last few days. It seemed to take an awful long time just to get to the top of one hill. There wasn't a thing to like about this path; down in between the hills, you couldn't see anything but the sand and rocks and scraggly trees here and there. Up on top you could see only too well how many more hills there were to cross.

Jamie smiled grimly as they approached the summit of another slope. A whole lot of men had gathered there; he saw Scurry on horseback, with a smaller, mounted form nearby that had to be Rose. A gun sat waiting while its crew and escort stood gazing southward from the ridgetop. With feelings of misgiving, Jamie strode on up among them, only to have his fears confirmed.

It wasn't a hill this time. It was a deep canyon, with steep sides of loose, pink granite rock. There wasn't even a stream in the bottom of it, not a trickle, though a wash of gray sand meandered its way eastward. Nothing to tempt them forward. Just a big, deep gash in the earth that had to be crossed. He looked at the gun—like Reily's, a six-pounder—close on nine hundred pounds of brass, with its carriage and limber, waiting to be got across somehow.

As he stood staring down, a horse came up beside him. He glanced up into Colonel Scurry's face.

"We're bringing these guns through, Captain," Scurry said, a slight rasp in his voice.

Jamie nodded. He walked over to where the first gun stood waiting, and put a hand on the barrel of the cannon. Gazing down at the carriage, he noted its numerous loops and bars, each designed to hold a particular tool or serve an exact purpose in the operation of the gun. He looked up just as Reily joined him.

"Ropes," Jamie said.

Reily nodded and shoved a foot at the pebbly soil, testing the footing. "Have to lower it by hand," he agreed.

"Sergeant Rose, give me that rope, and collect some others," Jamie called. "We'll need at least four."

Glancing at Scurry, Rose unlashed the rope from his saddle and tossed it to Jamie, who looped it around the axle. "Lock the wheels and unhitch the team," he said to the drivers.

By the time they were ready with the ropes, the civilian vehicles had begun to arrive. They'd been starting out later every morning, catching up to the straggling column usually by about midday. Today the first to appear was the Armijos' coach. It stopped just short of the canyon's rim, and the Armijo brothers jumped out and began an intense discussion in Spanish. Jamie ignored them. They weren't his responsibility. They could figure out for themselves how to get the coach across.

It took ten men on the ropes to control the descent of the artillery carriage, leaning back with all their weight as they slowly eased their way down the hill. The rest of A Company followed it down the steep slope, some leading the horses in small, mincing steps. Now and then a hoof slipped, sending a scatter of loose rock bouncing down into the canyon. Jamie watched it all from the ridgetop, keeping an eye on the progress of the gun. It reached the bottom safely, and the men with the ropes started up the other side, but the gun didn't budge.

"It's stalled, by God," Scurry said, shaking his head. He leaned forward on his horse to call over the cliff. "A Company! Lend them a hand with that!"

More men swarmed to the ropes, and began dragging and pushing the gun slowly up the far side of the canyon. When Jamie saw that it would work, he turned to Reily, who nodded and strode off to his own gun, calling to the drivers to unhitch the team. Scurry dismounted and led his horse toward the descent, clapping Jamie on the back as he passed.

Sibley's ambulance arrived. The general's voice could be heard from within, making plaintive inquiry. Jamie saw the driver respond, and walked over to give the man some brief advice on how to lower the carriage.

"All the passengers will have to get out and walk," he said. "Too dangerous to try to ride it down." Jamie noticed the Armijo brothers listening from nearby. "Tie your ropes to the axles, and go slowly. See how they did it with the gun?"

Sibley's driver nodded, and called out instructions to his shotgun, then knocked on the ambulance door and spoke quietly to its occupant. Jamie saw Sibley come out, blinking at the sun. He looked pale and unwell, and moved stiffly.

Well, it'll do him good to get some exercise, Jamie thought. He wasn't feeling particularly generous just now; his feet were tired already—he suspected he could feel a blister forming on one heel—and the day was far from over.

The pack mules were coming into view over the top of the last hill back. Jamie borrowed his horse from Reily and rode bareback to the train, collecting an armful of ropes and one of the mounted hands. The latter he told to observe the lowering of Reily's gun and to oversee the rest of the vehicles that would have to be lowered into the canyon. Jamie decided to continue with Reily, partly because he wanted to stay near the head of the column, more because he just wanted some companionship.

Jamie took hold of one of the ropes, because he had gloves, and Reily grabbed on behind him because he was Reily. The crew eased the gun over the ridge and started down the long, steep slope. Jamie's muscles were already complaining. He leaned back, his feet barely leaving the ground, shuffling along the treacherous footing. No one talked except to call out a warning or an instruction. The creak of the ropes and the scrabble of feet, and the pitter of pebbles tumbling down into the canyon were the only sounds. Once Jamie glanced up, when a cheer from the far slope announced the arrival of A Company's gun up top. They were not yet halfway down themselves, and Jamie confined his attention to his own two feet the rest of the way.

The descent seemed much longer than it had looked. Inch by inch, arms shaking, they worked their way until at last the gun came to rest on the bottom. Dropping the ropes, they paused to rest. Jamie leaned forward to stretch out his aching back. He felt dizzy, and his arms were trembling, little twitches running up and down the muscles. He took a swallow from his canteen, which was already almost empty.

Reily squatted next to him, resting his elbows on his knees, and peered up at the slope they'd just come down. "Here comes the general," he said.

Jamie glanced up and saw Sibley's driver and a dozen soldiers easing the ambulance down into the canyon. They were going faster than the gun crew had, but the vehicle was much lighter. Behind it, Sibley was picking his way down, accompanied by the ladies of the Armijo family, Señora Armijo on the general's arm. Ever gallant, our general, Jamie thought. Just not very practical.

"We'd better get out of their way, I guess," he said.

Reily nodded, and called the men back to the ropes. Jamie thought about leaving the work to the enlisted men this time, but in the end he resumed his place. Around him the men took up the ropes—he saw one private wince as his raw hands touched the rough hemp—and started up the canyon's south wall.

Hauling the gun up the cliff was possibly worse than lowering it, and it made a whole different set of muscles sore. Jamie maintained a grim silence and concentrated on not letting his mouth fall open, because that would make him drier and it was ten miles to water once they got out of the canyon. He wondered where Coopwood was—hadn't seen him all morning. Before long he stopped thinking anything at all except breathe, step, breathe. The rope bit into his shoulder and pinched his fingers together inside the gloves, and sweat dripped down his face from under his hat. The sun beat down on them—no shelter even in the canyon, which ran pretty much east-west—and it was midday or some little after.

Lord, let me make it up this blasted hill without falling flat on my face. Jamie began to fear that he really would fall, and knock into the man behind him, and send the whole crew and the gun tumbling back into the canyon. Terror of being responsible for such a disaster was about all that kept him going. He began to feel like that fellow—what was his name?—who had to push a rock uphill for all eternity. Better to let it roll backward and smash you, Jamie thought.

All at once the men up ahead gave out a startled cry. Jamie looked up sharply, and saw a hand reaching toward him. They were up, and in a moment they had the gun over, and Jamie pried his stiff hands away from the rope and sank down on his knees, panting. A feeble cheer went up from the crew. Jamie didn't take part, but instead drained the last drop from his canteen. He immediately regretted it, but it wasn't anything he could help.

Reily came and sat unceremoniously beside him, stretching out his legs. "Good work, Russell," he said, having the gall to actually grin. "You're a tough little scrap."

Jamie gave no answer, but sprawled on his back instead and lay there until he had caught his breath and could hear the horses coming up over the top. He sat up, retrieved his hat, and got slowly to his feet, looking back across the canyon. The column stretched back from it into the distance, and the sun glinted off the brass of another gun as it started down the far side. He sighed, clapped his hat on his head, and turned his gaze south, where more hills awaited them.

"We are ready," Juan Carlos said, coming into the house.

"Thank goodness!" Laura had just finished replacing the caps to her pistol after cleaning it. She put the gun away in her bag, put on her bonnet, and stood up. "Señora?" she said, gesturing for her chaperon to precede her.

Juan Carlos picked up the carpetbag and followed the ladies to the door. Laura paused to peep into the kitchen, hoping to find her hostess, for she wished to thank the Aragóns for their kindness. The kitchen was empty, however. Sighing, she turned away and went out into the bright sunlight.

A crowd of villagers had gathered around the carriage. As Laura approached, she saw the Aragóns among them. Señora Aragón smiled, and called out "Señorita Howland!" At this the others became aware of Laura and her companions, and crowded about them, proffering strings of onions and chili peppers, loaves of fresh bread, and other gifts, saying "Gracias" over and over. Laura blinked in confusion, and looked to Juan Carlos.

"They are thanking us for chasing away the ladrones," he said. "Last night some of the men went with us back to that camp. We found two dead men and buried them. The others were gone."

"It wasn't—oh, Juan, we cannot accept!" Laura said as a young girl with two long, black braids and a missing front tooth pushed a squalling lamb into her arms.

"If we don't they will be offended," Juan said. "They will think their gifts are not good enough for you."

"Oh, for heaven's sake, that's not the case! But we can't take their best things—their food—"

"They have enough to spare some. God blesses generosity," Juan said. "This is their best way to thank you, and Him, for protecting them."

Laura was about to protest that Juan deserved more credit than herself, but she bit back the words, knowing the argument was useless. No doubt Señora Sánchez's exaggerated tale had spread through the whole village, and the villagers saw Laura as the person who had freed them from harassment. She must accept the role of heroine, and be gracious to her admirers.

Which was difficult to accomplish with an armful of squirming lamb. She stood gazing at the villagers, who had fallen silent as she was speaking with Juan Carlos. Their faces were all turned to her, eyes hopeful. Laura was touched, and had to brush away a sudden tear.

"Gracias," she said. "Gracias por—por—Juan, how does one say 'kindness'?"

"Por su benevolencia," Juan said to the crowd. "Gracias por darnos refugio."

"Sí, muchas gracias," Laura said.

Smiles lit up the crowd of faces. They began to file past, and Laura clasped each one's hand while Señora Sánchez collected the chili peppers and onions, the bread, a double fistful of fresh goat cheese wrapped in cloth, dried herbs, and fruit. Juan Carlos fetched Mrs. Canby's picnic basket from the boot of the carriage, and soon it was filled to overflowing. Señora Aragón waited until all the rest had made their gifts, then came forward with a stack of tortillas wrapped in cloth, still warm.

"Thank you! Gracias," Laura said. "Juan, will you hold him?" She handed the lamb to Juan Carlos, and turned to hug Señora Aragón. "Muchas gracias," she repeated.

"Gracias a usted," the señora said, smiling. Her husband joined her, and held out a small, silver charm on a thin, sky blue ribbon to Laura.

"Oh, I cannot—"

"Por favor, tome," Señor Aragón said. "Ella le va a proteger."

The metal was cool against Laura's fingers. It was an image of the Virgin of Guadalupe. The little silver rays glinted in the sunlight. Laura slipped the ribbon over her head, and held the medal against her heart. "Gracias, señor, Señora. Yo—oh, Juan, please tell them I am deeply grateful."

As he did so, a thought occurred to Laura. "Wait here," she said to the Aragóns, and hurried to the carriage, where her bag sat on the floor. She dug into it, found her lemon drops, and returned. Opening the tin, she offered it to the Aragóns, then to their daughters. Each took a drop, their faces lighting with pleasure. Laura passed out the candy to the children and the rest of the villagers until it was gone, then helped Señora Sánchez into the carriage, settling the heavy-laden basket on the seat between them, and accepted the lamb from Juan Carlos, putting it on the floor where its feet skittered for freedom. The door, clean once more, closed upon them, and Laura released the lamb, then leaned out of the carriage in a most unladylike fashion, waving to the villagers as the vehicle started southward once more.

As they passed out of sight, she leaned forward to call to Juan Carlos. "Juan, what is the name of that village?"

"San Antonio," Juan called back.

"San Antonio." Such good, kind people. She had been very lucky.

Señora Sánchez was admiring the gift-laden basket. Laura remembered the tortillas, and unwrapped the cloth. The señora accepted one, and Laura took another for herself. She tore off a bit to offer to the lamb, which was having trouble keeping its feet in the moving carriage. It lay down, involuntarily she thought, and remained on the floor, chewing placidly.

Laura sighed with contentment. The morning's gloom had left her, and she gazed at the river, looking for signs of the army's passing. Her fingers found the little medal of Guadalupe and clasped it. Captain O'Brien was fond of omens, and she imagined he would take such a gift as a sign of good fortune to come. Well, so would she. Today, she hoped, would continue to be a most fortunate day for her.

O'Brien's mood had faltered, what with Ramsey clinging to him like a burr and a breeze picking up the column's dust and throwing it into his face. They had the rearguard again. O'Brien fumed to himself in silence. Neither F Company nor any of the Regular cavalry ever drew rearguard, it seemed. He'd not be surprised if the men began to blame him for the company's bad luck.

He could feel Ramsey's presence behind him, like an evil cloud hovering at his shoulder. He had spent the morning trying to think of some way to be rid of the man, and had ended convinced that he himself was not a bit clever, and that he was doomed to be trapped. Sooner or later Ramsey would catch him in some little error, and bring it to Chivington, who would use it to break him.

Into these happy musings intruded the sound of a vehicle driving up behind them. O'Brien called out an order to the company to draw aside and let it pass, but to his surprise it slowed to match the plodding walk of their horses, and came up beside him. O'Brien glanced at it, and thought he must be dreaming, for in it sat Miss Howland.

"Captain O'Brien!" she called, smiling and waving to him.

The black cloud that was Ramsey seemed to swell up behind him, threatening to swallow both him and the carriage. Before he could think, fear had unleashed his tongue.

"What the devil are you doing here!"

20

"Surely such a march over such a country and made by men mostly on foot, not accustomed to walking, was never surpassed."

—Private William Randolph Howell,
5th Texas Mounted Volunteers

Laura blinked, unable at first to comprehend the captain's angry tone. He glanced behind him, where a man in lieutenant's straps rode, watching. Laura had a vague memory of the face, but the straps were new; he must have been promoted to replace Lieutenant Franklin.

Swallowing, she drew up her courage and said, "I'm sorry to trouble you, Captain. I wanted to speak to you—"

"Not now!" Captain O'Brien hissed under his breath. He flashed her a hard look from beneath frowning brows, then turned his mount away from the carriage and clicked his tongue. The horse picked up a trot and headed up the column.

Laura found she was having trouble drawing breath as she watched the captain hasten away. The new lieutenant remained, gazing at her with measuring eyes as his horse sauntered along. She began to find him offensive, and retreated into the shade of the carriage top.

Had she made a terrible mistake? Should she not have come at all? Tears threatened but she bit them back. She would not be put off. She had come to give him an answer, and to warn him, and she would speak to him. If his feelings toward her had changed, so be it. She was entitled at least to be heard.

Feeling as though her bonnet would strangle her, Laura took it off and hung it by the ribbons from the door handle. She closed her eyes, leaning back against the cushioned seat.

How mortifying; she had not even seriously considered that the captain might have regretted his offer to her. After all, she was so far above him in breeding, he ought to be grateful indeed that she would notice him, never mind her lack of family connections or other useful influence, or the fact that, but for Franklin's generous gift, she was utterly penniless.

I am ashamed.

Laura felt her composure crumbling; she frowned, trying to stave off the tears. Reddened eyes would not make her more attractive. She must be patient, and find an opportunity to speak to the captain in private, and learn his true feelings. Much to her surprise, she found she couldn't bear to think of being turned away. She very much feared it would break her heart, in fact.

I am in love with him. Oh, dear.

"Señorita," Juan Carlos called. "Do you wish to stay back here with these men?"

Laura sat up, opening her eyes. Drifts of dust were coming into the carriage. "No, drive on," she said, looking for her shawl. The new lieutenant still rode alongside the carriage, watching her.

The animals picked up speed, and Laura watched the soldiers move out of their way. She recognized Captain O'Brien's back, saw him turn to glance her way as they passed. She did not wave this time; she did not wish to embarass him, which was why she had told Juan Carlos to continue. Better not to hang about his company, if he didn't want to be associated with her.

I will be heard, she decided, setting her chin high. She would know his position, and his reasons, before going back. She had gone to a great deal of trouble to see him, and he owed her that much.

Before long they had reached the head of the column. Colonel Canby should be here, but Laura hesitated to seek him out. There would be time enough to speak to him when they arrived at the fort, and she certainly didn't want to create a scene in the column. She therefore let Juan drive ahead, but soon the sound of pursuing hoofbeats reached them, and the carriage halted.

"I say, is that Mrs. Canby in there?" called a familiar voice. Laura leaned forward.

"Miss Howland!"

The lamb sprang for freedom, and Laura just managed to catch it. "Good afternoon, Lieutenant—I mean Captain. I beg your pardon."

Captain Nicodemus looked aghast. "Whatever are you doing here?" he said.

Laura was beginning to feel annoyed by this question. "Is Colonel Canby nearby?" she asked, ignoring it, and clutching the wriggling lamb to her. "I have a letter for him."

"Well, yes, of course. That is, he sent me over to see who it was. Thought it might be his wife, it being her coach, you know. Is she in there with you?" He leaned forward over his horse's neck, squinting.

"No, this is Señora Sánchez," Laura said, indicating her companion with a nod. "Shh," she added, addressing the lamb.

"Oh. How do, ma'am?"

"She doesn't speak English."

"Oh. Er—"

"Are we far from the fort, Captain?"

"No, no—not far at all. Less than a mile, in fact. That's it, just over there." Laura followed his gesture to a jumble of adobe visible east of the road. A track turned toward it from the main road a short distance ahead. Esteban glanced back at her from the driver's seat, his expression unhappy. She hadn't time to reassure him at the moment, but she would do so later.

"Will you be so kind as to tell the colonel I would like to speak to him there, when he has a free moment?" she said to Captain Nicodemus. "We'll drive on ahead."

"Oh, of course. Yes. Certainly."

"Thank you, Captain," Laura said, favoring him with a brief smile. The lamb squirmed free of her grasp, and bleated as it tumbled to the floor. Juan Carlos started forward again.

Captain Nicodemus galloped away, but he was soon back, trotting up to her side of the carriage. "The colonel's kindest regards, and I'm to escort you to the fort," he called.

Laura nodded, and mustered another smile for him, to

which he responded with a grin. She leaned back, feeling weary and cross, firmly holding at bay the sick worry that rose whenever she thought of Captain O'Brien.

A string of foul oaths, in both Irish and English, ran through O'Brien's head, but he couldn't find one that was bad enough for what he felt he deserved. The light of his heart, whom he'd thought never to see again, had driven up to him wreathed in smiles, and what had he done? He had sworn at her.

It crowned the day. He might just as well go and hang himself now, for there was no future for him, none at all. His commander hated him, Ramsey was turning his own men against him, and he'd tossed away whatever hope had remained—if indeed there'd been any at all—of winning Miss Howland. Saints knew what she was doing here, but she certainly deserved better than to be welcomed with curses.

He longed for a bottle of whiskey to drown himself in. Maybe Fort Craig's sutler would sell him one. He'd have to spend Miss Howland's money for it, which made him smile bitterly. He'd damned himself so far already, what difference would one more sin make?

But luck, or Chivington, or both, conspired to deny him even this small comfort. By the time he and his half a company reached the fort, orders were already circulating for the Colorado regiment to remove to a camp by the river, a mile's distance. Craig was filled to overflowing between the Regulars and Kit Carson's volunteers, and so the Pet Lambs must camp off alone by themselves in the sand.

O'Brien gazed at the earthen walls of the fort, an empty ache in his gut. Neither the sutler nor Miss Howland would see him tonight. He heaved a great sigh, and turned to lead his dusty, weary men away.

Laura stood beside the carriage, gazing about her at the utter confusion in the fort. Tents were being pitched between the buildings, some of which appeared to have been rather hastily constructed. Nearly every inch of ground inside the walls was taken up by soldiers' housing, and men hurried in and out of the barracks, or worked busily on what had been the parade ground but was now becoming a sea of tents. Laura berated herself for not thinking of how she and her companions were to be accommodated among this crowd.

Señora Sánchez remained in the carriage; she had refused to set foot outside it, and Laura was not entirely certain whether the bleating that issued from the vehicle now and then was the lamb's. One would think that the señora would wish to emerge and seek out her husband. One would think so, if circumstances within the fort were not quite so chaotic.

Laura stood by the vehicle, as it was the only place she could keep out of the way, waiting for Captain Nicodemus to return. He had seen them through the gate, then disappeared, waving his hand and calling out something unintelligible. Laura hoped he had gone to see about her lodging, but the hope was diminishing with each passing moment. She was just making up her mind to send Juan Carlos in search of assistance when a familiar figure appeared in the crowd: Lieutenant Anderson, another of her beaus from Santa Fé, making his way toward her.

"Miss Howland!" he cried, waving at her. Laura smiled and waved back. The lieutenant wove his way between two tents and past a cluster of men playing at dice in the dirt, and arrived at the carriage beaming, white teeth flashing in his tanned face.

"I thought it was you, but at first I could scarcely believe it! What are you doing here?"

Laura shook her head. "Wondering where I shall sleep tonight," she said, trying for a light tone, though she had to raise her voice over the babel of the soldiers.

Mr. Anderson grinned. He was as handsome as ever, like a Greek coin, though his face seemed a bit strained. Laura had not seen him since the autumn, long before the recent battles. She wondered what toll they had taken on him.

"Come with me," he said, offering her an arm.

"What about the carriage?"

He paused to give Juan Carlos brief instructions in Spanish, while Laura managed to coax her chaperon out of the vehicle. They left the lamb in Esteban's care, and Lieutenant Anderson led the two ladies away toward a small, squarish building that occupied one of the front corners of the fort.

"This is my office," he said, opening the door for them. "Nico's and mine, actually, but he's hardly ever here." The room was fairly large, with two desks, several chairs, and a number of makeshift bookcases along one wall. "You could stay here, or I can give you my quarters, but the office is larger," he added

"So you are an adjutant again? I don't wish to disrupt your work," Laura said, watching Señora Sánchez peer uncertainly about the room.

The lieutenant smiled. "And I can't let you, I'm afraid. But you'll have it to yourself from tattoo to reveille."

"That will do very well. Thank you."

She offered him her hand, and he pressed it warmly. "It's wonderful to see you here," he said. "Why have you come?"

Laura gently withdrew her hand. "I have some personal business to conduct," she said. "I also have a letter for Colonel Canby, when he has a moment to spare."

"He's just come in. Shall I let him know you're here?"

"I believe he's aware—"

"There you are!" cried Captain Nicodemus, bursting into the room. "Blast it, Allen, did you have to steal her away the minute she got into the fort?"

"Oh, so it was you who left her standing in the middle of the parade ground," Mr. Anderson replied calmly.

"I was trying to find her some quarters!" He turned to Laura. "I'm sorry, ma'am, but the guest quarters are all taken. There's not a room to spare, even the colonel's house is full."

"It's all right," Laura said. "Mr. Anderson has been kind enough to lend me this office. I'm not sure where Juan Carlos and Esteban will stay—"

"I think they'd be best off camping outside the walls," Anderson said. "They should be fairly comfortable there, and they can picket the animals. The stables are full, I'm afraid."

Laura nodded. "Thank you again."

"The colonel will receive you in half an hour," said Captain Nicodemus importantly, eyeing the lieutenant as he gave Laura a formal bow. She had to repress a laugh. It was almost like old times; they had spent the previous summer in what now seemed a whirl of frivolity and flirtation, even though Laura had not felt very frivolous at the time. It needed only Lieutenant McIntyre to complete the company.

Laura felt suddenly grave. Mr. McIntyre would not be joining them, ever again.

Mr. Anderson seemed to guess her thoughts, for he said, "We heard about Lacey, of course. I'm sorry."

"Don't be sorry for me," she said lightly. "He has harmed only himself."

"Well, I'm glad to hear that," the lieutenant said softly. "I had thought there to be an understanding between you."

Feeling herself on uncomfortable ground, Laura said, "Would you excuse me for a moment, Mr. Anderson? I'd like to tidy my hair before I go to the colonel."

"By all means." He bowed, even more graciously than Nicodemus had done. "I have an errand to run. Please make yourself at home. Come on, Nico, you have an errand, too, don't you?" he added, taking the captain by the arm.

"Mm? Oh, er, yes. I'll call for you in a quarter of an hour, Miss Howland," Nicodemus said as Anderson bundled him out the door.

She smiled after them fondly. An echo of summer, when everything had seemed much simpler, much easier. She'd been rich, then, she realized; housed in the Territory's best hotel by her profligate uncle, with nothing to do but pay visits to Mrs. Canby and dally with the colonel's staff. How had she dared to be discontented with that life?

War had brought so many changes to New Mexico, and to her own circumstances. Shaking off such gloomy thoughts, she looked about her and realized that she had not brought her bag. Señora Sánchez had her own little bundle, though, and she loaned Laura her comb. Laura sat in a chair by the empty fireplace, pulling the pins from her hair and dropping them into her lap. The scratch of the comb against her scalp was soothing, and she felt her spirits beginning to recover.

As she was pinning her hair up again a knock fell on the door, followed by Juan Carlos's voice. "Come in," she called.

Juan entered with her carpetbag, accompanied by Esteban

carrying the picnic basket. "The lamb ate two of the tortillas," Juan said apologetically.

"Wretched creature," Laura said, laughing. "I hope you
ate the rest yourselves."

"We took one each," he admitted. "We were very hungry."

"Have them all, please." Laura found the little bundle,
which showed signs of being nibbled, and handed it to him.
"I expect—well, I'm not sure what to do about dinner, but
we'll manage something, I'm sure."

"Gracias, señorita," Juan Carlos said.

"Thank *you*, Juan, for taking such good care of me. Have
you found a place to camp?"

"We will sleep in the carriage," he said. "It is just outside
the gate."

"Here, take some money," Laura said, giving him some
coins. "The sutler will sell you something more to eat. No,
I insist. Buy yourselves a treat. You've earned it."

Juan Carlos smiled and bowed before turning to leave.
Esteban bowed also, smiling shyly. His nervousness at being
near the military seemed to have finally gone. Laura nodded
as they left, and with a sigh, settled down to wait.

One foot before the other. Jamie started, and realized he'd
been walking with his eyes closed. He had one hand on the
gun barrel, still, from the last hill they'd come over. The soil
underfoot had been pinkish before, but now it was gray.
Looking to his right and squinting at the sun, he wondered
if it had stuck there a handspan above the horizon. Seemed
like it had been there for hours.

There was a whine in his ears, and a tight pain behind his
eyes. His lips were glued shut. His throat felt swollen, and
he couldn't get enough spit together to swallow. The men
around him must have all been in the same straits, because
no one talked at all. No one had talked for hours. It would
only hurt.

Men fell out all along the trail, and the column was so
strung out it was hard to consider it any kind of organized
thing. Each man struggled along as best he could. The companies of the 1st stuck more or less with the guns they'd
been assigned, but they all shrank by the hour. Jamie glanced

around, and saw that three of the men who'd been helping Reily's gun were missing, just of the ones he could see. Reily paced steadily alongside the limber, his face set, his eyes on the trail ahead. Jamie admired his fortitude. He himself was starting to think how nice it would be just to sit down for a while.

No! Can't stop, mustn't stop. No sense in stopping because he would only feel hungry if he didn't have to walk, and there was nothing to eat—he'd finished the last of his rations for breakfast. Somewhere back along the column the mule train had some flour left, but they were far behind. And he was too dry to eat anyway, so just keep walking.

He thought over his last letter from Momma—"Happy birthday Jamie and many happy returns"—he'd read it so often he knew it by heart. Now the words ran through his mind like a litany. Poppa well, Gabe well, Emma well and misses Stephen. Matthew still camped on the Potomac, and Daniel survived his first battle. The words had almost lost their meaning, and instead become just a river of sounds, a thing to cling to even if it made no sense. It ran over and over in his head, like a song that you couldn't get rid of; he set his feet down in rhythm with the words, and it helped him keep going.

In front of him a man dropped suddenly and lay beside the path, making a horrible gargling sound. Jamie dared a glance at him; the man's lips were black, and his whole face seemed swollen. His hands clawed at his throat. Jamie glanced at the limber and the gun carriage, already crammed with wounded in every possible space. There was no room for another. He trudged on past the writhing man, full of sick pity.

There's nothing I can do. Nothing.

Poppa well, Gabe well, Emma well. One foot before the other.

Shadows were getting long, lying across the hills to their left, and the awful heat was letting up a little. Everyone in the column stank like all hell; it had gotten worse through the hot day. Jamie made the effort of raising his head, and saw that the sun was now balanced just on the horizon, about to sink at last. Where was the water? he wondered. End of the day, there should be water, but they were still a ways off, apparently.

Starting up another hill. Jamie wanted to groan, but he didn't, and instead put his hands against the carriage axle between the legs of a wounded man who was riding there and leaned into each step, helping the horses what little he could. The pain inside his skull was increasing. He closed his eyes and just pushed the hateful carriage, the blasted gun. Threw his anger and frustration against the dead weight and followed it up the hill.

What if I die here? The idea sent a shiver through him. He didn't want to end up lying beside the trail, food for wolves, or in a shallow unmarked grave that Momma would never visit. No, he couldn't give it up, because who would get Stephen's last letter to Emma? She had to have her letters back, and the watch. So he had to keep going.

At the top of the hill, Jamie opened his eyes a crack. They were all gummed up with dust, but he didn't try to rub it away because that would only make them hurt. With an arm along the gun barrel to steady him, he fell back a little from the cramped confines of the axle. He could see the feet of the man in front of him, and the little curling cloud of dust that the gun carriage's wheels stirred up, and he didn't really need to see more to know he was still alive, still with the column, still in the right place. He had always known his place, been painfully aware of what he would and wouldn't get away with. Too small to bully his way in the world, so he had to make deals instead to get what he wanted, and keep his eyes open to avoid getting bullied himself. He would never be a hero, a dashing gallant like his brother Matthew or even a stalwart like Reily. His success would be just to get along without being trampled by all the heroes in their rush to glory.

Poppa well, Gabe well, Emma well. Pray for me, Momma. Pray to help me get home. I don't want to die here.

"Sorry we're in such a hullabaloo," Captain Nicodemus said as he guided Laura across the grounds toward the commander's quarters. "We're a bit over our normal capacity, as you see."

Cookfires had been lit in the fading light, and the fort was somewhat more settled, but still busy with soldiers passing back and forth, talking in groups or staring at their dinners as if watching would make them cook faster.

"It's quite all right," Laura said. "Are the Colorado Volunteers quartered in the fort?"

"No, they've gone off to camp by the river."

"By the river? Oh."

Aides and officers hurried in and out of the commander's headquarters, decidedly the center of activity within the fort. It stood opposite the adjutant's office, and Captain Nicodemus led Laura into a small outer room and knocked upon the next door. The colonel's voice summoned them in, and Laura straightened her back as she followed the captain into the office. It was modestly appointed, with a serviceable desk, several chairs, and a freshly lit fire on the hearth. Colonel Canby, dressed in a dusty civilian coat, rose from behind the desk to greet her.

"Miss Howland," he said, shaking hands. "What a delightful surprise. Thank you, Captain."

Nicodemus bowed himself out of the room. Laura glanced at the pile of papers on the colonel's desk, and felt a pang of guilt.

"Won't you sit down?" he said.

"Thank you, Colonel. I am sorry to intrude—I'm sure you have a great deal of business to attend to."

"Never so much that I cannot spare a few minutes for a friend," he said kindly. "Though I did wonder, when I heard you were here, what can have brought you at just this time. There is still a possibility that we shall be engaged in another fight."

Laura bit her lip. "Am I very much in the way? I will leave if you wish it."

"I would not presume to dictate to you, Miss Howland. If my wife has seen fit to lend you both her carriage and her servant, she must think your errand important."

To me, yes. I'm afraid you will think it foolish.

Laura drew Mrs. Canby's letter from her pocket. "She sends you this."

"Ah. Thank you." He gazed affectionately at the written

direction, then set the letter aside and returned his attention to Laura. "I received your letter also, about Mr. McIntyre."

"I wrote as a favor to him," Laura said. "I doubted you would grant his request to be exchanged."

The colonel nodded. "You were right. I cannot do it, but I'll see that he gets a fair trial." A hint of concern entered his voice. "You understand, I cannot suspend justice for a friend—"

"I wouldn't wish you to, Colonel. Mr. McIntyre is of no further interest to me. He must accept the consequences of his actions."

"Indeed." Colonel Canby leaned his elbows on his desk and laced his fingers. "Then, Miss Howland, how may I be of service to you?"

Laura felt a blush creeping into her cheeks. "Perhaps you are acquainted with one Captain O'Brien, of the Colorado Volunteers," she began.

One of the colonel's rather heavy eyebrows rose. "I am, yes."

"He is—a very good friend of mine, and I have reason to believe that some of his compatriots may be conspiring to discredit him."

"Have you indeed? Do you care to elaborate?"

Laura drew breath, and embarked on a somewhat jumbled explanation of all the various rumors she had heard, the accusations—mostly vague—of wrongdoing, and the expectation that Captain O'Brien would be brought up on some kind of charges. They seemed, in the colonel's calm presence, to be rather exaggerated, and Laura began to feel embarrassed that she had taken them seriously, but the colonel made no attempt to belittle her fears.

"He must be a very good friend indeed for you to have come so far to intercede on his behalf," he said softly.

"I do not ask you to interfere, Colonel," Laura said, "but I want to make it clear that he has not wronged me in any way. He has gone out of his way to protect me, in fact."

A small smile turned up one corner of the colonel's mouth. "And now you return the favor," he said. "Well, it so happens that this matter has already come to my attention. I am sorry to say it is not just his compatriots who seek to discredit him. Colonel Chivington seems to have an intense dislike of the man."

Laura pressed her lips together.

"I don't suppose you can tell me why?"

"Very likely it's because of me," she replied. "He's convinced I'm the worst sort of woman."

"Then I recommend you to be very careful."

"I am," Laura said. "I have brought a chaperon. María was with me until we reached Lemitar, but she is staying with her daughter, so I hired another."

"It's possible that even a chaperon may not serve to protect you. Do not attempt to approach the Colorado men's camp, Miss Howland."

Laura's eyes widened at this. "You think I will be threatened with violence?"

"Possibly. It certainly isn't worth the risk. Remember, you are surrounded by soldiers, and most of them could not be considered gentlemen."

Laura knew only too well what he meant. It was in just such a situation, and in rather alarming circumstances, that she had first met Captain O'Brien. She had been quite afraid of him at the time. She found herself smiling softly.

Colonel Canby rose and paced a few steps toward the fire. Looking down at it contemplatively, he said, "You say you do not ask me to interfere, but please allow me to assist you. Tomorrow morning I will summon Captain O'Brien to the fort. There's been a bit of nonsense concerning some wagons Colonel Chaves left in his charge. While he is here, you will have an opportunity to speak with him."

"Oh, thank you!" Laura cried. "Yes, that will be a great help, indeed. Dear Colonel Canby, I don't know how I shall ever repay you—"

"It's no trouble at all. Don't even think of it."

"You do not know the half of what I owe you," Laura warned. "Wait until you hear what we've done to your carriage!"

The colonel's smile rose to his eyes, making them crinkle at the corners. "Why don't you tell me about it over dinner tomorrow?" he said. "Perhaps by then you will have discovered another favor I can do for you."

Laura's heart gave a little flutter, and she glanced down, suddenly feeling shy. "I'm sure I don't know what you mean," she said, rising from her chair.

"You're an extraordinary young lady, Miss Howland," said the colonel as he saw her to the door. "All of your good friends must appreciate that, I believe."

"Thank you," Laura said, with a small curtsey.

"Captain Nicodemus?" he called, opening the door. "Would you see Miss Howland back to her quarters? I presume you found her some."

"Allen's got her set up in the adjutant's office," the captain said, hastening to offer his arm. "And I've got supper waiting for you there, ma'am."

Laura gave him a smile. "You are all much too kind to me," she said, with a glance back at her benefactor. "There are others who would have sent me packing. Thank you again, Colonel."

"Stay in your quarters, Miss Howland," Colonel Canby said kindly. "I'll send you a message in the morning."

Something was happening up ahead—angry voices—a fight? Jamie squinted. It was getting hard to see, but there was definitely some sort of commotion. The column was bunching up, and an argument was going on about the animals. His job; he'd better get up there. He left the gun and stumbled a step, tried to walk faster to get to the cluster of men up ahead. A man passed him going the other way, back along the column, his shirt all dark with wet.

With water.

Jamie looked wildly around for Reily, and saw him coming up fast. Reily grabbed onto his elbow and hustled him forward. They reached the group—it was the Armijos' coach, surrounded by men milling around and Sergeant Rose arguing with Manuel Armijo that the coach would block the way down, he should unhitch the animals—that was all Jamie heard before Reily had him over the edge of a small canyon and scrambling down to the stream glinting in the twilight below. Jamie could hear Reily panting beside him. He hurried as fast as his shaking legs would take him, sliding at times down the canyon wall and barking his hands on the rocks. Men climbing up cursed them as Reily batted them out of the way. At the bottom a mass of men and animals stood in the stream. Jamie didn't care. He followed Reily down to a flat rock that another man had just left, threw himself down on it and hung his face into the cool, clear water and drank. The cold hit his stomach like a fist but he drank on, feeling life flowing back into him, feeling the burning in his throat fade. Thank you, thank you, Jesus, was all he could think.

His hat's brim was dipping in the water. He sat up and pulled it off, and the motion made him notice that he was cold now and a little sick to his stomach. He bent down to drink some more anyway, and splashed water on his face and neck.

"Where are we?" he croaked.

"Heaven," Reily said, and put his face back in the stream.

Jamie laughed. No, not there, but at least we're not in hell.

The supper fire was burning down. O'Brien didn't bother to build it up. Old George would do it when next he passed by. The Negro was stalking through the grass out back of the tent, killing scorpions. Every now and then a muffled whack rang out of the darkness.

Their camp was in the river bottom, under trees just coming into leaf: cottonwoods and willows, with all manner of bushes clinging around their feet. It was a fair enough spot, but O'Brien was unmoved by its beauty. Sitting with his chin on his knees, staring into the coals, he was settling in for a cold night, with no liquor and no friendship.

He had gone into the river in the last of the day's light, to wash himself and his shirt. The water was running high, a bit treacherous. Someone had said that the river had already covered over the Valverde battleground farther north, so that nothing was left but the paths of the artillery through the woods. O'Brien had stayed close by the bank and scrubbed himself with handfuls of sand, and was now cleaner than he'd been in many a day.

You needn't have bothered, Alastar. You won't be going visiting on anyone who would care.

But he could feel the fort's presence, and knew that Miss

Howland was there, and it had made him unable to tolerate his own stench. So he'd bathed.

He could walk there. It was not far at all. Others had gone to visit the sutler despite Chivington's orders to remain in camp, and had brought back jugs of beer and tinned oysters and numerous other delights.

It was late, though, and likely she'd not want to see him. He wished he could send her a note—an apology—but had no one to write it for him. So if he walked to the fort at all, it would only be to buy whiskey, and while he wanted it badly, he knew he should not.

Whack. It was so close, it made O'Brien jump.

"Christ, man. Give it up."

"You want to find your boots full of these critters come morning?" Old George asked from the darkness.

"You'll never slay them all."

"I can sure try, though, can't I?"

Whack.

"Why don't you make some more coffee?" O'Brien suggested.

"River water's still settling out in that jar."

"I don't mind a bit of grit."

"Sure thing, then, Cap'n." The Negro came into the light, dropped his weapon—a stout length of tree-branch—and busied himself with the fire.

O'Brien glanced at Ramsey's empty tent, pitched nearby. Lately the man spent all his waking hours at headquarters, it seemed. He was thick with Chivington and his crew. O'Brien didn't mind not having to look at him, but feared whatever evil he might be designing.

He shifted his gaze to the Negro putting sticks of greasewood on the fire. The last thing I need, O'Brien thought, is for Chivington to question this fellow and get him to damn me. "Who's your master?" he asked.

"You are."

"No, I'm your employer. I pay you with food and coffee. You don't belong to me, understand?"

"Yes, sir."

"You don't have a master. You're free."

Old George looked up, his expression confused. "Free?"

O'Brien nodded. "You can go tomorrow, if you like," he said, half hoping the Negro would do it. The man stood staring at him, his mouth hanging open.

"Go where?" he said in a voice of dismay.

"Wherever you like," O'Brien told him.

Worry crumpled the Negro's brow. "Cap'n, I—I'd just as soon stay. I do good work for you don't I? And I don't really have nowhere else to go." He looked so lost and confused, O'Brien had to stifle a laugh.

"You can stay, then," he said. "But remember, whenever you wish, you can go. You're a free man, George."

"Yes, sir." The Negro nodded, and bent to poke at the fire, frowning in thought.

Fresh wood made the fire brighter and hotter. O'Brien closed his eyes, enjoying the heat. Soon the smell of coffee joined the woodsmoke. Comfortable scents. Home in the wilderness.

Whack.

O'Brien opened his eyes. Old George had picked up his stick and was back in the brush while the coffee boiled. O'Brien let him be. If it made the man feel better, he could murder all the insects he liked.

Time was when he himself would have been playing bluff poker on such a night as this. He remembered a game, not so long ago, with the other Colorado captains. Lately they'd left him alone, though, and if he sought them out he knew he'd be welcomed reluctantly. Bad luck hung over him like a cloud threatening rain, and no one wanted to be caught when the storm burst.

So he sat alone, musing and staring into the fire, wishing he'd done things differently. Easy to see your mistakes, looking back. If only he'd said something gallant to Miss Howland that afternoon, instead of shouting a curse at her, but he hadn't an ounce of gallantry in him. God hadn't seen fit to grace him with that gift. He had known it long ago. He sighed, and pulled out the little notebook that had been Franklin's, turning to the page where Miss Howland had written out the alphabet for him. Her pencil strokes were so tidy and straight, and his on the next page, where he'd practiced, so heavy and awkward. She'd made it seem like such a simple thing, but it wasn't. It wasn't at all.

He looked back at her writing, whispering the names of the letters to himself. He could hear her voice saying them. Closing his eyes, he sang softly,

> *"Siubhal, siubhal, siubhal a'rùin—"*

"Good evening, Captain."

O'Brien gave a violent start, and dropped the notebook. Ramsey was standing over him, and reached down to pick the book up, but O'Brien snatched it out of his way.

"Forgive me for disturbing you," Ramsey said in a tone not the least apologetic. "The colonel asked me to bring you these orders."

He held out a folded page, and O'Brien's heart sank. He took it, and glanced up at Ramsey, whose eyes gleamed in triumph.

O'Brien was still for a moment. "Have some coffee?" he said from a throat gone suddenly dry. "It should be near ready."

Ramsey's eyes flicked to the pot softly hissing on the fire, then back to the orders in O'Brien's hand. "Don't you think you should read that?" he said. "It's urgent."

"Oh, is it?" O'Brien said, rounding the fire. "Why? What did the colonel tell you about it?"

Ramsey frowned, his eyes narrowing.

"Nothing? Well, then, it can't be all that urgent now, can it?" O'Brien tucked the orders in his pocket and pulled the coffeepot off of the coals. He searched among the cooking gear for a couple of cups while he waited for the grounds to settle out and prayed for his heart to stop pounding so hard. "Nothing that can't wait for a cup of hot comfort," he said in a cheery voice that seemed not his own. He poured a cup full and offered it to Ramsey.

"Give it up, O'Brien," Ramsey said.

"You don't want it? I'll have it myself, then." O'Brien swallowed a mouthful, scalding his tongue.

"It's hopeless, you know."

"Nothing's hopeless. I don't like your tone, Mr. Ramsey."

"Give it up now and you'll walk away clean," Ramsey said. "Fight and you'll lose all." It was said softly, almost friendly like. O'Brien could fancy Ramsey using just such a tone with some criminal in a courtroom. It made his scalp bristle.

"You're talking nonsense, man," he said softly. "You need sleep, you've been marching too hard in the hot sun. Get a night's rest, you'll feel better. Dismissed."

"Excuse me, *sir*—"

"Have you orders to bring back an answer?" O'Brien demanded, his voice suddenly harsh.

Ramsey's brows twitched. "No—"

"You're dismissed, then. Good night."

Ramsey stayed where he was. O'Brien blew across the coffee and took a cautious sip, watching him.

"Come on, O'Brien," Ramsey said. "The game's up. It's time to admit it."

"Admit what?" called a voice from the darkness. "That Old George is making a pot of the best coffee in camp? Everyone knows that by now—you can smell it for half a mile."

"Denning!" O'Brien felt able to breathe once more. "Where did you spring from?"

Denning stepped into the firelight, smiling, and dropped his saddlebags at his feet. "Colonel Chaves sent us ahead. We just got in to Craig, and they sent us down here. First class accommodations, I see. Evening Ramsey," he added, giving his junior a measuring look.

Ramsey spared only a glance for him. To O'Brien he gave the full force of his malevolent stare. "Don't think it's over," he said, taking a step backward. "It's not."

Whack!

So loud it almost sounded like a pistol shot. Ramsey jumped violently, then peered toward the woods at his back.

"Whoo, that were a big 'un," Old George said, emerging from the brush and grinning as he brandished his stick, to which the remains of a large scorpion still clung. Ramsey made a face of disgust, shot one more angry glare O'Brien's way, then took himself off toward headquarters.

O'Brien watched him out of sight, a queasy feeling in the

pit of his stomach. He rubbed a hand over his face. "Thank you, Luther," he said quietly.

Denning walked around the fire, picked up the second cup, poured coffee into it, and sipped. "What was he pestering you about?" he asked.

O'Brien pulled the crumpled orders out of his pocket and handed them over. His knees felt soggy all of a sudden, as if he'd drunk a lot of whiskey after all, and he sat down beside the fire.

Old George put down his stick and went over to inspect the coffee. "Took it off too soon," he said, shaking his head. He put the pot back on the coals. "That Ramsey, he ain't no good to nobody." He spat for emphasis. "You want me to put up your tent, Mr. Denning?"

"No, don't bother," Denning said, perusing the orders.

"Sleep in mine," O'Brien offered.

Denning nodded. "That'll do. You could fetch my bedroll, if you don't mind, George. I left it on my saddle."

"Sure thing, Mr. Denning. It's a good thing you's back." The Negro strode off, whistling.

Denning folded the orders and handed them back to O'Brien. "Looks like we're scouting tomorrow. We're to report ready to ride at six, with three days' rations."

"Blast."

Denning sat down beside O'Brien and sipped his coffee. "Don't let Ramsey bully you."

O'Brien shook his head. "He'll have me out. Chivington wants it as badly as he does. It's only a matter of time."

"Not that easy. They have to have just cause."

"Don't they have it, then? All they want is the proof."

"I've been thinking about that," Denning said softly, stretching his feet out to the fire. "If all they wanted was to prove you can't read, they'd have just hauled you up and asked you straight out. I think they're trying to get you to make a mistake. If they can prove it keeps you from doing your job, they'll have a stronger case." He glanced up at O'Brien, smiling, and pulled at his coffee. "You've done an excellent job, you see. You're a good commander, and Chivington can't stand it, because you don't toadeat him like the others."

"Ah, Luther. You're making me blush." The coffee had cooled a bit, and O'Brien swallowed a mouthful. Old George was right; it had been taken off too soon. He put the cup down and took out his notebook, brushing dust from the pages. "Why do these letters look nothing like these?" he asked softly, holding Chivington's orders up beside the notebook.

"These are cursive." Denning tapped the orders. "It's a faster way to write."

"You mean I must learn two sets of letters, not one? Jesus wept!"

"It's not hard. They're a lot alike. Here, where's your pencil?"

O'Brien produced it, and watched Denning make a new list of the alphabet on a fresh page of the notebook. He wrote out a row of letters, big and small, as Miss Howland had done, then beneath it he wrote the same letters in the curving writing that Chivington used. Old George came back with Denning's bedroll meanwhile, and ducked into O'Brien's tent to lay it out.

"You connect them up when you want to make a word." Denning said, dropping his voice. "See, here," He took the orders and pointed. "What's that word?"

O'Brien frowned, looking from the paper to the notebook. He picked out the letters. "T-o. Toe?"

"To. Good," Denning said softly. "You see? You can read it, it just takes a little practice."

"There's not enough time," O'Brien whispered, shaking his head, staring at all the other meaningless strings of letters on the page.

"Then we'll do the best we can. Come on, try another. What's this one?"

O'Brien bent his head to the page, staring at the list of letters and picking out the matching ones. It made his head ache, but he kept at it, spelling out word after word under Denning's direction.

Old George came out, checked the coffee and nodded his approval, pulling it away from the coals. He picked up his stick and resumed his scorpion hunt. O'Brien and Denning refilled their cups, added wood to the fire, and worked on until Ramsey's returning footsteps made O'Brien hasten to tuck the notebook into his coat. Ramsey went straight into his tent without glancing their way. O'Brien pulled out his watch, and saw that it was late, past eleven.

"Best get some sleep," he said, and Denning followed him into the tent, where they rolled themselves in their blankets and drifted to sleep to the accompaniment of Old George's blows.

The next thing O'Brien knew was a jostle at his elbow. It was mostly dark still, and quite cold. He sat up and rubbed at his eyes.

"Time to get the boys up," Denning said, shrugging into his coat. His breath fogged a bit in the chill.

O'Brien nodded, and yawned, and reached for his own coat. Remembering Old George's scorpions, he shook it out before putting it on, and did the same with his boots, which he found to be uninhabited. He followed Denning outside, where Old George was hastily building the fire. "Just coffee," he said to the Negro. "And pack me up three days' rations."

Old George looked up apprehensively. "'M I going with you?" he asked.

"No, you'll stay with the camp. Someone has to keep the scorpions out of my bed."

As they passed Ramsey's tent, O'Brien took pleasure in calling, "Hallo, Ramsey, time to rise. We're riding this morning." Denning went on to rouse Morris, and the three of them got the company up and preparing to march. Denning's men, tired from a long ride the previous day, grumbled mightily, but they got into place for roll call by five thirty. Fifty-seven out of fifty-eight were present, Sergeant Fitzroy having gone to the surgeon complaining of stomach pains. O'Brien rode through the lines, glancing over his men to make sure they would pass an inspection, then sent Ramsey to lead them up to the plain where the orders had said to assemble, while he hurried with Denning to headquarters.

Chivington was alone in the headquarters tent, and seemed in a good mood; he actually smiled as O'Brien and Denning came in. "Good morning, Captain. Mr. Denning. Where's Ramsey?"

"With the men, sir. They're ready," O'Brien replied.

"Would you send him to me, Denning?" Chivington said, shuffling papers on his desk. "I have an errand for him."

Denning exchanged a glance with O'Brien, then said, "Yes, sir," and left.

O'Brien swallowed, preparing for whatever blow Chivington was about to deal him. He watched the colonel's hands—soft hands, preacher's hands—move through the papers, and was surprised when, instead of selecting one with which to doom him, they folded neatly on top of the pile.

"I have an important task for you, Captain," Chivington said. "A task which, if you perform it correctly, will bring you great honor."

"Sir?"

"The Texans were seen passing along the mountains south of the fort yesterday. They're moving very slowly, and should still be within striking distance." Chivington stood, and paced the length of the desk, his hands clasped behind him. "Colonel Canby has refused my offer to pursue them in force. For reasons I cannot surmise, he wishes to avoid engaging them, though it's clear we can whip them. My hands are tied in this, but he has not forbidden me to send out reconnaissance."

The colonel paused, and eyed O'Brien narrowly. O'Brien stood still, returning the gaze of the small, dark eyes. Chivington's beard made it hard to read his expression, but O'Brien thought he was smiling slightly.

"I want you to ride south until you locate the Texans. Canby's scouts have reported that they've buried all their cannon except the guns they took at Valverde," Chivington continued. "This is our chance to take them back. You'd like to be a hero, wouldn't you? Think of the glory you'd have if you saved McRae's guns."

O'Brien frowned. "With just my company? Can't be done, sir. We're fewer than sixty, against hundreds—"

"They're weak, they've blown up all their ammunition, and they're strung out for a mile or more. They've left dead and dying all along their path. If you struck now, they'd crumble before you. Unless you're afraid?"

"No, sir, but common sense—"

"Common sense be damned! I'm speaking of glory, Captain! If you're too much a coward to take up the challenge, so be it."

"I'm no coward," O'Brien said through clenched teeth. He took a step toward Chivington. "I'm not a fool either! Give me a battalion and we've got a chance, but with sixty they'll club us to death!" He took a steadying breath. "Sir, I know you don't like me, but don't take it out on my men. They're good lads, they deserve better."

"I've thought they deserve better for a long time," Chivington said in a voice of deadly calm. "Are you offering your resignation, Captain?"

Caught off guard, O'Brien stood gaping. Before he could form an answer, Denning burst into the tent, out of breath. Ramsey came in close behind him, wearing his smooth, lawyer's smile.

"Ah, Mr. Ramsey," Chivington said. "Would you be so kind as to visit the fort, and consult the adjutant's copy of Army Regulations? If Colonel Chaves has sold the property we captured, as I've heard he has done, then I believe we're entitled to some restitution." He turned, smiling, to O'Brien. "Forgive me, Captain, but I want Mr. Ramsey's legal expertise in this. You can spare him, I think."

Bastard, O'Brien thought. Bloody blue bastard! Taking his friends aside while he sends us to our deaths!

Denning looked uncertainly from Chivington to O'Brien. O'Brien kept his eyes locked on the colonel's, staring hatred. His ire had risen, and he was damned if he'd be forced into resigning. Let Chivington bear the responsibility of his own actions.

Chivington raised an eyebrow. "You have your orders, Captain," he said.

More than ever before, O'Brien wanted to throttle Chivington, beat him senseless, cut out his heart. He fair shook with the rage, but would not let it master him. Instead he stalked out of the tent with Denning hurrying up behind him.

"What is it?" Denning asked as O'Brien took the mare's reins from Chivington's orderly and flung himself into the saddle.

O'Brien waited until Denning had mounted and they'd ridden well away from headquarters before answering. "Luther, my friend," he said through gritted teeth, "we've been right well buggered."

21

"I'm sorry, Miss Howland," Colonel Canby said. "It appears Colonel Chivington has sent I Company on a scout. They left before my message reached the camp."

Laura pressed her lips together, resisting the urge to stamp her foot with frustration. "Do you know when they'll be back?"

The colonel moved aside the chili peppers and herbs Laura had brought him—selected from the basket of San Antonio's gifts—and picked up an open letter from his desk. He glanced through it, then shook his head. "He doesn't say. I expect he's sent them down for a look at the Texans, in which case I'd be surprised if they were away for longer than a day or two."

Laura sighed, and paced the few steps to the window. The light outside was quite bright, making her frown. "I don't wish to impose on you, Colonel. I could remove to San Antonio—"

"You may stay, Miss Howland, though it is a bit irregular, and I must ask you to be very discreet."

"Of course," she said, turning. The room needed sweeping, she noticed; the sunlight from the window illuminated dust on the plank floors. Many boots had trod them in the few hours since the colonel's arrival.

"My married officers will be pining for their wives whenever they see you," he said with a smile.

Laura bowed her head. "I'm sorry, Colonel. I don't mean to be troublesome."

"Then keep your promise to entertain me at dinner. That's your fee. I don't think you've met Colonel Carson?"

"Colonel Kit Carson?" Laura looked up, unable to help feeling thrilled at the prospect of meeting the famous scout. "No, I haven't."

"Not surprising. He's actually rather shy. He'll be joining us, along with a few others. I'm expecting Colonel Chaves to come in today, though I don't know if he'll be in time for dinner."

"All C's," Laura mused.

"Beg pardon?"

"Your commanders. Their names all begin with 'C.' They are all 'Colonel C's.'"

"Including me?" Colonel Canby smiled. "I hadn't noticed, but you're right."

Laura laughed. "I wonder if you have enough for seven? Seven C's around your table?"

"Hm. Myself, Carson, and Chaves are three. Carson's major is a Chaves as well. But I'm quite certain it will be inconvenient for Colonel Chivington to join us. I'm afraid you'll have to settle for three or four. Unless you don't mind my filling in with captains?"

"Dear Colonel Canby," Laura said, laughing. "Please don't go out of your way."

"Oh, I shan't," he said, raising his brows. "I'll have Allen do it. Poor fellow, he's only a lowly Lieutenant A, so he won't be able to join us."

"Oh, don't exclude him for that!"

The colonel's eyes crinkled. "I am teasing you, Miss Howland. He wouldn't be there in any case—I've got too many high-ups to entertain. I expect they'll find you quite charming." He smiled, then drew a blank sheet of writing paper toward him and dipped his pen in ink. "And Allen will enjoy filling up the table with C's for you. Will your chaperon be joining us?"

"She speaks only Spanish," Laura said uncertainly, "and I think she'd be rather intimidated. She would probably be happier visiting her husband."

"Then you shall have the Seven C's all to yourself." Colonel Canby's smile broadened. "I'll send Allen to fetch you at six. In the meantime—"

"I'll let you get on with your business." Laura nodded, starting toward the door. "Thank you, Colonel. No, don't get up—I'll let myself out."

"Thank you, Miss Howland," the colonel said, bowing slightly behind the desk. "I expect this will be a memorable evening."

Laura smiled, and softly closed the door behind her. The antechamber was filled with officers, who all stood at her arrival. She recognized Captain Graydon—looking dustier than before, if that was possible—but none of the others. Señora Sánchez was huddled into a corner by the door. Laura nodded to the room in general, took her chaperon's arm and walked out.

The fort was somewhat less busy than it had been the previous day. Soldiers rested in their camps, and many heads turned as Laura passed. She kept her chin high and her eyes forward as she made her way to the sally port, where the guards challenged her.

"We are just going to look in on our friends," she said. "They are camped close by, with our carriage."

"Oh, them," said a lean fellow in corporal's stripes. "You'll find them just up the wall there, Miss."

"Thank you," Laura said primly. She led Señora Sánchez outside, and they made their way through a few yards of dust and weeds to where the carriage stood. Juan Carlos and Esteban, sitting in the shade cast by the vehicle, rose to greet them. The animals had been staked out to graze, and the little lamb frisked up to Laura at their approach, knocking itself down as it reached the end of its tether. Laughing, Laura set it on its feet.

"What's this?" she said, pulling a bit of black straw from the wool at the side of its mouth.

"I am sorry, Señorita," Juan Carlos said, sounding unhappy. "We tied him in the carriage for the night, so the coyotes wouldn't steal him. I did not know he could reach your hat."

"Oh!" Laura hastened to the vehicle and found the remains

of her bonnet dangling from the ribbons, which still hung from the door. She turned to the lamb, who had followed her. "You dreadful little brute," she said, shaking the fragments of straw in its face. The lamb opened its mouth to reach out for them, and Laura whisked them away behind her back. "I have half a mind to offer you to the colonel for his dinner tonight!"

"Señorita, I am sorry about the hat. By the time I woke up, he had already ruined it. I will replace it."

"Juan, no. Oh, dear," she said, laughing at the shredded bonnet. "I was just thinking I needed a new one. Now I shall have an excuse." She looked up, and saw that he wore a frown of concern. "Please don't worry about it, Juan Carlos. It's nothing. How did you pass the night?"

"Well enough, except for the lamb."

"And you, Esteban? Cómo estás?"

"Bien, gracias." Esteban nodded. He did not smile, though, and Laura thought he looked a little nervous.

"I hope no one has tried to press him into the army again," she said to Juan Carlos.

The older man smiled. "No," he said. "He is homesick, I think. He has never been this far from Santa Fé before."

"Oh." Laura's heart went out to the boy, for she well understood his feelings. "Cómo está Miguel?" she asked him, gesturing toward the donkey.

" 'Stá mejor, gracias," Esteban replied, and this time he smiled a little.

Laura smiled back. She liked Esteban, and wished she were better able to converse with him. She was trying to remember the Spanish for "breakfast" when a commotion at the fort's entrance attracted her attention.

"Go on, get out of here," the guard shouted. "Last thing we need in here is a damned squaw begging all around!"

Laura walked a few steps toward the sally port, where she saw a curious sight: an Indian woman, mounted on a paint horse and leading a showy chestnut, was apparently seeking entrance to the fort. As Laura continued forward, she heard the woman call out in very good English, "I want to speak to Canby."

"Well, he don't want to speak to you," the guard answered. "Go on, git!"

The Indian woman looked quite fearsome. As Laura came closer she saw a rifle as well as a bow and quiver slung on the pinto's saddle. The woman's face was stern, strong lines chiseled into a rather fierce expression, framed by wild, uneven shocks of hair. Her limbs were bare beneath the fringes of her buckskin dress, save for boots of soft leather cross-wrapped with strips of hide. She was nothing like the modest, rather docile Pueblo women Laura had met; much more like the desert savage described in *Harper's Weekly* back at home.

The woman reached for the chestnut's saddlebags, and produced a blue uniform coat with blue infantry trim—a great deal of trim, all over the front—which she held up in the guards' view. "I want to speak to Canby," she repeated.

"Get out of here before I come whip you out!"

Laura hastened the last few steps to the guardhouse. "Excuse me, Corporal," she said. "Don't you think it unusual that she should be asking for the colonel by name?"

The guard merely blinked. Laura turned to the Indian, summoning her courage. "Where did you get that uniform?"

The woman gazed stonily down at her. "Kip Whistler," she said at last.

"Did Mr. Whistler send you here?" Laura asked.

A nod. "Sent me to speak to Canby."

"From where?"

The woman stared at Laura, then jerked her chin south and east, toward the river. Laura turned to the guard. "I think this may be important, Corporal."

"Ma'am, we get these varmints coming here all the time," the guard said. "All she wants to do is get inside, so she can panhandle everybody in sight and steal whatever she gets her hands on."

"If I escort her to the colonel, she won't have much chance to do that, will she?"

"But, ma'am—"

"I'll take responsibility for her," Laura said. Turning to the Indian, she took a step toward her. "I will take you to see Colonel Canby," she said, "but you must leave your horses outside."

The woman's eyes narrowed in distrust. Laura imagined what she must be feeling; she was all alone, had no one to assist her. Laura knew she was asking her to leave the better part of her property outside the fort.

"My friends will take care of your horses," she said, indicating Juan Carlos and Esteban. "I promise you they will be here for you when you return."

The woman turned her critical gaze toward Laura's comrades. After a moment, she gave a curt nod and dismounted, removing both sets of saddlebags and slinging them over her wiry shoulders. She draped the uniform over one arm, and unslung the rifle from her saddle. After glancing at Juan Carlos and Esteban, she led the animals to Señora Sánchez and surprised that lady by placing the reins in her hands.

"We won't be long," Laura said. She turned to the Indian woman, smiled, and started toward the sally port.

The guards were conferring as they approached. The corporal turned to Laura. "Ma'am, I really can't—"

"Will Lieutenant Anderson's authority be good enough for you, or do I have to send to the colonel?" Laura said briskly.

"I—ah—"

"I believe Mr. Anderson is in his office. Please don't keep us waiting."

"Well—oh, heck. Go on in," said the corporal in defeated tones. "Not with that rifle, though!"

Laura glanced at the weapon, and found the Indian woman's hard eyes on her. Black shocks brushed at her shoulders as she shook her head.

"Will you let me carry it for you?" Laura asked.

Another hard stare. At last the woman relinquished the weapon. Laura took hold of it carefully by the barrel, keeping her fingers well away from the trigger. "Will this do?" she asked the corporal.

Grudgingly, he stepped back and waved her through the gate. "You keep an eye on her," he warned.

"I shall. Thank you."

Laura led the Indian woman to the commander's quarters and into the antechamber. It was less full, but by no means empty, and the corporal who was in charge of the door opened his eyes wide as Laura and her companion entered.

"Colonel Canby has a visitor," Laura told him. "She has an important message for him."

"Uh—he's meeting with his staff," the corporal said.

"We can wait a little while."

Laura took a chair beside the window, resting the rifle's butt on the floor. The Indian woman followed her, but remained standing, her back to the wall, watching every movement in the room. Laura glanced covertly at her dress. The only jewelry she wore was a string of colored beads. Her hair appeared to have been chopped off randomly; it was several different lengths, which made Laura long for her scissors. She was pretty, Laura supposed, beneath her sternness. Laura was curious to know how she had become a messenger for, if appearances were correct, a Federal soldier.

The other men in the room either pretended to ignore them or stared openly. Laura frowned at the latter group, and hoped that the Indian's patience would not give out while those who were there before them saw the colonel. Luck was with her, for when the office door opened and the staff began to emerge the first out was Captain Nicodemus, who saw her and walked straight over.

"What've you got here?" he said, breaking into a grin. "Say, Allen, Miss Howland's brought us an Indian princess! Does she do tricks?" he added as Mr. Anderson joined them.

"Certainly not!" Laura said, rising to her feet and casting a nervous glance at the woman, whose lips had begun to curl downward. "She's here to see the colonel. She has a message for him."

"Apache, yes?" Anderson said to the woman, who gave him a sharp glance, then a single nod.

"Is that an army uniform?" he asked.

For answer, the woman displayed the coat. Mr. Anderson's troubled gaze skimmed over it, and he reached out to touch the cloth, which looked new. His eyes rose to meet Laura's. "I think we'd better show her in."

The corporal guarding the door made a weak protest, but was easily overcome by the two staff officers, who simply swept past him with Laura and the Apache woman following.

Laura pushed the door closed behind her, and moved up beside the woman, keeping the rifle just out of her reach. Colonel Canby looked up from his desk, rather startled, and glanced at each of their faces as he stood.

"Look what Miss Howland's brought you, sir," Nicodemus said.

"I am looking," the colonel replied, raising an eyebrow.

Laura took a step forward. "Colonel, this—lady—has brought a message to you from downriver. The guards were about to turn her away."

"Downriver? From whom?"

"From Kip Whistler," the woman said. She held up the uniform for the colonel to see. "He sent me to speak to Canby."

"I am Colonel Canby. Who is this Whistler? A musician, I presume, if that is his coat."

"A musician. Of course!" Laura said to herself. That was where she had seen such elaborately trimmed uniforms—on the military band that had played in the plaza at Santa Fé the previous summer.

"He has a flute," the woman agreed. "Two flutes." She dropped the coat on the floor and opened one of the saddlebags, revealing a longish, carved wooden flute and a brass-bound fife. At the sight of the latter, a frown settled on the colonel's brow.

"Did he give you his flutes and his uniform?" he asked quietly.

"They were on his horse. I take care of his horse until you get him out of jail."

"Jail!" Nicodemus cried.

"Shh, let her finish," Anderson said.

"Yes, please go on," the colonel said. "What message did Whistler give you?"

"He said to tell you there are many soldiers coming from California to help you. An army."

A moment's stillness was followed by a whooping cheer from Nicodemus and the shushes of the others. Canby strode out from behind his desk and stood facing the Apache, who held her head high and gazed at him warily.

"Whistler came from California?" he asked, his voice now

intent, and the woman nodded. "Did he say how many soldiers, or where they are now?"

She shook her head. "He left them at Picacho. They had a fight there with some other white men. Then Kip Whistler rode here with two others, but the others were killed."

"And Whistler was taken prisoner? By white men?"

"Yes. I caught his horse. It's a good horse."

A frown teased at Colonel Canby's brow. "How did he manage to send you with this message?"

"I talked to him. He said come tell you about the California soldiers, and you would get him out of jail."

"Where is he in jail?"

"Down the river there," said the Apache, with the same jerk of her chin. "You say Mesilla."

The colonel glanced at his two officers. "Well," he said, "the Texans have been trying to arrange an exchange. Clearly we must negotiate for this Whistler."

"Yes, sir," Anderson said. Laura noticed he had taken out a pocket notebook, in which he was scribbling furiously.

"Was there anything else?" the colonel asked.

The Apache gazed distantly for a moment, then said, "Yes. He is hurt."

"Whistler's hurt?"

She nodded. "Yes. They hurt him when they caught him."

"Expedite that letter, Allen," the colonel said, his frown deepening. "You know the arrangement we've been discussing. Tell them to add Whistler and they've got a deal. Send your fastest expressman."

"Yes, sir!" Mr. Anderson said on his way out the door.

Colonel Canby turned his attention back to the Apache woman. "I am in your debt," he said, bowing slightly. "How may I repay you?"

"Get Kip Whistler out of jail."

"That is what my assistant has gone to do."

"I will go with him," the woman said, picking up the uniform coat and turning toward the door.

Laura reached a hand out to restrain her. "No—he's gone to send a messenger to bargain for Mr. Whistler's release. It may take a few days."

The woman frowned. "You have many warriors here," she

said to the colonel. "You could lead them down there and take him back."

"I could, yes, but I prefer to bargain," Colonel Canby replied. "We've had enough fighting lately."

The woman's gaze dropped, and Laura saw something sad flick across her face. All at once she seemed less fierce.

"Are you hungry?" Laura asked gently.

The Apache glanced up. The sudden sharpness in her eyes was all the confirmation Laura needed.

"Let me find her something to eat, Colonel, if I may."

"Yes," he said. "Thank you. Captain Nicodemus, you'll assist them. Please stay near the fort," the colonel said to the Apache. "I may wish to talk with you again."

She gave him a hard look. "Kip Whistler will come here?"

"Yes, we'll bring him here, if he can travel."

The Apache nodded. "Then I will stay."

Laura led the woman to the door, which Captain Nicodemus hastened to open. Colonel Canby followed them.

"Thank you, Miss Howland, for bringing this to my attention," he said. "I am much obliged to you."

"I'm glad to have been of help," Laura said. "Perhaps it will make up in some part for all the inconvenience I've caused."

"My dear lady, the help you've just given me far outweighs any such trifles. You are worth your weight in gold."

"I wish Colonel Chivington shared your opinion," Laura said with a rueful smile. "Good morning, Colonel. I'll try not to intrude upon you again."

"You are always welcome, Miss Howland," he said, watching her step into the antechamber. "Yes, all right, Corporal. Who is next?"

O'Brien reined his company to a walk to let the horses rest. The mare blew a sigh, and paused to tear up a mouthful of dry grass. They'd been at a gallop for much of the morning, riding south down the dusty plain just above the riverbank. O'Brien had been glad to put distance between himself and the camp. Now his anger was fading, replaced by a sense of doom.

Denning came up beside him. "How long should we follow the river? Did Chivington show you a map?"

O'Brien shook his head. No map. No guide. Chivington had done all he could to ensure their failure. They're in the mountains, lads. Go find them and fetch back the guns. McRae's shade will watch over you, until you join him.

"I should go back and do as he wants," O'Brien muttered. "It's not worth men's lives. I'll resign."

"No, don't," Denning said. "I won't accept command under such circumstances. I'd have to resign as well."

"Then Ramsey would get the company!"

Denning nodded. "So we'd better go on."

"Blast it, Denning—"

"'Scuse me, sir," Rice piped up behind them, "I know I'm out of line, but we'd rather you stayed with us, Captain."

O'Brien glared over his shoulder, to find Rice and Morris riding side by side behind him. "Do you always eavesdrop on your superiors, Sergeant?"

"No, sir, but I can't really help if I happen to hear something. And, begging your pardon, we'd rather die with you than be under Ramsey's command. Sir."

O'Brien gazed hard at Rice, who had his chin set high. A shadow of stubble showed on the young cheeks, and a stubborn look was in his eyes.

"No one's dying, lad," O'Brien said gruffly. "I'll not feed my company to the wolves to please Chivington."

"The wolves'll be sorry for that," Morris remarked.

"Don't make me laugh, damn you," O'Brien told him, stifling a chuckle. "We're in the devil's own fix!"

"Well, he's your godfather, in't he?" said Morris. "He should be looking after you."

O'Brien cast his eyes skyward while Morris explained to young Rice about how he'd been born on All Hallows' Eve, and was therefore under the devil's protection. Surely the lad must have heard the tale before—it was one of those that passed around the company again and again—men told it to each other just because they liked the sound of it, and laughed as if they hadn't already heard it a dozen times.

A fierce love of his men surprised O'Brien, tightening his throat. I must save them, he told himself, and the devil won't help me do it, godfather or no, so I'd better start thinking.

Looking west toward the mountains, he wondered how far the Texans had gone. They must only be making about ten or fifteen miles a day, with most of them on foot and hauling heavy guns across country. The company had ridden perhaps twenty miles already, so they might be about opposite the Texans.

How can I take back the guns? It's not possible, but I can find out where they are, at least. Maybe I can get one gun back. Chivington would call that a failure, but he couldn't accuse me of not trying.

They came to the mouth of a creek that emptied into the Río Grande. To the west, its banks rose and grew steeper, growing to a deep cleft a mile or so on. If he could catch the Texans in such a place—and they might well go down for the water, being cut off from the river—he'd have an advantage.

"All right, Morris," he said, circling the mare back to come even with the sergeants. "Take two men and scout along the north bank for any sign of the Texans. Rice, you do the same on the south bank. No heroics, lads. Keep out of sight, and hurry back to us."

"Yes, sir!" Rice's eyes were bright with excitement as he hastened to tap two young sparks for the duty.

Morris gave O'Brien a wry look. "Punishment?" he asked. "Have I wounded you, then?"

"No, I need your sharp eyes. Don't be caught. I hear they can't cook a decent meal to save themselves."

"I'll take care, then," Morris said gravely.

"The rest can dismount," O'Brien called to the company. "Let your horses graze, but keep them close. We may leave at any moment."

He watched Morris and Rice head off westward, waiting until they were out of sight before sliding out of the saddle. Denning joined him, nodding approval.

"Well done, Alastar," he said softly. "You'll bring us through this."

"I wish I felt certain of that."

"Well, I do." Denning smiled. "You've got the devil's luck."

O'Brien shook his head. He felt distinctly unlucky of late.

He turned the mare loose to graze on the new grass in the
creek bed, and sat on a rock to watch her. It was the last
stroke of good luck he'd had, finding her. Since then he'd
lost Shaunessy, Ramsey was snapping at his heels, and Chivington wanted him dead, plain and simple.

Feeling morose, and not having liquor at hand, he could
not resist tormenting himself with thoughts of Miss Howland.
He wanted her as much as ever, and she seemed farther than
ever out of reach. The devil—his supposed guardian—had
given him a glimpse of her, just to torture him, then inspired
Chivington to send him away. He closed his eyes, imagining
the sunlight on her fair hair, her smile, what it would feel
like to take her in his arms. Imagined himself whispering
into her ear, what brought you down here, mo mùirnin?

O'Brien opened his eyes. What *had* brought her down to
Fort Craig? She'd been safe in Santa Fé with Mrs. Canby,
and with the Texans still prowling the mountains, the fort
was no place for a pleasure trip.

She'd said she had wanted to speak to him. At the time
he'd been so worried that Ramsey's mischief would extend
to her, he'd hurried out of her sight. But what could she want
to say to him that would bring her all that way?

Oh, don't do it, Alastar. Don't start to hope.

But he couldn't help the feeling that was rising in his
chest. By God, I will live, he decided. I'll bring my lads
home, and I'll see her again, and the devil and Chivington
be damned!

The circumstances were odd for a picnic, but because of the
crowding in the fort, and the various people Laura felt she
must look after, she decided it would be easiest. Hence, under a cool, clear midday she and Captain Nicodemus spread
a blanket on the ground in the shade of Fort Craig's walls
and invited Juan Carlos, Esteban, Señora Sánchez, and the
Apache woman to join them al fresco. The fare was simple
but plentiful: some cold beef, fresh bread from the fort's
ovens, the San Antonio goat cheese, and two jars of peaches
purchased from the sutler—very dear—for which Captain
Nicodemus had insisted on paying. To drink they had beer,

highly preferable to the somewhat silty water from the Río Grande, a mile to the east.

Captain Nicodemus spread some of the soft cheese on a slab of bread, covered it with a slice of beef, and took a bite. "Heaven on earth," he declared.

Laura laughed at him. "You must have been living on pretty poor fare to say so," she said.

"Oh no! I was referring to the company," he answered, leaning back on one elbow and taking another bite of food.

Laura gave him a mock frown, then prepared a similar slice for herself, and found it was indeed good, if not quite her idea of heaven. She offered the same to the others, and the three natives accepted. The Apache woman smelled the cheese, frowned, then took half a loaf of bread and a handful of beef away to where Esteban had staked her horses, and sat in the dust to eat. Laura watched her for a while, not staring, but glancing that way long enough to notice the woman tearing off bits of bread and giving them to the horses. As hungry as she was, she cared enough about the animals to want to supplement their meager springtime diet of dried desert grasses.

The Apache woman fascinated Laura, who kept comparing her to the Pueblo Indian women she had met at Tesuque, north of Santa Fé. Those women lived in houses, helped work the farms of their community, and wore long dresses of cotton in something like the American style, though without hoops. They were friendly although somewhat shy, and rather placid. This woman was not placid in the least. Laura wished she knew more about the Apaches. She remembered hearing mention of peace treaties and of raids, and that they were a nomadic people. Cochise was an Apache, she believed. His name was associated with great atrocities.

Laura opened the peaches and shared them around, hoping they would attract the Apache to the blanket, but she remained where she was, munching bread and watching the picnickers. At last Laura's curiosity won out, and she carried what remained of the first jar of peaches over to the Apache.

"Would you like some?" she said, smiling.

The woman regarded her suspiciously for a moment, then took the proffered jar and dug a peach half out with her fingers, watching Laura as she gobbled it. Laura did not wish to sit on the ground, as she was wearing her good green dress, but neither did she want to stand over the Apache woman. She compromised by crouching and folding her hands over her knees, a position which would soon become uncomfortable.

"My name is Laura Howland," she said. "What is yours?"

The Indian surprised her by swallowing politely before speaking. "Rain Weaver," she said.

"What a pretty name! Rain Weaver. And do you weave the rain?" Laura said, smiling.

The Apache nodded seriously, fishing another peach from the jar. "That's why I'm called that."

Laura wanted to ask how, but decided against it. She didn't want to annoy the Apache, for she wanted to learn more about her. All alone, this proud young woman, with strangers at war in her homeland. How dreadful.

"Where is your home, Rain Weaver?"

"Around here, and further south." There was a note of challenge in her voice, and her steady gaze took on a hint of suspicion. Laura found herself feeling slightly restless, and sought for a safe topic of conversation.

"Are you married?" she asked.

"No. I do better alone."

"Better?"

"We don't have many men left to be good husbands. They are all busy fighting. They think we are winning." Rain Weaver's gaze shifted to the walls of the fort, and Laura glanced up at it.

"Victorio is right," Rain Weaver said in a low voice. "We cannot win. There are too many of them."

As if a door had opened before her, Laura suddenly saw that another war was raging in this land, a war Rain Weaver's people were losing. She had heard of the Apache troubles, of course, but had never given them much thought. It had not seemed important. Laura's heart filled with pity for this woman whose way of life was dying, and shame that it was dying at the hands of her countrymen.

Rain Weaver went back to eating peaches. Laura watched her, wanting to do something, feeling helpless.

"Do you have a family?" she asked.

Rain Weaver froze for a moment, then stared into the distance, chewing mechanically. "Not anymore," she said.

"Oh, I'm so sorry," Laura said.

The Indian shrugged, and ate another peach.

"I've lost my family, too," Laura said, trying to think of something that would comfort her a little. "My father died just over a year ago."

"My brother died twelve days ago. White men killed him." Rain Weaver sounded angry, and very bitter.

"I'm sorry," Laura said again, unable to think of anything else.

"We killed the men who killed him." The Apache's eyes were on Laura, watching for her reaction.

Laura took a deep breath. "I'm sorry your people and mine are in conflict," she said. "I would rather be friends."

"Not all white men are bad," Rain Weaver said.

Laura accepted this concession with a good grace. It was probably the best she could expect, and was at least somewhat open-minded. Rain Weaver's experiences with white people must have been rather limited, although she clearly had learned English at a school.

Having finished the peaches, Rain Weaver drank the juice from the jar. Some dribbled down her face and throat, and she wiped it away with the back of her hand, then gave the jar back to Laura. "Thank you," she said solemnly.

"You're welcome." Laura smiled, setting it aside. "Would you like me to trim the ends of your hair? It's a little uneven."

Rain Weaver's face crumpled, to Laura's alarm, and she looked for a moment as though she were about to cry. She steadied herself, though, sighed deeply, and gave a single nod.

Laura took her sewing scissors from her pocket. She had fetched them when she'd gone back to Mr. Anderson's office for the cheese, and now she rose, walked around behind Rain Weaver, and crouched again, gently taking the thick black tresses between her fingers. They had clearly been cut recently, for each shank was all one length.

"Why did you cut off your hair?" she asked gently.

"Because my brother died." Rain Weaver's voice was hard again, and Laura decided not to press her further. Instead she hummed softly as she trimmed the Apache woman's hair, bringing all the different lengths even with the shortest. When she was finished, the black locks just brushed the nape of Rain Weaver's neck and lay along the edge of her jaw, with even bangs across the forehead. Laura took out her pocket mirror to show her the result.

Rain Weaver blinked at her image. The shorter hair made her seem younger, and made her eyes look rather large. She looked up at Laura. "Thank you."

"You're welcome." Reaching to put the mirror and scissors away, Laura found something else in her pocket. She took out a little bundle; the fragments of her ruined bonnet, wrapped in its ribbons, which she'd tucked away earlier. "This was my mourning hat," she told Rain Weaver, unwrapping it to show her. "We wear black for a year."

Rain Weaver handed her the mirror and took the ribbons, holding them up so that what remained of the straw dangled in the air. "You wear this on your head?"

"Not anymore," Laura laughed. "The lamb ate most of it."

Rain Weaver glanced at her, then pulled the straw fragments from the ribbon. When it was free of them, she ran the satin through her fingers, then leaned her head back and draped it over her eyes.

"Would you like to keep it?" Laura asked. "You may have it if you wish."

The ribbon fell to her shoulders as the Apache looked up, staring gravely at Laura for a long moment. She picked it up and tied it around her forehead, a duller black against the shining tresses. "Thank you, Laura Howland," she said.

Laura smiled. "You're welcome," she said, reaching out a hand. "Friends?"

A long look, and the ghost of a smile. "Friends," Rain Weaver said, shaking hands.

"They're crossing that canyon, all right," Morris said, opening his canteen for a deep swallow. He offered it to Rice, who was still out of breath from the ride back. Rice nodded agreement.

"They're lowering the guns down with ropes."

"What's to the south?" Denning asked.

Rice shrugged. "I didn't look that far."

"If there's another canyon . . ."

"Aye," O'Brien said. "We might be able to set up a trap. It's about our only chance."

"I'll go," Rice offered.

"Get the lay of the land," O'Brien called after him. "Find where's the levelest ground."

Rice nodded, tossing the empty canteen to Morris and giving O'Brien a half-wave, half-salute. He fetched his horse, hauling its head out of the stream and calling to his two scouts. O'Brien watched him away, then turned to Denning.

"Let's mount up. We must get further south."

The men were quiet as they followed the Río Grande. Its waters were muddy and fast, climbing high up its banks. They came to another stream, where O'Brien called a halt. The tracks of Rice's party turned away from the river on the south side of the creek, and O'Brien determined to wait for them there.

If they could cut off the head of the column, with the first gun, they might have a chance of succeeding. It would be more of a raid than a battle, but a raid was all they could manage with so few men. They'd need to run the gun along the firmest ground to get it away quickly. O'Brien looked up, gazing over his company.

"Any of you driven an artillery carriage?"

They all shook their heads, then Langston spoke up. "I've driven a portable forge," he said. "Used to do a little smithing."

"You never told us that, Joe!" Flannery cried beside him.

"Didn't want to get stuck shoeing all your damned horses."

"You'll do, then, Langston," O'Brien said. "Come here."

With Langston, Denning, and Morris, O'Brien crouched under a willow tree and started scratching pictures in the soft riverbank. They argued, discussed, and had formed a plan by the time Rice appeared coming down the streambed.

"This one's a canyon, too," he said, pointing back up the stream. "It's not quite as high as the others."

"Could a gun carriage make it over the bottom?" O'Brien asked.

Rice frowned. "There are a lot of bushes and trees, and it's pretty hilly. Best to bring the gun down the creek, I think."

"We'll try it. Denning, you'll take thirty men up the north side. Morris, take ten along the south. The rest with me."

"Sir," Rice said, "there's one more thing. Up toward the front there are some civilian carriages. If we could bottle them up, it might slow the Texans down."

"How many in front of the carriages?"

"Maybe a hundred, and two of the guns."

O'Brien tapped his thigh beside his holster. "All right," he said. "We cut them off at that point, threaten the civilians, and see if that stops them. Don't fire on them though. Fire only at military, unless someone else points a gun at you."

Denning nodded. "Why don't you send Rice along with me, and I'll send him back with a report once we're in position."

"Good. All right, then." O'Brien looked at his men, who were sitting along the riverbank and up along the creek. One man had taken out his tin plate and was panning idly in the creek. Another had cut a willow branch and slung a line into the river. Horses grazed along the bank. It was a scene most peaceful.

"Form up, lads," O'Brien called.

He climbed into his saddle and watched them gather, thinking of when they were raw recruits, full of excitement and ignorant of soldiering, he as much as the others. Now they had a couple of battles under their belts, and weren't in a hurry to get into the next, but they came. They looked to him, trusting him to lead them back out of danger. A cold knot of worry hung in his chest, for this fight was none of his choosing; he considered it insane, but he had his orders. When they went back to Chivington, every man of them must be able to say that their captain had led them brave into the fight.

McGuire rode up to him, brandishing the bugle which he'd grudgingly learned to play for the company. O'Brien nodded. "Keep back, and watch for my signal," he told the old fiddler.

"Or Denning's, or Morris's, if I fall. Blow retreat as soon as you see it from one of us."

"Aye, Captain," McGuire said. "That I'll do. It's a sorry business," he added, shaking his head.

The men were assembled; fifty-six mounted Pike's Peakers, every weapon loaded and ready. O'Brien looked them over, and was proud.

"All right, lads," he called to them. "We'll have only about five minutes to roll over them and take the gun. Follow your commanders, and run back to the river as soon as you hear the retreat. Anyone we leave behind is a dead man, so stay in your saddles. They're tired, but they hate us. Remember that."

That was a poor speech to fire up a soldier. O'Brien tried to think of something more, while the men watched him expectantly. What the hell would Franklin have said?

Movement in the sky caught his eye; a small hawk circled lazily over the men's heads and settled in the bare branches of a tree. Its tail feathers were ruddy, and it sat gazing at him.

"Look there," O'Brien said to his men, pointing. Those who hadn't seen the hawk turned their heads. "That's a good omen," O'Brien said. "We'll be like that bird there, and fall upon our prey before they know it, and get out just as quickly. We'll fly, lads. We'll be the wind."

He turned westward, ready to start. Behind him someone shouted, "Three cheers for Captain O'Brien!"

O'Brien felt his face reddening as he looked back at his cheering men. After all the hardships they'd suffered because of Chivington's enmity, they ought to be booing instead. He smiled at them, feeling a gratitude he couldn't voice, and waved them on westward.

As they lowered the gun yet again Jamie leaned back against the rope, trying to decide which part of him ached the most. Besides his stomach, of course. His stomach didn't count, and he was trying his best to ignore it. He'd had nothing to eat for twenty-four hours. Some of the men had killed snakes, and some had searched under rocks for whatever lived there. Jamie wasn't quite that hungry yet, but he was getting close. He kept hoping for a rabbit, but the head of the column must be flushing them all away.

His thighs protested as he eased step by step down the heavily wooded slope. This canyon wasn't quite as steep as the others, but the cedars and sagebrush were thick, so they had to go carefully. Suddenly a dozen bluebirds flew up the canyon, their bright color flashing amid the grays and pinks and dark greens. Jamie looked after them, disappearing as swiftly as they'd come.

The men below with the horses let out a shout: "Cavalry!"

Yankee cavalry, charging at them up the bottom of the canyon! Jamie could hear the rumble of hooves, then the snap, snap of gunfire began. The rope slipped in his hands and he had to get his attention back on the cannon. As one, the men on the ropes all increased their pace to a reckless scrabble down the last few feet of the slope. The gun jounced to a stop and B Company poured into a rough line around it, bringing rifles to bear on the attacking horsemen. Reily began shouting orders, and three artillerymen with him leapt to work, detaching the gun from its limber, swinging it into action. Not enough crew, Jamie knew, wishing he had learned more about the artillery. They could double up jobs, but it meant firing slower. He hurried to Reily.

"I can help! Tell me what to do—"

"Stay out of the way," Reily ordered.

Jamie stepped back, angry, taking care not to get in the infantry's line of fire. Captain Scarborough was yelling orders, and Reily was shouting furiously at his crew. The cannon fired, and Jamie winced at the unexpected shock through the ground. His ears rang. "Where did they come from?" he cried, not expecting an answer. It was unfair. Anger and confusion filled him. He took out his pistol and fired at one of the approaching horsemen. Three rounds didn't seem to have any effect. He kept firing.

A flurry of motion to the south—there were Yankees on the far side of the canyon, shooting down at A Company, who had their gun halfway up the hill. Jamie's heart lurched as the carriage slid a few feet backward, nearly crushing the men behind it. A minié ball's rising shriek recalled his attention. It struck the tube of the gun in front of him with a ringing clang and a scatter of sparks, and the cannoneer on the left side fell. Quicker than thought, Jamie sprang forward to pick up the sponge he had dropped, and held it while a sweating private poured water on it from his canteen. A glance up at Reily, who had his thumb over the vent and a lit punk held between his teeth. Reily nodded, and Jamie thrust the sponge down the tube, twisted the pole once, twice, as he'd seen the artillerymen do, and removed it with a low *thunk*.

He looked up. Reily shouted something he couldn't hear. Jamie backed away from the muzzle as the other two artillerymen loaded the gun and rammed the charge down. He saw Reily apply the punk to the vent and the gun crashed, a blinding flash of fire followed by clouds of smoke that enveloped him, the ball sailing in a perfect arc, flying over the heads of the leading horsemen and landing in the midst of their charge. Solid shot—all they had left, and not very effective—but still Jamie's heart thrilled to see it fly. They were fighting back, by God, and this gun would not be taken from them. He stepped forward, ready to sponge again.

The Yankees were almost on them now, only about a hundred yards and closing fast. Jamie squinted at the man leading the charge, and suddenly his mouth went dry. It looked like that damned Irish captain, except that Jamie remembered him riding a black horse, and this man was mounted on a liver chestnut with a star. . . .

"What are you doing?" Reily shouted at him. "Come back!"

Jamie ignored him, throwing away the sponge and drawing his pistol as he strode forward, then ran, craning to see the oncoming horse running straight at him, straight for the gun. His heart started pounding even harder than it had been.

"Cocoa!" he screamed, the name ripping itself from his throat.

22

"The possession of the battery was victory."

—Ovando J. Hollister

The mare reared, and O'Brien nearly fell, caught by surprise. He thought at first she'd been hit, but she plunged ahead without his asking, on toward the gun. O'Brien holstered his empty pistol and reached for his saber, but a shrill double whistle set the horse rearing again and he had to grab at the saddle to keep his balance. He was at the gun, and the mare had gone crazy. There was a lot of shouting amid the pistol and rifle fire, none of which he could make out. Horsemen scattered the small line of infantry and turned to charge again. He saw Langston on the ground, catching at the ropes that were tied to the gun's axle. The plan was to use the Texans' own ropes to bring the gun away, and getting them was Langston's task.

"Whoa, damn you!" he shouted to the mare.

A shot went off near him; his hat flew away and his ears were left ringing. He looked down at a face he remembered—sick in a wagon—angry now, and pointing a pistol at his chest. O'Brien let out a surprised oath and expected to die, but the pistol must have been empty, for the fellow threw it away with a snarl and leapt up at him, pulling him from the saddle. They fell heavily together, and O'Brien rolled, trying first to pin the Texan, and when that failed, to break away. The lad was small but he fought like a demon, cursing and kicking. O'Brien aimed a punch at his jaw that missed and hit the shoulder instead. It was enough to enable him to scramble away, get to his feet, and draw his saber. The Texan stood up as well, took one look at the blade, and screamed "Bastard!" He whistled to the mare, vaulted onto her back, and was gone.

O'Brien coughed, breathing powder smoke, and looked at the madness around him. His men on the south cliff were lying down, firing over the edge at the Texans who had a cannon stalled halfway up. To the north he could hear gunfire and see puffs of smoke rising, but Denning and his men were out of sight, holding the rest of the column at bay in the next canyon back. Near at hand his lads had used up their ammunition and were galloping back and forth, using sabers until they could get to the gun's ropes and haul it away.

The gun—only a few feet from him. Langston now lay beneath the carriage, soaked in blood. It looked like he'd been cut right open. O'Brien frowned in horror, then a prickling at his neck made him turn just in time to ward off a blow from a tall angry Texan with a short sword. Flecks of blood spattered on him from the blade. O'Brien cut back with his saber and the Texan dodged. O'Brien had the reach of him, but he was hot for the fight, almost mad, from the look in his eyes. They dueled, clumsy sword strokes from men who were more used to guns.

"Captain!"

O'Brien kept fighting, unable to spare a glance. Hoofbeats were coming up behind him. He turned the murderous Texan's sword aside and punched him soundly on the chin, rocking him back.

"Captain!"

O'Brien looked behind and saw Rice bearing down on him at a gallop. He parried another blow from the Texan, stepped backward and reached out his free arm to Rice, jumping as the lad caught him and hauled him up behind with a grunt. He clung to the sergeant's waist as the horse circled away.

"We're holding, sir, but they're organizing to flank us," Rice gasped. "Denning says we'll have to quit soon."

O'Brien looked over his shoulder. He could see the field better from horseback. A flash from a rifle came almost together with the shriek of a ball past their heads. O'Brien flinched. The line of rifles guarding the gun had re-formed now, two dozen at least, with bayonets glinting at their ends. The tall Texan stood by them, working the gun with a short crew. One of I Company's horses lay thrashing a few yards away, its rider pinned under it, still as death.

O'Brien felt cold doom descending. Possibly they could yet take the gun, but it would cost half his company their lives, and no chunk of brass was worth that. O'Brien reached for his hat and found that he'd lost it. Instead he snatched Rice's from his head and waved it in a long, high arc overhead. A moment later McGuire's bugle rose up over the din of the fighting, sounding the sweet notes of retreat. Glancing backward once more, he glimpsed the liver mare coming up to the gun, the young Texan astride her, taking aim at O'Brien with his own musket. Cursing, he ducked his head low.

"Veer off," he called to Rice, who obeyed at once, and kept changing direction every few strides, like a ship tacking, eastward, ever eastward. Amidst all the noise O'Brien didn't hear that particular musket fire, nor did he feel a bullet in his back, for which he thanked whatever saintly power might be watching over this wretched fight.

The lads in the canyon bottom thundered and clattered along the creek bed, making hard for the river. O'Brien glimpsed Morris's handful galloping along the southern cliff. Denning's lot were out of his sight, and he worried about them, hoping they'd heard McGuire's signal. Even as he thought it, he saw McGuire urging his horse up the cliff farther on to the east. Brave man; he hoped to sweet Jesus he didn't get killed. McGuire meant a lot to the company.

O'Brien turned his eyes eastward. Best not to think of such things. There was naught to do now but get to the river, and figure out what to tell Chivington.

Jamie kept loading and firing until the Colorado men were out of sight. He hadn't been used to using a musket much lately, and the Irishman's piece was heavy, but he thought he'd struck one of the retreating cavalrymen. Two had fallen from their horses as they rode away, and four others lay near the gun. They'd be dead soon if they weren't already; the angry men of the 1st would make sure of that. B Company cheered as the last Yankee disappeared down the canyon, and Jamie cheered with them, a wordless cry of victory. Reily joined him, shouting and clapping his back. Jamie couldn't tell what he was saying, but it didn't matter. They had won. Wild elation swept through him. He threw down the musket and flung himself at Reily, locked in a bear hug, feeling waves of joy and relief. Finally Reily released him, grinning.

"You're not bad, for fresh meat," Reily shouted, and Jamie grinned back.

The noise of celebration subsided. The men surged forward to claim the property of the fallen, and Jamie turned to Cocoa, waiting patiently behind him. Tears sprang to his eyes as he rubbed his face into her warm neck, and she gave a low nicker and nuzzled his shoulder. He clung to her, laughing, amazed at her return. She nudged him again, and he turned to look into her huge brown eyes.

"At least the bastard took good care of you," he said, stroking her nose. She looked well, brushed to glossiness and obviously well fed.

Well fed! Jamie grabbed at the saddlebags, pulling the one on his side open and finding soft bread, cold beef, and a small sack full of coffee beans, already roasted. He ripped off a chunk of the bread and gobbled it as fast as he could cram it in his mouth, his stomach screaming at him for more. Cocoa craned her neck around to watch him, ears pricked forward with interest. He gave her flank a pat, and started on the beef. He should share it, he realized. Others were hungry too. He didn't want to, and he had to fight down an animal urge to hoard it all to himself.

Looking around for Reily, Jamie saw him talking with Scarborough and Colonel Scurry, who'd been back with Sibley's ambulance when they were attacked. He pulled the rest of the bread out of the bag and carried it over to them, munching all the way. Cocoa followed; he could feel her warm breath on his shoulder.

"—don't know what the damn hell they were thinking," Scurry was saying to Reily in an irritated voice. "If we were mounted, I'd go teach them a lesson!"

"Bread, sir?" Jamie said around a mouthful, and both their heads turned toward him.

"Where'd you get that?" Reily exclaimed, reaching for it.

"Captured it," Jamie said, and tore the loaf in three pieces, handing one to each officer.

"Much obliged," Scurry said. Reily nodded agreement, his mouth already full.

Jamie looked at the gun, standing in the canyon bottom. A dead Yankee lay underneath it. "They were trying to take the gun," he said.

"Why in hell?" Scurry exclaimed. "What good would it do them? They're not going to fight us again, or they would have brought a bigger force."

Jamie drew a shuddering breath, surprised at the tumult of his feelings. "Maybe they were trying to spoil it for us. The Valverde battery. By breaking it up."

Scurry's eyes narrowed. "Well, they won't do it! Nothing will break up this battery. The Valverde guns are ours!"

Jamie nodded, gazing at the gun, knowing they'd soon be taking up the weary march once more. "Damn right they're ours."

O'Brien stared westward, the river at his back, hoping to see one more horseman come riding toward them. The sun was getting low enough to make him squint. He was worried. Denning had lost one man killed, and a handful of O'Brien's were missing, besides Langston. Too many.

"I think that's everyone we'll see," Denning said softly at his side.

O'Brien closed his eyes briefly. "Call roll," he said. "Then we'll be off."

Denning took out his notebook and began calling names. When a silence was heard instead of an answer, he made a note. O'Brien kept watching the canyon, but no others came.

McGuire and Kimmick knelt on the creek bank tending to Dougal, who'd taken a ball in the thigh. A couple of others had bad wounds, and many had flesh wounds, O'Brien included. A ball had brushed his cheek, leaving a burning scrape which he was trying his best to ignore. It was nothing compared to what others had suffered. He bent to drink from the creek and splashed a little water on his face, which just seemed to make it burn more. He loaded his pistol, and as he was finishing Denning came up to report.

"Seven missing," he said softly. "Presumed dead?"

"Aye." O'Brien nodded. "We'll come back tomorrow and

find them." Whatever was left of them, after every soldier in the Texan army paid his respects. Anger lay in O'Brien's gut like a stone. Seven brave men gone out of his company, worse than the fight at Glorieta, but this time it was Chivington's doing. He was lucky, he supposed, to have lost only seven.

Madness. It was sheer, spiteful madness. Chivington would hear no reason, and that meant O'Brien's doom, unless he made sure someone else knew of it. Someone outside the regiment.

"Mount up," he said, and Denning repeated the order. The men obeyed wearily. McGuire and Kimmick helped Dougal to his feet, his leg bound with a tourniquet. "Can he ride?" O'Brien asked.

"Yes, sir," Dougal said in a shaky voice. "I'll ride." The others helped him into the saddle, and Kimmick mounted and stood near him, watching him with a worried frown.

O'Brien took Langston's horse, which had run with the others in the retreat. The men had assembled themselves in a column, ready to ride.

"You did well, lads," he called to them. "You did bloody well. It was a gamble, and we lost it, but we're here still, and that's all that matters. You're the bravest damned lot of Trolls in all Colorado."

A shaky laugh rippled through the company. They're frightened, still, O'Brien thought, and he grieved for them. No one should have to face the odds they'd faced this day.

"Right, then. Back to camp. Last one in buys the whiskey," he called, and spurred forward. Someone cheered half-heartedly, and others took it up, and it grew at last into a shout, a wordless roar of joy, as the horses galloped up the riverbank. They were alive, and on their way back to safety. It was enough for now.

"Miss Howland? Is something wrong?" Colonel Chaves inquired.

"Oh, I beg your pardon," Laura said. "I was thinking of something else."

"Your adventures have wearied you, no doubt."

Laura smiled. The colonel, like the rest of the men assembled around Colonel Canby's table, had expressed admiration for her tale of her party's encounter with the ladrones near San Antonio. She had been hard pressed to maintain a ladylike poise while recounting the gruesome story, but the gentlemen had paid rapt attention, and she even thought she had detected Colonel Carson smiling a little. The famous scout was indeed very quiet, rarely speaking, and Laura remained in awe of him, though his person was not imposing. His light brown hair was trimmed neatly, his face clean-shaven and rather serious above his carefully brushed uniform. He was only slightly taller than she, and not in any way flamboyant. It was hard to imagine him having any of the adventures attributed to him.

"I only wished to offer you some wine," Colonel Chaves said softly, "but perhaps you are tired of us."

"Oh, no," Laura said, and pushed her glass toward him. "Yes, I'll have some wine, thank you."

She gazed around the table, trying to recall all the gentlemen's names. Colonels Canby, Chaves, and Carson, of course, and Major José Francisco Chaves, a relative of Colonel Chaves. Also Captain Chapin, whom she was very glad to see again, and Captains Clafin and Chacón, whom she had not previously met. Colonel Paul was also present, his rank being too high to permit his exclusion despite his lack of a "C." He was holding forth at present on the shortcomings of the Colorado Volunteers, a subject on which she had little to say. Or rather, little that a lady should express. She had no criticism of the regiment, but she could not like its commander, hero that he was. She gathered Colonel Paul shared her opinion.

Laura sipped her wine. The dinner party had been pleasant, but she was anxious, and it spoiled her enjoyment. She had not eaten much, despite its being the best meal set before her in many a day: roasted goose, wild asparagus, rice and baked onions, and the obligatory chile-spiced dish, which on this occasion was too hot for her even to attempt. The dishes had been removed, and the waiters now brought in dessert—a trifle soaked in rum. Laura tasted and found it good, but she laid down her spoon. She was too tense to eat.

Watching the waiters move about the room, she noticed

Mr. Anderson slip in with them and bend to whisper in Colonel Canby's ear. The colonel looked up sharply at the lieutenant, then glanced around the table, his gaze crossing hers. He replied briefly to Anderson, who nodded and went out.

"Colonel Paul," Captain Chapin said, "may I suggest that you recruit Miss Howland here to command the Pike's Peakers? She has demonstrated her mettle, and would doubtless make an excellent colonel."

"I am afraid that will not be possible," Colonel Chaves interjected. "Miss Howland and I are negotiating over her command of my new operations. I have decided to purchase a ship and take up piracy, since it is obviously so profitable."

Raucous laughter went up all around the table. Colonel Chaves was alluding to the fact that he was presently under house arrest pending investigation of his handling of the Texans' wagons. Laura was unsure of the circumstances, but knew that Colonel Canby was exasperated with the entire issue. Colonel Chaves seemed unconcerned.

"You may laugh," Laura said, contributing her mite, "but an adventuress must be careful what she agrees to. I have my reputation to consider, after all. I think command of an army regiment, even one of volunteers, might be entirely too respectable."

Another laugh greeted this mild jest, and Laura determined it was time she left the gentlemen to their brandy. She rose, saying, "Colonel Canby, thank you for a delightful evening. I have enjoyed meeting all of your guests."

The men all stood, and Colonel Carson raised his wineglass. "To Miss Howland, Queen of the Seven C's!"

"Miss Howland!"

Laura smiled as they drank. "How appropriate," she murmured to Colonel Chaves. "I shall have to accept command of your ship, I see."

Chaves bowed, a wry smile lurking on his lips. He assisted Laura in arranging her shawl about her shoulders and escorted her to the dining room door, where she was met by Mr. Anderson.

"How did you enjoy the party?" Anderson said, smiling as he led her away. "Were the C's entertaining?"

"They were quite delightful, all of them. They've been

making plans for the continuation of my descent into ruin."

He laughed. "Well, I hope they didn't offend you. They're soldiers still, underneath all the brass."

"I wasn't offended. I think I should enjoy being a pirate queen."

"Oh, dear."

"You did an excellent job," Laura assured him. "It's too bad you couldn't be among the party."

"Too much to do," he said. A frown flickered across his brow, but was gone at once. He led her outside, where the tents and the barracks were lit by the flicker of dying camp-fires. A crescent moon was rising over the hills to the east, its color pale gold. Somewhere a soldier was singing low and soft. It made her homesick for, of all things, I Company's camp; the music, the fires under star-scattered skies, and the smells of horses and dust and wood smoke. And Captain O'Brien.

"Mr. Anderson," she said as they passed along the front wall of the fort, "have you had any news of Captain O'Brien's company? The colonel told me he'd gone on a scout."

When he did not answer immediately, Laura glanced up, and saw him frowning.

"Dear me," she said. "You must disapprove of me a great deal."

"I don't disapprove of *you* at all," the lieutenant said.

"That's comforting. Do you have grounds for disapproving of the captain, other than rumors you may have heard?"

Mr. Anderson's frown deepened. "He's not a gentleman."

Laura walked a few steps before answering. "I've come to think there are different kinds of gentlemen," she said. "Some of those who've been bred as gentlemen have little true nobility of spirit. Others less fortunate are sometimes more gracious. I do not speak of you, of course, Mr. Anderson. You have always been a true friend."

"Then take this in the context of friendship, Miss Howland. You would do better not to associate with Captain O'Brien."

Laura hesitated. "Thank you. I know your intentions are good." They reached the office, and she turned to her escort offering to shake hands. Instead he clasped her hand in both of his.

"Miss Howland, if you are in any difficulty—"

"No difficulty," she hastened to assure him. "None whatsoever."

His eyes searched her face, and while she could not but be gratified by his concern, the suspicion that her friends seemed to think she was either lost to all sense of propriety or totally unable to control herself made her cross. She gently removed her hand from his grasp. "My friend is in trouble, and I wish to help him," she said. "Surely you can understand?"

"I don't want to see you hurt."

"I'll take care to avoid it. I'm not quite completely helpless, Mr. Anderson."

He smiled resignedly. "Call on me. For anything."

"Thank you," Laura said, returning his smile. "I trust I shall not need to trouble you. Good night."

Señora Sánchez stirred as Laura entered the dark office. Laura murmured a greeting, and prepared for bed herself. The remains of a fire put out inadequate warmth, and she shivered as she undressed and brushed out her hair. She must not allow her spirits to be depressed; that would not serve to help the captain. As she lay down, she clasped her little silver medal of Guadalupe, whispering words of prayer until she drifted to sleep.

The door opened, and O'Brien got to his feet as Colonel Canby came in. His dress uniform was immaculate, new by the looks of it. It made O'Brien conscious of his battle dirt, but that couldn't be helped. He followed the colonel through an inner door into his office. Canby went around behind his desk and took a cigar out of a box that lay on it. He didn't offer one to O'Brien.

"Well, Captain," he said, carefully closing the box. "I understand you wish to report some casualties. What I do not understand is why you wish to report them to me."

O'Brien took a deep breath. "Sir, I only want you to know the orders I was given, before you hear something else."

The colonel frowned, then seated himself. "Go on," he said, and placed the cigar in his mouth.

"Last night I received orders to report with my company at first light for a scout. I did so, and Colonel Chivington told me I was to go find the Texans and take back McRae's guns."

Canby was still for a moment. "Did he? That's interesting."

"I told him it couldn't be done with one company, sir. I offered to try it if he'd give me a battalion, but he cursed me and called me a coward—"

"Our gentle preacher cursed you?"

"Aye." O'Brien's anger rose at the memory. "He suggested I should resign. He's been wanting me out of his regiment ever since Glorieta—"

"Captain, I'm afraid I cannot interfere in the colonel's management of his regiment."

"I know, sir. I just wanted you to know what I'd been ordered to do." O'Brien swallowed. "I thought I might be able to get one of the guns. We set up a trap in a canyon, and it almost worked."

Canby leaned forward, and took the cigar from his mouth. "Good God. You actually attacked the Texans with one company?"

O'Brien nodded, and felt his throat tightening. "I lost seven killed. Haven't counted the wounded—we may lose another."

"Captain, I am more sorry than I can say." Canby's frown deepened, and he stood. "Particularly as it was entirely unnecessary. Chivington knew I did not wish to engage the Texans again. We discussed it yesterday."

"He was setting me up to fail, sir."

"Apparently. May I see the orders he gave you?" The colonel extended his hand.

"Orders?" O'Brien felt his chest getting tight. "There were no written orders."

"Well, did you write them down yourself?"

A curtain of darkness seemed to be reaching for O'Brien. His stomach did a slow flip, and he felt as if he might sink right through the floor. "No, sir," he said.

"Was anyone else present when Chivington gave you these orders?"

O'Brien shook his head.

The colonel's mouth became a thin, grim line. "Then you have no proof. It's your word against Chivington's."

O'Brien stared at the floor. Wood planks, set too green, for they were starting to gap apart a bit.

I've lost my company. My poor Trolls will have Ramsey for captain.

"I'm sorry," the colonel said with a sigh. "I don't see how I can help you."

O'Brien nodded numbly. "Sorry to have troubled you, sir," he said, and turned to go.

"Captain."

O'Brien stopped. He turned, and found Canby's gaze hard on him.

"Why didn't you write down the orders? You know that is the standard procedure."

The gray eyes demanded an answer. O'Brien licked his lips. "I can't," he whispered.

"Can't?" The colonel sounded puzzled. A horrified expression came over his face. O'Brien looked away. He was ruined for certain, now. There was not a thing left to him.

"Does Chivington know this?" Canby said in a stern voice.

"He suspects, I think," O'Brien said miserably.

"Well, no wonder he wants you out of his regiment!" The colonel began to pace slowly behind the desk. "How have you managed to conceal it?"

O'Brien shifted his weight from one foot to the other, wishing the interview would end. "My lieutenants helped me. Except Ramsey," he added bitterly. "He wants to be captain in my place."

Canby was frowning now. "I've had to make allowances for the native volunteers, but a white man—Captain, you must surely know that a commander is expected to be literate!"

"I'll resign if *you* tell me to," O'Brien said roughly.

"You must either resign or learn to read and write!"

"I've been trying to learn," O'Brien protested. "We've been in the saddle so much—" Catching himself, he straightened his shoulders. "I'll make no excuses, sir. I'm doing my best, that's all."

A soft knock was followed by the door opening, and one of the colonel's staff looked in. "In a moment, Allen," Canby said, and the fellow withdrew.

The colonel stood gazing at him, frowning in thought. O'Brien waited, unable to think of anything more to say. At last Canby spoke, in a voice so quiet O'Brien could scarcely hear him.

"I am concerned about this, Captain, make no mistake. About all you have told me. I'm not quite sure what to make of you. With one notable exception, everyone to whom I have spoken about you has expressed a good opinion."

O'Brien glanced up at him, surprised. "Thank you, sir," he said in a hoarse voice.

Canby sighed. "Well, you'd better go report to Chivington. I will see him tomorrow, I expect."

"Sir."

In the outer room O'Brien found the colonel's staffer lounging on one of the hard wooden chairs. The lieutenant gave him a long, measuring glance, then got up and went into the office.

O'Brien stood in the empty room, staring blindly at the walls. There were rumors of gold in New Mexico, if you didn't fear the Indians, or perhaps the army could use a good teamster. Not Chivington's regiment, though. He was damned if he'd ever work for Chivington again.

He sighed. Last one in buys the whiskey, and my poor lads have earned a stiff drink. With his bootheels ringing hollow on the wooden floor, he left headquarters in search of the sutler.

"Here it is," Captain Coopwood said. "They stopped just short of it."

Jamie peered down the cliff in the dim moonlight and heard water rushing below, feeling sorry for the men who had given up and made a dry camp three miles back. Cocoa shifted beneath him, nickering softly. "You want some, girl?" he said. She was tired, but seemed willing to do whatever he wished of her. He stroked her neck.

"Best way down's over here." Coopwood led the way into the canyon, the horses carefully picking their way down in the darkness. Dismounting to let Cocoa drink, Jamie hissed as he set his feet on the ground. Two days of marching had made them a mess of blisters; he was soft, he admitted, and guiltily grateful to be mounted again.

The stream ran lazily along the wide bottom, the water surprisingly cold. Melting snow running down from the San Mateos, Coopwood had said. All the streams and rivers ran high in the spring, as if this bitter, dry land disdained to soak up the moisture. Jamie wasn't so proud. Even though he wasn't thirsty he squatted to suck up a few mouthfuls of water. He figured he would never pass a stream again without taking a drink. As he straightened he gazed down the canyon, eastward and a little south.

"This is the Alamosa?"

"Yep," Coopwood said. "Next valley's our route to the river. Easy going all the way."

"We're that close?" Jamie said, which was stupid, he knew. It was just that they'd been so far from anything comfortable for so long, finding out they were almost back to the Río Grande was a bit of a shock.

"I figure on riding ahead and letting Steele's pickets know we're here," Coopwood said. "They can send up some food for the boys."

Jamie nodded, his gut twisting just at the thought.

"Care to come along?" Coopwood asked. "I can find you a bed."

A bed. Heaven on earth. A bed, a bath, a hot meal—

"No," Jamie said. "I'd better go back. I want to make sure the guns get through."

Coopwood nodded. With a wave of farewell he mounted and rode out of the canyon. Jamie watched him gallop away across a flat plain under the waning moon. With the Río Grande ahead, the world seemed a little less hard. We'll make it now, Jamie thought, smiling for the first time in days as he turned Cocoa back toward the column.

O'Brien sat with his chin on his knees, staring at the flicker of the dying fire through a half-empty bottle of whiskey that stood on one of the rocks of the firepit. It was all that was left of the spree he'd brought home to his Trolls. He'd watched them drink, get angry, grow sad, toast their fallen comrades, and at last stumble off to their beds after pressing the last of the liquor into his hands. They were better, he thought, than they had been. They might wake with bad heads, but likely they'd not suffer nightmares. Not this first night, anyway.

He himself hadn't touched a drop. Chivington had been abed by the time he'd reached camp, and had left orders for him to report at six sharp, no doubt to receive the colonel's abuse for doing exactly as he'd been told. He no longer cared. He stared at the golden fire in the bottom of the bottle, thinking about swallowing it and letting it burn all down his inside. He wanted to, sure, but he also wanted to call on Miss Howland and if he wasn't arrested he meant to do it, if only to bid her farewell. The least he could do was refrain from breathing whiskey fumes at her as he told her that all of his hopes had been broken.

Once, just once, I'd like to try something and not fail.

A soft sound made him look up. The Negro stepped into the firelight. "You going to bed, Cap'n?" he asked.

"No," O'Brien said, looking back at the fire. Likely Old George would be out of a job tomorrow, but he'd have no trouble finding another patron. Word that he could cook had got 'round. Maybe Ramsey would hire him. O'Brien closed his eyes.

"That were a bad fight today, weren't it?" the Negro said.

"Aye. Very bad."

"I'm right sorry for it, Cap'n."

A rustling of canvas preceded Denning's appearance from his tent, his greatcoat thrown over his shoulders, shirtsleeves beneath. "Can't sleep," he said, crouching beside O'Brien and holding his hands to the fire.

"Want me to make you some coffee?" the Negro offered.

"No, thank you, George."

"You want some, Cap'n? Or something to eat?"

"No," O'Brien told him. "Don't fuss, man. Go to bed."

Old George hesitated. "Well," he said, "you call ifn you want anything."

"That I will," O'Brien said. "Good night."

"Night, Cap'n. Night, Mr. Denning."

"Good night, George."

O'Brien waited until the fellow's footsteps had faded back to his own little camp a few yards away. "Look after him for me, will you?" he said softly to Denning.

"You're assuming the worst."

"I want you to look after the lads, too. Don't let Ramsey win all." He turned. Denning's face was cut deep with shadows by the feeble firelight, making him seem older than he was. "They like you," O'Brien said. "You'll be a good captain."

Denning sighed. "I would never have joined if it hadn't been for that idiotic duel. You saved my life, Alastar. I'll whatever you wish."

Remembering the duel drew a smile from O'Brien. It seemed an eternity ago, though it had been only a year. He'd thought himself right clever, then, to charge the pistols with powder only, and the look on the adversaries' faces had been priceless. He wished for a bit of that cleverness now; he needed it, what with Ramsey against him. He sighed, staring into the coals, trying to see some brighter future there than the one Ramsey'd planned for him.

Powder only.

A coldness poured down through his veins—a cold that no fire had the power to banish. He began to see what might be a way out of his troubles, but it was a dark way, a lonely way. He drew a sharp breath, let it out in a sigh, and then swallowed.

"Luther?" he said.

"Yes?"

"Tomorrow I want you to go fetch back our dead. Take Morris and a dozen men, and ask the quartermaster for a wagon."

"All right," Denning said.

"You can take the road. It'll be faster."

"We'll still be back late."

O'Brien nodded. "Take a day's rations along in case of trouble."

"You'll be all right alone?" Denning asked.

O'Brien managed a laugh. "What could you do if you were here?"

"Nothing, I suppose."

"You bring back our heroes," O'Brien said. "I'll be all right." *And you'll be out of harm's way.*

Denning sighed. "I guess I'd better try to sleep, then." He got to his feet and reached down a hand. "Good night," he said.

"Sleep well." O'Brien held the grip for a moment, then released Denning's hand and watched him go back to his tent.

The last flame was flickering in the bottle, on its way to death. O'Brien watched it, part of his mind planning, part of it dreaming of gold running through his fingers, a river of gold, now dust, now shining golden hair.

23

*"But since it falls unto my lot
That I should rise and you should not,
I'll gently rise and softly call,
Good night, and joy be with you all."*

—*The Parting Glass*, Irish Traditional Song

In the blue-gray before dawn O'Brien walked quietly through the camp, taking care not to disturb his sleeping men. The great table mountain across the river loomed dark, shadowing the forest at its feet, with only the barest promise of sunrise outlining the ridge.

O'Brien crouched beside a blanket-wrapped form and gently shook its shoulder. "Rice," he whispered.

The young sergeant woke with a start. O'Brien gave his arm a warning squeeze, then beckoned him away from the others, into the woods. Rice stood up, shedding his blanket, and followed. When they were out of earshot, O'Brien stopped and spoke softly. "I've a favor to ask you," he said. "If you don't like to do it, you've only to say so."

Rice rubbed at his shoulders to warm them, and glanced around at the trees. "Sir?"

O'Brien drew a breath. "Have you seen Ramsey's pistol? It's like this one, isn't it?" O'Brien held out his own navy pistol.

"Yes, sir." Rice nodded. "It's exactly like that one."

"When he goes for to shave this morning, will you slip into his tent and change this gun for his?"

Rice looked up at him. In the dim light O'Brien could just see his frown. "Are you going to kill him?" the lad asked.

"No," O'Brien answered. "I'll not harm a hair of his head."

Rice took the pistol, and checked the cylinder. Every

chamber was loaded, the cartridges rammed deep. He looked up at O'Brien, questions writ on his face, but said only, "I'll do it."

O'Brien sighed. "Thank you, lad. You'll understand why before long."

Rice merely nodded. He took his own gun from its holster, and held it out to O'Brien. "Take mine. It'll look strange if you walk around unarmed."

Touched, O'Brien accepted the pistol. His throat threatened to close, but he managed to say, "Thank you. Go on back to bed now."

Rice put O'Brien's weapon into his holster and stood gazing at him a moment. At last he turned and strode back toward the camp, dry leaves crunching softly under his boots. O'Brien watched him away.

The sky was already much lighter, the sharp, flat mountain more clearly outlined through the gray tree branches. New leaves were starting all along their edges, O'Brien noticed. A promise of green in this desolate land. Suddenly his heart yearned for home—for Ireland—for the music of its brooks and the soft grass of its hills. If he closed his eyes and listened to the river, he could almost imagine himself there.

He'd no time, though, for sighs and remembrances. He took out his watch—Franklin's watch—and saw it was close on five-thirty. He strode back toward Officer's Row and his camp, for he had his own shaving to do. Today, he thought wryly, he must look like a gentleman, no matter what fate brought his way.

Hoofbeats approached, and Laura looked up to see Colonel Canby on horseback coming toward her. She had come outside the fort's walls in order to allow Mr. Anderson the use of his office, and she and Rain Weaver had been playing with the lamb. Señora Sánchez watched from the shade, with Juan Carlos beside her whittling a cottonwood root.

"Good morning, Miss Howland," Colonel Canby hailed Laura.

She stood up and brushed the dust from her skirt. "Good morning, Colonel." She smiled up at him, shading her eyes with her hand.

"I wonder if you would mind being without the carriage for a day or two?" the colonel said. "I'd like to send it on an errand. We're exchanging some prisoners with the Texans, and one of ours is wounded."

"Mr. Whistler?" Laura asked, glancing at Rain Weaver.

"Yes."

"Do you need the team as well?"

"No, I'll use our stock. A team of four will travel faster."

"Then I don't mind at all, Colonel," Laura replied. "It is your carriage, after all, and I imagine Juan Carlos would like to ride back to Lemitar."

"Thank you. Captain Nicodemus will fetch it." More hoof-beats; Colonel Carson and Colonel Paul rode together through the sally port and joined Colonel Canby.

"Are you going hunting?" Laura asked. "It's a fine day for it."

Colonel Canby glanced eastward, then down at her. "No. Business, I'm afraid. Do you hunt, Miss Howland?"

"I cannot claim to, though I have been out twice."

"Coyotes offer fairly good sport, I am told."

"They must be harder to catch than foxes," Laura said. "They are the same color as the terrain."

This won her a reluctant smile from the colonel. "May I count on you again for dinner this evening?"

"I'd be delighted."

He lifted his hat and rode off, with his companions close behind. Eastward, toward the river.

Toward the camp of the Colorado Volunteers. Laura frowned, watching the dust kicked up by the cantering horses. "What sort of business?" she murmured.

"You should eat something, Alastar," Denning said softly.

O'Brien shook his head. It was all he could do to sip at a cup of Old George's coffee. His stomach had been tied all in knots, even before his interview with Chivington, who had listened in stony silence to his report, then informed him of his intent to prefer charges and demanded his saber.

"I've done some wicked things," O'Brien said gloomily, watching Old George remove his frying pan from the fire, "but never in all my life have I been arrested."

"It's just a formality," Denning told him. "You've got a better chance, now, because Chivington can't sit on the court-martial, and neither can any of his officers."

"It's my word against his. D'you think they'll favor me over Our Mighty Hero Chivington, with God sitting on his right shoulder?" O'Brien spat into the fire.

"At least you'll get a fair hearing."

"How's Dougal?" O'Brien asked, wanting to speak of something else.

"In a fever. Kimmick's looking after him."

"Bloody hell."

"You sure you don't want some of this bacon, Cap'n?" Old George said, waving the sizzling meat under his nose.

O'Brien drew back. "No. You eat it."

The Negro looked crestfallen. Denning reached across to take a piece of bacon before Old George carried it away.

"He's worried about his reputation," Denning remarked, crunching a bite. "Wouldn't do for word to get around that you hadn't eaten your breakfast."

"Hadn't you ought to be going? It's a long ride ahead of you."

"Morris is fetching the wagon," Denning replied. "He'll come for me."

"Captain O'Brien?" It was Shoup, standing over him. "You are to report to Colonel Chivington at headquarters," said the colonel's aide.

O'Brien gave Denning a long look, then stood. Old George reappeared and began brushing at the shoulders of his coat.

"Leave it be," O'Brien said. "You got every speck off it already."

"Cap'n . . ."

O'Brien looked back at the Negro, whose face was screwed up in a frightened frown. "It's all right," he said, and managed a smile. He turned to Denning, gripped his hand silently, then followed Shoup to Chivington's camp.

Not just Chivington, but Canby and two others sat waiting inside the main tent. O'Brien glanced around, looking for Ramsey, but he was not present. To one side sat Captain Chapin with his pen at the ready. O'Brien stood at attention and fixed his eyes at the row of feet beneath the table. The grass within the tent had already been trampled to death, he noticed.

"Captain O'Brien, this is Colonel Carson. You are acquainted with Colonel Paul," said Colonel Canby. "They are here to take part in a hearing to determine whether a court-martial is indeed appropriate in this instance."

O'Brien glanced at them. Paul he remembered from Fort Union when they'd arrived—an older fellow, had been Regular Army before becoming a colonel of volunteers—and Carson was small and stocky, probably a scrapper from the looks of him. Have to be, with the reputation he had. Neither smiled.

Colonel Canby looked O'Brien in the eyes and said, "Colonel Chivington informs me that you have exceeded your authority in leading an understrength force in an attack against the Texans. What do you have to say?"

O'Brien licked his lips. "The colonel ordered me to retrieve McRae's guns," he said.

"I did not," Chivington said. "I ordered you to find the Texans, that is all."

"You spoke of glory and honor to be won," O'Brien said angrily. "This is your chance, if you're not a coward, you said!"

"Captain—" Canby warned.

"I may have speculated about retrieving the guns," Chivington said coldly, "but all I ordered you to do was scout, as indicated by the written orders I sent you to have your company report for reconnaissance."

Bastard! O'Brien stared cold hatred at his commander.

"May we see those orders, Captain?" Canby said.

O'Brien reached into his pocket for the paper that would confirm the colonel's claim. He'd planned it carefully, Chivington had. From the start, every word had been calculated to shape O'Brien's ruin. It smacked of Ramsey's wiles.

As he pulled the orders from his pocket, another bit of paper came with them and fell to the ground. He handed the first to Chapin, then stooped for the other.

"What is that?" Chivington demanded. "Bring it here."

Chapin looked at O'Brien with apologetic eyes, and held

out his hand. O'Brien gave him the crumpled scrap, which he took to Chivington while Colonel Canby looked at the orders. Chivington smoothed out the paper and held it up, his eyes fairly gleaming.

"Ten dollars," he said. "That's a lot of money, Captain!"

Canby glanced up, frowning. Chivington passed the scrap to Carson, who handed it to the commander.

"Who gave it to you?" Chivington demanded.

"No one," O'Brien said. "I found it."

"Found it? You mean some Texan left his ten dollars lying in the road?"

"Not in the road." O'Brien fair squirmed in his boots, for he knew his next words wouldn't help him. "In a whorehouse."

"A whorehouse?" Chivington's tone was iced with disdain.

"I was cleaning it out," O'Brien explained, "to make it a hospital, but we took the Texans to Socorro instead."

"So if we went to this house there would be no one there to confirm or deny your story? How convenient." Chivington turned to Canby. "Colonel, I think I must modify my charges. I believe this man to be guilty of treason!"

"For possessing Confederate scrip?" Canby asked mildly, raising an eyebrow. "Then we'll have to arrest half our troops. The men are buying it for souvenirs, Colonel, in every town on the river."

"I found it in La Joya," O'Brien insisted, keeping a rein on his temper. "The Negro was with me. Ask him."

Chivington dismissed it with a wave of his hand. "You could have prompted him what to say."

"Come, come, Colonel," Paul interjected. "That would hardly be worth the trouble. If he feared discovery of the note, he could simply have destroyed it!"

"We are straying from our purpose, gentlemen," Canby said.

No one answered. Someone shifted in his chair, a creak over the constant scratching of Chapin's pen.

"Colonel Chivington, may I presume that you withdraw the charge of treason?" Canby asked.

Chivington frowned. "I do not. That note may be part of

a bribe. He may have been paid to destroy his company."

Colonel Paul cleared his throat. "Attacking the Texan column would be an inefficient way to commit treason," he said. "He might much more easily have surrendered to them."

"Either way, he would hardly have returned to face these accusations if he had planned to betray his company," Canby added.

"Unless he has further betrayals in mind," Chivington said darkly.

Canby sighed. "Send for the Negro," he said to Chapin, who nodded, put down his pen, and went out of the tent. No one spoke for a moment.

"Permission to step outside, Colonel?" O'Brien asked.

"Granted," Canby said. "Stay within call."

O'Brien avoided Chivington's baleful gaze as he left the tent. Outside it was bright enough to make him blink, even beneath the trees. A cluster of men with Ramsey at their center stood nearby, waiting for gossip or creating their own. Rice was among them; he looked at O'Brien and gave a tiny nod. Feeling a mixture of relief and apprehension, O'Brien glanced away at Ramsey. He made sure to catch the lieutenant's eye, scowled, then strode off into the woods behind headquarters.

Ramsey did not follow at once, so O'Brien chose a tree stump to sit upon, took his little notebook from his pocket, and sat gazing at it as if reading the Lord's very word. A cautious glance told him Ramsey had observed this, and in fact a moment later the man's footsteps could be heard approaching. O'Brien kept his eyes on the page, one where he'd writ many a's in succession. The last dozen or so looked half decent.

"Interesting reading?" Ramsey asked.

"You wouldn't think so," O'Brien replied, meeting his gaze.

Ramsey smiled—a cold, nasty smile—and said, "How's your trial going?"

"It isn't a trial," O'Brien said. He put his notebook away and stood up.

"It will be, soon enough," Ramsey said.

"Will it, then?" O'Brien gazed at him, measuring this little, vicious man; a puller of strings, a puppeteer. He'd gone in fear of the fellow too long. He feared him less now, and in another way, more.

Because now I will pull the strings, he thought. It only remained which to pull to achieve the result he desired.

"I thought of sending you to fetch back our dead heroes," he said. "I thought you should see the place where we fought yesterday, and where our lads bled. But I sent Denning instead. Do you know why?"

"I don't profess to be a mind reader," Ramsey said coldly.

"Because you don't deserve to go."

Ramsey frowned, which gave O'Brien secret pleasure. "You don't deserve to set foot on that ground," he continued. "You stayed away from it on purpose, to avoid the danger. You're a coward."

Ramsey's eyes narrowed. "Colonel Chivington—"

"Oh, aye, Chivington sent you on some little errand, but you knew what was in the wind. I'm sure you both planned it together. You took care to be out of harm's way."

"That's ridiculous," Ramsey declared, but he did not smile.

"Coward," O'Brien called him.

A little breeze caught up a bit of Ramsey's hair and blew it across his forehead. He blinked. "This is pointless," he said, turning to leave.

"You'll never get the lads to follow you," O'Brien said, taking a step after him. "They want someone they know they can trust."

Ramsey stopped, and looked back. O'Brien wished that his heart would quit pounding so fast. "You're a 'Go-on,'" he said. "That's not what they want."

"You don't know what you're talking about," Ramsey said, sneering. "You don't have the first inkling what is necessary for command. You'd be lost if you ever made major, which thank God you won't."

"It's you who'd be lost," O'Brien answered, "Lost and alone, for you'd have none of the men behind you. They'd never trust you. You'd find yourself like Slough, with your own men to fire on you in battle, if you ever had the courage to stand before them instead of behind!"

Anger flared in Ramsey's eyes. Good, O'Brien thought. Strike again.

"You think it's a game that we're playing," he went on, crowding him closer, and Ramsey fell back. "You think you're sitting at a chess board, with all the little men before you, to play with their lives. It's no game, Ramsey. It's blood and terror and triumph, but you'll never know that. You'll never succeed at it because you haven't got the guts!" O'Brien raised his voice on the last words, fairly spitting them into Ramsey's face.

"Stay away," Ramsey said in a wild voice, and took another step backward. O'Brien's gaze flicked to the tents behind him, some twenty yards away. He stepped closer to Ramsey.

"How many men did you kill at Glorieta?" he demanded. "How many in the charge? How many at the train?"

"I was with Chivington—"

"With Chivington." O'Brien sneered, and advanced another step. "You're nothing but a lily-livered bootlick. You couldn't kill a dog." Another step. He was almost within arm's reach.

"Stop it!" Ramsey cried, stumbling backward, a hand at his hip. O'Brien followed.

"You couldn't kill me, if I came at you!"

Crack!

O'Brien blinked, blinded by the blast of the pistol. He'd been struck in the chest, a sharp blow that had set him off balance. He'd not been expecting that, he realized as he fell.

24

"The feeling and expression of the whole brigade is never to come up here again unless mounted and under a different general."

—Alfred B. Peticolas

Laura watched the carriage trundle away toward the road, escorted by a dozen cavalrymen. The morning was not yet half gone, but the day was warming already, and she wished for her poor, shredded bonnet.

"Captain Nicodemus," she said to the gentleman standing beside her, "do you know what business took Colonel Canby to the Volunteers' camp this morning?"

"Course I do," he said, gazing after the vehicle. "Everyone knows."

"Not quite everyone. Will you enlighten me?"

The captain turned to her with a startled expression. "Oh, it's nothing," he said hastily. "Nothing you need concern yourself with, ma'am."

Something snapped within her. "I have had enough of being sheltered," she declared. "If you will not tell me, I will go to the camp and find out for myself." To emphasize her intention, she took a step in the direction of the rutted track that led toward the river.

"No, no, Miss Howland," the captain said. "You don't want to go there! Not the sort of place for a lady."

Laura smiled wryly. "You have forgotten, perhaps, that I am quite familiar with the Colorado regiment and their camps."

"No, I haven't!" The captain sounded exasperated. "It still ain't the place for you! Never was! Please, Miss Howland. Think what your intended would say if he learned you'd gone there."

"My intended *is* there, Captain. He is an officer in the Volunteers." Having dared to utter these words, Laura felt exceedingly brave, and continued. "Is the colonel's business something to do with Captain O'Brien?"

Captain Nicodemus looked uncomfortable. "Well, yes," he admitted. "It's only a hearing, though. Nothing to worry about. I daresay it'll all blow over."

"What sort of hearing?" Laura demanded.

"A preliminary hearing."

"Preliminary to what?"

The captain's brow crumpled up and he smoothed the ends of his mustache. "Well," he said unhappily, "Chivington don't like him much—"

"Preliminary to *what*, Captain?"

Nicodemus sighed. "Court-martial."

A cold fear gripped Laura's heart. "Rain Weaver?" she cried, spinning away from the captain.

"Miss Howland—" he began.

Rain Weaver stood up, suddenly alert, and the lamb skittered away from her feet as Laura hastened to her. "I must go to the camp," Laura said, nodding toward the river. "Will you come with me? And may we ride your horses?"

"That red horse, he's spooky," Rain Weaver said.

"I believe I can manage him. Please, my friend? Please?"

Rain Weaver gazed at her with sober eyes, then gave a short nod and started toward the horses grazing nearby. Laura followed, finding she was unaccountably short of breath.

Captain Nicodemus caught up to them. "Miss Howland—"

"Thank you, Captain, but I've no time to waste," Laura told him firmly.

"At least let me escort you!" he protested.

"Certainly, but we are leaving at once." Laura strode up to the chestnut, which Rain Weaver was already saddling, and stroked its nose. "What a pretty boy you are," she told it, smoothing the pale forelock. "You may help me to mount, if you care to, Captain," she added over her shoulder.

The captain muttered something—"Dash it," perhaps—but folded his hands into a step for her and tossed her neatly into the saddle. Laura slipped her feet into the stirrups without a blush and arranged her skirts as decently as was possible, then reached down a hand to Captain Nicodemus. "Thank you," she said taking up the reins.

"Wait for me," he pleaded, and ran toward the sally port, shouting for his horse. The chestnut jibbed. Laura murmured soothingly to him and glanced up at Rain Weaver, mounted on the paint.

"You won't like that horse," the Apache warned.

"Well, I haven't much choice, have I? It will take too long to walk."

Rain Weaver shrugged and they started together, eastward toward the river. As they crested the first hill Laura glanced back to see if the captain was following.

"Oh no! Brutus!"

Laura reined in, and waved over her shoulder at the little lamb, who had trotted after them. "Go home!" she shouted.

Instead the lamb frisked forward. The chestnut uttered a shrill whinny and reared. Laura clung to his neck, her heart pounding. Rain Weaver was shouting, the chestnut kept plunging, and Laura felt herself slipping sideways, then suddenly she felt a jolt and a firm arm caught her around the waist, holding her up. She thought for a moment that Captain Nicodemus had caught her, but the next moment she saw him galloping toward her from the fort. The horse calmed at last, and Laura was able to sit up. Rain Weaver had leapt onto the horse behind her, and now held the reins.

"Th-thank you," Laura managed to say.

"I better ride with you," Rain Weaver said. "This horse is spooky."

"What about your horse?"

"He'll follow. You hold on."

Rain Weaver turned the chestnut, started him forward at a canter, and without breaking stride she leaned down and scooped up the lamb in one arm, turning back toward the river the next second. Filled with admiration, Laura held the lamb close and spared a final glance toward Captain Nicodemus, faithfully following, then looked to the river ahead.

A hand grabbed at O'Brien's shoulder. He couldn't see whose, for he lay with his face in dead leaves, but it must have been Ramsey's. The shot had addled his wits some, and his ears still rang, but now he could hear someone shouting. The hand released him abruptly.

"Stand back, sir!" cried the voice, coming to O'Brien as if muffled by cotton. "Drop your weapon!" It was Rice, he realized. Good lad, Rice.

Others were coming; he could feel their feet pounding the earth beneath him. Slowly he moved, getting his arm free so he could put his weight on it to sit up. Before he could do so more hands were upon him, helping hands this time, gently turning him, keeping him from rising. He was stunned yet, and did not resist them. Hands searched over his chest, which was smarting like hell. He propped himself on his elbows, and had the satisfaction of seeing Ramsey held between two men. Ramsey's eyes met his, and grew wide, and his lips moved. There was much noise and confusion, but O'Brien distinctly heard him cry, "Devil!"

"What is the matter here?" It was Canby's voice. O'Brien glanced up to see the commander standing over him, with Chapin and the others behind him. Chivington gave O'Brien a poisonous glance before striding toward Ramsey. O'Brien tried to sit up.

"No, no," someone said. "Lie still."

It was Hamilton, the surgeon, on his knees beside O'Brien, still searching for his wound.

"I'm all right," O'Brien told him. He pushed the man's hands away and sat up, brushing leaves from his coat. This evidence of his still being among the living created a stir among the men gathered around.

"Ball must have gone over his shoulder," someone said.

"Did anyone see what happened?" Canby demanded.

"I did," Rice answered, then gestured to a handful of others standing nearby. "We all did. Lieutenant Ramsey fired his pistol at Captain O'Brien."

The lads with him nodded agreement. Canby gave Ramsey a long, measuring glance. O'Brien got to his feet, which drew Canby's attention. "Did you threaten him?" the colonel demanded. "Did you draw your weapon?"

"No," O'Brien answered. "I was telling him he hadn't the

courage to shoot a man. Seems he thought he would prove me wrong."

"Bastard!" Ramsey cried.

"Silence," Canby commanded. "You are under arrest, sir, for assaulting a fellow officer. Do not leave this camp, nor take any military action. Captain Chapin, take charge of his saber, if you please."

Chapin moved to do so. The two men holding Ramsey released him. His eyes stayed on O'Brien, burning hatred. "Demon bastard," he said. Chapin took him by the arm and led him away.

Colonel Canby turned to O'Brien. "Captain, in view of the circumstances, I think we should postpone your hearing—"

"Begging your pardon, sir, I'd as soon have it over and done with."

"Are you sure you feel fit? Do you not wish to compose yourself?"

"I'm all right," O'Brien said. "Let's get on with it."

Canby's eyebrows twitched. "Very well. We will reconvene in five minutes." He and the other colonels strode away back to headquarters. Chivington hung close by Canby's side, talking urgently. O'Brien lost sight of them as his own men crowded around him.

O'Brien nodded, and shook their hands, only half-hearing their jumbled words. Worried words, words of admiration, words of praise. He accepted them, feeling a bit dazed, but satisfied at having achieved his end. He had an odd, light-headed sensation, no doubt the result of having stared down a pistol barrel at point-blank and lived to remember it.

"Go away now, lads," he said to his men. "Go back to the camp. I've got business to attend to." They protested, but he promised to speak with them later, and at last they took themselves off. O'Brien stood staring down at the trampled leaves. Quiet was falling back into the woods, making them peaceful once more.

It had worked. Ramsey was finished, or so O'Brien hoped. He himself might not be permitted to stay in command of his Trolls, but at least they'd not fall into Ramsey's hands.

The rustle of a footstep startled him. Rice had stayed behind, and now he walked over to where Ramsey'd been standing, and crouched, picking up the pistol Ramsey had fired.

"Think he'll be cashiered?" he asked, turning the weapon over in his hands.

"We can only hope." O'Brien joined him, carefully placing his back between them and any curious eyes in the camp. "You'd best let me take charge of that," he said, reaching for the gun. "Here's yours."

Rice accepted his own pistol, and gave over both O'Brien's and Ramsey's.

"How did you do it?" he whispered.

"Tell you later," O'Brien said, standing up. "Or you can ask Mr. Denning about his duel."

Rice's brow wrinkled in confusion, but he said no more. Good, steady lad. They walked back to headquarters together, and as they came near O'Brien noticed a commotion brewing. Ramsey couldn't have found some new trick already? Frowning, he lengthened his stride.

"Then where is he?" a woman's voice demanded. "I wish to speak to him immediately."

"Sweet merciful Mary," O'Brien muttered, and in a moment his suspicion was confirmed. They came around the corner of the headquarters tent and before it, her hair all awry and her eyes flashing magnificently, stood Miss Howland.

"Here he is," the orderly said to Laura, and without further ado he ducked into the tent.

Laura turned to find Captain O'Brien approaching, accompanied by a young sergeant. She was suddenly conscious of her wind-blown appearance, and smoothed a hand over her hair.

"Good morning, Captain," she said. "I came as soon as I heard."

"You shouldn't be here," he told her gruffly.

"I can help you," Laura insisted. "I am ready to swear that you did not kill Lieutenant Franklin—"

"That's kind of you," the captain said, "but that's not what it's about."

"Oh," Laura said, taken aback.

"My men and I were cut up yesterday, attacking the Texans," he explained quietly. "I was given no choice, but I can't prove it now, and Chivington—"

"That despicable man!"

The captain smiled reluctantly. "Aye. So you'd best not be here."

Feeling frustrated, Laura glanced around. There were several soldiers nearby, all of whom became suddenly busy with adjusting tent ropes and similar tasks. Captain Nicodemus, also, stood watching from a short distance.

"I wish to speak privately with you," Laura said to Captain O'Brien, lowering her voice. "I never had the chance to answer you—"

"Don't," he said, and the pain in his voice stopped her short. His forehead drew up into a frown. "I may not have a job come tomorrow. You'd best just forget me."

"Captain—"

"I'm sorry for all the trouble you've been to."

"Captain O'Brien?" a voice said. "We're waiting on you."

Laura glanced up to see Captain Chapin holding open the flap of the large tent. Captain O'Brien glanced at him, then looked back at Laura.

"Go back to the fort," he said, eyes pleading, then turned and went into the tent.

Laura watched the flap fall shut behind him, a lump rising in her throat. Not wishing to cry in the presence of soldiers, she turned to the woods and strode briskly away. Her feelings were tumultuous, and it was not until she tripped on a root that she realized she was not looking at where she was going. She stopped, surrounded by gray trees, and stood listening to the sound of the river and the hundred little sounds of the camp. All so normal, as if the world were not ending, but would continue blithely on regardless of her feelings. So unfair.

A bird peeped, a hopeful sound. Spring was coming. Laura leaned against a tree trunk and wept.

O'Brien faced the line of colonels again, his teeth grimly clenched. He was tempted to resign then and there, for even if this farce came out in his favor, he'd still be under Chivington's command and subject to his whims. It was only a matter of time before Chivington would have his way.

But damned if he'd give in. He was just stubborn, he supposed. He hated yielding when he knew he was in the right. Realizing he was still holding Ramsey's pistol, he shoved it through his belt and stood at attention.

Old George was there, standing off to one side. The Negro cast a frightened look at O'Brien, then hunched his shoulders and peered at the four colonels doubtfully.

"Now then," Canby said, glancing up at the Negro. "Mr.—?"

"Old George, sir. Don't have no last name."

"I see. Can you tell me where you have seen this before?" Canby held out O'Brien's Confederate note.

"That's Reb money," the Negro said.

"Do you remember this particular note? Take it to him, Chapin."

Old George took the money gingerly, as if it would bite. He turned it over, and shrugged. "No . . ."

O'Brien closed his eyes.

". . . less it's the one the Cap'n found in that house up the river."

O'Brien had to struggle to hold his tongue. He glanced at the Negro, silently pledging to shower gifts upon him, if it remained in his power to do so.

"What house was that?" Canby asked quietly.

"Well, sir—there was some bad women in there, and the Cap'n he said we had to clean it out, 'cause the Texans was sleeping on the ground and one had up and died. But then we went on south after all."

"And you found the money in that house?"

"The Cap'n found it. Under a mattress. Asked me what it was, 'cause he'd never seen any before."

O'Brien held his breath, and glanced from one to another of the colonels. Chivington was stroking his whiskers, staring with narrowed eyes at the Negro.

"Thank you, George," Canby said, and turned to Chivington. "Well, Colonel? It seems clear that the Texans did not bribe the captain. I Company's attack on their column was not planned in advance."

"Yes, it was," Old George said.

"What?" O'Brien cried, and took a step toward him.

Canby held out a hand to stay him. "What do you mean, George?"

The Negro's eyes grew wide, and he glanced at O'Brien. "Well, sir," he said slowly, "it was planned the night before anyway, 'cause I heard Mr. Ramsey telling Sergeant Fitzroy he should report sick. Said the company would catch hell tomorrow, and to stay out of it."

"Fitzroy did report sick yesterday, sir!" O'Brien said. His heart began pounding. "And Colonel Chivington sent Ramsey to Fort Craig!"

"Yes, I saw him there," Canby said grimly. "George, when and where did you hear this?" he demanded.

"Out by the picket ropes, night before last," Old George said. "I went to fetch Mr. Denning's bedroll from his horse, and I heard them talking under a tree."

"Did Ramsey mention Captain O'Brien?"

Old George frowned thoughtfully. "Yes. He said, won't old O'Brien be surprised. Don't think they knew I was there, or he wouldn't have said that."

"I should think not." Canby turned to Chivington. "Well, Colonel? This is an interesting development. Did you share your speculations with Mr. Ramsey?"

Chivington rose, fuming, and placed both hands upon the table. "I know nothing of this," he said grimly. "This man could be making it up."

"Hm. I suppose it's possible he could. We'd better speak to Mr. Ramsey, and this Fitzroy." Canby took out his watch and frowned at it. "You may go for now, Captain, and so may you, George. We'll send if we need you again."

His gaze shifted to Chivington. "I think we can resolve this matter to everyone's satisfaction."

"No, I do not wish to return just yet." Laura pressed her handkerchief to her eyes, knowing they must be quite red.

"But you've seen O'Brien," Nicodemus protested. "He told you himself you shouldn't be here!"

"I have seen him, but I have not spoken with him." She turned to face the captain, and was surprised to see a line of tents not far away—Officer's Row by the looks of it, though the line was imperfect, being pitched among trees. "I do understand and appreciate your concern, Captain Nicodemus," she continued, "but I really must speak to Captain O'Brien. I've come a long way for that purpose."

Nicodemus's expression softened, and he suddenly seemed quite young, and a bit lost. "You really love him, don't you?"

Laura pressed her lips together. "That, sir, is—"

"None of my business." He nodded. "Sorry." He looked around, as if seeking something he'd dropped in the woods. "Well, I ought to go find King and give him a drink," he said, putting on an awkward smile. "That Apache gal's already had your horses down to the river. Here she comes."

Laura glanced eastward and saw Rain Weaver leading both horses, with the lamb under her arm. By the time she looked back, Captain Nicodemus was striding toward headquarters. Sighing, Laura went to meet Rain Weaver and took the lamb from her, hugging it to her and stroking its soft ears.

"We go back now?" Rain Weaver asked.

"Not yet, please. I'm sorry."

The Apache shrugged, and allowed the horses to graze along the forest floor. They made an immense rustling as they nosed leaves away from last summer's grass, pale and yellow. They walked toward the soldiers' camp, where Laura saw blankets strung between trees for shade, or as hammocks.

"Look, there it is!" cried a voice from the camp. "I told you!"

A half dozen soldiers started toward them. Laura recognized one of them as a member of I Company. He spoke as they came up to her.

"It is a pet lamb, isn't it, Miss?"

"Why, yes," Laura said. "I suppose it is." She set the lamb on its feet, and the soldier knelt down to touch it. The lamb nuzzled his hand. Other men came forward from the camp and crowded around, reaching out to the tiny creature. One held out a scrap of bread, which the lamb gobbled enthusiastically, to the delight of the rest.

"What's its name?"

"I've been calling him Brutus," Laura told them.

"Is it for us?"

Laura glanced around the circle of faces, all beaming at the little animal. "That depends," she said slowly. "Do you want him for your supper?"

"No!" was the indignant chorus.

"He'd make a fine mascot," an older man said. "The Pet Lambs' pet lamb!"

"You may have him, then, if you will promise not to eat him."

A cheer greeted this pronouncement. Laura made her way out of the crowd as the soldiers pressed forward to meet their new mascot.

"You've just made a hundred new friends."

It was Captain O'Brien's voice. Laura turned to see him standing quite close by. At once her heart began to thump alarmingly, and she took a couple of short breaths before saying, "And relieved myself of a burden into the bargain."

Rain Weaver folded her arms, frowning. "He would have been good to eat."

"Oh, I'm sorry," Laura told her. "If you want a lamb dinner, I'm sure we can find another, but I don't think I could bear to eat little Brutus, for all the trouble he's been."

"Hmph."

Laura glanced at the captain, feeling awkward. There was much she wished to say to him, but she had great difficulty finding the words. "You're not wearing your hat," she said at last; an idiotic remark.

"I've lost it."

"Oh, I've lost mine, too," she said, laughing nervously. "That is, Brutus there ate it. We shall have to go shopping together."

How foolish, Laura. Whatever must he be thinking?

The captain didn't smile at the jest, only nodded gravely.

"What happened to your cheek?" Laura asked.

His hand moved toward his face, then he put it down again. "It's nothing," he said.

"Musket ball," Rain Weaver said bluntly, and the captain glanced at her.

"Rain Weaver—" Laura began.

"I'll go get those horses," the Apache said, looking from

O'Brien to Laura. "They shouldn't walk in the camp." She turned and marched away, leaving Laura alone with Captain O'Brien. By silent accord, they strolled farther from the crowd of soldiers and their lamb.

"Is your hearing concluded?" Laura asked softly.

"No," the captain replied. "They're still at it, but they've done with me for now. It's looking a little better. I don't want to say—that is, I shouldn't expect—"

"It doesn't matter," Laura said. "If you lose your position, we shall simply find you something else."

The captain stopped walking, and stood staring at her with familiar intensity. The green gaze made her feel a bit giddy.

"I have faith in you, Captain," she said earnestly. "I believe you can accomplish anything you set your mind to, if only you will believe in yourself."

Silent still, he looked at her wonderingly. "Now," she said, straightening her shoulders. "I think we did not quite understand each other when last we met in Santa Fé—"

"Miss Howland, I wish you'd forget that day."

Laura's words caught in her throat. She pressed her lips together.

"I made such a great fool of myself," the captain continued. "I wish it had never happened."

"Oh," Laura whispered. "I see." They had come to a stop beneath a cottonwood tree, and a sudden breeze rustled the new leaves, sounding like rain. Laura blinked, trying to keep back a tear. A stray bit of cotton drifted down, and her hand came up to catch it, but was instead itself caught and pressed warmly.

"I'll do it proper this time." Captain O'Brien knelt beside her, gazing up at her, and said, "Miss Howland, will you do me the honor of being my wife?"

Laura drew a deep breath. She felt laughter bubbling up inside her, but managed to quell it, and said, "Yes."

"Dang it, O'Brien, what sort of a great gaping gaby are you!" called a voice from beyond the tree. "Proposing to ladies in a fellow's backyard!"

Laura's laughter escaped. "Good afternoon, Captain Logan," she called back, as Captain O'Brien got to his feet.

Logan came around the corner of his tent, his mustache

spread wide by a grin. "Afternoon, Miss. Nice to see you again. Congratulations, O'Brien. You don't deserve her."

"I know that," the captain said, gazing down at Laura in a way that made her feel quite light-headed.

"Say, O'Brien," Logan said, becoming serious, "I just wanted to tell you, we all wish we'd been with you yesterday."

Captain O'Brien grimaced. "So do I."

"There's been a deal of discussion. Most of us are of the opinion you're being given the little end of the horn."

"I'm of that opinion myself."

Logan glanced past them, and gave a nod. "Here comes Colonel Canby. I expect he's looking for you. Best of luck," he said, shaking hands with Captain O'Brien. "Ma'am," he added to Laura, lifting his hat before going back to his tent.

Laura smiled after him, then turned to face Colonel Canby, standing beside Captain O'Brien. Her fiancé, she realized with a flutter.

"Good morning, Miss Howland," the colonel said. "I see you have decided to ignore my advice."

"I did not come alone, Colonel," she answered. "Rain Weaver came with me, and I doubt anyone would trouble me in her company."

"I doubt it, too," he said. "Please excuse me, but I must confer with Captain O'Brien."

"If you please, sir," the captain said, "you might as well speak to us both. We . . ." He flushed, and glanced at Laura.

"We mean to be married," Laura said, feeling her own cheeks redden.

Colonel Canby's brows rose, and he smiled. "Do you indeed? Congratulations. In that case let us step to your camp, Captain, where we may have a little privacy. I have news for you."

O'Brien had to keep himself from staring at Miss Howland. She sat on an upended log, just as she'd done a month ago, that first morning up at Las Vegas, and gazed expectantly at Colonel Canby. O'Brien made himself do the same.

The colonel stood with his back to O'Brien's tent, looking

stern. "Captain O'Brien," he said, "I'm afraid you won't be commanding I Company any longer."

O'Brien felt the blood drain from his face. He swallowed, thinking now Miss Howland would surely change her mind.

Canby's face softened into a smile. "You'll be on detached service for now, with my staff, until we find the best place for you. We all agreed you'd be better off out of the Colorado regiment."

Feeling a weight lift from his chest, O'Brien dared to breathe again. "And the charges?" he asked.

"Colonel Chivington has agreed to drop them," Canby said, "and in turn I have overlooked the little irregularity with Lieutenant Ramsey and Sergeant Fitzroy. It's the best we could do, without dragging the whole sordid mess out indefinitely."

O'Brien felt a pang for his lads—he'd miss them, sure, but at least he'd his rank, still, and Denning would take care of them. "Thank you, sir," he said hoarsely. "I don't know how to thank you enough!"

"I'll tell you how," Colonel Canby said, his voice growing stern again. "Attend to that matter we spoke of."

O'Brien glanced up sharply, then nodded. "Right away, sir. You'll have no cause to complain of me."

"Good. Mr. Ramsey will still stand trial for attacking you, of course." The colonel frowned. "I would like to know exactly how that came about."

O'Brien licked his lips. "It's a bit complicated," he said.

"Perhaps you can explain it over dinner. It'll just be the staff tonight, so we can all relax, and you'll have a chance to get acquainted with everyone."

"Thank you sir," O'Brien said. "I'd be honored."

A smile hovered on Canby's lips. "Well," he said, looking at them both. "I'd better go ask my cook if we have any champagne. Good afternoon, Miss Howland. Captain." Nodding, he turned and strode off.

O'Brien watched him away. I'm going to be married, he thought. It had not quite struck home before, and all his failings rose up to haunt him.

"What are you thinking?" Miss Howland asked shyly.

"That I haven't any way to buy you a wedding ring," he

said. "I've spent all the money you gave me."

"It was yours to spend," she replied. "It was for the burro, and you didn't let me give you enough."

He shook his head, and sat down, frowning into the fire. "Can't even put my own ring on your finger."

"I have a ring that will do," she offered. "It was among the things Lieutenant Franklin left to me."

He glanced up at her, eyes hard, then looked away again. "Franklin," he said with a bitter laugh. "I'll never be what Franklin was to you."

"That's true," she said softly. "You'll be much more. Do you know, I only knew the lieutenant for six days? Hardly enough time to become friends."

He looked at her, searching her face. Was she taking him only because Franklin was gone?

She must have heard his thoughts, for she said, "I could never have married Lieutenant Franklin, Captain. Please don't let that worry you."

"He'd have given you more than I'll ever have."

She shook her head. "It was impossible that we should be anything more than friends," she said sadly. It made him want to take her in his arms, to protect her from all sadness, to give her everything her heart desired. He had nothing to give her, though. Nothing. Except—

He stood up, and strode to his tent. Old George had kept it tidy, and in two steps he had what he wanted, and returned.

"This is for you," he said. "A wedding gift."

Miss Howland cried out, and leapt from her seat. At first he feared she was angry, but she reached out for his gift, and held it close. "Where did you find it?" she cried.

"In a wagon we took from the Texans," he said.

She raised her face to him, and it was covered with tears. "This clock was my father's," she said. "I thought I'd lost it forever. Thank you, Captain! Thank you!"

He put his arm around her, and reached up to wipe the tears away. "Shh, mo mùirnin. Shh," he whispered, then with a queer dizzy feeling inside him, he said. "Call me Alastar."

"Thank you, Alastar," she said meekly, leaning against him and clinging to her little clock. He kissed her brow, holding her close, and smiled. It seemed he'd at last done something right.

Jamie sat in a real chair, eating fresh baked bread and re-reading his five letters from home. It was shady under the many-arched portal of Colonel Steele's headquarters, and the trees on the plaza and down along the river here were leafed out completely. It was as if the army had toiled through a death land to come suddenly alive again.

The column was trickling in to Mesilla, and would be yet for a day or two, he figured. Some—mostly the 2nd—had already started down the river for Fort Bliss. Word of the Federal column approaching from California had set the seal of defeat on the campaign; there was no more talk of trying to hold even Bliss. General Sibley had taken to his bed.

Meanwhile there was a great mess to be straightened out. Food and clothes were in short supply, and would be for some time yet. Jamie had sent out a train and a detail to collect up stragglers back along the mountain route. There would be more of that, he expected, but he counted on not having to worry about it.

Lane crossed the plaza toward him, waving a hand. "There you are," he said, and pulled up another of the hide-and-wicker chairs. "Wanted to make sure I saw you before we left."

"We'll miss you," Jamie said, swallowing the last bite of bread. "Colonel Scurry's taking the best of the staff with him. You, Rose—"

"But not you, so not the best," Lane said cheerily. "We still haven't found a Q.M. for the new regiment, and we won't get one as good as you. Sure you won't change your mind?"

Jamie shook his head. "I've got other plans."

"Too bad for us." Lane nodded toward Jamie's letters. "How're your folks?"

"Fine, thanks. Yours?"

"Fine, except my sister's getting married to the biggest clown in Victoria. Going to have to talk to her when I get back."

Jamie's smile faded. His own sister would not be getting

married at all. There were three unopened letters in his pocket that Emma had written to Martin. He didn't like to think about it.

"Where's Reily?" he asked.

"In with Colonel Reily, I expect," Lane said, nodding toward the building. "Putting in for his transfer."

"Not anymore," Reily said, stepping out of headquarters to join them on the portal. "It's a done deal."

Jamie turned his head to look at him. "Why'd you transfer? I thought you loved the artillery."

"It's fine when you've got guns to command," Reily said bitterly. "No sense in having a unit without any weapons. All the regimental artillery's being disbanded."

"I figured you'd be joining the new battery," Jamie said.

Reily shook his head. "I think I'll like staff work better. Now that father's back, it'll give me a chance to be near him."

"Fine," Jamie said. "*You* can worry about getting the army back to San Antonio. I'm staying with the guns."

"Jamie!" Lane exclaimed.

"You don't know anything about artillery!" Reily said, laughing.

Jamie put away his letters, and stood up. "I know enough," he said. "Sayers said he'd train me, and give me command of a section."

The laughter went out of Reily's eyes. "You're serious, aren't you?" Jamie merely nodded. "You'll have to resign your brevet," Reily said.

Jamie shrugged. "I only got it because Martin was killed. Not a good reason to be promoted."

"Jamie, Jamie!" Lane said, frowning. "Why? You never wanted combat duty!"

With a sigh, Jamie strolled out into the sunshine, to where the Valverde Battery was on display in front of headquarters. He put a hand on the nearest—one of the field guns, its brass barrel warning in the bright southern sun. "All the trouble we've been to over these damned guns," he said. "Martin died in the charge when we took them, and we've lost so many others . . . they just have to be worth it." He turned to his friends, unsure of how to make them understand his feelings. "They have to be worth it, don't you see?"

Lane nodded, and came forward to grab him in a tight hug. Jamie closed his eyes, frowning. He wasn't quite sure he understood all the reasons himself, but he knew this was what he had to do.

"Buy you a drink?" Lane said, releasing him. "I've got a couple of hours before we leave."

Jamie nodded. "Give me a few minutes first?"

"Sure. Come on, Reily. You can help me pack up my kit."

"Already I'm being treated like a drudge!" Reily protested.

"Better get used to it," Lane told him, grinning.

Jamie waved as his friends started across the plaza, then went back to his chair. On a little table beside it were two sheets of letter paper that he'd borrowed from headquarters, weighed down by an inkwell. Real ink. He hadn't used any in weeks. He picked up the quill—borrowed as well—and rubbed his thumb back and forth across its tip, making a small scratching sound, as he frowned at the blank paper. At last he opened the inkwell, dipped the pen, and started to write.

Dearest Emma—

Kip rode with clenched teeth, despite the carriage's being well-sprung. His fellow passengers had given up trying to converse with him, since he hadn't the breath to give long answers and had stuck mostly to "yes" and "no." There wasn't much he could tell them anyway. The Texans had made themselves acquainted with the contents of Calloway's letter and had made no secret of it. Consequently the Federal officers riding with Kip discussed the column coming from California—its numbers and equipage and its probable effect on the Texans' campaign—as if they knew more about it than himself. He didn't bother correcting any of the little errors in their assumptions, as he was occupied in keeping from cussing every time the carriage hit a rock. The last couple of miles, since they'd turned off the Camino Real, had been especially bad.

Finally the walls of an earthwork rose into view. The vehicle slowed, and voices challenged, and after a bit of hubbub they rolled into the grounds of Fort Craig. Kip waited for the others to vacate the carriage before easing himself down the steps. There was quite a commotion going on in the fort, and when he'd got down he looked around, blinking in the slanting light of the day's end.

It was a party, he gathered. There were tents all over the place, but a large space had been cleared in the center of the parade ground, and dozens of officers in their dress blues were gathered therein, with a lot of enlisted men watching from the sidelines and passing around canteens that Kip suspected were filled with something stronger than water. A fiddler was playing a reel, and the officers formed in two lines, clapping time while one of them danced down the set with a pretty gal dressed in green. Kip watched, a slow smile spreading on his face. This festive scene brought home to him, more than anything yet had, that he was free again and back among friends.

"I have your horse."

Kip turned to find Rain Weaver beside him. Instantly he was assailed by a confusion of feelings: gratitude, relief, and, oddly, a revisit of the fear he'd felt in captivity. It left him shaken, and all he could say was, "Thank you."

She nodded, and a corner of her mouth curved up slightly. "Now you owe me a debt."

Kip laughed, a little nervously. "I certainly do." Feeling awkward, he nodded toward the dancing. "Is it a wedding?"

Black eyes flicked toward the party, then back to Kip. "Yes. Your people have strange customs. When my people have a wedding, the man and woman stay apart during the feasting, to hear the advice of their elders."

"We do the advice part ahead of time, I think," Kip said. "Your hair looks nice."

Her eyes widened a little, and she looked away at the dancing. Kip felt the old silly grin settling in on his face.

"How do your people decide to get married?" he asked. "Do the parents arrange it?"

Rain Weaver shook her head. "The man leaves his horse staked outside the woman's wickiup. If she accepts him, she takes care of the horse. If not, she lets it starve."

"That so? You took care of my horse—"

She spun on him, eyes flashing furiously. "That is different!"

"I know, I know," Kip said, laughing. "I was joking!"

The fire died in her eyes. She blinked, and looked away, frowning.

"Sort of," Kip added. "I'd like to hear more about your customs. Will you tell me?"

Rain Weaver gave him a long measuring glance, then slowly nodded. He reached for her hand, but she pulled it away.

"White men are like mice," she said. "Always in a hurry going nowhere."

Chastened, Kip turned to watch the dancing. At least she wasn't leaving. That was good enough for now, he guessed. She stood next to him gazing at the celebration, and he watched her sidelong, relieved to see the frown ease from her brow.

He started as her hand slipped into his. Happiness brimmed up inside him, but he kept silent, as together they watched the wedding party dance down the sun.

Epilogue

Dear Momma, Poppa, Emma, and Gabe,

I hope by now you have my first letters. We are resting here in Franklin while we recruit our strength for the journey home. That, as you can imagine, is the sweetest word any of us can think of. Thank you for the packages of clothing and the quilt—all arrived safely and are much appreciated. I once thought it possible for Momma to knit too many socks. I will never think such an ungrateful thought again! Your socks have saved the feet of many a soldier, your son included. I hope to make some of the others known to you when we return, so they can thank you themselves.

Have you had a letter yet from Daniel? I was glad to hear your news that he survived Corinth. We have had some other news of the battle and it must have been a terrible fight. Please send him my kindest regards, and the same to Matthew when you write to him.

I am making good progress in learning my artillery duties. Captain Sayers is about my age, but he has had the advantage of a military education, hence he lords it over me and all the others. He works us till we're just about to drop, then shames us into working harder still. Most of my crew know the drill better than I do, but they kindly overlook my inexperience and treat me with the greatest respect. I think it's left over from my having been in control of the comforts of life for so long. We shall see if it lasts.

We should be starting for San Antonio by the end of this month (officially) or more likely early June. Horses and transportation are our biggest problems, besides the large numbers of sick and just bone-weary men, too weak to march yet. I thank the Lord every night for giving Cocoa back to me. Without her I would probably have to continue on foot. They are saying our march, once we're back at home, will have been longer than Napoleon's army marching out of Russia. Poppa will think I'm soft, and he's right I guess, but I'd rather finish the job in the saddle than afoot.

Please keep writing whenever you have the time. Your letters make me feel closer to home. I think day and night about seeing you all again, and being back at the ranch.

> Your loving son and brother,
> James

Author's Note

Historical fiction, by definition, does not reflect historical events with perfect accuracy. While it is a major objective of mine to bring the history of the New Mexico Campaign to the attention of those who might not otherwise encounter it, the process of fictionalizing these events necessarily involves a bit of tampering with the facts.

Fictional characters in this novel include Kip Whistler and his friends (except Semmilrogge, who really was wounded at Stanwix Flats, though not badly), Laura Howland, Alastar O'Brien, Jamie Russell, Juan Carlos and María Díaz, Esteban Gutíerrez, Rain Weaver, Old George, Lacey McIntyre, Joseph Hall, Captain Owens, all of I Company of the 1st Colorado Volunteers, and various minor characters. The real I Company, 1st Colorado, was an infantry company, not a cavalry company.

In *The Guns of Valverde,* the greatest variance from historical fact is I Company's attack on the retreating Texans below Fort Craig. No such attack was made, although Chivington proposed harassing the retreat and was forbidden to do so by Canby. A scouting party of cavalry did parallel the Texans down the Río Grande for a few days, but returned without incident.

Another departure from strict history is Kip Whistler's ride: carrying Captain Calloway's message to Colonel Canby with a sergeant and a Mexican guide, being ambushed in Apache Canyon and losing both companions, capture by Confederates, imprisonment in Mesilla, and managing to get word of the California Column to Canby. These events did take place; they happened not to Kip Whistler, who is entirely fictional, but to John Jones, a Unionist civilian resident of Tucson who became a scout for the Federal army under

Colonel Carleton. Jones's ride, ambush, and capture took place not in April of 1862 (as did Kip's) but in June of that year. Its ultimate effect was as I've depicted: the Confederates, learning of the approach of the California Column, abandoned all hope of retaining New Mexico or the Confederate Territory of Arizona, and began the last stage of withdrawal. The Sibley Brigade, largely on foot, returned across southwestern Texas in the heat of summer to San Antonio, bringing with them the Valverde Battery, their only tangible gains from the New Mexico Campaign.

For information about efforts to preserve the Glorieta Battlefield, please visit *www.pgnagle.com.*

Suggested Reading

This short bibliography represents a selection of references which the author recommends to readers wishing to learn more about the New Mexico Campaign.

Alberts, Don E., *The Battle of Glorieta: Union Victory in the West* (Texas A&M University Military History Series, No. 61), Texas A&M University Press, College Station, Texas, 1998.

————, ed., *Rebels on the Río Grande, the Civil War Journal of A. B. Peticolas,* University of New Mexico Press, Albuquerque, New Mexico, 1984.

Carmony, Neil B. ed., *The Civil War in Apache Land, Sergeant George Hand's Diary,* High Lonesome Books, Silver City, New Mexico, 1996.

Colton, Ray C., *The Civil War in the Western Territories,* University of Oklahoma Press, Norman, Oklahoma, 1959.

Frazier, Donald S. *Blood & Treasure: Confederate Empire in the Southwest* (Texas A&M University Military History Series, No. 41), Texas A&M University Press, College Station, Texas, 1997.

Hall, Martin Hardwick, *Sibley's New Mexico Campaign,* University of Texas Press, Austin, Texas, 1960.

Hollister, Ovando J., *Colorado Volunteers in New Mexico,* (orig. published in 1862 as *History of the First Regiment of Colorado Volunteers*), The Lakeside Press, Chicago, Illinois, 1962.

Josephy, Alvin M., Jr., *The Civil War in the American West,* Alfred A. Knopf, Inc., New York, New York, 1991.

Simmons, Marc, ed., *The Battle at Valley's Ranch, First Account of the Gettysburg of the West, 1862,* San Pedro Press, Sandia Park, New Mexico, 1987.

Simmons, Marc, *The Little Lion of the Southwest,* The Swallow Press, Chicago, Illinois, 1973.

Thompson, Jerry D., ed., *Westward the Texans, the Civil War Journal of William Randolph Howell,* Texas Western Press, El Paso, Texas, 1990.

Whitford, William C., *The Battle of Glorieta Pass: Colorado Volunteers in the Civil War,* (orig. published in 1906 as *The Colorado Volunteers in the Civil War*), facsimile edition by The Río Grande Press, Glorieta, New Mexico, 1991.

About the Author

A native and lifelong resident of New Mexico, P. G. Nagle has a special love of the outdoors, particularly New Mexico's wilds, where many of her stories are born. Her recent historical novel, *Glorieta Pass*, and its sequel, *The Guns of Valverde*, are set during the New Mexico Campaign of the Civil War.

Nagle's work has appeared in several anthologies, including collections honoring New Mexico writer Jack Williamson, who lives in Portales, New Mexico, and the late Roger Zelazny, who lived in Santa Fé. Her short story "Coyote Ugly" was honored as a finalist for the Theodore Sturgeon Award.